TAPESTRY OF THE BOAR

Sir Walter, listening to expressions of appreciation and gratitude, eyed his guest from those hawk-like eyes and came up with an unexpected suggestion and request.

"I am told that you Swintons won your name and style from your famed ability to deal with wild boars, my young friend. The swine from whence comes Swinton. Your ancestors helped rid the Merse of many. Is that so?"

"Our arms, yes, bear the three boars, sir. And supporters, two boars also."

"And do you still so deal? Still kill boars?"

"There are not many left, now. But, yes, I have myself killed two, sir."

"And, think you, could you kill another? You see, we have one here, at Smailholm, a savage brute. It has some sort of den up at the Pictish fort, yonder. And only yesterday it savaged a child picking marsh-marigolds down at the lochan. Where its other swine, the sows, live, I know not. But it does much damage, kills many calves. If you could rid us of the brute many would thank you. None of my people here seem able to deal with it."

Hugh blinked. "I . . . I do not know, Sir Walter. But – I could try, yes. If I could find it. I would require a spear . . ."

Tapestry of the Boar

Nigel Tranter

CORONET BOOKS
Hodder and Stoughton

First published in Great Britain in 1993
by Hodder and Stoughton Limited
A division of Hodder Headline PLC

Coronet edition 1994

10 9 8 7 6 5 4 3 2 1

British Library Cataloguing in Publication Data
Tranter, Nigel
Tapestry of the Boar.
I. Title
823.912 [F]

ISBN 0 340 60105 1

Printed and bound in Great Britain by
Cox & Wyman Ltd, Reading, Berkshire

Hodder and Stoughton Ltd
A Division of Hodder Headline PLC
338 Euston Road
London NW1 3BH

To
John, Viscount of Arbuthnott
and
Major General Sir John Swinton
who both helped

List of Principal Characters

In Order of Appearance

Hugh de Swinton: Second son of the Sheriff of the Merse, or Berwickshire

Duncan: Illegitimate son of the sheriff

Sir Ernulf de Swinton: Chief of the Name, uncle of above

Cospatrick de Swinton: Sheriff

Cospatrick, Earl of March: Distant kinsman and powerful noble

William, Prince of Strathclyde: Brother of King Malcolm the Fourth

Edward, Bishop of Aberdeen: Chancellor of the realm

Robert de Bruce, Lord of Annandale: Powerful noble

Lord Patrick Home: Second son of the Earl of March

William, Abbot of Melrose: Vice-Chancellor

Meg Cockburn: Daughter of the Swintons' chief shepherd

Malcolm the Fourth, King of Scots: Known as Malcolm the Maiden

Lord Waldeve of Dunbar: Elder son of the Earl of March

Earl Fergus of Galloway: Great Celtic noble

Walter fitz Alan: The High Steward

Sir Walter Olifard of Smailholm: Justiciar of Lothian

Dod Lumsden: Steward-farmer of Aldcambus

Tam Robson: Steward-farmer of Redheugh

Somerled mac Fergus, Lord of the Isles

Malcolm MacEth, Earl of Ross: Great noble of royal descent

Countess Ada: Mother of the King and Prince William

Princess Ada: Sister of the King

Count Floris of Holland

Sir Osbert Olifard: Thane of Arbuthnott and the Mearns

Margaret Olifard: Daughter and heiress of above

Gelis: Maid to Margaret Olifard

Roger, Archbishop of York

Hugh de Swinton dismounted from his horse and handed the reins to his illegitimate half-brother, foster-brother, friend and associate – he would never call him servant – Duncan, and ran lithely up the steep, stepped slope of the motte or mound within the strong palisade of timber, to the keep or tower-house of Swinton which crowned that artificial hillock. This was not his home, but he knew it well, for it was his uncle's seat, there in the wide Merse, or March, which separated the rest of Scotland from Northumbria across Tweed. The summons to him had been urgent.

The gatehouse before the keep was open, and the duty guard, grinning to him, waved him in, towards the tower door, reached by a little outside flight of steps and a bridge-like gangway, the door being above ground at first-floor level; for all here was for defence, so near the former border with England whence raiding had been so apt to come. The keep itself, although also built of timber, was thickly coated with clay, and whitewashed, the hardened clay being to prevent fire-arrows from setting the wood alight. Five storeys high it towered.

Past the porter in his tiny cave-like chamber within the doorway, and getting another smiling salute, Hugh raced two at a time up the narrow stairway. He had long legs and energy at twenty years, and could have run three at a time, only the tight twisting of the turnpike stair made that impossible, for this also was a defensive feature, constructed thus so that it could be held by one man with a sword, however many sought to climb, himself two-thirds hidden behind the central pillar. Swinton Castle, as were so many in that borderland, was like that, had to be to have survived.

On the next floor up a door stood open, for although a fire smouldered on the great hall hearth within, it was almost early summer and not cold. Hugh entered.

Three men sat there, not at the high dais-table at the far end of the chamber, on its platform, but on settles near the fire, beakers of ale in hand, one elderly-seeming, one in later middle years and one young, little older than Hugh.

"You have taken your time, lad," his uncle, Sir Ernulf de Swinton said.

"I was hawking on the Blackadder haughs beyond Kimmerghame, sir. I came so soon as your man reached me. In all haste."

"Aye, well. There is need for haste apparently, see you. The prince requires all landed men to assemble at Roxburgh this very day. Short notice, but William mac Henry mac David is like that, ever in haste."

"Roxburgh? Today! Assemble in arms?"

"No, no. Not in arms – yet! That may come. This is for a council, it seems. I do not think that the prince will require *your* advice and guidance," and Sir Ernulf favoured his two nephews with one raised eyebrow. "But his courier says all landed men. So you had better go with your father. I cannot so much as sit a horse, old bones forbidding. But it will be good for you, forby, to learn how these matters go, the debating and contentions of men, your seniors and betters – aye, and their follies! Eh, Pate?"

His brother, Cospatrick de Swinton, Sheriff of the Merse, nicknamed Pate, shrugged. "These two need to learn nothing about contention and debate, Ulf – they never cease at it!" But he smiled at his sons. "I agree that they should go, however. Time that they took some weight from the shoulders of their ageing father!"

Both young men gazed at the lusty and forthright man, their sire, whose greying hair was the only sign of his years, and exchanged looks.

"Ageing!" Alan said. "If that is ageing, then *I* am still in my bairn's cot! I, who have indeed come of age, myself!" He was rather proud of this distinction, so recently won, especially in front of his brother. "Show us the signs of it, Father, and we may believe you." Then he bit his lip, glancing at his uncle, who was indeed ageing, although only in his early sixties. Had he been tactless? Alan, just one year older than Hugh, was dark, almost swarthy, slight of build but good-looking with it, taking after their late mother; whereas Hugh was taller, more powerfully made, like their father, fresh-featured, and his mane of long hair so fair as to be like white gold – indeed he was known locally as Hugh the Fair. *He* forbore to comment.

Sir Ernulf said, "It is eighteen miles to Roxburgh Castle, three hours' riding."

"I must go back to Swinton Parva first," Hugh declared. "I cannot appear before Prince William clad so, for the hawking."

"Think you that the prince will even *see* you in that throng? Or, yes, he may see your hair, lad, and stare! But your clothing is of no account. He is not one for caring for gear, leaving that to his brother. No, go you straight to Roxburgh."

"May I ask the reason for this council? In such haste."

"We do not know, were not told. Only that it was urgent, needful. All landed men. With so many away with the King in France, as are my own sons, William will be seeking all that can be raised."

"It can scarcely be good news," the father added.

"No. I will be waiting to hear from you, at the earliest."

That clearly was as good as their dismissal.

The sheriff rose, nodding. "Probably the morrow, then, Ulf. Come, you two."

Gulping down the last of their ale, the two young men sketched bows to their uncle, the head of the line, Swinton of that Ilk, and the late King David's friend, and followed their father out.

Their ride thereafter although lengthy was not difficult, the Merse being good country for horsemen, rolling pastureland, cattle-dotted, with no great heights and passes to negotiate, the rivers draining it swift-running and creating few bogs, with fords aplenty, even a bridge or two, much of it Church

3

land now. Swinton lay all but in the centre of it, midway between the great Priory of Coldinghame and the splendid Abbey of Kelshaugh, or Kelso as most pronounced it, and between Berwick-upon-Tweed with its Dominican and Cistercian friaries and the holy burgh-toun of the Kaimes. That this vast tract of fine country, the largest plain in all Scotland, should be so largely under the sway of Holy Church was a sore point with many, even the faithfully inclined, Swinton itself having to pay St Cuthbert's dues, as they were called. The Swinton family did not complain, for it was all the good King David's doing, of hallowed memory, and he had been Sir Ernulf's friend. Yet they had been settled at Swinton for four generations before David, for his own good reasons, made the churchmen supreme in the Merse. Not all the other landholders there were as accepting, patient, understanding.

The trio, with their suitable half-dozen of escort, including Hugh's foster-brother Duncan, rode west by south, good going by drove-roads which led to the great Kelshaugh cattle-markets, where again Holy Church gained its tithe of the takings. They went by Swintonhill and Leitholm, where they forded the Leit Water. As an enquiring boy Hugh had asked why this was not called the Greyadder, for the name Leit, or *liath*, in the Celtic tongue, meant grey, and they had in the Merse the Whiteadder, or White Water, and the Blackadder – to be told not to ask daft questions. Then on by Eccles, which meant church, so anciently there must have been a religious shrine here, and there was now a large convent of nuns. Further, at the Eden Water, which Hugh had once assumed to be something to do with the Garden of Eden, especially as he had had another uncle named Adam, and had again been accused of being silly, they forded at Edenholm or Ednam – and had to pay for the privilege of crossing, again to Holy Church. For this small but important fording-place on the great drove-road had its especial importance above others such. Here King David had, thirty-two years before, established the first parish in Scotland, in his notable concept of limiting the too-great power of the lords, barons and landed men who could often invalidate the royal decrees, by

4

instead putting power, temporal power, into the hands of the Church, as a counter-weight. He devised the idea of dividing all his kingdom into parishes, in addition to its baronies and lordships, and having a parish kirk within each, as centre for the common folk – and Edenholm was the first of them all. It was for these, not only out of his genuine piety, that the King had built all those magnificent abbeys, Kelshaugh, Jedburgh, Dryburgh, Melrose and the rest, to be not only monuments to the faith but seminaries, colleges, for the training of the host of priests needed to staff and serve all the new parish kirks. It all had started here in the Merse – whatever the Merse barons and lairds thought of it. Yet the King had been well beloved, as well as respected and obeyed, the finest monarch Scotland had had since MacBeth. The same could hardly yet be said of his grandson Malcolm.

After Edenholm, they left the drove-road, to follow up the south bank of the Eden Water, due westwards now, to avoid Kelshaugh, so as to come down to the great River Tweed above the abbey-town, near Roxburgh itself – this not the palace-castle but its large township upstream. For there was no ford at the castle, again deliberately for defence. Reaching the river, they splashed over its artificial shallows on a causeway of underwater stones, and not alone now, for two other groups of visiting magnates were crossing also, one none other than the great Cospatrick, Earl of March himself, from Ersildoune, a distant kinsman of the Swintons, after whose mutual ancestor Sheriff Cospatrick was named. The Swinton brothers fell suitably and modestly to the rear.

Downriver the enlarged party trotted for over a mile. Roxburgh Castle was extraordinarily and dramatically sited on a narrow peninsula where that other great river, the Teviot, joined Tweed, to form a lengthy and narrow arrowhead of steep rocky ground protected by deep, rushing water on all sides except for the access at the west end, this guarded by a deep fosse or water-filled ditch, with drawbridge. The resultant stronghold, stone-built, this one, not timber and clay, was necessarily long-strung-out, a succession of towers and keeps and a hallhouse within enclosing curtain walls topped by battlemented wall-walks, a strange principal seat for a monarchy, and within a few miles of the border with England, while the rest of the kingdom stretched northwards for nearly three hundred miles. Yet so it had been chosen by David mac Malcolm, partly as a gesture to indicate that he was no longer at war with the old enemy of England, but also to emphasise the Scots claims to Northumbria and Cumbria, ceded by English King Stephen. Previous Scots monarchs, David's own brothers, Alexander and Edgar, had seated themselves at Edinburgh, and their father, Malcolm Canmore, at Dunfermline and Stirling; but David, after his long exile in England as hostage, had settled on this Roxburgh on the edge of the Merse; and his grandson now on the throne, Malcolm the Fourth, the Maiden, did the same.

The visitors had to dismount and leave their horses, amongst scores of others, on the grassy riverside haughs, for there was no room for all these beasts within the castle itself. It ill became the mighty Earl Cospatrick, who claimed more royal blood than the King himself, to have to climb on foot up the brae and walk into the castle, but there was no option. Under the two gatehouse arches and below the portcullises, they strode, sentries on the watch. Across three courtyards of this elongated fortress, past two keeps, they came to a larger but lower building of only two storeys, the doorway guarded by servitors in the royal livery. Brushing these aside, the Earl of March pushed inside into an already crowded great hall, which dwarfed the one of Swinton needless to say. More servants were, with difficulty, moving amongst the noisy throng, seeking to dispense viands and drink. Up at the far end, on the raised dais, only a small group sat at table, six men, two of them clerics, although the one in the middle could only just be called a man, tall for his age and heavily built as he was, Brawny Will as his grandfather David had called him, Prince of Strathclyde and, in name at least, Earl of Northumbria.

Shouldering his way through the crush with no apologies, the Earl Cospatrick headed for that dais; but although his namesake, the sheriff, and his sons moved after him, it was

6

only to a fairly frontal position. They gladly accepted some refreshment after their eighteen-mile ride.

The talk around them was patchy, incoherent and interspersed with greetings. But they gathered that there was serious trouble in the air, sundry great names being bandied about, Fergus of Galloway's in particular. The Sheriff of the Merse left his sons, to go and converse with intimates.

Whether or not Prince William and his advisers had been awaiting the arrival of the Earl Cospatrick they did not know, but it seemed likely, for soon after the latter's arrival at the dais-table, a horn was blown for quiet and the prince beat on the board with his tankard.

"My lords spiritual and temporal, barons and gentles," the youth said in a loud and jerky voice, but notably confident for his seventeen years, "I have ill tidings for you. There is shameful revolt in the land – treason to our lord the King. And by those who should lead in their loyalty, I say. Six earls have raised the standard of rebellion against my royal brother, at St John's Town of Perth, the Earls of Strathearn, Atholl, Angus, Mar, Moray and Fife. And we have just heard that this revolt has been joined by Earl Fergus of Galloway."

At the prince's pause there was a hush, as the significance of that statement sank in. For all these named earls were of the ancient Celtic polity, indeed the descendants of former mormaors or sub-kings of Alba, under the *Ard Righ*, the High King. Whereas most of those present at Roxburgh were only partly Celtic by blood, with a strong admixture of Norman and Flemish, brought up from England by David on his return to take up the throne thirty-six years before. Most had adopted Scottish names, usually those of the lands they had been allotted, or had married the heiresses to – such indeed as de Swinton; although these last did have more of the Celtic in them, and royal blood also, however far back.

Prince William went on. "In my brother's unfortunate absence in France, these have taken their opportunity to . . ."

He got no further on account of the growls arising from the

gathering. King Malcolm's decision to go to the assistance of King Henry the Second of England, his far-out cousin, in his efforts to win back control of the Plantagenet lands in France, and with a Scots army, was highly unpopular.

William banged the table. "Hear me! I have already sent off couriers, to take ship to the Rhône and Toulouse, where we understand King Malcolm is at present, to urge his return with all speed, and with his force. But this will take time. Meanwhile we must act, in his name."

Again there was the growling, but of agreement this time, largely indicative of the great north–south division of Scotland between the Lowlands and the Highlands, for of course almost all those present were from south of Forth and Clyde, the Lowlands, whereas those earls named as rebelling were all from the north – that is except Fergus of Galloway. He was the odd man out, although he was of sufficiently Celtic ancestry. But he was comparatively near at hand, whilst the others were far off. And Galloway was a very large earldom and its men renowned warriors.

Edward, Bishop of Aberdeen, the Chancellor or chief minister of the realm, one of the two clerics flanking the prince, rose to speak; but almost contemptuously the Earl Cospatrick waved him down and spoke first, eloquent in more than his words, and representing the hostility of so many there to the power to which the ecclesiastics had been deliberately promoted in the kingdom.

"The upstart Fergus must be dealt with, and at once," he declared. "The others can wait – they are distantly placed. He is not. He should never have been granted Galloway. It belonged to *my* house! We all must arm, and march. And swiftly, before there can be any coming together with these northern earls, any warfare of two fronts. Assembly must be called, at once, in fullest possible numbers, for those Galloway men can fight! Give me three days, four, and I will bring one thousand!"

Grinning his approval at the engendered shouts of acclamation from all over the hall, with men vying with each other to name numbers also, not only the great ones seeking to outbid,

8

Prince William, seeing the Chancellor still on his feet, thumped the table for quiet.

"Good!" he cried. "Good! We need all." He turned. "You, my lord Bishop, wish to speak?"

"Yes, Highness. I say that in this sorry situation, while assault should be made to teach my lord of Galloway where his loyalty should be, our backs must be protected while it is done. As my lord Earl has indicated. A line should be formed, and held, at the narrows of the Forth, at Stirling, to face north, to deter these rebelling earls. There they must cross, if they march south." The Chancellor, a plump, round-faced man but with shrewd eyes, paused. "Holy Church can help in this, I judge, as in so much. My lord Bishop of St Andrews, the Primate, can have many men at his command. And the College of Bishops can, I am sure, proffer a sufficiency of moneys to hire many more to arms. We might even outdo my lord Earl's thousand!"

The hint of mockery in his bow towards Cospatrick told its own story, and roused varying reactions from the company, with many murmurings. The uneasy balance between Church and state was emphasised.

"I think that I may confirm my lord Chancellor's affirmation," the other cleric on the dais, Herbert, Bishop of Glasgow, said smoothly, an elderly prelate, richly robed and of a remote bearing.

Beside him a man of a very different sort jumped up. "That is well enough. But I say that Galloway is what we have to decide on here. We will require every man; I *know*, who sits on Fergus's doorstep!" Robert de Bruce, second Lord of Annandale, a big, burly character, red of face and hot of temper, exclaimed. "If you march against Galloway by Nithsdale and Annandale, I will have five hundred awaiting you. Five hundred, I say!"

That set the tone of the further proceedings, with the Chancellor summoning clerks to set down on paper the numbers promised by all the magnates, barons, knights and landed men, a lengthy process and less orderly than might have been advantageous. In Sir Ernulf's and his own names, the sheriff offered one hundred – which was stretching matters, with his nephews already away with the King in France, and seventy men with them.

While all this was going on, the senior lords were discussing timing, places and tactics. From the first it was accepted that while the prince would be nominally in charge, the Earl Cospatrick, the only one of that rank, other than Fergus of Galloway himself, south of Forth and Clyde, should actually command the forces in the field, experienced in border warfare as he was. They would assemble at Melrose, more central and spacious for their purpose, and convenient for the earl, at Ersildoune, in five days' time, and march up Tweed right to that river's source on Tweedsmuir, then over the watershed and down Annandale beyond, to assail Galloway from the north; that is, unless they heard that Fergus had moved in the interim, in which case they would have to adjust their plans.

Thereafter more feeding was provided in one of the keeps. Many, with further to go, would be staying overnight at the castle; but the Swintons decided that they could make it back to Kimmerghame by early dark. The young men would be busy, on the morrow, riding round, summoning and gathering their Merse mosstrooping tenantry, while their father went to acquaint Sir Ernulf with the position and gain his authority to assemble maximum numbers of the Swinton men.

Excited at the prospects, Hugh and Alan discussed it all at considerable length as they rode home, their father, somewhat cynical as became a sheriff and judge, less voluble; and declaring that the situation was as good as made for his namesake the earl, who had long wanted the Galloway lordship added to his own. After all, his forebear and their own, Maldred, brother of King Duncan whom MacBeth had slain, had been Earl of Northumberland and Cumberland on marrying their heiress thereof, granddaughter of King Ethelred the Unready, of England; whereas Fergus was a mere incomer from somewhere in the north-west, who had married a daughter of the Norman Henry the First, son of the Conqueror, and whom King David had found useful and promoted because he had founded Dundrennan Abbey and Whithorn Priory. The ways of monarchs could seem curious to lesser men.

2

They mustered one hundred and three men from Swinton and Simprim and their outlying properties, some fairly old for the business but nowise prepared to be left out, Sir Ernulf grieving that his incapacity prevented him from taking part. All were mounted, for a Merseman lacking a horse was as good as crippled – even though all too often they were apt to use the said steeds for raiding other folk's cattle.

On the fourth day, then, they set off for war, in high spirits and fine style, most of them, although the sheriff was only moderately sanguine, as by nature. They were not going directly to the rallying-place at Melrose, for they had received a message from the Earl Cospatrick requesting them to join his array at Ersildoune on the River Leader, before it joined Tweed; why was not stated. The sheriff had his own notions as to the reason.

This time they went, in column, due westwards, by Charterhall and Greenlaw and the wide moorlands of Gordon, to descend to the valley of the Purves Water at the Earlstoun of Ersildoune, thirty miles no less, through the Merse. Here was a sizeable township, cradled in a hollow below the White Hill thereof, a quite lofty summit and representing the very western boundary of the Merse with Lauderdale. As expected, they found the town overflowing with the assembling horsemen, not all the townsfolk appreciative, idle mosstroopers not always the most welcome visitors for well-doing residents, and their horses excessively hungry for carefully stored forage. Leaving their party down at the River Leader's bank beside the small Learmonth tower of Ersildoune itself, the sheriff and his sons made their way up to the much larger castle of the earl, on a spur of the White Hill, crowded inevitably.

Cospatrick made them welcome, more heartily than was his usual perhaps, for although his namesake was his sheriff and distant kinsman, the earl was not of an effusive nature. But, as was rather anticipated, he was glad to have the Swinton five score to add to his total, for it seemed that he had had difficulty in raising the promised one thousand men, and his array required this topping-up. His son, of course, the Lord Waldeve, had six hundred away with him in France with King Malcolm. But a suitable front had to be maintained.

In the absence of the said Waldeve, they found that the earl had chosen his second son Patrick Home to be second-in-command of this force – which could have given offence to the sheriff who in fact ranked senior not only in years. But presumably this young man, only a year older than Alan de Swinton, was to be given experience in his leadership of men, as was no doubt desirable. Moreover, he had brought a major contribution of Home manpower, for the Homes of that Ilk were a powerful Merse clan, and Patrick had married the heiress a year or so before, and taken the name of Home. The sheriff accepted the situation.

A noisy, boisterous evening was passed by the castle guests, to rival that of their followers in the township. They would march at sun-up, for Melrose.

Trotting down Lauderdale, then, the ever-enquiring Hugh, riding now beside Learmonth of Ersildoune and wondering why the vale was not called Leaderdale, gained no satisfactory answer; but he did learn that his companion, although a loyal vassal of the earl, rather resented his superior's appropriation of the style of Ersildoune. After all, the Learmonths had held the admittedly minor barony of that name long before the first Cospatrick – this was the fourth – was given overlordship of the Merse and built his great castle nearby. *He* was Ersildoune, not the earl, even though he could bring only a score of men to this host.

It was only five miles down to the Tweed at Melrose. They found the level haughlands north of the great abbey thronged with men, tents and pavilions sprouting up everywhere, long horse-lines dividing the various units. There was no real

13

township here, only the abbey's monastic quarters and the lay workers' hutments, the local community being sited some distance off, two miles eastwards, at a steep bend of the Tweed, and known as Old Melrose, meaning the great headland.

Finding the necessary quite extensive space for their large company – even though it was still not quite the promised one thousand – the earl gave orders for his pavilion to be pitched, his banner hoisted over it, and went in search of the prince, his gentry with him. There was no difficulty in locating Brawny Will's tent, with the black boar on silver of the royal standard flapping above it, ancient symbol of the Celtic High Kings.

The prince had been informed of their arrival, and was thankful to see them for, despite all the noisy estimating of numbers that other day at Roxburgh, not quite as many as expected had turned up, indeed only some eighteen hundred so far. So the earl's contingent, the largest single force there, was welcomed. The monarchy was dependent almost entirely on the levies of its lords and barons, there being no national standing army, and the royal guard, a modest array anyway, was mainly away with King Malcolm in France.

A few more small groups came in before dusk. They would march in the morning.

The Abbot of Melrose provided what approximated to a banquet for the prince and the army's leaders that evening, his monks and lay brothers doing their best for the mass of the soldiery, Holy Church having its uses on occasion. The provision was sufficient for quite a few of the participants to achieve drunkenness, Prince William included. There was much boasting over what they would do to Fergus of Galloway in due course.

Next day there was the usual problem of marching a mixed force. Being largely Mersemen, this was mainly a horsed army; but there were some hundreds of foot from the higher lands of upper Lauderdale, Teviotdale, Selkirk, the Gala Water and even Lothian, all but despised by the mosstroopers, and these of course went much more slowly than the horsemen and could not cover more than one-third of the distances daily. This dichotomy always provided headaches for commanders, so

14

that there were in fact usually *two* armies, horse and foot, with different priorities, even routes to follow, and little love lost between them. And, also, the lords and lairds of the foot were themselves mounted and apt to ride with the horsed leadership, so that the bands of pikemen and spearmen were often less than well controlled, as the inhabitants of the countryside passed through tended to discover.

With mainly mere drove-roads to follow, and these fairly narrow usually, an army on the march could be strung out over miles, and as such vulnerable to assault by ambush from an enemy in place beforehand. So scouting parties were always out well in advance and on the flanks. In this case, however, there was little likelihood of any attempt to halt them, for they were a long way from Galloway, and Fergus, even if he knew that they were coming against him, would scarcely come all this way to challenge them; and if he was intending to march northwards to join or meet the other rebel earls, he almost certainly would go by the western side of Scotland, by the shires of Dumfries, Ayr and Renfrew to the Clyde and into the Highlands from there.

The royal route, then, was up Tweed, by Faldonside and Yair, to Caddonfoot and Elibank, to Traquair and eventually Peebles, where, twenty-five miles on their way, they halted for the night. How far the foot had got none knew. There was no convenient abbey at Peebles to provide catering, but there was a little-used and small royal castle, and the quite large church and monastic establishment of St Mungo, and these had to serve. Actually they had passed, only a mile or so to the east, at Eshiels, the major hospice of St Leonards of the Knights of St Lazarus; but this was for the care and treatment of lepers, so its services had to be shunned. The churchmen were always better provided with food and drink than anybody else, probably because they worked harder, and this was accepted by the laity as a suitable contribution, after all the tithes, tiends, tolls and dues Holy Church collected from them; and not only the lairds and barons, for ordinary travellers were beholden to the clerics for the wayside hospices which, dotting the countryside, made long journeying possible.

The following day's riding took them, still up Tweed, past its junctions with the Manor and Lyne Waters, to Drumelzier, where the great river took its major turn southwards, coming down from its source on high Tweedsmuir, wild upland country now, and all but impassable for any army in winter snows. Even in this early May it was bleak and difficult going up there, and with some twenty miles covered they camped at Oliver Castle, the remote small fortalice of the Frasers, where there was another hospice and little church, and where they collected a posse of exceedingly wild-seeming Fraser adherents under the laird's son. These would be their guides for the next part of their lengthy journey. The hospice was, they were told, used as a penance-place for recalcitrant monks sent from Melrose, so grim were the surroundings.

They did indeed cross the roof of Lowland Scotland the next day, finding Tweedsmuir all that it was reputed to be, and more bare, harsh, extensive and waterlogged heights, under mighty Hartfell, where in fact rose not only Tweed but the other great rivers of Clyde and Annan, to flow in different directions. Thankful all were when, in mid-afternoon they began to follow the last-named stream down towards the vast spread of lower ground now before them opening, which represented Annandale and Nithsdale. They reached Moffat for the night, a market-town renowned for its sheep-sales.

From now on a different attitude began to prevail, especially amongst the leaders, for this land ahead of them – and they could see right to the blue hills of Westmorland in Cumbria – although the shire of Dumfries, was under the sway of Galloway, and so could represent danger. Admittedly Robert de Bruce was Lord of Annandale, and was presumably waiting for them and would, it was hoped, send to warn them if he learned of any advance northwards by Fergus; but they could not be sure of this, and readiness was the order of the day, the scouts to be extra vigilant.

The Bruce had two main castles, at Lochmaben and Annan itself, some twenty-five miles apart. But since the latter was situated just across the narrows of Solway from Galloway proper, and only another twenty-five as the crow flies from

Fergus's principal castle of Urr, it seemed likely that he would be mustering at Lochmaben. Thither they would head, guided by the Frasers, but watchfully, a score more miles.

It was much easier riding now, and they made Lochmaben by early afternoon, being met by a party of Bruce's men led by his son, also Robert. All was well, so far, this young man told them, no word of Fergus massing his forces.

They found Lochmaben, near the right bank of Annan, an extraordinary place, for no fewer than seven lochs were grouped here, with two other rivers entering them, and the township amongst them, irregularly placed and all but surrounded by water. It was already full of armed men, for young Bruce explained that the castle, almost a mile away, was in too narrow a defensive position for the assembly of large numbers and, he asserted, they had done even better than his father had promised, gathering almost seven hundred men, most of them Johnstones and Maxwells, for the royal army.

Leaving the troops amongst the meadows of the various lochs, young Bruce led the magnates to the castle, which they discovered occupied a peninsula jutting into one of the lochs, with a narrow isthmus which, ditched by a wide fosse, turned the site into an island, highly defensive. Here the prince and his lieutenants were welcomed by its lord.

Now, in this watery place, they must await the arrival of the foot. Meanwhile tactics fell to be discussed. Bruce had his scouts out probing fairly deep into Galloway, but seemed to rely more on the word brought by mendicant friars who traversed all the land and were the recognised source of news for great and small alike. These had informed him that the Earl Fergus was indeed massing men in various parts of his wide domains, the general belief being that he intended to march north with them to join the other rebel earls, first to seal off all Scotia – that is, Scotland north of Forth and Clyde – from the Lowlands, and to re-establish the Celtic supremacy there; and then to strike southwards in major force to take over the entire kingdom from the present Anglo-Norman-Scots royal house. Whom they would then set upon the throne was not clear.

All this was of no great help to Prince William's advisers

in planning their strategy. Galloway was a vast earldom, a province indeed, and Fergus might be planning his main assembly-place anywhere therein. All that was certain was that his two main seats were at Mote of Urr and Kenmure, these two locations being fairly central and not much more than a score of miles apart, more or less at either end of long Loch Ken. It seemed reasonable to assume that Fergus would muster, finally, at one or other; and if indeed he was going to march north, then it would probably be at the northernmost, Kenmure. That was as far as they could assess the matter, lacking more detailed information.

So what to do? The general opinion was that their best course was to strike due westwards from this Lochmaben, across Nithsdale into Galloway, in the high, empty area of the Glenkens, and then swing southwards, heading for Loch Ken itself, midway between Fergus's two castles. By then they should know more of the enemy's moves and probable intentions; and if Fergus was mustering at both places, at least they would be in a position to prevent these two assemblies joining up. On the other hand, admittedly, it could throw themselves open to attack from two sides. They would have to take precautions as to that. No other plan of campaign was forthcoming.

They had to wait for four days for their foot to catch up with them, and then another two while these had their very necessary rest. In the interim the visitors exploited the possibilities of Lochmaben in varying fashion which, as far as the Swintons were concerned, involved much fishing for a special kind of white fish, unique, strangely, to the castle's loch, known as vendace, this providing excellent and unusual sport; at least this activity did not upset the local population as did much of that of the rank and file.

But at length all was ready, and the westwards march began, out of Annandale and over the low hills of the Forest of Ae into Nithsdale, crossing that river, and then the Cluden Water and on to Irongray, nine miles, where they passed the first night. At least in this good pastureland the army was not going to go short of meat, cattle in ample supply if not always paid for, the mosstroopers wishing that it was all a deal nearer to the Merse, for their convenience. These had ample time for such gleaning, for now the mounted men must go at the pace of the foot, for safety's sake. This was wearisome, and Hugh, Alan and Duncan were glad to take their turns out with the scouting parties, under local guidance.

Soon after Irongray, they crossed from the sheriffdom of Dumfries into Galloway itself, and now they were the more watchful. Sometimes on their out-ridings the scouts saw more than cowherds and cattle – horsemen in the distance, although none approaching close. Almost certainly these would be scouts also, but Galloway ones; so that the probability was that Fergus would not be uninformed as to his invaders' whereabouts.

There was much computing as to what size of a force that the earl could raise against them. Bruce, alarmingly, said that, if he was to summon his full strength from all over his extensive province, he could probably field ten to twelve thousand; but that would take much time and was not likely at this stage, for any march north; half that, perhaps? With their own force at barely five thousand, this was more than enough for consideration, for fighters on their own ground usually held the advantage. The Earl Cospatrick was notably more concerned than was Prince William.

They were averaging only some ten miles a day now, in rolling Glenkens country, with many streams to ford and bogs to avoid; so it took two days more to reach and cross the Old Water at Shawhead, and then over to the Crocket at Auchenreoch Loch. Here they saw the first sign of the enemy, apart from the probable scouts, a sizeable body of cavalry, on a neighbouring ridge. The earl sent a strong force of his Merse mosstroopers to challenge this, the Swintons included; but the other squadron made off northwards at speed into the low hummocky hills; and the sheriff strongly counselled Patrick Home, in charge, not to pursue, for in those little valleys they could easily be ambushed or circled behind. With no very good grace, the young lord acceded, and they turned back.

His father was interested, when he heard, that it was

19

northwards that this party had ridden off. Did that imply that Fergus was massing at Kenmure, not Mote of Urr? It could be both, of course; but this might be a pointer – and they needed pointers.

Still wondering, they halted for the night, the fourth out from Lochmaben, in the valley of the Urr Water itself, at Glenlair, some twelve miles they were told above Fergus's principal castle, and roughly midway between it and Kenmure – although the last was on the other side of Loch Ken, still six miles to the west. They were all very much aware of this position, deep in enemy country, and with possibly large forces no great distance away on either side.

A council of war that night decided that, until they knew where the main Galloway force was assembled, they should remain here. They had found a major bend in the river, all but a loop, which offered a good defensive position where they could be reasonably safe from any surprise attack. In the morning, two groups should be sent out, fairly large companies of horse, since these might well come up against the enemy, mere scouting parties inadequate now, one to go north, the other south, their task to discover, if possible, where was Fergus's major assembly. Once that was known, a decision on attack could be made. Lord Patrick Home would lead the southern probe, towards Mote of Urr; Sheriff Pate the northern, towards Kenmure.

So next day the sheriff and his sons, with two hundred Mersemen, rode off up the Water of Urr, with young Robert Bruce as guide, he having been hereabouts on occasion with his father's cattle-herds for the large markets at St John's Town of Dalry. He reckoned that they had some fifteen miles to go, to Kenmure, following the river up for three miles or so then swinging off north-westwards over more of the Glenkens Hills for Balmaclellan, quite a major township, where they would be wise to go carefully, skirting it to the south, then on six or seven miles. They would reach the River Ken thereafter and follow it down to the loch. Kenmure Castle stood a mile down the western loch-shore.

Hugh, for one, found it satisfying to ride free again, after all

20

the holding back for the footmen, although he was not unaware of the tingle of excitement occasioned by the fact that they were riding into danger. If indeed Fergus was assembling at Kenmure, then the nearer they got to it, the more risk there was of falling in with companies of Galwegians making therefor. Their objective was not to assail any such but to gain information; but they might have to fight, nevertheless.

Crossing the high ground of Mochrum Fell and Glenhead, they got their first glimpse of the dozen-miles-long Loch Ken, glittering in the May sunlight, narrow as it was lengthy, and dotted with islets, therefore evidently shallow. Well short of Balmaclellan they found the Shirmers Burn to take them down to the lochside.

The sheriff, nearing the shore and perceiving that the water was less than half a mile across, decided that the narrowness presented them with a real advantage. They need not, now, go on up and round the head of the loch to learn what they wanted to know. Opposite Kenmure they would be able to *see* any large encampment of men. On the other hand, though, if they could see, they could also be seen. However, as Bruce pointed out, at half a mile's distance they would not be recognised as enemy, and would probably be taken for a company on its way to join the Galloway muster – *if* indeed there was a muster at Kenmure.

This was accepted, and reaching the shore they turned north again up a fair road. The width of this road revealed it as a major highway, which warned them that there might well be armed men coming up it, or down it. So they sent out scouts to front and rear. Bruce said that they ought to be up level with Kenmure in a couple of miles.

They did not have to go half that distance before they saw men on the other side of the loch, many men, a large column of mounted troops heading southwards. It was difficult to calculate numbers at that range, but they guessed it as at least five hundred. And going *from* Kenmure, not towards it. So – Mote of Urr?

The sheriff thought that although this looked as probably the main assembly-place, it was not certain. He decided that

21

they must go on further, to see whether there was any large concentration at Kenmure. The Earl Cospatrick would have to know this.

Half a mile further and there was another numerous body of men marching south across there, foot this time, strung out for a long way, in file. This seemed to confirm the notion that the Mote of Urr was Fergus's chosen gathering area. But, round a bend in the loch-shore just ahead they ought to be able to see Kenmure Castle itself, Bruce said. So they rode on.

Their forward scouts were waiting round that bend, and pointing. There across the gleaming water less than a mile away rose a lofty mound crowned by a tall castle. And around its base was a large encampment, black against all the greenery of waterside birches and alders. Many men were still there, obviously. Fergus of Galloway did not lack manpower, that was all too clear.

Even as they stared, another company issued from that concourse of men and tents, again heading southwards, cavalry once more. That was enough for the sheriff. He gave orders to turn back whence they had come, and fast now.

They had barely gone two miles, heading for the Shirmers Burn again, when two of their rearward scouts met them with alarming news. From high ground looking south these had seen men and horses crossing the loch in boats, scows, from west to east, at a very narrow stretch, no more than two hundred yards wide. They had watched this ferrying process, to see what developed; but when quite a substantial number had come across, the enemy had started to head *northwards*, in this direction. So they had hurried to warn of it. The other three scouts were keeping an eye on the advance, from cover.

Bruce began to declare that the crossing would be at the well-known narrows of the Airds, where there was a ferry, when the sheriff interrupted him to demand of the scouts how many were crossing, and how far away would they be now? Answers were distinctly vague, perhaps inevitably.

Presumably these men had been sent across to investigate who it was that had been riding north on this wrong side of the loch. They might well be a smaller party than themselves

22

and so could be dealt with. But the main objective of this exercise was to gain information and return with it as quickly as possible, not to engage the enemy. So, could they get back to the Shirmers Burn and off into the hills before these Galwegians caught up with them?

The scouts did not know. It depended on how fast the enemy were advancing. They reckoned it still over a mile to the burn's junction with the loch; and when they had left their companion scouts it had been more than a mile on the other side . . .

Orders were given to ride at the fastest.

But they were too late. Round another major bend, at a spur of the hillside, there, not a quarter-mile ahead of them, were the oncoming horsemen, how many they could not see for twists in the road, but scores at least. A clash was inevitable, head-on, steep slopes on the right, water on the left.

The road was broad, for large cattle-droves, but it still was no place for an armed cavalry encounter, four abreast being as many as could ride, so that only the front ranks could engage effectively. The sheriff, experienced in borderland fighting, if scarcely real warfare, decided swiftly.

"Arrowhead!" he shouted. "An arrowhead! Alan! Hugh! To me. Flank me. No – back, back." Still cantering on at speed, he waved his already drawn sword right and left, to indicate an inverted V-shaped formation, himself the point of it. "An arrow, I say! Quick! Arrowhead. Shields up!"

Even though not all hearing him, sons included, had ever actually experienced such formation-fighting, they at least knew what the term represented. Whether those towards the rear of their column heard the sheriff's orders, those in front knew roughly what was expected of them, Hugh and Duncan on the sheriff's left, not alongside but half a length to the rear, Alan and young Bruce on the right, others pushing forward to flank them similarly. For, of course, where riding abreast allowed only four, in this arrowhead formation they could double that, spurring almost knee to knee. It involved some confusing trial and error admittedly, to get into approximately the required position, riding forward at speed the while – and all the time the two columns bearing down on each other at

23

the canter, horses' hooves drumming; but a fairish arrowhead was achieved, at front, however vaguely so it was behind. And involuntarily, a great shouting arose from scores of throats, the spontaneous battle-cry.

Hugh was following his father's example and drawing his sword, when he thought better of it. In this position wielding a sword effectively would be difficult, as apt to strike friend as foe. A lance or pike would have been better, but he was not so equipped, although many of the mosstroopers behind were. His mace would be best. Reaching back for the spiked iron club hanging from his saddle, he drew it and raised it high. At his side, or just back a little, Duncan, seeing it, did the same. Perhaps others would emulate.

All this, at speed, brought the enemies down upon each other in a deal less time than it takes to tell. Was it Hugh's imagination or did the oncoming foe seem to be slowing down somewhat? At any rate they were not forming any V. No doubt their front ranks did not contain any leader capable of so deciding and ordering. They were nowise shrinking back or aside – they could not, with the pressure of their companions from behind; and it was now evident that there were many in the rear and unfortunately some had lances couched. But they came on abreast, however unsure as to orders.

The headlong clash was shocking, explosive, breathtaking. Hugh was aware of a lance-tip thrusting at him, a man's contorted features behind a wide-nostrilled rearing horse before his own. He flung up the shield, painted with three boars' heads within a chevron silver on black, strapped on his left forearm, to ward off the thrust, and swung the mace in his right hand. In fact, the lance did not strike it, for the other's horse, rearing, threw it off-aim and it went high, well above the intended victim's left shoulder, and there it was smashed down by Duncan's mace, on that side. Then the enemy horse, pawing the air, allowed Hugh to swing a sidelong blow at the lance-bearer, who had been jerked around in his saddle by the jolt on his weapon, and, unsteady as now was his seat, this crashing swipe toppled the man quite over and he fell to the ground, to be trampled on by friendly and hostile hooves alike.

Not that Hugh actually saw this little first victory, for the pace of the chase carried him onward without pause. A large part of the principle behind the arrowhead formation was the driving impact and speed of the charge, pressed on from behind. In fact it was mainly the horses that decided the issue at this stage. The attacking beasts, being driven at their hardest, so often alarmed the enemy mounts that these reared and shied and tried to sidle, to the fatal weakening of their front ranks, and these, abruptly piled into from behind, produced chaos, crashings and fallings, whilst the arrowhead bored on into the mass, necessarily slowed up somewhat but driven forward themselves by those in the rear.

Much depended on the leader, the apex of the arrow. If he fell, or his mount did, or if he was somehow pushed aside, then the entire formation and assault was endangered, and it would be essential for a replacement to take the lead immediately. The sheriff well knew it. Not for him to get into combat with any, his duty to smash on regardless of the enemy, using his sword in figure-of-eight swing, yes, but uncaring whether it struck, purely to drive aside any lance or pike or sword which might thrust at him. This he did now, as he and his ploughed into and through the press of rearing, neighing horses and shouting, yelling and falling men. The charge did lose impetus, but still a forward thrust was maintained. At his sides, Hugh and Alan and the others managed to keep their positions approximately. Not that they either were able to do much actual battling, mace or sword work, but that was for others coming on, their task to break up the enemy column.

This they found they had achieved in an astonishingly short time, when ahead of them they saw only a few horsemen, turned and fleeing. They had had no opportunity to gauge the size of the company they had driven through, but it was probably somewhat smaller than their own. Glancing back, they could see only a confusion of men and animals behind; but in it all there was one positive and distinct current – their own files, however scattered, driving their way through after them.

Biting his lip, the sheriff stared, assessing, still without drawing up, his companions with him. Then he was gazing forward again, looking for possible further enemy parties. Because of the bends in the road, they could not see far; but they did see, high on a lochside knoll, their three missing scouts, and these were obviously waving to them. What they were waving about was not very clear, but it looked as though they meant that the main group should turn eastwards, inland.

The sheriff nodded, looked back again, and then gestured onwards with his sword. No time nor occasion to linger; if they were leaving any casualties behind, they must see to themselves – if they could. That was the warfare code, main objectives first, in this case the earl and prince to be informed of the situation. Somewhat straggling as they were now, the mosstroopers came on, shouting triumphantly. It had been some sort of a small victory.

Round two bends and they could see the gap where the Shirmers Burn came down and their track turned off eastwards. There was no sign of more enemy ahead. At the burnside they found their three scouts awaiting them. These reported that there *was* another body of Galwegians coming on, but these were foot. Did the sheriff wish to wait and assail them?

That man decided without difficulty, no. Looking back, he could see only three riderless horses amongst his grinning Mersemen, and then perceived one man riding pillion behind another. Only two casualties, then? That was very well. There might be some wounded, but these must wait. He led the way on and up into the Glenkens Hills, to much chatter and laughter and hooting from behind.

It had been Hugh de Swinton's first experience of battle, although not of border raiding, to be sure.

Safely up amongst the heights, they halted for a brief break, to assess their state and situation. There were a few wounds, none serious and mainly bruising, for the mosstroopers wore padded leather jackets which could turn and lessen many a

26

glancing blow. Two men were seen to have gone down, both transfixed by lances, and therefore probably dead. How many of the enemy had fallen it was impossible to say, for there were greatly varying accounts, and not a few undoubtedly would have been only unhorsed and unhurt, as had their own one pillion-rider, who now regained his own mount. But there was no question that the Galwegians had suffered severely – first blood for the royal forces.

They retraced their outward route over to the Water of Urr, and then down its valley. But when, at length, they reached the camp-site at Glenlair, it was to find no army there, only a couple of men left to tell them to go on southwards towards the Mote of Urr. It seemed that the south-probing company under Lord Home, having a shorter and simpler road to travel, had sent back word quite soon that the main enemy muster was indeed taking place at the Mote, and being added to all the time. So the prince and earl had decided that the sooner they attacked the assembling host the better, before it got still further reinforced, and had marched, this some three hours ago.

So it was on again for their company, still down the Water of Urr, the sheriff somewhat doubtful as to this development. He quite realised that the policy of assailing the enemy while they were not fully assembled might be effective; but it could well mean fighting on a disadvantageous battlefield. After all, if the Galloway muster was at and around Fergus's castle of Urr on its mote-hill, then the enemy might be very strongly placed, for the castle itself would undoubtedly be so. It could, in fact, develop into almost a kind of siege, for which the attackers were nowise equipped, or indeed capable. There might be little room for manoeuvre, for tactics, merely head-on assault against large numbers in a strong defensive position. Sheriff Pate emphasised the dangers and risks of this to his sons and young Bruce as they rode on. He hoped that the Earl Cospatrick would be recognising it, and seeking to coax out the enemy to some more favourable battleground.

They had gone over five miles further down Urr, and were approaching the village of Croys, itself no more than four miles apparently from Mote of Urr, when they saw a party of horsemen coming towards them, and fast, upriver, no large company, perhaps fourscore. Something about that party, the way they were riding, heads down, spurring hard, rang an ominous bell in the sheriff's mind.

"These look like coming for help!" he jerked. "In haste. I do not like this. Coming back for us, I think. And fast!"

Cospatrick de Swinton was both right and wrong in his reaction to the sight; right in that it was not good news, wrong in that these were coming for help. When the newcomers came up with them, they proved to be a troop of Bruce horse – or what was left of one. Their leader, with a bloodstained shirt showing, was a far-out kinsman of young Robert, and he was in a state of mixed anger and all but despair.

"Fools!" he shouted, hoarsely. "The fools! All is lost! They attacked. Headlong. Would not wait. Heeded us not. Struck at the Mote itself. And they knew – the Galwegians knew of us. Knew that we came. Had forces behind us and to flank. It was slaughter, I say! Fools!"

As they all stared at the man, the sheriff thumped his saddle-bow. "Quiet, man!" he ordered sternly. "Keep your head! Tell us first – are you pursued?"

"No. No, I think not . . ."

"There has been disaster? Were you coming to warn us?"

"No. Yes. We were making for Kirkpatrick and Auchenreoch Loch. Back to Nithsdale and Annandale . . ."

"You are fleeing home, then? But not pursued, you think. No great haste, then. So, tell us what is done. Tell us quietly, man. In some order. There has been battle, defeat?"

The man swallowed, and sought to control his voice, while others behind him were shouting their versions of it all.

"The Lord Home sent word that the main muster was at the Mote. We marched south, well past this, beyond Haugh of Urr. My lord of Annandale and your Earl Cospatrick were for waiting. To choose a strong position. To have the Galwegians attack *us*, not us them. And seek to outflank their attacks. But your young Prince William, the fool, he said they must assail the assembly-place. Before more men arrived, before the

28

enemy were ready for us. He, the prince, insisted. And it was disaster . . ."

"You are saying that the prince's army was defeated? And now in flight?"

"Yes. We were split into two, to attack the Mote from north and south. The castle is at a bend in this river, where a burn joins it, a strong site. We approached it on the wrong side, the wrong side of Urr. Many enemy massed on the far side. There are fords, underwater causeways, we knew naught of. And Fergus of Galloway knew that we were coming – it is his country. We could see his people. Thousands! But could not reach them. And while we were seeking ways of crossing, both our forces were attacked from the rear. While fighting off these, the others came across by the hidden causeways. We were trapped. It was calamity. And all folly. Defeat, and needlessly so . . ."

"Folly indeed! So, now? Are we reassembling? *You* are not, it seems!"

"No. It was flight, all flight. All for themselves. No orders reaching us. Two forces. Many fell."

"And the prince? And the earl? And your lord?"

"God knows! We were in the north force. We saw all that could fleeing eastwards. For Dumfries, the Nith, the Annan. We came this way, as best . . ."

"So-o-o!" The sheriff looked at his sons and the others. "Failure! Brawny Will playing the leader, and the fool, together! When princes know best!" He shook his head. "Now what? If all are fleeing back out of Galloway, no purpose in our going on. Nothing that we can do. Back to Lochmaben, then? With these."

Shaken, unhappy, none could say otherwise. They turned their horses' heads, to ride eastwards out of the Urr valley. There was still no sign of any enemy troops.

With no foot to delay them, and with May's long evenings, they were able to reach Lochmaben in Annandale before darkness – to find others there who had been equally expeditious, these including Prince William, Earl Cospatrick and Bruce

29

himself. And in the castle the atmosphere was tense indeed, blame being freely allocated, and few seeming to feel like bed, despite physical weariness and mental turmoil.

Although none could verbally berate the prince, he was left in no doubt that in the opinion of most his was the blame for the defeat, his overruling of the earl's strategy mainly responsible. There was dissension also over the failure to rally again afterwards.

Although they were in no fit state to discuss future plans adequately, there was inevitably some discussion. All seemed agreed on one issue, at least – there was little point in waiting there at Lochmaben and seeking to assemble another army there. Fergus would have to be dealt with, and effectively; but the next attempt must be better planned and led. That was as far as agreement went. And they were none of them forgetting the five northern earls also in revolt.

So next day most of those who had won back to Lochmaben from the Urr set off again for the east and the Merse and Roxburgh, the Swintons included, a somewhat defiant prince and a disgruntled earl at their head, and leaving behind an apprehensive Lord of Annandale, who now feared that further reaction from Galloway might well fall upon himself in the first place.

Hugh, for one, returned homewards but little encouraged by his first experience of warfare. Admittedly his father's party had won their small sally against the enemy; but that was a very minor engagement compared with the dire defeat of their army as a whole. And by no way could he or his imagine that if they had been with the main body the ultimate result would have been any different, the sheriff's military advice being even less likely to have prevailed than had that of his noble namesake the earl.

They made a distinctly subdued journey of it, up long Annandale, over the heights of Tweedsmuir and down Tweed thereafter, however confident Prince William declared himself to be that it would not be long before they showed the wretched Fergus of Galloway who was master in the land, and those northern rebels likewise. The sheriff privately hoped that nothing would be attempted until King Malcolm arrived back with his army from France, with its seasoned warriors, some of them the late King David's practised generals. How long that would be, who could tell, although couriers had been told to urge haste.

3

Back at Swinton Parva, or Little Swinton, martial ardour much cooled, it was good to return to normal living. This subsidiary seat of Swinton Castle, reserved for second sons and the like, lay less than two miles south of Sir Ernulf's fortalice, across the Leit Water, on a gentle ridge, a much less defensive establishment, a hallhouse indeed, long and comparatively low, of only two storeys and an attic, whitewashed and reed-thatched, but commodious and more convenient to live in than the lofty tower-house on its motte. It also had a bailey, or curtain-walled enclosure, around it however, for protection, providing a large courtyard which contained lean-to outbuildings, stablings, dairy, brewhouse, stores; and nearby was the hatton, or hall-toun of the supportive folk, with cot-houses, byres for milk-cows, barns and a horse-mill, the water-mill of the barony, on the Leit, belonging to the castle. It made a pleasant place to dwell in, with open woodland around and splendid views southwards to the Cheviots, the Tweed only six miles away, and northwards to the Lammermuirs beyond the Blackadder a similar distance.

With May now nearing its close, much work, neglected by the military interlude, fell to be dealt with by the Mersemen, mainly cattle country as theirs was, but with sheep flocks on the higher ground. Lambing was over, but now the lambs, with their ewes, had to be moved up to the hills proper for the summer grazing. Calving was still going on, and with the winter-flooded haughlands and valley floors now drying out, cattle had to be moved thereto and the lush pasture. On the runrigs or cultivation rows the oats were sprouting green, but had to be cleared of weeds from the intervening furrows. And so on. In all of this the Swinton brothers were much involved, for they were as dependent on farming for their living as were all their people, including the menfolk who had so recently been playing the mosstroopers in Galloway.

Hugh, as the younger son, had for the past four years been allotted the duty of leading the Lammermuirs May-time sheiling. This was a quite major task, moving the huge flocks of sheep and lambs northwards for almost twenty miles to their high summer grazings. Practically all the Merse lairds did this, for the Lammermuirs, as their name implied, were lofty moorlands of mixed heather and grass, neither rocky nor boggy, excellent pastures for sheep from May until October, indeed the principal sheep-ground of all Scotland. The Cheviots, to the south, were good also; but these hills suffered from two handicaps: one that the flocks had to be got across wide Tweed, where there were no fords passable for sheep, and two that they were all too open to the attentions of acquisitive English border raiders. So it was to the Lammermuirs, an almost empty upland area of some three hundred and fifty anything but square miles, that the Merse flockmasters turned. They had to share them with their Lothian counterparts of still further north, not always amicably. Most lairds and lords had their own well-defined areas, however far detached from their Merse estates and baronies, even the Earl Cospatrick concerned with this process, grazing vast numbers of sheep; but he had extensive uplands on the eastern edge of the range, near his secondary seat of Dunbar, on the Norse Sea coast. The Swintons owned the property of Cranshaws, fairly centrally situated in the southern foothills, comprising some three thousand acres of hillsides and heather and sheltered little valleys, excellent sheep country.

So two days after their return, Hugh, with Duncan his foster-brother and over a score of temporary shepherds, lately men-at-arms, set off for Cranshaws, with their dogs and baaing charges, from their more enclosed winter-time pastures. It was reckoned that two sheep per acre was about a suitable density, which would have allowed the Swintons to take some six thousand animals. But it had not been a very successful lambing season, and they had not reached these numbers;

they had four thousand, however, and moving four thousand silly animals for almost twenty miles was no light task. They went in separate flocks, of course, a dozen of these, each with a couple of men and four or five dogs, and it was Hugh's and Duncan's duty not only to lead the way by the best routes, not necessarily the shortest and quickest with so many streams to cross, but to ride up and down the very extended column of flocks to seek to right any problems and difficulties, of which there were apt to be many. One of the worst of these was when there was convergence with other groups of flocks going in the same direction, especially at fords. On this occasion, with so many of the Merse lairds having been involved in the Galloway adventure, and their sheiling activities likewise delayed, this complication was particularly likely.

It was, of course, no task for horsemen, and Hugh and his foster-brother walked most of the time, but took their horses with them for the frequent inspections of their outstrung procession of slow-moving flocks, these extending necessarily over miles; also they took two or three pack-horses with them, to carry the provisions necessary for their sustenance. Five miles in a day was as much as they could hope to cover, for the lambs, sprightly enough to start with, quickly got tired, lagged, and became separated from their ewes. It was a taxing and wearisome business until one got, if possible, into the patient rhythm of it, so much slower and more demanding than was apt to be the return journey in late autumn, when the lambs were all grown into sturdy near-adults. Yet Hugh, for one, enjoyed these sheiling excursions, having managed to find compensations.

From Swinton village, where the flocks assembled on the haughs between the little church and the Leit Water, they started off north-westwards over undulating country, by Harcarse, to make for their first major hurdle, the crossing of the Blackadder. Sheep could swim, although they did not like to do so, but lambs could drown all too easily; so, since there were few bridges in the Merse, or indeed anywhere in the land, shallow fords and underwater causeways had to be used; and getting the reluctant flocks across these was a patience-trying and lengthy process. There was a ford at Nisbet, four miles on, but although good enough for horses and cattle it was not for sheep and lambs; so they would have to divert westwards for over a mile – and every extra mile counted in this procedure – to Cairn's Mill, where there was a weir to divert a mill-lade, and at this time of the year this could be used as a causeway of sorts. The Blackadder in fact would be the most difficult crossing of the entire journey, it being quite a major river.

It took them most of the day to get that far, many of the sheep seeming excessively stupid and tending to flounce off in any direction except the required one, so that the dogs were kept busy rounding them up and back and the shepherds hoarse and dry with shouting and whistling. But at least the loud baaing and bleating did sink considerably as the day wore on and short legs got weary; and they all could hear the larks carolling and the cuckoos calling hauntingly, and so savour the summer to come.

At Cairn's Mill the enormous task of persuading four thousand sheep to cross fifty yards of river began, and went on for hours, men and horses standing in the water to form a kind of alleyway, while other shepherds, with the dogs, tongues lolling out by now, herded them in, protesting. The water, over the weir, was no more than a foot deep at this season, but the lambs' legs were not even that in many cases, and much coaxing and driving was necessary. Some had to be picked up and carried across, to the alarm of their mothers.

Fortunately there was a semicircular haugh at the far side, a large water-meadow but dry now, where those ferried over could wait, more or less unattended, allowing their shepherds to assist with the crossing of the other flocks; indeed where they might all spend the night. All the men had done this before, but Hugh well remembered his first involvement, and near-despair at the follies and frustrations of it all.

At length this stage was over and not one lamb drowned, although some, bolting in fright into even deeper water, had had to be rescued, wetly. Camp-fires were lit and a plain but substantial meal produced, the so-useful dogs not forgotten. Hugh could have spent the night in the nearby miller's house, to which he was invited; but he preferred to stay with his men. For it was not going to be any quiet and slumbrous occasion, but a matter of watch and ward. For the Merse was apt to be a prey to more predators than just the human variety, wild boars a particular menace. These seemed to prefer the thickets, mosses and scrub forest of the lower ground – one reason why the Lammermuir heights were so valued, and which they appeared to avoid – and thousands of sheep and lambs, conveniently assembled, might well be a major attraction for them. The dogs would assist with the guarding of course, but not even sheepdogs would necessarily be prepared to tackle a wild boar. Nor for that matter would every shepherd, for the creatures could be savage indeed, and powerful, with great menacing tusks, and many had been the human victims. So fires were to be lit at intervals round the landward perimeter of the haugh, boars misliking fire, and patrols kept up throughout the night, Hugh and Duncan prepared to take their turns at this.

As it happened, these two had a particular interest in this guarding against boars. For, according to tradition, this was how they had come by their name. The Merse had always been notorious for infestation by the animals, and the first of their line to come up from Bamburgh in Northumberland, to settle in Scotland, were said to have taken it upon themselves if not to exterminate the pests at least to reduce their numbers drastically. This they had done, to the gratitude of the local inhabitants, and earned them the style of Swine-slayers, and their property and eventual barony the name of Swiners'-toun, or Swinton. Or so went the story. Hugh indeed had killed two boars in his day, on horseback and with a spear. So he felt an especial obligation over this night's guardianship duties.

In the event, the seven hours or so of darkness passed without incident, the sheep too tired to stray and no predators making an appearance. The fact that their human protectors lacked sleep was not important, for although the day's activities had been trying on their patience, it had not been taxing for them physically, whatever it had been for the dogs.

Next day they had no such major obstacles to surmount, but

plenty of minor ones, mainly connected with burns to cross, for, after the trials and alarms of the Blackadder crossing, the flocks seemed to take fright at the sight of any running water at all, and sought to avoid it, which called for much vigorous herding, the dogs being kept very busy; for this was a land of burns and streams. By Crunklaw they came to the Howe Burn and then the Nisbet Burn, in their heading for Gavinton on the Langton Burn, this to avoid the quite large township of Duns, which would have presented great problems for the through-passage of thousands of sheep; and between these three rivulets, they had to negotiate innumerable lesser small watercourses. Yet this Gavinton was not much more than three miles from Cairn's Mill.

And here, with the Lammermuir foothills beginning to rise before them, they met with another complication – competition for passage-way, in the form of another series of flocks heading in the same direction. Such meetings could produce clashes amongst impatient, rival herders, and arguments as to which had the right of way; but fortunately this column proved to be that of Home of Wedderburn, some eight miles north of Swinton, and being Homes, connected to the Swintons by marriage, they were on friendly terms, and no troubles eventuated. No man-made troubles, that is; but inevitably there were plenty of the other sort, sheep-made, for of course the wretched animals tended to associate with each other, whichever flock, and tremendous efforts had to be made to keep them apart, and where this was only partially possible, to define ownership, one blackface sheep or lamb looking exactly like another to the uninitiated, and not all being adequately marked with coloured keels for the different proprietors. However, the Wedderburn lot having come a shorter distance from their home ground that day, Hugh conceded them the passage; and since this would take a considerable time, with numbers approximately as large as his own, it would mean the Swinton flocks stopping for the night at this Gavinton, or a little westwards at the mill thereof, not much more than three miles covered. The same guard against boars was mounted here, although this area was not much troubled with the brutes.

The Wedderburn contingent camped within sight, but at the other side of the Langton Burn. In the morning these ought to be no problem, for the Homes had their Lammermuir pastures almost due north, in the Cockburn Law and Abbey St Bathans area, whereas Cranshaws was still well to the north-west, deeper into the hills.

The following day's journey involved crossing the high ground of Harelawcraigs Hill and down the Mill Burn's valley, a tributary of the Whiteadder. From the heights, looking north, they saw all the spread of the Lammermuirs stretching before them, seemingly to infinity, ridge and summit, cleft and cleuch and valley, green mainly but dotted with the brown of old heather, a fair and all but challenging sight which always stirred Hugh de Swinton. He knew the names of many of these hills, indeed he had climbed most of them over those four years, and sheepish names they tended to be, like Lammermuir itself – Ewelaw and Ewelairs, Lammer Law and Lamb Rig, Wedderlie and Weddersyde, Tuplaw and Tuppiesyde, wedder and tup being castrated and whole rams respectively; Hoglaw and Hog Rig, hogs being yearlings; Rammerscales, Herds Hill, Woollands, Sheeppath, and the rest.

Now they had only some seven miles to go, in the main to follow up the course of the Whiteadder; but they could cut off a sizeable corner by crossing a low ridge at Windsheil and reaching the river again at Ellemford. They got that far by the third night.

Here, in fact, amongst the ever-heightening hills, they were on their own land, although still three miles from Cranshaws. So, once across Whiteadder, in the morning, Hugh left two of the flocks to take over the pastures hereabouts, and moved on with the rest up the quite wide vale, very lovely country with a great sense of space despite the enclosing hillsides, the skies and the ridges and summits seeming to marry in remote unison, with the slopes away ahead of them steepening to enclose the river.

A mile or so up, two more flocks were shed, at Fellcleuch, right and left, into the hills, the shepherds well acquainted with their chosen terrain. They would use local help in their

38

task, of course, for although there were no townships, villages or even hamlets here, the valleys were not entirely empty, and cottages and shacks housed little families with their own cow or two and a few sheep, these eking out a precarious but contented existence amongst the uplands and usually glad to supplement their livings by aiding at the summer-sheiling flocks from the lower country.

Cranshaws itself, reached at last in mid-afternoon of the fourth day, was the nearest thing to a community that the herders had seen since leaving Gavinton, with a tiny church, a mill and a scatter of cot-houses, with one larger house up on a slight ridge above the river which was now beginning to narrow and take on the character of a cascading torrent. This larger house was Hugh's destination.

Their approach had not gone unnoticed apparently and they were met by a welcoming trio, a spare, keen-eyed man of later middle years, a very similar-looking younger man, obviously a son, and a very differently built young woman, rounded without being actually plump, sturdy, sonsy, lively and notably roving of eye where her menfolk were keen – Dod and Jock Cockburn, and Meg.

Greetings were varied, Dod's a grave salutation for Hugh and a nod for Duncan, with a wave for the others, Jock's a wide grin and Meg's a punch on the shoulder for Duncan, a quick squeeze of the arm for his foster-brother and a skirling cry for the shepherds. There were cheers and chuckles all round.

Dod Cockburn was resident chief shepherd for the Swintons and had been for long, who had indeed taught Hugh his trade as far as sheep were concerned. If Jock had not done much teaching, undoubtedly his sister had, in her own way.

Hugh began to explain why this year the sheiling had been delayed, but the Cockburns had heard the news, indeed knew of the fiasco at Mote of Urr, to the wonder of their visitor who never failed to be astonished at the speed with which tidings got around the countryside to even the most remote localities. Meg interrupted to announce that, once they had got the sheep settled down in the riverside haughs, there would be a hearty meal awaiting them all up at the house. Hugh got

39

another squeeze as she departed to see to it all, Duncan noting it levelly.

Later, they all ate together round the long kitchen table, mutton broth, cold roe venison, oaten scones with honey, and ale in plenty, indeed no shortage of anything.

Dod wanted to know for how long Hugh would be staying with them. This was always a question, for to be sure, with the Cockburns there to take charge, there was no real need for the Swintons to remain with the shepherds and flocks, their task to get them all here and take them back in the autumn. But Hugh had always enjoyed a few days in the hills, looking on it as something of a holiday, its delights of sundry sorts to be savoured rather than duties to be performed. But on this occasion, his father and uncle had warned him not to delay his return overlong, as there might well be further military activities ahead. He said as much – three days or four – to cries of disappointment from Meg.

The shepherds were installed in hutments nearby, but the Swintons were given a room in the house. They were escorted thereto by Meg eventually, and each awarded a goodnight kiss, not each of identical quality.

"That one could teach a man much, I think," Hugh observed judiciously, when they were alone and getting into bed.

The other did not comment.

"Do you not agree, Duncan? She is alive, has spirit. And is not afraid to show it. Unlike most of the young women we know."

"Perhaps."

"You do not sound eager! I say that she would make a good guide to more than the Lammermuir Hills!"

"And I say that she would make a man a good wife."

"Wife . . . ?"

"Aye, wife. Goodnight."

Hugh looked at the other's turned back thoughtfully.

Next day was spent inspecting and allocating the various pastures for each flock, this covering the catchment area for the Whiteadder, with its innumerable tributary burns flowing out of a jumble of rounded hills, some major heights, Dod Cockburn and his son leading. Hugh and Duncan knew it all, to be sure, but year by year conditions could vary, different stretches of heather carefully burned to encourage grasses to grow through it for better feeding for the sheep, bog spread or diminished, natural drainage changing, and the like. Just to the north of their ground here was Lothian, and with no marked boundaries, the shepherds had to be very careful, for sheep were inveterate strayers and had to be brought back frequently from neighbours' ground – this of course applying to both sides of the march. So the keel markings were very important here, black double patches for Swinton. Fortunately their land marched with that of Gifford of Yester, a baron with whom they were on good terms, indeed Gifford had been with them on the recent Galloway campaign. He used double red keel markings on the fleeces; so the shepherds along the line had to do much separating and recovering of straying stock.

There was really no need for the Swintons to remain at Cranshaws any longer, save for the making of a brief tour round the perimeter of their three-thousand-acre property to ensure that there were no problems with other neighbouring proprietors, and a checking that all was well with the flocks and shepherds left further down the Whiteadder, but Hugh could do this last on his way home, and he might leave Duncan to see to the former, which was more of a gesture than anything else. However, Hugh was determined that he should have at least one day as it were off duty; and on their inspection this day he had noted something which he had never seen before, certain protuberances on the summit of one of the hills of their terrain, not viewed from quite that angle previously. This was called Priest Law, which was an unusual name, not in the least sheepish; and when he had asked Dod why it was so called and what those projections up there represented, he was told that they were ancient stones referring to some long-past religious foundation, strange site for such as this high and remote hilltop. So that became Hugh's objective for the next day.

He had no intention of going alone, of course. Meg Cockburn was a great hill-walker and climber, for a woman, and often accompanied the men on their shepherding duties, and declared that she roamed the Lammermuirs on her own. She it was who had led him on many an interesting excursion, in the past, not all connected remotely with sheep, a major part of his attachment to the area. On this occasion, Meg showing no reluctance to going along. Hugh had not intended that his foster-brother should accompany them, and might instead start on his round of neighbouring proprietors; but Duncan seemed to take it for granted that he was to be one of the party, and the other could by no means say him nay. Hugh was very fond of Duncan, however dourly uncommunicative he could be at times. At least Jock Cockburn did not offer to make a foursome of it.

Next morning, then, with a parcel of honeyed scones to sustain them, the three of them set off, not up the Whiteadder as they had done previously but due westwards, starting to climb almost at once, directly into the heights, to mount the shoulder of Cranshaws Hill itself and over the heathery gap between it and the lesser Dog Hill, from which they could see the quite imposing outline of Priest Law prominent ahead, across the Kilmade Burn, less than two miles off as the crow flew, but a deal more to walk. Meg climbed nimbly, her ever-long skirts adapted for convenience in the tall heather by the simple expedient of hitching up the rear lengths through between her legs and tucking the tails into a belt at the front, much freeing her movements – and revealing a fine, long pair of shapely limbs for appreciative male eyes. Also not to be ignored was the heaving of a prominent bosom occasioned by all the exercise.

There was a notable dip into the Kilmade Burn valley, representing some waste of energy, but it had its compensations, for down at the burnside amongst rocks and splashings, Meg discovered some inability to get across without help which, with a young man on either side aiding her, ended by her landing bodily into Hugh's arms owing apparently to strangely unskilful footsteps for that one, there to be clutched, cherished and comforted appropriately.

The climb thereafter up Priest Law was quite steep and

taxing on muscles and lungs, for there was no daundering and delay, not with those white female legs leading the way at a lively pace, tumultuous upper half not appearing to hold up the process in the slightest. Meg had been born and bred in these hills, of course. No assistance seemed to be called for, at this stage.

Breathless at the top, they found the curious features which Hugh had spotted from far below, two arrangements of stones. One was circular and wide, broken-down walling and ditches and ramparts, obviously once a Pictish fortlet; and the other an arrangement of flat stones in the form of a cross, which seemed like gravestones, a very old conjunction, and in such a lofty and inaccessible situation. Meg said that her mother had told her that the circle was the remains of a sun-worshipping pagan temple, and that the priest referred to was probably a druid. But Hugh demurred, pointing to the three-cross formation nearby, and adding that the burn they had so recently crossed was called the Kilmade. Kil always referred to the cell of a missionary Celtic Columban Church saint. What 'made' represented was not clear, but he had heard of a St Medan, early Abbot of Melrose, before the Roman Catholic Church had been introduced. So this might well be a retreat-haunt of his, such as these ancient clerics all used to have; and he had chosen this site to counter the influence of the previous pagan worshipping represented by the circular Pictish enclosure. Meg accepted the likelihood of this, especially as, she told them, the next valley they had to negotiate, of the Faseny Water, held the ruins of a chapel which was reputed to have been an outpost of Melrose Abbey. These slabs could well be the graves of its monks, who chose to be buried on this spot on the way to heaven dedicated to St Medan. Satisfied with their assessments, they sat there eating their scones, and admiring the stupendous vistas, the girl between the two men, although it was perhaps noticeable that Meg tended to lean more often against Hugh than against Duncan.

It was far too soon to head back for Cranshaws, all agreed; so Meg suggested that they should pay a visit to another ancient circle of stones, the Craw Stanes on Nine Stanes Rig. They could actually see it from here, although it was three miles away, to the north. Was that too far for the Swintons?

With that challenge, of course, there could be no answer but one, and they set off downhill there and then, on the opposite side from their ascent.

This was a deeper and steeper descent and the subsequent glen a wider one, with a larger stream to cross at the bottom, the Faseny Water, with the ruined chapel on the other side. This watercourse, with Meg prospecting a possible place to wade over, presented Duncan with his opportunity. He offered to carry the girl over, insisted on it. And grinning at Hugh, she agreed that he should – if he could!

So there was much grappling, hoisting and clasping, as with arms round the man's neck Meg was ferried across, a slow process inevitably with Duncan having to base his feet very carefully on the slippery stones and getting very wet, while his passenger made faces at the other man, in no hurry to get down once the far bank was reached. Hugh smiled.

They examined the chapel ruins, which were obviously not so ancient as the relics above, and then proceeded northwards. Apparently they had still another obstacle to negotiate, over the shoulder of Pensheil Hill, the Kell Burn, beyond Pensheil. Knowing the ground best, Meg led the way to an area of shallows, and without waiting for any argument as to who should this time act ferryman, hitched up her skirt-arrangement still higher and strode in, beckoning. It was Hugh's turn to get wet. She warned them that there were still innumerable small watercourses and trickles ahead of them before they reached the escarpment of Nine Stanes Rig.

At least there was no problem in finding their destination on that long bare ridge, for the stone circle, known as the Craw Stanes, stood out prominently from the heather. Inspecting these upright monoliths, they were disappointed to discover no Pictish carvings and symbols thereon. No suggestions were forthcoming as to why these relics were called the Craw Stanes, when crows frequented all these hills.

A discussion developed as to the meaning and significance

44

of these monuments. All knew that they were connected with pre-Christian sun-worship, of course; but there were various ideas as to the number of stones used, for that could be anything from six to thirteen; their alignment as to sunrise and sunset in different months; whether there were always recumbent slabs in the middle, altars for sacrifice, human and otherwise; and the siting of individual indicator monoliths outwith the circle, for whatever purpose in the druidical ceremonies which took place.

Hugh also wondered why there were so few stone circles and symbol stones in the Merse itself. Surely these ancient peoples did not avoid the low-lying ground deliberately, and occupy only the hilly territories? Duncan suggested that this might be a defensive policy to escape the attentions of seaborne invaders, the Vikings and their like, who did seem to avoid the hills.

Their return to Cranshaws, seven miles, was accomplished without any actual hill-climbing, although with the uneven ground, Meg, tiring or not, often seemed to find it helpful to walk hand in hand with Hugh, the men engaging in fairly friendly rivalry in the burn-crossings. It had all been a good day, by any standards.

Next morning, reluctantly, Hugh made his farewells, leaving Duncan to his visiting duties. Meg accompanied him out of sight of the house, where they could embrace in more thorough fashion, and pleaded with him to come back sooner than the autumn sheep-gathering. He promised to try.

Alone and mounted, despite making quick calls on the flocks pasturing lower down the Whiteadder, the man was able to cover the twenty-odd miles in remarkably different time than on the outward journey, home at Swinton Parva in mid-afternoon. There his father told him that the Earl Cospatrick had had word from Prince William that King Malcolm was indeed on his way home, with much of his army, and that the fullest strength of all loyal men was to be mustered to deal with the deplorable Fergus of Galloway. So all the Merse was to be raised, for after Galloway was subdued they were to march north, a great host, to tackle these other rebel earls and put down such shameful revolt by the Celtic lords. There was more work for Hugh de Swinton to do than sheep-herding.

4

The assembly, three weeks later, was again at Roxburgh, however cramped a terrain it was for a major army to muster in the restricted Tweed valley floor. Much of the host had to encamp at Kelshaugh nearby, where the abbey's monks helped to supply sustenance and forage. Almost all the Earl Cospatrick's force were sent there, so Hugh and Duncan did not see the King until the second day, when he came to inspect them all, although Alan, as elder son, went with the sheriff to the castle.

Malcolm mac Henry mac David, Malcolm the Maiden as he was termed – for he was not only unwed but had taken a vow of chastity, much against his mother's pleading, for reasons uncertain – was now in his twentieth year. He was notably different from either of his brothers, in character as in appearance, slender, reserved, slow of speech, wary, but with the occasional swift sweet smile, an unlikely leader of armies. In fact he was scarcely that, a figurehead rather, although with his own quiet strengths, for he had inherited sufficient of his grandfather's fighting Norman commanders to act generals, such as Hugh de Morville, the High Constable, Walter fitz Alan, the High Steward, and Hervey de Keith, the Marischal. Malcolm had indeed only gone in person on the recent expedition, to assist the King of England to recover his Plantagenet territories in France, in order to be knighted by that monarch, odd as this might seem. For only a king could decently confer knighthood on a king, and Malcolm felt that it was time that he was so dignified. And, they had been told, once actually knighted, at Tours, after a skirmish, he had promptly created thirty of his own nobles' sons knights in turn, which he had been unable to do before, for only a knight could make a knight, be he king or not.

Now he came round all the Merse companies camped in the abbey environs, with his youngest brother, David, Earl of Huntingdon, a sixteen-year-old lumpish youth, and escorted by de Morville the High Constable and de Keith the Marischal, veterans both and much more critical of what they saw amongst the mosstroopers than was their liege-lord.

Cospatrick presented Hugh but not Duncan, saying that he had distinguished himself in the fighting at Mote of Urr – which was not strictly accurate but which possibly might help to give the impression that all there had not been quite such a shambles as had almost certainly been reported.

"Sir Ernulf de Swinton was my esteemed grandsire's friend," the King said, nodding. "A gallant knight."

"Sadly much crippled now, Sire, or he would have been here with us. But he has sent every man who could be raised."

"I believe it of him, my friend. And we shall need them all, I think, to deal with these rebels." And he moved on.

Hugh told Duncan that he liked what he had seen of their monarch, preferring him to Prince William or the other, the Earl David, who seemed to be aloof.

Later, their father informed them that the plan was to march in two days' time, for Galloway, again via Lochmaben, where Bruce of Annandale would be likely to have any available word as to Fergus's movements. Such a large army as this being assembled could not move all those miles, and necessarily slowly, without the news getting to the Galwegians, and Fergus's reactions could only be guessed at. He would recognise that this time he would be faced with experienced commanders and much greater numbers, so he might well decide to withdraw into the far and mountainous depths of his province, where he would be hard to bring to battle and the land could be used to fight for him. There was no careless optimism amongst the veterans, although the Princes William and David boasted that they would make Fergus pay for his previous actions.

So, after much marshalling and arranging in order, they

moved off, again up Tweed, in late June now, a large array, four thousand horse and six thousand foot, the Earl Cospatrick distinctly disgruntled at being given only junior command although the only earl present, unless the purely titular English earldom of Huntingdon belonging to Prince David was counted. Admittedly he had scarcely distinguished himself in leadership at Mote of Urr, but he blamed that on Brawny Will. So, offended, he rode not with the royal party but with his own Merse lairds. Anyway, he tended to look down on the present Anglo-Scots ruling house as much inferior to his own more lofty line.

It took the cavalry five days to reach Lochmaben Castle, where they waited for the foot to catch up. The Bruce was able to tell them that the reports said that Fergus had indeed retired deep into his territories, where he was alleged to be gathering greater forces at Borgue, near the Solway coast, where reinforcements from all the Galloway peninsulas could reach him by sea.

This was not the best news for the newcomers, even though half expected. Borgue was fully sixty miles down, well beyond Dalbeattie and even Kirkcudbright, a long way to march their army, and through much country eminently suitable for ambushes. But at least it meant that most of the eastern and northern parts of Galloway would be open to attack and unlikely to be well garrisoned. They ought to be able to make a punishing assault on the rebel earldom.

It was four more days before they could move westwards to cross Nith and into enemy territory. The orders now were for the foot to sack and burn, whilst the cavalry pressed ahead. Actually Hugh and Duncan did more than that, for, with young Rob Bruce again, they volunteered to act scouts, and roamed far and wide spying out the land, much to be preferred to reined-in riding on the march, or harrying and ravishing.

This time they went south-west for Dunscore and then Crocketford, the intention being to reach and if possible sack the Mote of Urr castle, as lesson for Fergus, and then to head on southwards to cross Dee soon after it emerged from long

49

Loch Ken, at Threave, and so to make for Kirkcudbright and Borgue.

It felt strange to be riding free in all this country through which they had so recently fled as a defeated army. They had no trouble with the local inhabitants, most of whose young men would no doubt be away with their earl. And they saw no signs of enemy troop movements.

When at last the scouting-party heedfully approached Mote of Urr, it was to discern no large number of men thereabouts. When a small company of horsemen did emerge from the stockaded enclosure, presumably to challenge themselves, they sheered off discreetly, their duty to gain information not to engage the enemy. But they could tell the King and his advisers that Fergus's principal stronghold was now open to attack.

In fact, when two days later the main cavalry host assailed it, they found the Mote of Urr deserted. What would burn of it was given to the flames and the rest cast down, something of an anticlimax as it was, but their main objective achieved.

The scouts were crossing Dee next day, at Threave, when they met a mendicant friar, who presumably owed no allegiance to the Earl Fergus, for he informed them that the Galloway army was on the march, and heading north. They had left Borgue three days earlier, and were said to be making for the Rhinns of Kell mountains, and further still.

This was important news indeed, which had to be rushed back to their main body; heading north, *away* from them; and making for the mountains. Was this an attempt to lure the royal host into dangerous territory where it might be readily assailed, split up, ambushed and destroyed piecemeal? It could be that. Or it might be that Fergus was heading north a long way, to join the other rebel earls. Or again, he might be meaning merely to work round and get behind the King's array. Whatever it was, Malcolm had to learn about this at once.

Back at the Mote, there was great concern and debate amongst the leadership. First of all, was it true? Could that friar be trusted? And if so, which was most likely to be the correct answer?

Some guessed one course, some the others, most favouring the idea that it was an enemy move to coax them into the Kells heights, a range almost of mountains. But until they were sure of the truth of the report, there was no action which they could usefully take.

Rob Bruce promptly again volunteered to lead a small fast-riding group north to the Rhinns of Kells to discover the facts, Hugh and Duncan offering to accompany him, Alan de Swinton also. This was seized upon at once, and they were told by Keith, the Marischal, to be off right away, haste of the essence, and quite a long way to ride.

So, with fresh horses and some food and drink, the four set off, no escort being desired, quicker without one, and being speeded on their way by King Malcolm himself, wishing them well.

Hugh for one had no doubts as to the size of the task they were undertaking. Bruce said that the Rhinns of Kells were at least twenty-five miles to the north, and extended for a long way further. Once therein they would have to discover if indeed the enemy host was taking up positions in those high hills, still making for the north, or swinging round eastwards and south again in an encircling move. Not any minor responsibility for four young men.

Bruce led them up the east side of Loch Ken at a cracking pace, past the area where they had been engaged with the enemy those weeks before, and where they had looked across to Kenmure Castle. Whether it was still being garrisoned they did not know, nor were concerned now to discover – so long as they were not interfered with in their onward progress. Thereafter, at the head of the loch, almost twenty miles covered already, at Kells itself, they turned off westwards into ever-heightening hills, actual mountains ahead culminating in the mighty peak of Merrick, the highest summit south of Forth and Clyde. They met with no problems other than the terrain itself.

Bruce said that, marching north from Borgue, the Galwegian force would almost certainly proceed up the Water of Fleet, which would bring them to the Fell of Fleet and the Clatteringshaws area. Then up the lesser Water of the Black

51

Dee into the Rhinns, then on through the high pass between the summits of Meikle Milyea and the great Merrick. This would lead eventually down to Loch Doon and at length to Dalmellington, in the shire of Ayr, a long and arduous journey, but necessary if they were heading for the Clyde crossings and up into Perthshire and Atholl and Angus, where were the other rebels. On the other hand, if they were only making a round-about diversion to get behind the royal army, then almost certainly they would have to swing eastwards this way by the head of Loch Ken's twenty-mile barrier – so care here was vital. But if it was just a matter of disposing his forces in the Kells mountain ranges, then they must try to discover where Fergus was making his base therein. All very testing work for scouts.

Going warily indeed they headed westwards for some three miles, seeing nothing significant, but ready to bolt into the hills, until they came to the Black Dee in the Clatteringshaws vicinity. And there they saw sufficient to assure them that they were on the right track, for a large force cannot march over country without leaving its traces, down-trodden grass, damaged bushes and reeds, horse-droppings and the like, and here there were such in abundance; and in muddy patches of the riverside, it was clear that the passage had been northwards.

So that was something ascertained. Fergus had marched this way, and not swung eastwards. How much further?

They discussed procedure now. Whether to follow up in the tracks of the Galwegians? This would be quickest, but might be dangerous if they were to run into any rearward parties of the enemy. On the other hand, ahead of them the hillsides flanking the Black Dee were becoming progressively steeper, with little or no cover available for horsemen. Bruce thought that they should go on. It was evening now, but the late June nights were never really dark, and they ought to be able to avoid stumbling upon any rearguard. Alan thought that it was too risky, and they ought to try to find some parallel route northwards; there must be some such, on one side or the other? It was Hugh who pointed out that there was a distant cottage on a hillside, isolated and almost certainly a shepherd's house. Ask there how long it was since the Galwegian force had passed. The horse-droppings did not seem fresh. When his brother said that was dangerous also, in enemy territory, Hugh maintained that if they said that they were Galloway men hastening to join the earl's army, there would be no suspicions. That was accepted.

They rode on up to the cottage, and found only an elderly woman there. Without hesitation she told them that a great host of men had passed northwards two days before, going where her husband had no notion. But up there was only the pass of Mullwharchar, over to Loch Doon and Ayrshire.

Another debate, as they rode on. Two days ago. How far would the enemy have got in two days in this high country? It would depend on how many were foot. They could be fifteen or twenty miles ahead. And if they were, was there any way that they could still turn and swing round southwards again? Bruce thought not, for east of Loch Doon were only the empty mountain ranges of Cairnsmore of Deugh and Alharig. If they had been going to attempt an encircling move they would surely have struck eastwards before this. So, it looked either a mountains campaign, or Fergus was indeed heading for the Clyde and the Highlands. And if it was the former, they might come across men-at-arms anywhere. They could only go on, cautiously.

That they did, as the dusk settled on the uplands, easily following the tracks of an army. Hugh said that they might get warning – camp-fires. Surely even a rearguard, halting for the night, would light fires? They would not expect to be followed, thus.

They saw no fires, nor any men, as they followed the river up, it now no more than a rushing stream, the hillsides becoming vague, uncertain, in the gloaming. All this certainly would make good fighting ground for defenders, with innumerable places to hide in, for surprise attacks, ambushes, with the invaders inevitably far strung out.

How far to go, then? Go right to the pass, Alan suggested, this oddly named Mullwharchar. If the enemy had not halted by then, surely they would not be going to turn off, their destination the north? Agreeing, they proceeded.

It might have been midnight before they reached the summit of the pass; and however murky the light, or lack of it, the horse-droppings and other signs still persisted. And there was no glow of camp-fires visible ahead. Satisfied, the four of them turned their mounts' heads round and headed back whence they had come. They reckoned that they were almost forty miles from Mote of Urr.

At least they knew their way back. They could not ride fast, until dawn; but by following the rivers, the Black Dee, the Fleet and then Loch Ken, they should be able to cover it in five hours. The King and his commanders ought to be interested in their report.

There was much praise for the four young men, weary indeed on tired horses, when they reached the just-stirring royal camp. King Malcolm declared them worthy sons of their fathers and leal subjects.

A hasty conference of only half-awake leaders was convened to hear the news and to decide on action. All agreed that it looked as though Fergus was heading to join the other earls in their revolt. So what was the best course? To follow after him? The Lord of Annandale said no. Marching an army through those mountains was a slow process, slow for Fergus and slow for them to follow also. Much better that they should take the shorter, quicker route and try to get *ahead* of the Galwegians, to prevent them from joining up with the other rebels, prevent them crossing Clyde, in fact. That would be the worthwhile move.

The Marischal and High Constable agreed — if it was possible? Bruce asserted that it was; he would show them the way. Leave the foot to come on at their own pace. Fast riding by the cavalry, back into Nithsdale and up that river by Thornhill to the Enterkin pass and so over to Sanquhar with the lower lands of Ayrshire ahead. Thereafter north-east by the Crawick Water to Crawfordjohn and up to Douglas. So they ought to reach the Clyde well before Fergus's array, which was having to take a much longer and hillier route, and would be delayed by their foot. Much would depend on where he intended to cross Clyde. He might well make for the first crossings where the estuary and firth narrowed in, at Glasgow, but might choose further upriver. But cross Clyde he must.

So it was decided. It was all move – except for the weary scouts that is. They could sleep for a few hours and come on later; they would catch up. They were too tired to appreciate all the acclaim heaped upon them, it is to be feared.

Undoubtedly it was their own fault for having proved such useful and effective probers of the situation, for the young men were not long in finding themselves allotted further scouting duties; at least three of them were, for Alan was not really inclined that way, and preferred to remain with the army as a captain of mosstroopers. After some hours of sleep and a good meal, it took them some time to catch up with the main body, the cavalry that is, for they passed the foot before ever reaching Nithsdale; indeed it was over the Enterkin heights and on past Sanquhar before they did so, the commanders having clearly forced the pace. The host was intending to turn off north-eastwards up the Crawick Water north of the Lowther Hills; but the leaders wanted to be sure that Fergus was indeed still heading northwards, and by what route, however far to the west he might be, the necessary Clyde crossing their question-mark. If they were going to confront him and prevent him crossing, they had to know his direction. So – information again.

The trio were nothing loth in fact, for mere riding in convoy, as it were, seemed dull to them after all their ranging abroad, whatever Alan's preferences. And this undertaking, although it might prove lengthier, would not be likely to be dangerous, for they were not in enemy country now, and their task simpler. They were approximately level with the Dalmellington area here, where Bruce had said that the Mullwharchar pass led down to, past Loch Doon, although they were nearly thirty miles to the east. So if they headed thither they ought to come across the

55

tracks of Fergus's force, follow these up and discover his onward route.

It meant hard riding again, of course, for the royal host could not risk getting too far north-eastwards towards the upper Clyde if it proved the wrong course and they had to swing back and lose precious time. Fortunately there was no lack of good horses for the scouts.

They pounded westwards then, by Kirkconnel and below the Knipe past Dalleagles, and were able to reach Dalmellington in three hours. There they again came on the tracks of an army, and local folk told them that the Galwegians had passed there two days before, a great host, where going they knew not, but they had proceeded on down the River Doon.

So far, so good. There seemed to be no doubt now that Fergus was bound for the Highlands. They followed on.

An hour's riding and they found that the army had left the Doon valley at Mill of Shield, to head due northwards towards Stair, on the River Ayr, camping for the night just short of there. So they were catching up. By midday they were at Tarbolton. Clearly Fergus was avoiding Ayr and the coastal routes. If he continued thus, Bruce said, he would pass Kilmarnock and up the Fenwick Water towards Mearns. The Clyde crossing near Glasgow, then, at a narrowing where there was a causeway. It looked almost certain that was the enemy plan.

At Hurlford, south of Kilmarnock, they came across the traces of another large camping-site where most evidently the host had spent the previous night, indeed camp-fire embers still smouldering. That was it, then – Fenwick, Mearns, Langside, Glasgow. It was enough. At the rate that they seemed to be marching, say twelve miles in a day, three more days to reach the Clyde crossing. Could the royal army intercept before that? It ought to be possible.

All haste, then, back to their own people. Wherever they were by now.

Without Rob Bruce knowing the country as he did, they would have needed to retrace their steps; but he said that by heading almost due eastwards, by the hilly drove-road which led from the cattle-rearing heights of the Airds Moss and the Blackside Hills, they could reach the Douglas Water in about thirty miles. The King's force probably would not have got that far by the time they reached it, but they could turn up it and meet them. Thirty miles, then, with their news.

They made it by dusk to Douglas, found their army not yet there and, turning upriver, met their people where the Glespin Burn joined the larger river. Great was the satisfaction expressed at their report, and loud the acclaim again. Weary once more, they listened to the plans being made. The High Steward, Walter fitz Alan, knew the territory south and west of Glasgow well, for much of it was his great barony of Renfrew. He suggested that the place to try to reach and wait for Fergus would be in the Langside area, open ground where they could marshal their cavalry to best effect. It was near the excellent Clyde crossing at Rutherglen. There was none better, for miles on either side, for a host to go over. Heading the way he was, that would be Fergus's objective. How quickly could they get to Langside?

There were various assessments as to that. They would have to give men and horses a brief rest, then on through the night. How far? To Lesmahagow ten miles. To Strathaven another ten. Blantyre ten more. If they could make Blantyre by the following night, they ought to be in a position to intercept the enemy. All agreed that they could effect that.

Hugh and his companions foresaw themselves being called upon to undertake more scouting duties, to discover the whereabouts of the Galwegians by tomorrow night. But in fact they seemed barely to have closed their eyes when they were awakened and informed otherwise. They were to go back, not forwards, this time. Their task now was to contact the foot, and lead them over north-westwards, to get behind Fergus's array and advance to threaten its rear, so that the enemy would be caught between the two royal forces.

Actually, the trio were less than happy with this new order. Tired as they were, they would have preferred to have acted in their former role again, especially when they learned that they had to take Patrick, Lord of Home, Cospatrick's younger son, with them, by royal command – this in case the foot commander, his elder brother the Lord Waldeve of Dunbar, refused to consider the young men of sufficient authority for him to have to obey their instructions. Home was, of course, far-out kin to the Swintons, but scarcely beloved. He, in turn, seemed no more enamoured of this mission than they were.

However, in their still sleep-affected state, converse was at a minimum anyway as they rode off southwards again. Just how far the foot were likely to have got they had little notion, but Bruce thought probably somewhere between Auldgirth and Closeburn. In fact, they proved to have done rather better than that and a meeting was effected near Thornhill that evening, in the haughs of the Nith.

Lord Waldeve of Dunbar was very different from his brother, a friendly enough character in his early thirties, however chafing he was at being left to command these slow-moving thousands. Almost certainly he would have accepted without demur Hugh's and Bruce's instructions to change course and make north-westwards to get behind the Galwegians, lacking his brother's authoritative telling. Anyway, he commanded a crack-of-dawn start for the troops, and told the trio that they must lead the way, for he knew nothing of this country.

Conferring that night, Bruce, Hugh and Duncan came to the conclusion that it would be best to go back once more over the same route followed by the cavalry, until they reached Crawick, where they should head off westwards, as they themselves had done on their last scouting, to follow up the enemy trail on their apparently chosen course to the Clyde. How far they would have got in the interval, they could only guess.

It was galling, of course, for horsemen to move so slowly as the infantry, after all their dashing about, and they sympathised with Waldeve and his lieutenants who had been so constrained all along. Ten miles a day was the maximum that they could cover; so they had at least four days' marching ahead of them. Patience was the order of the day.

For three frustrating days, then, they made their deliberate way north-westwards, on the trail of that other army, wondering – wondering how much further, wondering how the King's force was doing, wondering what would be the outcome of it all; and all the time fretting at the pace. Not that they could blame the men-at-arms, burdened with their weapons, gear and blankets, who had to trudge all these endless miles with no certainty as to the end. They were seeing warfare from a different angle.

It was the fourth day, on the Earn Water in the Broadlees vicinity, that suddenly all was changed. They had come down to the lower ground from the loch-dotted high moorland of Ballageich, and were looking over to more of the same rising ground to the north, when they perceived movement, widespread movement. And as they gazed, they saw that it was movement on a large scale, by no means disciplined movement. Men, hundreds of men, were streaming approximately in their direction, and although most were on foot, there were some horsemen amongst them. Soon they seemed to cover the moorland.

"Sakes!" the Lord Waldeve cried. "See, there is flight! Flight, I say! What . . . ? Who . . . ?"

"They are not *our* people," his brother jerked. "They are foot. Few horse. Our host forward all horse. So . . . !"

"They can only be the Galloway men," Bruce exclaimed. "In such numbers. It must be defeat! For Fergus. There has been battle, and these are fleeing. While we, we but marched! The two hosts have met, somewhere north. And these are fleeing back."

"Then we are too late. Battle joined, and over!"

"Too late, yes . . ."

"Not too late to deal with these!" Home cried. "See, we can halt their flight."

"To what end?" his brother demanded. "To slay a few more folk who now threaten nothing."

"They are the enemy. And they could rally. What have we come all this way for?"

"They may be only a small part of Fergus's force. A wing,

defeated. All may not be so. We should press on, I say. Leave these. We may be needed still . . ."

There was much exclamation from Waldeve's other leaders. It was clear that most agreed with Home. Attack these evidently fleeing men. Teach them to rebel against their king! More might well be coming . . .

Personally Hugh agreed with Waldeve that there was little point in seeking to assail these fugitives, who represented no sort of menace. They were their own fellow-countrymen, after all, even if their earl had raised them to rebellion against their sovereign-lord Malcolm. Better to press on, in case they were needed ahead.

But the other viewpoint prevailed. They should be intercepted, assailed, cut down. And it was obvious that more were coming.

Not that interception was a simple matter. These fleeing men were scattered over a wide area, in pairs, small groups and larger clusters, but in no recognisable formations and under no evident command. Moreover, now they were tending to veer away westwards, for the mass of the royalist infantry ahead would be very evident to them. To deploy thousands of foot suddenly to deal with any proportion of these would be difficult. Cavalry would have been different, but the only horsemen here were about a dozen lairds and leaders. Without enthusiasm, Waldeve despatched a few troops of men to make a gesture at interception, but it was only that. Patrick Home and two or three others spurred off with them; Hugh, Bruce and Duncan remained behind.

More horsemen were now appearing over the low ridges of moorland ahead, from the north-east, but none in any compact formation, further evidence of defeat. There was nothing that an infantry force could do about these.

They waited.

In time the punitive parties returned, blood-lust partially satisfied. But Home brought information, from the mouth of a young wounded McCulloch lairdling who, interrogated, told of a grievous surprise for the Earl Fergus's host in the Cathcart area, south of Langside, trapped while they were crossing the River White Cart on their way to ford Clyde. A great cavalry force had struck at them, on both sides of the water. It had been chaos, disaster, the earl's array wholly broken up. Where Fergus was now, who knew? But all was lost, his army dispersed.

This confirmation of their assessment of the situation left Waldeve, however gratified, unsure what his role should be now. There did not seem to be much point in leading his footsore marchers further northwards if the victory was thus won and they all had to head south again whence they had come. He adopted the obvious course, to wait where they were meantime, and send messengers ahead to the King for instructions. As obvious was the choice of couriers, the Swintons and Bruce.

These went gladly. It ought not to be difficult to find the victorious army.

It proved not to be so. They found the White Cart readily enough, and following it down in due course came to the great encampment of the royal host.

Triumph reigned of course, the only disappointment being that they had not captured the Earl Fergus. But his cohorts were destroyed, although the Marischal tempered that declaration by substituting the term dispersed rather than destroyed. They had gained a complete surprise and had inflicted great damage and slaughter, with remarkably few casualties themselves. Bruce of Annandale commiserated with his son over having missed it all.

What now, then? The King's experienced advisers were urging him to go on, having got thus far, themselves to do the crossing of Clyde and marching on northwards, instead of Fergus. Strike at the other rebels while the iron of victory still was hot. On to the Highlands with them.

This policy seemed to win general acceptance, in the present euphoria of success. But there was the complication of the infantry host. This had marched far enough already. To order it onwards for at least another hundred miles was out of the question, and its slow progress would hold up any action anyway. So it should turn back, and the men-at-arms revert meantime to being farm-workers, millers, smiths, cowherds and the like – with harvest-time coming they would be needed thereat. So, an order sent to that effect. The Lords Waldeve and Patrick to come on, leaving others to lead the infantry homewards. Bruce, Hugh and Duncan were the inevitable couriers again, since only they knew just where the foot was waiting. Then they could follow on northwards, with the Earl Cospatrick's sons.

The trio at least were left in no doubts as to their usefulness.

5

Delays over getting the infantry leadership arranged and the host on its way southwards resulted in Hugh and his companions not catching up with the cavalry army again until they reached the vicinity of Cumbernauld, in upper Strathkelvin, well on the way to Stirling, for Waldeve and his brother were scarcely as urgent horsemen as were the younger men. These lords did not make the most congenial fellow-travellers.

This was all unknown country, north of Glasgow, for Hugh and Duncan. And their first sight of Stirling, with its great fortress-crowned rock rising out of the Carse of Forth, the blue infinity of the Highland mountains behind, was unforgettable, dramatic. Here the advancing army had to begin to go warily.

This was, of course, the very waist of Scotland and, for armies as for even ordinary travellers, a very narrow waist it was. For here the Scotwater, or Firth of Forth, cut in some eighty miles from the Norse Sea, on the east, and narrowed fairly abruptly into a river, to provide the first possible crossing-place other than by ship. And westwards, for twenty-five miles the Flanders Moss, a five-miles-wide stretch of bog and swamp and lochans created by the River Forth coming from its Highland source on Ben Lomondside, was impassable save by one or two secret and winding routes known only to the MacGregor clansmen to the north. So here, at Stirling, any who would move from Lowlands into Highlands, other than by sea, must cross; a situation which largely accounted for the fact that Scotland all but consisted of two nations, Lowland and Highland.

Here, then, if the rebel Celtic earls knew of this advance of their spurned monarch, the Lowland Norman-Scots Malcolm, they could effectively hold up the array by simply blocking the narrow bridge and the mile-long causeway beyond. Here even a small force could halt a large one, one reason why earlier Scots rulers had fortified the great castle rock overlooking the passage. So now a fair-sized advance guard was sent forward to prospect. They sent back word that all was clear. It was, admittedly, unlikely that the earls could have heard of the sudden decision of the royal force to move into the Highlands against them.

As they crossed Forth and moved on up the Allan Water beyond, making for Strathearn, Sheriff Pate explained to his sons just what was behind this northern revolt. Ancient Scotland was a Celtic nation, from the Picts and Dalriadans onwards, and had been ruled by a High King, the *Ard Righ*, and his lesser kings, the *ri*, these using the style of mormaors, seven of them. In time, with the uniting of Bernicia – that is, the Merse and Lothian – and Strathclyde with the High King's Alba and Dalriada, the Scotland as they knew it was born, and these mormaors or *ri* had adopted the title of earls. In emulation, later, two earldoms were created by the monarchy in the Lowlands, but only for nobles with the Celtic background, these the Earls of March and of Galloway. These Celtic earls were very jealous of their ancient rank and privileges, and they claimed that the present line of kings, descended from Malcolm the Third, Canmore, had failed to respect these. Religion entered into it all also, for of course the earls had all been reared in the original Columban Celtic Church, whereas Malcolm Canmore had introduced the Roman Catholic faith, through his queen Margaret, the present King's great-grandmother, and that Church had put down the Celtic one. Now many of the offices of state were held by Catholic bishops, to the offence of these northern magnates who formerly had held them. Apparently the last straw had been King Malcolm's taking of a Scots army to France to aid the King of England's warfare there, and this revolt had broken out.

Hugh, for one, got the impression that their father, of

part-Celtic blood himself, was not entirely out of sympathy with the rebels.

The King was heading for St John's Town of Perth, where the earls were reported to be assembling, this presumably because it was near the head of Strathearn, and the Earl of Strathearn, Ferteth, was their leader. The others were the Earls of Atholl, Angus, Mar, Moray and Fife. That left only Ross, whose attitude was uncertain and delicate, but highly important. For he, Malcolm MacEth, was of the royal blood himself, descended from King David's brother, Ethelred, who had rebelled against his mother and become a Celtic Church cleric. The Earl Malcolm had already rebelled against his kinsman, the late king, had been captured and imprisoned in Roxburgh Castle; but, eventually freed and restored to his earldom of Ross, he had married the sister of the great Somerled, Lord or King of the Isles, who ruled the Hebrides and the West Highland seaboard. Somerled was in an uneasy relationship with King Malcolm; but if Ross joined the other earls, and managed to bring in his brother-in-law, then matters would be serious indeed, for Somerled controlled vast numbers of warlike Islesmen and clansmen and was himself one of the most renowned warriors in Christendom. So much was in the balance as far as the northern part of the kingdom was concerned, the main reason why this present venture was being proceeded with without delay. Ross must not be persuaded to join the others.

The Allan Water, a major tributary of Forth, took them northwards for over twenty miles, until they crossed a sort of watershed, to the young Ruthven Water which flowed down into the Earn and so on to the Tay estuary. They were here entering Strathearn, and could look for trouble perhaps. They thought it prudent to camp at Tullibardine.

Although Bruce, Hugh and Duncan knew nothing of this country, neither was anyone else in the company very know-ledgeable – and since these three had proved such able scouts hitherto, they were chosen to go ahead once more, prospecting. If the earls were assembling at Perth, then it was not likely that any large numbers of men would be left in Strathearn itself,

65

but precautions must be taken. Also it was vital to discover, if possible, just where such muster was taking place, since it was improbable that it would be within the city itself.

So the trio rode ahead once again, and were not averse to doing so, although here they felt themselves to be on more dangerous ground, mistakenly perhaps, but because it was all unknown to them.

Very much aware of the mighty barrier of the Highland mountains drawing ever nearer, they went, eyes busy, past the ruined chapel of Columban St Kattan and on to Aberuthven, the first sizeable community they had come to. Here they saw another chapel, not ruinous. The folk wore ragged tartans and there was very much the feeling of another land. They were eyed with suspicion rather than with hostility. But pointing to the chapel, with a thatched cottage attached and smoke rising from the latter's chimney, Hugh suggested that it probably housed a Roman Catholic priest or monk, and if so he might be more prepared to inform them than would be these other villagers. They turned aside thereto.

Sure enough, a young monkish character, hearing horses' hooves, met them at the door, and whether as a self-protective gesture or out of habitual custom, raised an arm to make the sign of the cross and wish them peace. Since they were hardly there with peaceful intent, this was slightly off-putting, but Hugh spoke in friendly tones.

"We are seeking the Earl of Strathearn. On King Malcolm's behalf. Do you know where we may find him?" he asked.

"The Earl Ferteth is not at Ruthven Castle, sirs," they were told, without hesitation. "He is, I understand, gone to Scone Abbey."

"Scone? That is near to Perth, is it not?"

"North of St John's Town three miles it is, yes. There is a great meeting there, it is said."

"Ah, not at Perth itself? That meeting is what brings King Malcolm to these parts."

"Scone Abbey it is. Other great ones there."

"And many men?"

The priest sounded more guarded now. "As to that, I am not informed, sir. But some are gone from here, yes."

"M'mm. We thank you then, Father. We shall tell the King of Scone." And they rode on.

Scone was a likely enough assembly-place they decided, especially with the religious aspect of this revolt. Scone had been the traditional crowning-place of the Scots monarchs since Kenneth MacAlpin's time three centuries before, its abbey the sanctum of the renowned Stone of Destiny, the coronation seat, of enormous symbolic significance for any challenge to the throne's present occupant. And of course, since large numbers always attended coronations, there had to be ample space available for the magnates' escorting companies there, which there could not be in the narrow streets of the walled city. This was important information, for the trio knew enough of that famous place to be aware that it was on the other, eastern, side of Tay from Perth, and this situation would almost certainly affect the royal strategy.

They did not proceed further, only to the crossing of Earn at Ford of Dalreoch, to ensure that it was not held by guards, before turning back with their news; for the army's approach might well have to be altered. They rejoined the host in the Auchterarder vicinity, and great was the discussion aroused by their report. This of Scone, and having to cross Tay, one of the greatest rivers in Scotland, altered ideas considerably. The recognised crossing was the ancient bridge at Perth itself, alleged to have been built by the Romans; but that would almost certainly be well guarded. However, it was well known that there were fords some way upriver, the main one just opposite Scone itself, the Dorders Ford, barely three miles up; and another at Luncarty, two miles more. These, probably, were where they should make for.

The Marischal and other tacticians decided that a three-pronged approach was advisable. Two large forces should head all but due northwards, well west of Perth, to get round to these two fords, one to aim directly at the Dorders for Scone itself, the other to Luncarty, to get over and behind the assembly area, and to threaten from the north-east. But the third and smaller group should approach the city of Perth openly, from the south here, to distract and preoccupy the earls' attention so that they were more open to attack from flank and rear.

An interesting aspect of the situation became evident in this discussion. The Earl Cospatrick and his two sons, supported by some others of the leadership, those with a more Celtic background, made it clear that they were not happy with the warlike expressions and threats put forward by many of the Norman-Scots lords and echoed by the Princes William and David, if not by their brother. It was one thing to deal drastically with Fergus of Galloway, whose earldom they coveted and who, by his proximity to their own lands, constituted a grave danger; but these northern earls were in a different category altogether. Their rising must be put down, admittedly; but the less bloodshed and battle involved the better. After all, they represented more than half the land area of all Scotland, and the native Celtic part of it; and some of their protesting had an undoubted validity. Let them see the King there in strength, and hear that Fergus had been defeated, and give them opportunity perhaps to negotiate, without major fighting. Sheriff Pate backed this attitude, to his sons' approval.

Although this aroused a contrary reaction in many there, King Malcolm saw wisdom in it and voiced moderation. So decisions were made. The Marischal de Keith would lead the Dorders Ford main assault; the High Constable de Morville command the Luncarty encircling move; and the King himself would make directly for Perth with about one thousand horse, to demonstrate an obvious presence and to hope that the overall position would lead the earls to negotiate for some consideration of their grievances.

In the circumstances, the Earl Cospatrick and the Mersemen elected to go with the King's party, Hugh, Duncan and Rob Bruce with them.

They had some dozen miles to go, the other two forces further; and since it was advisable that all should make their presence known to the earls at approximately the same time, for maximum effect, there was no hurry for the royal company. While the other two arrays went due northwards, by Dalreoch and Gask and Glen Almond, they themselves rode by Dunning, where they saw one of the original Columban churches still entire, and on to ford Earn near Forteviot, which had been the capital of the mormaordom of Fortrenn, the precursor of the Fife earldom. From there it was only some three miles over the shoulder of Moncreiffe Hill, to Perth and the Tay.

With the two princes gone with the other forces, and most of the Norman lords likewise, the Cospatrick faction were able to come much closer to King Malcolm than hitherto, and found the young monarch agreeable and even companionable. His was a comparatively gentle nature to be King of Scots, a position which had always called for strong characters. Still only in his twentieth year he was scarcely the war-leader; but perhaps in the present situation he was the better for that. Clearly he was looking for some acceptable compromise with his Celtic earls rather than outright battle.

Moncreiffe Hill's ridge surmounted, they looked down on the attractively placed city beside the winding Tay suddenly narrowing from its estuary, a mere mile off now, within its strong walls. In fact, Malcolm was the only one of the party's leaders who had ever been here before, brought as a boy of twelve to be crowned, on the death of his grandfather David; so he knew something of the features of the place, in especial that the fairly modest royal castle stood outwith the walls, and this side of the town, a convenience in the present situation, for almost certainly they would find the city gates shut against them. They could take up position at the castle, and seek to come to some reasonable arrangement with the earls, threatened as these would be by the other arrays. Malcolm confessed however that his one great fear was over the Earl of Ross and his links with Somerled of the Isles. If these were brought in against him, then the kingdom would be in jeopardy indeed.

Nearing the walls, they could see the castle rising near the waterside and not far from one of the city gates. Saw also that the said gate was closed and men watching from its parapet above. The King sent forward the Earl Cospatrick to announce his presence, taking a few horsemen with him.

"I am the Earl of March," he shouted. "I come in the name of His Grace Malcolm mac Henry mac David mac Malcolm mac Duncan, your High King, here present. He requires this, his city of St John's Town of Perth, to be opened to him forthwith."

There was no response.

"I repeat – open! In the name of the King. And at once."

Still no one answered him, and the gate remained closed and barred.

"You shall pay for this!" the earl cried, and returned to the waiting company. It was indeed only what had been anticipated.

The thousand men dismounted there in one of the Inches, as the open spaces north and south of the town were named, prepared to encamp and set up horse-lines, while the monarch and his officers made over for the castle. Now they must wait, perhaps for quite some time. Scone and the Dorders Ford were three miles away to the north.

The castle, however royal in name, was little more than an empty shell, its keeper an old man who clearly scarcely believed that here was his master in person. He and his wife did the best they could for the visitors, but that was not much. The new arrivals doubted whether this was better than camping in the field. They also wondered how the other two detachments were faring.

Waiting, Hugh, Duncan and Rob Bruce went on a circuit of the walls – or a semi-circuit, for these went right to the river-bank on the east side. They ascertained that all the gates were shut, although possibly the one which they could not see from this side of Tay, that which opened on to the bridge, was not. What the citizens of Perth, in there, were thinking they could only guess.

Back with the King, they all discussed what was best to do if there was no response, their waiting strategy unavailing. Malcolm was certainly not in favour of an attack on the city, seeking to storm those walls and gates. That undoubtedly would entail much loss of life for his men and also for the townsfolk. Nothing was to be gained by such slaughter, and Perth itself in royal hands would not improve the situation as regards the earls. All that they could do, probably, was to work their way round the walls northwards, and so join the Marischal's force at Dorders, or wherever it had got to in the interim.

It was early evening before there were any developments. Then a creaking and clanking at the gate nearest the castle heralded the arrival of one man. Once he was out, the gate was promptly slammed shut again. The lone visitor was a richly clad cleric.

He was brought to the castle, an elderly man looking distinctly uncomfortable despite his fine garb, and announced himself to be Rembold, Abbot of Scone, seeking the King's Grace.

Malcolm, flanked by his lords and lairds, received him stiffly for that young man. "So, my lord Abbot, what brings you, a rebel, to my presence?" he demanded.

"No rebel, Sire, I assure you. But your faithful leal servant."

"Yet you harbour these rebel earls, I am told – you the custodian of my coronation stone."

"I have had no choice, Your Grace. They descended upon my abbey. Enforced their wills upon me and my canons and monks. Indeed claimed that I am interloper, impostor, that Scone belongs to the Old Church. And . . . they are strong."

"So? And now you come to me? For aid?"

"No, Sire. Or . . . not aid. But for your royal heed and concern. They, these earls, have sent me. To speak with you, for them."

"Ha! And to what effect, my lord Abbot?"

"They are constrained. By two of your armies, Sire. There has been fighting. Men dead. They would have you to know that they are not in revolt against Your Grace. Only that they seek reform of rule and governance. They believe that they and their people are wronged in certain matters of state."

71

"They assemble their thousands of men against me, and you say that they are not in revolt?"

"Only by so doing, they believed, would Your Grace hear their plaint and heed them. They say that they have complained before and gone unheeded."

"They are ever at it! Harking back to ancient times. Judging all by the past."

"So say I, Sire. But they see it . . . differently. So, to save further bloodshed, they send me to Your Grace."

"To seek to effect what?"

"The Lord Ferteth — that is, the Earl of Strathearn — would have you to call back your armies. And heed their requests, consider them. If Your Grace will do that, then they will disperse *their* forces. And there need be no more blood spilled."

"And these requests? These complaints? What are they, that I have to consider?"

"I do not know, Sire. They have not told me, in any detail. My task is to learn if you will hear them. And hold back your armies meantime. If so, they will send their requests, name them, for your consideration."

Malcolm smoothed his already fairly smooth chin. "Aye. Well, leave us for a space, my lord Abbot, and I will think on the matter. You will be called when I have decided. Leave us."

The cleric gone, the King smiled to the others. "So, it serves — thus far! We shall hear what are their demands. How say you, my lords?"

"It is what we sought," the earl said. "They are concerned. Probably the Constable has placed himself between Scone and some of their support. It remains to be seen what their demands may be."

"And whether they are such as may be met!" Bruce of Annandale added.

They waited a little before calling back the abbot, and told him that the King would consider the earls' request when they were brought, promising nothing. Meantime, however, he would order the other two arrays to refrain from further attack, but to remain in their present positions.

The abbot was clearly relieved, a relief demonstrated by his revelation now that it all might have been otherwise; for at one stage the Earl Ferteth of Strathearn had proposed a sally in force by a sufficiency of their clansmen to capture the King. The impression given was that this dire proposal was rejected largely on the abbot's own urgings, and this more worthy course adopted. How much of this to believe they did not know.

The cleric departed, promising to return on the morrow.

Hugh and his friends were allotted another task, to go and inform the Marischal and the Constable, and to command them in the King's name to halt hostilities meantime.

Making the half-circle of Perth's walls again to the northern of the two so-called Inches, they proceeded up Tay three miles to the Dorders Ford. They found the Marischal's force encamped for the night on the wide haughland at the far side of the crossing – so they had at least won the passage over what was bound to have been a well-guarded approach. The abbey was to be seen on the high ground half a mile away, presumably still in rebel hands.

Fording the underwater causeway they reached Keith, who proved not unhappy to receive their news and orders, for he admitted that the earls were in a strong position up there and his two previous attempts to storm the place had been beaten off with quite heavy losses. He would be well pleased not to have to repeat the process.

Reaching de Morville thereafter, in the dusk, was less simple. Since they were now across Tay they did not have to go up the couple of miles to the Luncarty ford but could head straight north-eastwards to get around and behind the abbey area. Just where the other array was, the Marischal had no idea.

The trio rode cautiously. They had no guide, and all they were told was that there was an old Roman camp, easily recognisable, some way up, not far east of the Luncarty ford, where they were bound to come across the tracks of the Constable's force. They could only follow these up.

This they did, thankful as ever for the propensities of any cavalry host to leave very obvious trails of hoof-marks and horse-droppings, easily traced. This took them now in an easterly direction amongst woodland and small hills, past stone circles and some standing-stones, evidently a Pictish settlement area, and on past a hamlet called Balboughty. It was the camp-fires shining in the gloaming which brought them to their goal eventually, beside a mill and its stream, where they were challenged by watchful guards and escorted to the High Constable.

That man heard them out more critically than had Keith. Clearly he was for attack and teaching these Celts a lesson. There was a force of Highlandmen, apparently, a mile or so to the east, and he had a detachment out watching them – reinforcements for the earls undoubtedly. For how long was he to hold back his assault? Until ordered to resume, he was told. But the abbot had said that he would be returning to the King on the morrow. De Morville muttered something derogatory.

They spent the night at this encampment, an undisturbed night, and were up early for their return to Perth.

There they were not long back when Abbot Rembold did reappear, with the earls' demands, or proposals, as he more tactfully put it. First of all, he said, they protested their loyalty to the King, in person; their complaints were about the policies imposed on a young monarch by his present advisers. They wanted a better sharing-out of the offices of state; the rights of what remained of the Columban Church to be recognised and respected, its surviving monasteries and chapels protected from Roman Catholic encroachments; some substantial reduction of the sokage, or dues paid to the crown for lands held, a feudal conception never known before in Scotland, especially where these payments were, as so often, made over to the Catholic Church, as had been the policy of the late King David, to help pay for his parish-ministry conception; justiciarships or dempsterships, with sheriffdoms or thanages, to be held, in Scotia – that is Scotland north of Forth and Clyde – mainly by Celtic nominees; a limiting of the powers of feudal barons appointed by the crown to newcomers, for instance the power of pit-and-gallows; and more similar.

Listening to this catalogue, Hugh de Swinton came to the conclusion that these northern earls had indeed something to complain about, especially in the matter of the Church. They, in the Merse, were critical of the ever-increasing power and dominance of the clergy. But here in the north, still Celtic, the situation must be the more trying. David had been a good and able king, but his methods of controlling his lords and barons by promoting the churchmen's power, and the parish system, were not without their problems and drawbacks.

Again the abbot was asked to retire, while Malcolm and his advisers considered all this. In fact, no great deal of consideration was necessary, for none of these complaints was so difficult to concede as to be worth going to battle over. Perhaps it was as well that de Morville and the others of purely Norman background were not present, or they might have advised differently. But the Earl Cospatrick, his sons, and the Mersemen were strongly in favour of agreement to most of it; and Bruce of Annandale, although of Norman ancestry had Celtic blood also, made few objections. So the abbot was called in again and told that if the earls sent a written list of their requests to the King at Roxburgh, they would be sympathetically reviewed and concessions made. Meanwhile the royal army would return southwards and deal finally with the recalcitrant Fergus of Galloway, once they saw the earls' forces were dispersing.

The Abbot Rembold took his departure, with vehement protestations of loyalty and esteem.

So it was back again for the scouting friends to inform the Marischal and the Constable as to the royal will and decision, whatever their reactions, with orders to reassemble at Auchterarder for the march south.

They went in cheerful mood.

6

It had been a strange campaign, frustrating for the warlike, satisfactory for those who saw peace as preferable, with the only actual battling having been fought against Fergus of Galloway. But this matter of Fergus still preoccupied the leadership. He was still likely to be a thorn in the flesh, a constant danger, for although his force had been defeated at the White Cart, no great numbers had been slain, and the great majority of his people would have been able to make their way back home, the earl included unfortunately. And Galloway was a vast territory, a whole province which, with the outlying parts of the shires of Ayr and Dumfries which it tended to dominate, extended to perhaps four thousand square miles, and quite heavily populated. So Fergus could easily raise another and much larger army. Not only this, but there was a complication which demanded some solution swiftly. Fergus had married Elizabeth, an illegitimate daughter of King Henry the First of England, which meant that he had especial relations with the English – indeed, his two sons, Uhtred and Gilbert, were still with King Henry the Second in France, not having come home with Malcolm. For all concerned, it would be wise to deal with the Galloway situation before these two returned, for the English monarch had not been happy about the Scots army's leaving of him; and the last thing wanted now was some trouble with England over Galloway. Practically all, therefore, agreed that Fergus should not be given time to rally his forces and assemble his full strength.

So it was back southwards for the royal host, almost exactly by the route over which they had come. There was little hope of overtaking their own infantry which, by this time, would probably have reached their home grounds and disbanded.

But their thousands of cavalry ought to be capable of coping with Fergus, in his present disorganised state.

They had perhaps one hundred and twenty miles to ride, even to Loch Ken, and Fergus might have retired considerably further south, possibly to Borgue, to lick his wounds. Four or five days, then, for a horsed host could not hope to cover much more than twenty-five miles in any day.

This time there was little need for prospecting ahead by scouts, not until they reached Galloway itself that is; so Hugh and his companions had to put up with the dull routine of a host on the march, day after day. With the King now surrounded again by his Norman-Scots, they were relegated to a humble place in the entourage, Sheriff Pate declaring that this was all very good for them, or they would be getting altogether too uppish, with all this association with royalty and great ones.

However, on the fifth day, when they turned south-westwards from the upper Nith, for Moniaive and into Galloway proper, the trio were called for and sent ahead once more to resume their scouting duties, in especial to try to find out where the Earl Fergus was now.

There was no convenient trail of droppings and other marks of passage to follow this time, for the Galwegians would have fled homewards in no sort of order or groupings; so it was just a matter of probing onwards, being watchful and asking.

They obtained no hint as to their quarry's whereabouts until they reached the upper Ken valley in the vicinity of that other St John's Town, of Dalry, where, enquiring of the local priest where they might find the Earl of Galloway, they were told that, so far as was known, he was at his castle of Kenmure, none so far away. Clearly the cleric assumed them to be friends of the earl.

This, if a fact, was highly important news, to be imparted to the King just as swiftly as possible. Back they turned, up the Garpel Water, in haste.

They reached the main body on the Moor of Craigmuie, and great was the satisfaction expressed by all. How best to deal with the situation? A direct assault on Kenmure Castle, lacking siege machinery, bombards and the like, could be ineffective – not that Kenmure was reckoned to be any very strong hold. But starving out is a lengthy process. And Fergus, anyway, if he heard of their approach, would probably flee deeper into his south-western fastnesses before they could reach him. Some sort of encirclement *before* any close approach was made should probably be their aim; but Kenmure's situation at the north-western top of long Loch Ken made anything such difficult. How could any double approach be contrived from the south, other than by a force going all the way down the nearly twelve-miles-long loch's east side and then up the west, entailing unacceptable delay, in which the waiting main body would almost certainly be discovered, surprise lost and Fergus escaping?

It was then that Hugh and Rob Bruce came up with their remembered information as to the narrows of the loch and scow-ferries at Kells, scene of their encounter in May when they had won their little victory. If a flanking force could be got down to that area, unseen from the loch previously, and somehow got across those narrows, then it could approach Kenmure Castle from the south, and with only minimal delay, for Kells was no more than five miles down. They had ascertained, at Dalry, that there was no way that a force could get round the castle north-abouts without being very visible to its occupants.

This suggestion was accepted. But how to get a horsed force across even two hundred yards of narrows if the scows were berthed at the far side?

That produced some discussion, with even a proposal made that a group of strong swimmers might swim across, swords strapped to their backs, to force the ferrymen to bring the scows over. Hugh, however, suggested that if only one or two horsemen made an appearance at the narrows at first, the rest remaining out of sight, and hailed the ferrymen to bring a boat over for them, it would not be evident that they themselves were not Galwegians seeking Fergus, and ought to arouse no suspicions. Once one scow was over, an armed party could cross back and compel the other craft to come over.

None could better this proposal, and a detachment, mainly

of Mersemen under Earl Cospatrick, was detailed to go off southwards, well east of the loch and hidden from it by the intervening low ridges, hiding in some valley until the scow problem was resolved. Then to send back word, and both forces would advance on Kenmure at the same time. It was to be hoped that, meantime, Fergus, if he was indeed at Kenmure, would not be warned of their coming.

It was not difficult to lead the Merse contingent southwards through the low hills, parallel with Loch Ken but not visible from it, for this was terrain traversed those weeks before by Hugh and his companions. The mosstroopers made good time of it.

After some seven miles, the scouts mounted a ridge, to peer over. That they had judged none so badly they discovered, for they could see the shining waters of the loch narrowing in only about half a mile further south.

The force found a fairly suitable hiding-place to wait, a short distance on, and the three scouts rode forward, openly now, prepared to do some shouting across the water. But to their surprise, they found one scow tied up at this eastern side of the loch, with a cot-house nearby. They could also see a number of other boats moored at the far side, where were the few houses of the Kells ferry community. Whether this was a customary arrangement, they did not know; but it did make sense to keep at least one scow always on this east side.

How best to deal with this situation? At least there would be no need to swim across. Four ferrymen were watching them from the cottage. Ask, or command? They rode down to them.

Obviously armed and knightly riders, their approach was eyed warily. They announced that they had a body of horsemen wishing to cross the loch to go to see the Earl Fergus at Kenmure. They would require all available scows. They would pay.

That produced no positive reaction.

"Either you ferry us over or we take the scow ourselves," Hugh declared. He had noted that the long sweeps had been left in the boat.

"Who are you?" one of the men demanded.

"Is that any concern of yours?" Hugh reined his horse round, hand warningly on sword-hilt, and led the other two over to the boat. There he and Rob sat their mounts eloquently silent, while they sent Duncan back to inform the Earl Cospatrick of the situation.

The ferrymen watched, silent also.

Duncan arrived presently with only half a dozen others. The earl said that if they all appeared, the ferrymen on the other side might well be alarmed and refuse to let their scows be used, hide the sweeps possibly. Let them row this boat over, with these men, who would take armed possession of the other craft, and leaving them there come back to this side. Then the company would come down, and send over as many as the boat would hold, to bring across the other scows.

This seemed sound policy, and the newcomers, dismounting, piled into the scow, Hugh with them, leaving Rob to watch the ferrymen and guard the horses.

The inexpert oarsmen made but a doubtful job of rowing across, the long sweeps being awkward to handle; but the distance was only some two hundred yards. A group of the opposite ferrymen were watching their passage critically; but no doubt noting how well armed were these unskilful oarsmen and themselves quite unarmed, they limited their evident hostility to mere looks.

Landing, Hugh declared that they were taking over all ferry-boats in the name of the King. Any trouble would be met with a dire response. Then he and Duncan re-embarked and made a splashy, laborious and zigzag return to the east side.

Their arrival there coincided with that of the earl and his force, the eastern ferrymen promptly disappearing into their cot-house. Without the horses, some thirty men were able to pile on to the scow and be ferried across, equally ineptly, with instructions to bring back the other craft.

And so the major crossing began, and with the horses, quite a lengthy process. Couriers were sent back to inform the King that the double advance could begin.

It had all been an involved undertaking – but almost certainly worth it.

Up the west side of the loch there was no option but to string out close to the water's edge, for here very shortly hillsides came down almost to the shore for practically all the way up to Kenmure. The Mersemen rode fast, concerned that the ferrying had taken overlong, and desiring that their arrival on the scene should more or less coincide with that of the King's host.

In the event, when they reached the only minor valley and opening of their four-mile ride, where a stream came down to the loch, and across this, on its higher site, the stockaded castle rose, it was to see the main host already massed at the further side, banners, armour and weaponry glinting in the late afternoon sunlight, troop and squadron and phalanx making an imposing, threatening show. The Earl Cospatrick ordered his people to spread out in a crescent formation to fill the valley, which, with the others half a mile off, as nearly encircled the castle as the terrain made possible. Sitting their mounts, they settled themselves to await orders, signals, the next move up to the King, the Marischal and the Constable.

There was no sign of any assembly of men at the castle itself. How many might be within its walls and stockading was anybody's guess. To be sitting there idle, after all the activity and urgency, felt strange indeed. Was the King waiting for nightfall? Was any sort of storming of the palisading possible, without unacceptable losses? Had Fergus been summoned to surrender? Was he there, indeed? It was all indeterminate to those waiting, unreal-seeming.

Reality, when it did come, was heralded by the distant blaring of trumpets and horns. They could only speculate on what this signified, and hope. But as the noise continued, they could scarcely doubt. Surely this could mean only triumph, victory, Kenmure yielding, Fergus's surrender?

When they could see movement of some part of the royal host towards the castle, there could be no question. Cospatrick, raising an arm, waved his people forwards.

Because of the siting of the place and its stockade, there was no way round between it and the loch-shore save in single file – the reason for their long detour southwards. But now, with most evidently no danger of attack from that walling, they could so ride. No heads appeared above the palisading to watch them.

When they reached the assembly around the royal standard of the black boar on silver, and all the other banners, it was to find the Earl Fergus there in person, standing before King Malcolm. He was a tall, noble-featured man in his early sixties, with a proud bearing despite his humiliating situation, expressing neither depression nor defiance, but schooled to a sort of accepting dignity, listening to what was being said to him. Some of the Normans were hectoring him, mocking, but Malcolm was not. With the Earl Cospatrick coming up, the King raised a quietening hand.

"Here is one, my lord Fergus, who believes that *his* should be your earldom of Galloway," he announced. "How say you to that, now?"

"I say, Sire, that I have yielded up my person, at your royal command, but not my earldom. Cospatrick of March has no claim to it, only covets it. Has it not belonged to my line for long? Has he not sufficient, with the Merse and Lothian? And some of Northumbria and Cumbria? And I – I, Sire, have two sons supporting my kinsman, King Henry of England!" There was no attempt to hide the warning in that.

His fellow-earl frowned, but only tightened his lips.

"If I forbear to dispose of your earldom, and leave it for your sons, *you*, a rebel, I must punish," Malcolm asserted. "Where, my lord, do you choose to be imprisoned?"

"Put him in Ross's former cell at Roxburgh," de Morville jerked.

"I will hold him secure at my castle of Renfrew," Walter fitz Alan, the High Steward, volunteered, grinning.

There were other offers.

Fergus looked only at the King. "Your Grace, like your royal grandsire, is a man of the Church," he said levelly. "I would choose, if I must be captive, to be a prisoner of Christ.

82

Send me to a monastery. I will take vows. And make a large donation to Holy Church, found another abbey if you will. King David, I think, would have had it so."

Hugh recognised shrewd judgment when he heard that, even though others there hooted and scoffed, including the Prince William.

Not his brother, however. He was his grandfather's successor in more than just blood. He stilled the noise again, with raised hand. "You would do that? An abbey, and become monk. For the remainder of your days?"

"I would, yes. My word on it. So be it that Galloway remains with my sons."

"So! We will consider it, then. Consider it well. Meantime, you remain prisoner." He gestured. "Take him away."

Fergus bowed carefully, and turned around. His guards did not actually lay hands on him. He was an earl, and earls were not to be manhandled, any more than executed; they were, after all, of the kingly stature, whatever the Normans thought of it. He looked back as he was led towards his castle.

"The hospitality of my house is at Your Grace's disposal," he declared.

Hugh and Duncan exchanged glances. Who had had the best of that exchange? they wondered.

They took Fergus of Galloway back with them to Roxburgh, *en route* for a form of incarceration in the Abbey of the Holy Rood, founded by King David at Edinburgh while his own abbey of Soulseat and his priory of Whithorn were being enlarged. He went, not like any prisoner, and quite frequently Hugh rode beside him, admiring the man's self-possession and calm acceptance of his fate.

Parting with Rob Bruce at Lochmaben was quite a wrench, for they had become good friends. They would endeavour to maintain their association – although not necessarily in a warfare state, it was to be hoped.

It took three more days to reach Roxburgh, shedding various contingents on the way. It would be good to be home at Swinton Parva.

That evening, at the castle, the King sent for Hugh to come to his personal withdrawing-room off one of the stronghold's great halls. Only his two brothers and one other man were present, this latter elderly, stooping and hawk-eyed. Malcolm introduced him as Sir Walter Olifard of Smailholm, Justiciar of Lothian. Hugh had heard of him of course, although they had never met, for Smailholm was none so far from Swinton, overlooking the west side of the Merse, near to Melrose; but he was seldom there, his onerous duties up in Lothian preoccupying him presumably.

"I have come to think well of you, Hugh de Swinton," the King announced. "As my grandsire thought well of your father and Sir Ernulf. You have proved an excellent scouting-informant, reliable. I would show my appreciation of your services. I have spoken with Sir Walter here, and he has agreed to hand over to you certain lands which he holds of the crown. They are not in the Merse, but not far off, on the coast – Aldcambus and Redheugh, where Coldinghameshire joins Lothian. These are not large lands, and only a modest house goes with them. It is not a barony. But it will make you your own laird, since you have an elder brother to inherit Swinton Parva. How say you?"

Surprised indeed, Hugh could only stammer his gratitude, wagging his head.

"Sir Walter will give you a charter, under my royal seal. Call for it at Smailholm in a few days' time. Do you know Aldcambus?"

"No, Sire. But . . . I am greatly honoured. Nothing that I have done deserves this. It was all only my simple duty . . ."

"Not all do their duty so well and so effectively, my friend. And, who knows, I may well require your services hereafter – but, I hope, not in more battling! Now, Sir Walter will instruct you further." And he nodded their dismissal.

The older man led Hugh out, bowing, into the hall.

"I know your father, the Sheriff Cospatrick," he said. "A good man. I could do with one or two like him in my justiciarship of Lothian. His Grace clearly is pleased with you. *I* am no fighting man, never was, so do not know to what he refers. Now, this of Aldcambus and Redheugh. Two properties, on the edge of Coldinghame Muir. Where the Lammermuirs come down to the sea. One of a thousand acres, the other four hundred. You keep sheep on the Lammermuirs, I am told, so this may be of some advantage to you. There is no castle, but a small tower on the cliffs. The House of Aldcambus will serve you well enough – when you have refurbished it, for I fear that it is neglected. My chief shepherd has been dwelling in Redheugh – *my* sheep graze on Coldinghame Muir. So, come you in a day or two to Smailholm Tower, and I will have your charter, signed, sealed and witnessed, for you."

"I thank you, sir. This is wholly unexpected, I assure you. My gain, it seems, is your loss!"

"No great loss, boy. My son is already well provided for with the great Lanarkshire lands of Bothwell. And my brother is a thane indeed up in the Mearns of ample estate. And I grow old, with more than enough on my hands. Aldcambus is neglected, as I say . . ."

Hugh went hot-foot to tell his father, Alan and Duncan of his good fortune. He discovered that the sheriff already knew of the situation, but had kept silent, deeming the surprise preferable. He got congratulations, although he gained the impression that Alan was scarcely overjoyed at it all. And it did not fail to occur to him that Duncan, who deserved as much, got nothing, only a foster-brother and illegitimate at that. He would have to see what could be done about that.

It was on to Swinton Parva, then – but would life be returning to normal, after all?

7

A few days later, Hugh rode across the Merse to Smailholm, a score of miles only, by Eccles, Edenham and Nenthorn. It was strange how the comparatively low-lying, undulating plain, so large and fair, at this western side began to produce quite notable craggy eminences, rising like islands out of the green, fertile sea, these tending to soar perhaps one hundred feet above the rest – Sweethope Hill, Home Craigs, Stichil, Brotherstone Hill and Smailholm, these gradually leading up to the high and really hilly ground which flanked the Tweed. And, inevitably, for defensive purposes, these isolated heights tended to be crowned by castles and towers; and as well as being defensible, they were very useful as beacon sites. On these were established a line of beacons, so readily visible from afar, which, on invasion from over the border from England, could be lit, and with smoke by day and flame by night could send warnings right across the Merse, and on beyond, in a matter of only minutes, so that all learned of danger and were readied to repel raiders.

Smailholm Tower was on one such height, one of the most westerly, and especially dramatic as to site. In fact there was a close clutter of rugged little hills here, three miles from Tweed, these enclosing a lochan, and on the top of the loftiest spur above this water soared the tower, not large but stone-built this one, and enclosed within a curtain wall which seemed to be almost part of the rock summit itself, and following the irregular outline. The iron beacon-cage on the tower-top was prominent. At least Smailholm Tower was not hard to find. Nearby, on another of the cluster of hillocks, were the remains of an early Pictish fortlet, indicating that this had always been recognised as a defensive site.

Riding up the steep ascent to it, Hugh perceived that he was being watched from the tower's parapet, and recognised that this would be a hard place to approach secretly as it would be to capture. However his reception this day was friendly enough, the justiciar offering his visitor refreshment, as well as the precious signed and sealed charter, which the young man unrolled and inspected with something like awe, so impressive did the parchment look, with the royal beeswax seal attached by a ribbon and the names of no fewer than five important witnesses appended, these being those of the Bishop Edward of Aberdeen, the Chancellor of the Realm, Bishop Ingelram of Glasgow, the Earl Cospatrick, Sir Bernard de Baliol and Walter the High Steward. All in Latin, it began:

Malcolmum Dei Gracia rex Scottorum omnibus, sciatis nos dedisse dilecto nostro Walterus Olifard . . . resigneverint . . . Hugo de Swinton.

This in hand, Hugh had to accept what he had hardly taken in before, that he was now the laird of quite extensive lands, no longer just the younger son of a younger son, held in his own right where even his father's Swinton Parva was held of Sir Ernulf. It made something to think about.

But shortly afterwards he had something very different to think about. For Sir Walter, listening to expressions of appreciation and gratitude, eyed his guest from those hawk-like eyes and came up with an unexpected suggestion and request.

"I am told that you Swintons won your name and style from your famed ability to deal with wild boars, my young friend. The swine from whence comes Swinton. Your ancestors helped rid the Merse of many. Is that so?"

"Our arms, yes, bear the three boars, sir. And supporters, two boars also."

"And do you still so deal? Still kill boars?"

"There are not many left, now. But, yes, I have myself killed two, sir."

"And, think you, could you kill another? You see, we have

87

one here, at Smailholm, a savage brute. It has some sort of den up at the Pictish fort, yonder. And only yesterday it savaged a child picking marsh-marigolds down at the lochan. Where its other swine, the sows, live, I know not. But it does much damage, kills many calves. If you could rid us of the brute many would thank you. None of my people here seem able to deal with it."

Hugh blinked. "I . . . I do not know, Sir Walter. But – I could try, yes. If I could find it. I would require a spear . . ."

"We can give you that. And a couple of dogs to help rouse it out. It appears to sleep by day, usually – although not yesterday, when it attacked the little girl. Up there, somewhere at the fort, it lives. The dogs will none of them face it, but they could rouse it out for you, probably. Will you do it?"

"I can try, yes."

"Then I will call for the dogs. And find you a spear . . ."

So presently, and none too confident, Hugh, spear in hand and two shaggy cattle-dogs eyeing him as warily as though he had himself been a boar, mounted his horse and, to the well-wishing of Olifard and his servitors, set off for the neighbouring and less craggy hill, extremely doubtful as to the entire attempt. It was one thing for a hunt to comb scrub woodland, with hounds, to put up possible boars, corner one or more against some barrier or thicket, and ride them down with spears; and altogether another to seek out a brute alone, with untrained herd-dogs, and cope with the creature on its own ground. Fortunately his horse, an old friend, was a reliable beast and could be expected not to panic, as it had proved in action at Loch Kenside and elsewhere; but faced with a charging boar . . . ?

Down into a dip and on up the fairly steep, grassy slopes beyond, he rode, calling on the two dogs to follow, which they did only half-heartedly. No doubt they normally would tend to avoid this hill. They kept close to the horse's heels.

Up on the summit, not extensive, although more so than the tower-knowe above the lochan, the green ramparts and ditches of the ancient fort occupied much of it. The remains of stone hutments foundations were still visible; and presumably it was amongst those that the boar had its lair. The dogs were notably reluctant to go near.

Only a little less cautious, Hugh had his mount to circle the area, his spear at the ready. Peer as he would, it was impossible to see into all the corners and crannies of the stones. The creature might be asleep, might not be there at all . . .

He had made his first circuit and was beginning a second, closer in, when doubts were resolved, in a fashion. A snorting roar emanated from the far side of the fort, and out therefrom charged his quarry – if such it could be described; which actually was the quarry might be debatable.

For so hulking and ungainly-seeming an animal, the wild boar is extraordinarily swift on its small feet, its massive, heavy forequarters looking as though they would topple it forward, overbalancing its slighter hindquarters. But no such upset was developing. Head down, tusks gleaming, the brute came out, pounding forward and, fortunately, at the pair of cowering dogs, which were at that side.

These turned and fled, yelping, to be sure. It was as well that they had a start, for the attacker had the greater speed, strange as this might seem.

Hugh reined round and, couching his spear, spurred off in pursuit. Could his horse, at the gallop, catch up with that boar? If so, it would much simplify his task, in assailing it from the rear.

Alas, despite its own snortings, the beast presumably heard the sound of horse's hooves, for suddenly it all but rose on its comparatively puny hind legs to wheel round, abandoning the dogs for the larger quarry. The reversal of direction only slightly reduced its speed.

Hugh had only moments to adapt to the new situation, his mount likewise – for his steed would undoubtedly seek to take its own avoiding action, which meant that its rider would have to adjust to this also. The boar would aim for the horse's legs, and if it struck, the rider would be thrown from the saddle inevitably, for the mount would fall. Then it would be a question as to which the boar would savage first, horse or man. Spear poised, Hugh prepared for instant reaction.

The horse, at no urging from him, with the boar barely a dozen yards off, more or less repeated the other creature's tactics, rearing up on its hind legs, to swing abruptly right-angled to the left. As well that Hugh was prepared, for he could easily have been thrown. The boar changed course in turn, but at its speed could not do so sufficiently effectively to make contact with the horse's legs, and swept past close on the right, swinging round. And from the saddle, stooping, Hugh drove down with the spear.

But the speed of it all prevented an effective thrust. The spearhead struck home, but made only a glancing contact with the brute's haunch, ripping it open but just superficially and all but being wrenched out of the thruster's hand in the process. Hugh retained his seat and his grip only with an effort.

The boar, already circling as it was, regained the initiative first, for the horse plunged onward on the new course, with its snorting assailant only a few yards behind.

Over that uneven ground the horse could not reach its fastest gallop, only a canter after the sudden rearing turn. The boar would catch up, and its hurtling weight and those tusks would contact with the rear legs, and Hugh and his mount would go down.

The man, desperate, saw a gorse bush half-ahead, and took the chance. Jerking his reins savagely, he dragged his mount's head in that direction. The beast did change course, enough to head directly for the bush – probably it perceived its possibilities. Straight at the quite large clump Hugh spurred, and left the horse to cope.

The animal rose to the occasion, and literally. It took to the air, to leap right over the spread of thorns, a rough circle of some twelve feet in diameter, a major hurdle indeed. Its jump did not quite cover it all, landing down into the jagged greenery at the far side, but not so much as to cause it to stumble or delay its canter.

Retaining his seat demanded an effort, especially as on landing Hugh sought to look back. He saw what suddenly he had hoped for, blessing his mount. The boar came directly on, straight into the bush after the horse. And that gorse made all the difference. The creature's comparatively short legs, despite its weight and the speed of its entry, tripped and became entangled with the tough lower branches of the shrubbery. This did not halt the brute but caused it to stagger and lurch as it crashed through, greatly reducing its speed, indeed causing it to veer and plough its way. Seeing this, Hugh put his horse to the test, wrenching at the reins to pull its head up and then to swing it round in its tracks. It said a lot for that animal that, in the circumstances, it obeyed its master's so urgent and abrupt commands. Fore-hooves pawing the air, it reared and somehow teetered round without overbalancing, to face in the opposite direction, thereupon to confront the danger anew.

The boar was temporarily at a disadvantage. Stumbling through the prickly thicket, feet catching in the dense lower growth, impetus lost, it twisted this way and that to get through the tangle. And horse and man bore down upon it.

Hugh, spear high, had only seconds. But he used them effectively, as indeed he must to survive. In its twistings, the boar momentarily presented itself sideways on; and down the spear drove, just behind the shoulder, deep into the brute – to be jerked right out of the man's hand.

But this last mattered nothing now, the blow struck. The boar plunged on, but wildly erratically, still in the bush, its snorting changed to a gasping squealing, after a few paces to crash over on its side, kicking fitfully. As Hugh reined up, he saw its jerkings lessen and stop, and the creature lay still. The spearhead had almost certainly pierced through to the heart.

His horse doing the snorting now and actually quivering beneath him, Hugh waited for a minute or two, just in case. But no, the boar lay where it had fallen, almost certainly dead.

Patting and stroking his sweating steed, and murmuring praise to it, the man dismounted and moved over to retrieve his spear. He was, he realised, himself trembling just a little as he stared down at the fallen menace. He said a little prayer of thankfulness.

He had some difficulty in extracting that spear, the head caught between ribs. Then, back at his horse, he removed the rope always coiled behind his saddle and apt to be required for emergencies. Taking this, he went and tied it to the boar's hind legs, and returned to hitch the other end to his saddle-bow. Rubbing the horse's still-flaring nostrils, he remounted, and urged the animal forward. That heavy carcase took a deal of dragging out of the bush's entanglement and onward, but the horse proved itself entirely capable of doing so, and even gave the impression of satisfaction with the process. They moved off slowly and soon were heading downhill,the boar bumping behind. There was no sign of the two dogs.

Up at the tower their approach was again observed; probably all had been watched as far as was possible from afar. Anyway, a cheering reception awaited horse and rider, Sir Walter foremost with acclaim.

"Ha! Swinton, boar-slayer!" Olifard greeted him. "A worthy bearer of your name and arms. What a creature! What notable tusks! Save us – I will have that head on my hall wall. And give thanks to Hugh de Swinton who put it there!"

"My horse did most of it," Hugh declared. "I merely drove in the spear."

He rode homewards thereafter, charter tucked within his doublet, wondering why he should have been so favoured.

8

Eager to visit and inspect his new lairdship, Hugh was not long in riding northwards, with Duncan. Now mid-August, the oat harvest was in progress, but this did not really demand their activity, and their father excused them.

They went by the town of Duns, and by Bonkyl, crossing Whiteadder at the Cumledge Ford, and over the little pass of the eastern Lammermuirs, guarded by its former Pictish fort, and down to the quite major Eye Water valley, beyond which lay the coastal plateau of Coldinghame Muir. Aldcambus was situated on the north-western slopes of this, they had been told, where it slanted down to the sea.

Up a tributary of the Eye Water they turned for nearly three miles, to where the valley began to narrow in and the hillsides draw close, and here they turned off eastwards, as instructed, to climb to the sheep pasture of Penmanshiel, making for an ancient artificial mound known as Andrew's Cairn, from which they could look down on Aldcambus. Who Andrew had been they did not know; they did not think that it could have anything to do with Saint Andrew, Scotland's patron, for he had certainly never been here, and there was no shrine nor chapel.

However unclear as to the name's origin, the cairn did not disappoint as to prospects. For north, east and westwards, abruptly after the constriction of the valley, a vast panorama appeared before them, of slopes and moor, cliffs and ocean, as far as eye could see, heather moorland sinking to green grazing land and then to a dramatic, precipitous seaboard, that to the east showing only the clifftops, but to the north-west an endless succession of reddish crags, headlands, reefs, stacks and skerries, where the tides surged whitely, right to the mighty

Craig of Bass, and northwards over the wrinkled blue of the ocean to the far-off Isle of May in the mouth of the Scotwater or Firth of Forth. If Aldcambus was similarly endowed as to views, it was going to be a notable place to own.

Actually it looked as though this would be so, for they could see what must be the house and surrounding property a mile or so directly below them on the slopes, another mile back from the coast, with no higher ground between it and that vista. Down thereto they rode, exclaiming at it all.

Past a tiny loch cradled in a hollow, with cattle grazing around, they came down its outflowing burn into a widening scoop of the braeside, in which, flanked by a few trees in an otherwise fairly bare landscape, sat a long, low hallhouse on its grassy shelf, timber-built and clay-covered, not unlike Swinton Parva in design but smaller, two storeys and a garret in height under a slated roof. It had been whitewashed, but long since, and this was now patchy and stained, with other signs of neglect, slates missing, a window-shutter hanging askew, the orchard overgrown. There were outhouses and a stable-block nearby, and a farmery a little way further down the slope. Eyeing it all, Hugh nodded.

"Neglected, as Olifard said, but a fair place. Work for us here, Duncan. The site is splendid, is it not? A fair domain to have won, all unexpected."

"In an easterly gale off the Norse Sea it will catch it all!" the down-to-earth foster-brother declared. "See those uprooted trees, how they lie."

"No doubt. But most of the trees have survived – as shall we! I like it here. And the house is larger than I had thought, from what Sir Walter said. I count eleven windows at this side, and three in the garret. Enough and more."

They rode on down.

Dismounting, they walked round the outside of the house, Duncan pointing out that there were fewer windows facing east, doubtless wisely, views notwithstanding. They tried the door, westwards-facing, but found it locked. Crossing to the stableyard and outbuildings, they saw a stockily built

94

middle-aged man watching them, who had obviously come up from the farmery.

"Ha, friend," Hugh called. "You belong here? I am Hugh de Swinton and this is my brother. I am the new owner of this place, given me by King Malcolm and Sir Walter Olifard. You will not have heard, I think. We come from Swinton in the Merse. Do you farm here?"

"Aye, lord. I am Dod Lumsden. I keep all here for Sir Walter. These many years. You say that Aldcambus is his no longer? Yours, now? I . . . I canna just take it in, lord. I, I canna . . ."

"I can understand that, friend Lumsden. But it is so." Hugh patted his doublet. "I have the King's charter here, signed and sealed, if you wish to see it? No? Then, we would see the house. You keep it secure."

"Secure, yes. But no' in that great order, just. Sir Walter doesna come that often. I havena seen him in two year . . ."

"He told me, yes. It is locked, the house. You have the key?"

The man went over to a circular-walled well-shaft in the yard, and reaching down, produced a large key.

The House of Aldcambus had the musty smell of disuse, but it was less neglected-seeming within than without, not richly furnished but what was there was good, sheepskin and deerskin rugs on the flooring, woven hangings on the walls. There was a quite large hall, a withdrawing-room off, with a corridor giving access to a large kitchen, larder and storeroom. Up the twisting stairway were five bedchambers, none of the beds looking as though they had been slept in for long, but all rooms with fireplaces, chests, alcoves and arras. The further ladder-like stair took them up to the garret area, all one lengthy apartment under the roof timbers. This was littered with gear and plenishings, even old rusty chain-mail and helmets and weaponry.

"As I said, work for us here, Duncan. But this will make a good place to live. How say you?"

The other shrugged. "I prefer Swinton Parva," he said. "And Cranshaws."

95

"Ah! But we are none so far from Cranshaws here, man! A dozen miles, no? Across the hills."

They went out to inspect the stables, dairy, barns and orchard. All told the same story, basically sound and useful but requiring attention. The man Lumsden was at pains to point out that the fault was not his. He ran the Mains, the demesne farm, and kept an eye on the laird's property, but only that. He had no orders to maintain the house – although his wife on occasion went therein to see that all was in some sort of order, and lit a fire or two in winter. Sir Walter had other properties than this which would see more of him. And his duties as Justiciar of Lothian did not bring him here into Berwickshire.

In the orchard, noting that the apple, pear and plum trees were pruned, trim and bearing fruit, Lumsden admitted that he had looked after these, no doubt so that he could enjoy the yield. He told them that he tended some seventy stirks, six milk-cows and two bulls, with around four hundred sheep up on Penshiel Muir. Did all these come to the lord with the property?

"I am no lord, friend Lumsden. As to the stock, I do not know. That was not mentioned. I would think not. Sir Walter may sell the cattle and sheep. But there is another place, is there not? A smaller property – Redheugh? Is that nearby?"

"Aye. You can see it, yonder, sir." The man pointed, almost due eastwards by a little north, just over a mile off. "Down near to the cliffs, and the sea."

"I see houses, yes. And it is empty also? Like this?"

"No. Tam Robson bides there. He's the chief shepherd here. I'm no shepherd, sir. I tend the cattle and till the rigs. Mind, I keep an eye on the high-ground flocks, too, and help at the dipping and shearing. For Tam has plenties to do watching the sheep along yon ill coast!"

"Coast? Sheep on the coast?"

"Aye. Redheugh's a right scunner for the sheep! Och, there's guid pasture too, mind, inland a wee. But the crittirs ay drift ower to the clifftops, the daft-like brutes. It's an unchancy place, is Redheugh – the land o' it, no' the house. It reaches

96

along the coast a guid two mile, cliffs and craigs a' the way. And doesna reach far inland, see you, a bare half-mile. There is Coldinghame Muir and that belongs to the Church, to the Prior o' Coldinghame. So the Redheugh sheep are ay at the clifftops – when they're no' halfways doon or drowned-deid at the foot! So Tam's kept at it."

"It sounds a strange place to run sheep, to me!"

"That's right, sir. But, some way, the best sheep in a' this land are bred there, the best lambs, in threes as often as no'. Tam says it's something to dae wi' the grasses that grow there, the turf, at the cliffs. He says it's pairtly the sea-spray and pairtly the birds, the sea-fowl. The birds, see you, thousands o' them, nest on the cliffs, all along, right to St Ebba's Head. Their droppings make the ground grow this girsage, these grasses, Tam says. And they do right well by the sheep."

"Here's a curious matter. We must go and see this Redheugh. Tomorrow."

"You are biding here the night, sirs? Aye – well, I'll get the wife to make you a bit supper."

"You are kind. No need to bring it up here. We will eat it down at your house . . ."

The motherly Eupham Lumsden did them very well, indeed offered to give them a bed but, when they decided to sleep in the larger house, said that they would find clean blankets in more than one of the bedchamber chests.

They had a walk round some of the property, noting the sheep-folds and dipping fanks, well pleased with what they saw, before turning in to spend their first night at Aldcambus, empty-seeming as the house felt to them.

In the morning they rode to Redheugh, much concerned to see this strange-sounding place. Before reaching it, however, they paid a visit to another building which they had spotted on the lower ground half a mile to the north and obviously close to the sea, the little Chapel of St Helen's, Dod Lumsden told them, seldom used now, since it was an appendage of the monks of Durham. When Hugh expressed surprise at this, he was informed that King Edgar, the strange elder brother and predecessor of the late King David, had given it to the English,

97

for reasons unknown, some sixty years before, this then all being royal land, David having thereafter handed the rest of the regality to the Olifards – which was how it came about that King Malcolm still held some rights of sokage over it, and had been able to require Sir Walter to transfer it to Hugh.

The small church, of the vivid red stone so locally prominent, seemed very much isolated and alone down there beside a tiny lochan, and only a few hundred yards from the coastal clifftops, a strange monument to a strange man who had been a costly monarch for Scotland in many ways, so very different a character to his brother David. What the Durham monks thought of it all was anybody's guess, although this generation possibly had completely forgotten that they owned it.

With the sound of waves breaking nearby, they rode on to the cliff's edge, anticipating something worth viewing – but quite unprepared for what they saw. It was not the height of the precipices which impressed, no more here than seventy feet or so, and those a short distance to the east rising vastly higher and more dramatic; it was the extraordinarily striking redness of the stone, almost scarlet indeed, such as neither of them had ever seen before, and its meeting with the blue waters of the sea producing an almost unbelievable and challenging clash of colours and also a peculiar blending of shades and tones in the underwater shallows until the blue took over. Long they stared, wondering.

The brilliant red faded somewhat in a mile or so, after rounding a small headland, although the cliffs thereafter took the eye in their spectacular upthrust to great crags and stacks, these a darker red, nearer to crimson. And just before these greater heights commenced, they could see their destination, the cluster of houses of Redheugh.

Picking their way along the clifftops thereto, they marvelled at all this colour and exciting scenery, never so much as mentioned by King Malcolm or Sir Walter. To have come by such a heritage, actually to possess it all, was scarcely to be credited.

Redheugh itself lived up to its name, for the largest house here was indeed built of the red stone, although the subsidiary cottages and hutments were of timber and clay. The house was not so large as Aldcambus, but of a fair size nevertheless, more than any farmhouse. There was no orchard here, so near the cliffhead, but there was a walled-in garden. Another stone wall enclosed a small grass pasture for three milk-cows. And nearby were timber-fenced folds and fanks for sheep.

The noise of hammering above the regular subdued roaring of the waves on the reefs and skerries of the shore, which would be the ever-present background sound of this place, led them round the back of the house, to find a man repairing some of the fold fencing, an elderly man this but wiry, and far from frail. He eyed them critically.

"Are you Tam Robson?" Hugh asked. "The shepherd here?" They dismounted.

"I am, ay. And who asks it?"

"We are your new lairds, Swinton by name. Aldcambus and Redheugh are now ours, of King Malcolm's gift. Dod Lumsden told us of you."

The other digested that, unspeaking.

"We find it all of great interest. This place, this seaboard, these cliffs. We did not know of it, when granted the lands. Sir Walter Olifard said little of it all."

"It is good, good!" That, strangely, was Duncan, who did not usually demonstrate enthusiasm; he would have implied criticism of east winds and storms here. "I like it here. All this." He waved a hand. "You live here? Is it wild of a winter? A challenge? The onset of the sea's fury? I think it will be."

"You could name it that, aye. Windy, just."

"More than that, no? You have lived here long?"

"All my days, maister."

"And you do not . . . mislike it?"

"I like it fine."

"*I* could live here," Duncan said, with quite an emphasis.

Hugh looked at him thoughtfully. "I think that you shall," he said. He turned to the older man. "We hear that you graze many sheep here, along these cliffs. Summer and winter. That is extraordinary. We winter ours down in the Merse, at Swinton, but summer them up at the sheilings in the

99

Lammermuirs, at Cranshaws. Your sheep must be hardy indeed, to survive the winters here."

"They're that, aye. Blackface, mind. They get the winds. And the spume, the spray. Even the kelp, the seaweed, gets thrown up. But they dinna get the snows here, like on the higher ground. And the snow's the killer. O' the lambs. Och, our lambs do fine, here. And grow right hardy. Grow guid wool, too."

"This much interests us, being sheep-folk ourselves. Would you show us your flocks and grazings, friend?"

"If you're the lairds now, I maun do as you say, sirs."

"We ask it, not order it." That was Duncan, and again his brother looked at him interestedly.

"Aye, then." Robson gestured at the horses. "You'll need to walk, mind. It's nae place for your beasts."

They tethered their mounts to the railing which the man had been repairing, and expressed themselves as ready.

Their guide led them on almost due eastwards, by a well-worn track, and quickly they came again to the clifftops, much higher here but still more so, obviously, further on. Far below, the tide surged and broke whitely on an almost continuous array of red reefs and rocks. But not exactly continuous, for here, at a brief declivity, a sort of steep green corrie in the precipices, a little less-than-sheer path wound its way downwards. And at the foot was a tiny beach where a boat was drawn up on the shingle.

"Yours?" Duncan demanded.

"Aye. A bit fish, flukies, haddies, aye and crabs and lapsters, ay make a change frae the mutton and beef, see you."

"The seas are not too rough, here?"

"No' a' the times!"

Hugh pointed. "There are sheep down there now! And there, on the cliffside itself. How do they get there?"

"Och, aye. They're guid climbers, my sheep."

That was astonishingly well proved as they proceeded, the cliffs ever heightening. Although most of the sheep they saw were grazing along the tops and a little way inland, many were to be discovered down on grassy little ledges and re-entrants of

100

the steep crags, amongst the roosting, wheeling and screaming birds. Why should they so do, in such dangerous and intricate descents, was a mystery, until Robson explained that it was the fowls' droppings, white on all the ledges and projections, which caused special herbage to grow, which the sheep seemed to find to their taste, and which was evidently very good for them, for they throve on it. The same applied here on the tops and a little way inland, where the fowl circled. There was the proof of this, he pointed out, up yonder at the Craig of Bass. Bass mutton was famed, fetching higher price than any other, and just because the sheep which pastured up on that great stack in the sea fed on grisage growing out of the droppings of the innumerable gannets roosting there.

No gannets, or solan geese, roosted on these Redheugh cliffs, but many varieties of other sea-fowl did, all but sufficient to darken the air in their screaming, sailing, diving thousands – kittiwakes, guillemots, petrels, fulmars, shearwaters, razorbills and every variety of gulls, their excretions indeed having occasionally to be dodged by the wary. No question but that all this deposit must have a major effect on the plant-life.

The visitors were interested, also, to discover just how far inland from the cliffs their property extended. They learned that it was not far, however extended lengthwise; indeed they could see their boundary, not much more than a quarter-mile away, marked by a continuous grass-grown quite high bank running parallel with the coast, thrown up their guide said by the Coldinghame Priory monks to make very clear where *their* sheep-grazings commenced, Holy Church jealously possessive. Redheugh might stretch for miles, but it was a ribbon-like property.

Robson named various landmarks for them, eastwards from Siccar Point, Meikle Poo Craig, and the Hirst Rocks, past the Black Bull and Little Rooks Head to Dowlaw. It was east of the last, almost three miles, up-and-down miles, from Redheugh itself, that he pointed out, ahead, the only actual building they had seen, and an extraordinary one, in siting as to construction. It was, in fact, not on the clifftop but halfway down, a little redstone tower crowning

101

an isolated stack or spire of rock which soared out of the surging waves.

"What is that? What, of a mercy, is that for?" Hugh wondered. "Built there. Here is a madness!"

"We ca' it the Fastness," they were told – and certainly it was that, whatever the reason for it. "Nane kens for why it is there, or whae reared it. Auld it is. But there maun hae been a guid reason, for it would tak a deal o' building on top o' yon rock. Mair stanes, aye, and men tae, would fa' in the sea than got set in place!"

"There must have been a reason for it. Is it a watch-tower? But – would one such have been better on the clifftop than halfway-down?"

"Maybe no'. What were they watching for? See you, there's a big cave right underneath yon stack. And there's a bit shaft cut in the rock up frae it to the tower. That would tak as meikle cutting as the building above. Why a' that? Aye, and the stack itsel' is just the point o' a bit craig, a headland. Boats, then? A tower up here on the top couldna see doon baith sides o' the craig, into the wee bays there. Yon one does. And the cave – boats can win in there. And what they carried could be hoisted up the shaft into the tower. I jalouse it was built there because o' that, some way. There's no' a haven or a sheltered boat-landing on a' this coast for ten mile – that bit where *my* boat lies isna possible eight months o' the year. But the cave has a right bend in it, and can gie shelter frae breaking seas at a' times. I say yon tower's there because o' the cave and boats landing."

"But what were they landing, that was so important that they required a tower to watch and protect it?"

"Guid kens, sirs. Could it be yon Danes? Them they ca' the Vikings? Raiders o' a' this coast. It's auld enough."

"I suppose that it could be . . ."

"Can we get down to it?" Duncan demanded. "We must see this. How do you get on to that rock-top?"

"There would be a bridge o' sorts that they could lower. Noo, I keep a bit planking handy. Mind, I'm no' that often doon to it . . ."

102

Nothing would do but that they must get down to see this improbable feature – if Robson could do it, so could they. There was a track of sorts part-way, oddly enough through heather, which seldom grew so close to salt water as this, and which the sheep seemed to approve of, for there were many hereabouts. Thereafter it was just a case of scrambling down, as best they could, seeking not to slip, and grabbing at such handholds as were available. This slippery process brought them to a shelf of grass at approximately the same level as the tower – only there was a yawning gap between the land and the stack-top, which the visitors eyed with major doubts, doubts which were not greatly lessened when Tam Robson went over to a hollow and dragged out a length of planking, no doubt salvaged from the tide, fully ten feet of it, which he proceeded to toss, almost casually, across, its further anchor-point looking less than secure.

"It'll no' break," he announced reassuringly, and strolled over to climb the quite steep and bare rock beyond.

The pair eyed each other. That fact that the plank was unlikely to break was not their principal concern. It was the width of the thing, a foot at most. Crossing that was going to demand some faith as well as resolution and a steady tread. But the older man had done it, and often, apparently. They were not to be shamed – even though it all might not be worth it.

Duncan, who seemed to have developed some unexpected affinity for all this Redheugh terrain, went first, chin jutted.

"Do not look down," Hugh advised, helpfully. "Look right ahead." But he held his breath as the other edged over. Duncan did not seem to be taking good advice and not looking down. But he made it, however slowly.

Then it was Hugh's turn. A purposeful but unhurried stride was to be recommended, that edging and creeping was not the way, destination, not the means of getting there, the preoccupation. Unfortunately, riding-boots with spurs were not the ideal footwear for this sort of thing – as they had discovered in the descent so far.

Stepping out, he became quickly aware of a complication. There were uneven patches, callosities, on that planking, knots in the wood in fact which could affect his tread in those boots. So it was necessary to look down, to avoid them. And a stomach-churning emptiness gaped on either hand of the foot-wide passage. Preoccupations adjusted themselves. If his heel caught in one of those lumps? And the plank undoubtedly swayed up and down . . .

It was Duncan at the other side offering his hand in aid which got Hugh over in any style, even in a final little rush – for of course that hand had to be ignored. But it was good to feel solid rock underfoot, even though further clambering was now called for, with little in the way of grips.

Actually there was not a great deal to see in the tower itself, after all this, for it was of the simplest construction, square, thick walls, four storeys but its stairway collapsed. It was in a lower extension northwards that the interest lay, for here, on the naked rock flooring, was the mouth of the shaft which led down to the cave, an awesome hole up which echoed the swish of the tides far below. Peer down as they would there was nothing to be seen but blackness. What had been hoisted up that grim funnel? Or lowered down it?

In the circumstances, there was no request to be taken to that cave; that must await a boating excursion. But they did move down the few yards to the very lip of the stack, to peer over it, to find themselves staring into the beady eyes of sundry sea-fowl sitting on ledges and protuberances right up to this edge, these apparently seeing no reason to stir at this intrusion on their living-space. All the way down to the boiling surf the creatures roosted, such as were not diving into the sea or swimming about.

"What is that wailing sound?" Duncan asked. "I heard it before."

"Seals, maister. That's them singing. There's plenties o' them along this coast. Ower many, for they kill the salmon. Right greedy, they are. They just eat a bit bite oot o' each and leave the rest. I'm no' yin for the seals."

Look as they would they could see no signs of these sinful animals, however vocal they were.

It seemed that they were nearing the edge of the Redheugh

104

territory here, Robson announcing that soon they would come to the march with the Lumsdaine property, this not unlike their own. They decided to turn back, much impressed and indeed excited by all that they had seen.

At Redheugh and the horses again, they bade farewell to Tam Robson, thanking him and assuring that they would be seeing more of him, much more. Looking back as they rode for Aldcambus, Hugh spoke.

"You like this Redheugh, Duncan – I can tell that. How say you to being laird of it? Redheugh is yours, if you want it."

His foster-brother stared. "Mine? You mean . . . all mine? The whole property? Mine!"

"Just that. I have thought on this. You should have been given some token of the King's esteem when I was. Why myself and not you? You did as much as I did . . ."

"But I am a bastard!" That was harshly said.

"What of it? You served the King as well as I did. You should have been rewarded, if I was. So, I was given *two* lairdships. You shall have the lesser, this Redheugh. Although I deem it the more . . . interesting!"

Duncan said nothing, too overcome for words.

"Swinton of Aldcambus, and Swinton of Redheugh! As one laird to another – how sounds it?"

"It is too much . . ."

"Not so. You may have to put this Tam Robson out of the house. But he will have a cottage, no doubt."

"No. He can stay. I feel that I could work with that man. He is my sort. No, leave him there."

"That is for you to say. But – this of the sheep there. And the cattle here. The stock. These belong to Olifard. This Robson, and Lumsden too, they look after another's flocks and herds, not ours. If Sir Walter decided to sell these, what then? We have not the gold to buy them. These great ones never think of the like!"

"Could we borrow the moneys? And pay it back, in time. Sir Ernulf, perhaps?"

"Would he . . . ? I am only a second son of his brother."

"You could ask."

They decided that, since they were so comparatively close, they would go back to Swinton Parva, on the morrow, by Cranshaws. They had, after all, something to tell Meg and her father and brother.

The Lammermuir Hills could almost be said to start at Aldcambus, rising swiftly behind, once the valley of the Eye's tributary, the Heriot Water, was passed, to quite major heights, and so continuing for twenty-five miles and more. So they rode up by Andrew's Cairn again, down into the vale, and then commenced the real climbing, a great bend in the Heriot Water assisting. By Eweside and Ecclaw and the upper Eye Water, they came in time to the great escarpment of the Monynut Edge, whereafter they were on the Swintons' own grounds, and Cranshaws only two miles ahead.

Their welcome by the Cockburns was sufficiently warm, especially by Meg, who hugged them both, whether or not equally was hard to assess. Their news, of course, was acclaimed, although the young woman at once asked whether this meant that they would be seeing less of them, now that they had their own lands to look after? She was told no, that in fact she might be seeing the more of them, for they would still have the Swinton flocks spring and autumn herdings to attend to – they could not just abandon this duty; but they would now most of the time be based at Aldcambus and Redheugh, only a dozen miles away. This seemed to please Meg not a little.

Duncan was very earnest about informing her of his new status as a laird in his own right, Hugh noted.

When they headed for their couches that night, as usual Meg saw them to their chamber floor. She embraced Duncan first, enthusiastically enough, but when she turned to Hugh, it was to whisper in his ear.

"I wish that you . . . did not have to share the same room!"

He answered that by squeezing her breast, whilst eyeing his foster-brother's back.

They were off in the morning southwards, assuring that they would be back in just over a month's time, if not before, to collect the Swinton sheep. They were urged to come for a longer stay next time.

9

It was with some hesitation, a few days later, that Hugh approached Sir Ernulf at Swinton House. The sheriff had said that he saw no reason not to, although he did not know how his brother would respond. Sir Ernulf was fairly rich in lands, but not necessarily in money. Hugh thought it best not to take Duncan.

His uncle, after enquiring after the size, features and possibilities of the new properties, asked whether Hugh intended to go and live there, and if so, what of the Swinton sheiling-herding?

That gave the opening required.

"We, Duncan and myself, will not fail you in the herding, sir," he assured. "Even though we hope to have our own herding to do. But with no great distance to move our beasts, as here . . ."

"So, you have won flocks and herds as well as lands, have you?"

"No-o-o. Leastways, I think not. They are there, the sheep and cattle. But naught was said as to them. By either the King or Sir Walter Olifard."

"If naught was said, then it is much to be doubted that the stock is yours, boy. Land and stock do not usually go together, unless so stated. So what do you do for beasts?"

"H'rr'mm. We . . . I wondered whether we might borrow, Uncle. Either some stock, to start us. Or moneys to buy them."

"So that is why I am favoured with this visit, lad! You want moneys to set you up as a lairdie!"

"Only to borrow, sir. We will pay it back so soon as we can."

"Perhaps – so soon as you can! How much?"

"I, I do not know. Do not know how much Sir Walter may ask for his stock. Any or all of it."

"Is there much?"

"Not much as you would count it, Uncle, here at Swinton. Four hundred or so sheep at each property, I think. Seventy cattle-beasts. These are the numbers there at present."

"So. Then see you Olifard, what he says. I will consider the matter . . ."

With that, Hugh had to be content.

When he got home, thinking to ride to Smailholm the next day, it was to find a still more urgent call awaiting him. It was from King Malcolm no less. Hugh de Swinton was required to wait upon His Grace at Roxburgh Castle at earliest convenience. No reasons were given.

Not a little surprised and intrigued, Hugh had to adjust his priorities. At least he could call in at Smailholm on his way back from Roxburgh.

He rode alone, next day, wondering what the monarch would require of him. Nothing anent armed men demanded, nor scouting duties. They had heard naught of any national crisis.

At Roxburgh he learned that the King was out hunting in Teviotdale, and had to wait. None there enlightened him as to why he had been summoned.

It was some time after the hunting-party had returned before he was summoned to the royal presence. He found Malcolm alone with one other youngish man, a cleric. Hugh was greeted in friendly fashion, and informed that the priest was William, Cistercian Abbot of Melrose, formerly the King's personal chaplain. Hugh was waved to a bench, to sit down.

"I have a project, my friend," Malcolm began. "A great project, with my lord Abbot here. I desire to establish a hospital, a great hospital. You understand? Not a hospice – there are many of these, scores. But no hospital, in all Scotland. I saw one such in France, near to Toulouse. A sanctuary for the sick, the deprived, the poor and needy, aye and for travellers also. My grandsire, the saintly David,

109

founded the abbeys – Melrose, Kelshaugh here, Jedburgh, Dryburgh, the Holy Rood and the rest. Others have followed his lead, even Fergus of Galloway. I would emulate his good work. There is a sufficiency of abbeys now, to train the necessary priests, but no single hospital. So that is the task that I have set myself."

Hugh was duly impressed, but wondered what all this might have to do with him.

The Abbot William nodded. "A noble and pious endeavour," he commended. "His Grace is greatly to be praised, in this."

"I would have it a Cistercian foundation," the King went on. "The Cistercians are the Order most concerned for the needy and the sick.. The good Abbot William, here, is a Cistercian. Now, where to establish this hospital. You, de Swinton, I am told, know Lammermuir well?"

"I know some of it, yes, Sire. But the Lammermuir Hills are a great area. I know well only the eastern parts of them."

"How far to the west do you know?"

"I have been right to where they join the Morthwaite Hills, Your Grace. But I do not know that part so well."

"Better than we do, I swear! See you, we want it, this hospital, to be set up near to the main highway between this Roxburgh and my city of Edinburgh. Yet it must be remote from all other communities, for the folk are always fearful of disease and plague, foolishly, shamefully so. No township or village would wish to have such a place near to them. There would be trouble with the monks who would serve it. Monks from a Cistercian monastery will have to maintain it and tend the sick. Melrose is such. So, somewhere between Melrose and Edinburgh would be best, and that takes us through the Lammermuir Hills. You understand me?"

"Yes, Sire. But there must be places amany where a hospital could be built, without any great knowledge of the hills . . ."

"Not so." That was the abbot. "Not where it would meet all our requirements. It will have to be searched for. Heedfully."

"See you," the King went on. "This community and

110

establishment must be carefully sited. And large. For it is to aid travellers also, a part set aside for them at some distance from the quarters for the sick. So it should be near the highway where the travellers must pass. Convenient for supplies to reach it, and in winter. But not near to any village. There is no hospice nor shelter thereabouts meantime, as I know to my cost! It is some forty miles from Melrose to Edinburgh, so two days' journey for most horsed travellers, much more for on foot. And after Lauder, no resting-place other than hovels, until the Benedictine hospice at Cranstoun. In Lothian. This is not good, a trial for wayfarers. We must find a suitable place for our hospital, then. I ask you and Abbot William to go find it, my friend. You have served me well hitherto. I will be in your debt if you can do so again."

That word debt did not fail to strike a spark of hope in Hugh's mind with regard to sheep and cattle stocks to be acquired. "I will be happy to attempt this, Your Grace," he said.

"Then see you to it, with the Abbot William. And earn my thanks." That was clearly the end of their audience.

Outside, the pair consulted. The abbot's duties at Melrose would prevent him from embarking on this exploratory task for a few days. Four days hence, then? Would that suit? Come for him at the abbey, and they would set out northwards. It might take them some time to find the best site. And in the circumstances, they would have to be prepared for rough conditions, in the hills, sleeping out perhaps. He would provide the necessary sustenance.

Not a little surprised at the notion of a mitred abbot talking thus, Hugh agreed. In four days, yes. He would bring his foster-brother, Duncan, with him, who could be useful. Sizing the other up, he came to the conclusion that he might well make an effective travelling companion, despite being a clerk in holy orders.

On the way back to Swinton Parva, he did call in at Smailholm Tower, but found Olifard gone to his duties in Lothian. So that matter had to remain in abeyance meantime.

* * *

111

Hugh and Duncan duly presented themselves at the great and splendid Melrose Abbey four days later, its size and magnificence causing further doubts as to the suitability of its master as a colleague for the exploration of wild and trackless hills. However, when Abbot William appeared, to join them, he was clad approximately as they were themselves, in plain travelling garb, the only hint of his profession and status a small golden crucifix on a chain at his neck. At their greeting he promptly told them that they could dispense with my lord Abbot and just call him William, as he would address them as Hugh and Duncan; which made a hopeful start.

They rode off, just the three of them, although the abbot led a pack-horse laden with blankets and provender, to cross the high ground eastwards where once the Romans had established their marching-camp called Trimontium, referring to the three Eildon Hills which soared above Melrose. This brought them to where the Leader Water came down to join Tweed, and they turned up Lauderdale, on the highway from Roxburgh to Edinburgh.

They passed Learmonth's tower of Ersildoune, and close to the Earl Cospatrick's town and castle nearby, but halted at neither, the abbot declaring that these and other folk hereabouts, high and low, would not be happy to hear of their project of establishing a hospital for the sick anywhere in their vicinity. There was great and sad general misunderstanding, indeed superstition, about illness and disease, the assumption frequently being that this was the hand of God upon the sufferers for their sins; and the association with such was dangerous, for they could transmit the affliction to others. So they must be shunned, kept at a distance, lepers not permitted to come within a mile of communities. This was, of course, a nonsense, most sicknesses not being infectious. The Cistercian Order had always made an especial study of ailments and diseases and their remedies, and knew that only such as leprosy and two or three plagues were to be transmitted by association, and that by close contact only, these requiring their own infirmaries where the sufferers had to be looked after separately. But the vast majority of ailments were not so, and should be treated

112

by trained carers; they were of no danger to their neighbours. But getting the folk to understand and accept that was difficult indeed, however hard the Order tried. Hence the need to site this hospital of the King's well apart from any populated area, and with space to keep the allied overnight hospice for travellers at a fair distance from the sick quarters.

Hugh asked if the abbot had any ideas as to where they should start their search, to be told that the Melrose monks had their own chosen route northwards to Edinburgh and to the other Cistercian abbey of Newbattle in Lothian, this not following the general highway through Lauderdale but heading westwards from Melrose to the Allan Water's confluence with Tweed, and up this narrower vale by Colmslie and Langshaw to join the ancient Roman road of Dere Street, thus cutting off a great corner, a route suitable for hardy walkers but less so for ordinary travellers and horsed folk. The monks even had a resting-house, a little shelter on a ridge near a sheiling farmery called Clints. If they could find a suitable route from the main highway to that area, it might serve; but it might be too far off.

So they rode on as far as the little burgh of Lauder, with the hills drawing ever closer, there to leave the highway to head westwards by tracks through the heights, making for the upper Allan Water valley. Four or five miles of this and they came to the conclusion that here was no area to consider, the going too rough to expect normal travellers to cross.

"There is a greater valley of the Gala Water further to the west, which also runs north to south," Duncan suggested. "There is a drove-road up that. Could that not be the best approach?"

"I spoke of it to the King," he was told. "But he said that it was longer to reach Edinburgh. And it winds and twists more than does the Leader. So, no – our choice of ground must be reached from the main Lauderdale highway."

Over Lauder Common they found a fairly good track heading north and south. An area they came to thereafter, high moorland between what a shepherd told them were the hills of Whit Law and Pot Law, seemed a possible site, with

113

much levelish space and two streams for water; but the abbot felt that it was rather far from the highway – almost two miles. Hugh said that he did not see that they could gain the sort of isolation required without such distancing. And they could place the travellers' part of the establishment nearest to the road. Then they noted a high farmery hitherto hidden by a crest, and this perhaps would count against the area. When they rode down to this house they learned that it was called Cathpair, and belonged to the large property of Hoppringle. Moreover, it seemed, the community of Stow-in-Wedale was not much more than a mile away, on the Gala Water. So this was ruled out.

Obviously finding an area with all the necessary conditions was not going to be simple. They decided to go down to this Stow-in-Wedale, where there was one of King David's parish churches which the abbot knew of, there to hope to spend the night at the priest's house.

The young priest of Stow, however unready for unexpected guests, was much gratified that one of them should be the illustrious Abbot of Melrose, and did his best to give them hospitality in his modest house by the Gala Water. He told them that this Stow had been the site of a major battle long ago, in which the great King Arthur was involved against Saxon invaders, of which his visitors had not heard. They were more interested in finding out if he knew of any place to east and north of this which might measure up to the needs of their quest. After some debate, he came up with the suggestion of the Overhowden area, some six miles through the hills to the north-east, where there was a large Pictish stone circle set on an eminence in a heathy moor. This was not much more than a mile, he gauged, from the Lauderdale highway. If the Picts had had a settlement there, it must have offered the necessities for a community, water, wood and peat for fuel, grazing and the like.

So in the morning the trio retraced their steps, back up past Cathpair and on into the ever-higher slopes of these southern Lammermuirs. In time they reached the Melrose monks' track, and in fact came to the resting-house which the abbot had

114

mentioned. Oddly enough, he had never before seen it, for he had come from St Andrews, in Fife, on his appointment to the abbey, and on any journeys thereafter had always gone on horseback. They found the simple, low-set building of stone, on its quite lofty ridge, basic indeed as to features but at least providing shelter for hardy walkers.

They did not linger here but headed due eastwards, down to what the priest had called the Mean Burn, across which, after some two miles from the resting-house, they could see the monoliths of a stone circle crowning a knoll which rose out of fairly level moorland. They made therefor.

Overhowden itself proved to be only a shepherd's isolated cottage, quite close to the highly impressive stone circle, which ought to cause no problems. The surrounding heathery expanse was large enough to provide for the necessary many separate buildings of the hospital envisaged. And the henge on its mound would make a notable centrepiece for a religious establishment for, as the abbot pointed out, these stone circles had been places of worship before Christianity was brought to the Picts, even though the pagan ceremonies conducted there had been grievously mistaken, often including human sacrifice. So a good Holy Church refuge for the sick and the needy imposed on the site would worthily wipe out the errors of past sun-worship. Here then was what they were looking for – thanks to the young priest of Stow.

Alas, on making their way down, eastwards still, towards the highway, topping an intermediate rise they suddenly came in sight of a village below them, hitherto hidden, and only a mile from their chosen site. Overhowden, then, would not serve, too near to a community. Disappointed, they rode on down.

The village, they discovered, was called Oxton, and they had not known of it because it was sited well back from the highway, with an intervening slight ridge. It was a pleasant little place; but the horsemen found themselves deploring it because of its proximity to their Overhowden.

Hugh pointed across the valley, which the villagers told them was named Glen Gelt, formed by a headstream of the Leader. They had been confining their search to the westwards side of Lauderdale. Why not try the east side? After all, these Lammermuirs went on for at least another score of miles eastwards.

The abbot was doubtful. The hills looked steeper there, and more crowded together. But they did go down, to ford the Gelt Burn, and started to climb the other side, steep indeed. Soon they passed another Pictish feature, but this was a fort not a stone circle, set on a high and strong position for defence, not on an accessible site for worship.

Soon, up there, they realised that the abbot had been right. This eastern side was altogether too hilly for their purposes, ridges and deep hollows no site for a hospital. Soon they turned back.

The abbot was now anxious to get on to the Roman road, Dere Street, which in fact they had crossed in reaching Overhowden. There was said to have been a marching-camp along it somewhere, which implied level ground and drinking-water. They might find something there.

So it was down to cross the Gelt again and turn northwards on to the higher ground on the west. At another shepherd's cottage they learned that this area was called Childinchirch, where once there had been a Celtic Church establishment named after St Cuthbert as a child, which the abbot saw as a hopeful sign. At least they knew that there was no further village or community now existing near to the highway, this now beginning to rise steadily towards quite a pass at Soutra – they had all passed this way often enough to be sure of that.

Up on the west side high ground again they found themselves on what amounted to a sort of plateau, an all but level heathery expanse, miles of it, Dere Street threading its centre. Along this they rode, looking right and left, judging, assessing. Was there water here? Fuel? And where was the marching-camp?

They did not find anything recognisable as a Roman camp-site; but they realised that this plateau was narrowing in here almost like a great arrowhead, the ground obviously beginning to drop sharply on either side, to the Soutra pass on the right, and to who knew what on the other. But with these drops there would almost certainly be water, running water, and possibly woodland in that further valley. This was beginning to look hopeful.

They were nearing the tip of that great arrowhead when suddenly they all drew rein. A slight crest of heather had obstructed their view. Then abruptly, with the ground dropping away before them hugely, an overwhelming prospect opened, all but catching their breaths. After the comparative constriction of hills and moors, here was seeming infinity spread out for them, the green plain of Lothian reaching far and wide for almost twenty miles to where the lion-like outline of Arthur's Seat rose to mark the site of Edinburgh's city, lesser heights flanking it, the castle rock etched against the blue waters of the Firth of Forth beyond, then all the green hills of Fife and far, far off, the long purple mountains of the Highland Line, ridge upon ridge, limitless.

Silent they all gazed, until Hugh exclaimed, "This is it, then! Here, here at Soutra is the place. With this to view . . . !"

Abbot William nodded slowly. "Yes. God is good. To bring us here. Yes, here we have found what we sought, and more. This prospect could serve many, as a glimpse of heaven to the lost, the sick, the dying! A church here, facing all that. And the hospital stretching back over the level moorland – better than Overhowden. If we can find springs, running water, this is it . . ."

They split up, then, to go and explore the immediate area and its possibilities. Hugh took the further north-westwards side, and quickly found himself descending into a quite deep hanging valley, or more of a wide corrie, clothed with scattered scrub woodland of birch and hawthorn, with many small burns contributing to a fair-sized stream. So, if this was anything to go by, there would be no lack of water and fuel, for the higher moorland would provide all the peat required. He rode further and found similar conditions, before returning to their chosen viewpoint site, where he was presently joined by the others, both equally satisfied.

They decided that they need look no further. Back to Roxburgh with them, to tell the King.

They made Melrose Abbey by nightfall, and the brothers had the new experience of being entertained in the abbot's own handsome quarters.

They decided that while the Cistercians might be very good at looking after the sick, poor and needy, they were also quite good at looking after themselves and their guests.

On the morrow they all three rode on down Tweed to Roxburgh, to find King Malcolm at the nearby abbey of Kelshaugh, engaged in a conference with Abbot Arnold thereof and other senior clerics, mainly bishops. It seemed that this had been called to recommend to the Pope in Rome the appointment of this Arnold as the new Bishop of St Andrews, and Primate of Holy Church in Scotland. Just why was unclear to ordinary young men like Hugh and Duncan, and why the other bishops should agree to it likewise; but no doubt there were adequate reasons, and no obvious clash of opinions was in evidence.

Although Abbot William joined this royal company in debate, it was some time before the King was able to send for the two brothers, by which time of course he had learned something of the success of their venture. He was very appreciative and said that, the matter of the primacy over, he wanted to see for himself their suggested hospital site. On the morrow, then, they would all ride north to this Soutra, to inspect it. That seemed to be a royal command.

So that night was spent in Roxburgh Castle as humbler guests amongst the great ones, seeing nothing of the monarch nor abbot, in the small angle-tower in which they were disposed. They made no complaints.

But in the morning it was very different, royal company indeed, for Malcolm had his brothers William and David accompany him northwards to see the proposed situation of his great new and pious project, and quite a cavalcade escorted them, Hugh and Duncan starting out very much in the rear. But

118

presently the King sent for them to ride beside himself and Abbot William, eager to hear about all the exploring, and the other sites considered but rejected.

The other royal brothers seemed less interested, but Brawny Will did enquire of Hugh as to another matter – the killing of that wild boar at Smailholm. It seemed the word of that had spread abroad, even to these royal ears, and probably the incident had developed in the telling. But the prince wanted to hear details, declaring that it had never been *his* good fortune to come across a boar. He would like to have instructions as to the best way of slaying such a brute, so that if he found one he would have the satisfaction of killing it effectively.

Malcolm, listening, at that, only part playfully, reproved him. Was not the wild boar the symbol of their ancient royal line, dating back beyond the mists of time? Not for *them* to slay. To which his brother declared that it was the most unsuitable symbol for a kingly house, one of the most objectionable of beasts. They ought to do better than that. A lion, perhaps . . . ?

It was all of thirty miles from Roxburgh to Soutra, but all there were practised horsemen, and on that well-trodden highway they covered the distance in just over four hours. At Childinchirch they left the road to mount to the high ground, Abbot William explaining how the place had got its name, strange as it sounded. Now comments began to be made about barren moors and desolate heights, by the uninitiated, these ignored by Malcolm who gazed about him keenly.

When, of course, they came to the Soutra edge and the vista burst upon their sight, even the most sceptical were impressed, and the King all but ecstatic. Here, yes, was all that he could have hoped for, and more. He congratulated his three searchers warmly and promised that he would reward them in some appropriate fashion.

They did not linger, for it was a long road back to Roxburgh, Malcolm announcing that he would come back here one day soon, with Abbot William, to go over the ground in detail and plan where the various buildings and structures should be

119

sited. He agreed that the church of the establishment should face that wonderful God-given view.

Riding southwards again, with the September evening upon them, Abbot William dropped off at Melrose, and Hugh and Duncan with him, for it was closer to both Smailholm and Swinton here than was Roxburgh. On their leaving the royal party, Malcolm again expressed his thanks, and asked the two brothers what he could offer them to prove his gratitude for services rendered. Some minor offices of profit in the gift of the crown, perhaps?

Hugh drew a deep breath. "Nothing such is called for, Sire. And I am all unworthy. But . . . of your great generosity you gave us the properties of Aldcambus and Redheugh. My brother and I are greatly beholden. But – these are stock-bearing lands, sheep and cattle, and we have not the moneys to purchase the necessary flocks and herds. A . . . some assistance to do so would be greatly esteemed, Your Grace. Some small help . . ." He stopped, biting his lip and glancing around him. Was he committing *lèse majesté*? Was this a grave offence, asking the monarch for money?

The King seemed nowise upset, despite the expressions of those around. Indeed he smiled. "This is a modest request, indeed, Hugh de Swinton," he said. "You need how much?"

"Oh, I have no notion, Sire. No great sum." He was all but stammering. "Just to help us buy some beasts. They are there now. If Sir Walter Olifard will sell them . . ."

"So! Then I will tell the keeper of my privy purse to send you a sufficiency, never fear. And who knows, I may think of other ways of showing my goodwill. To you both. And, it may well be that I may require your services on another occasion." And he waved his cavalcade onwards.

"That was featly done," the abbot observed, to Hugh's surprise, for it had seemed anything but that to him.

Duncan nodded approval. It was noticeable that he had been included in the King's remarks, by no means ignored this time.

So they spent another night as the abbot's guests, and set off in the morning, hopefully, for Smailholm.

This time Sir Walter was in residence again, and seemed pleased to see them, wondering whether they had yet visited their new properties at the knuckle-end of the Lammermuirs. At their glowing response, especially as to Redheugh, he nodded, but said that they had to be young fully to appreciate that cliff-girt terrain. A place for goats – not that he had ever kept any there.

Their talk of cliff-happy sheep gave Hugh the opening he required. Would Sir Walter consider selling these sheep, and the Aldcambus ones also, the cattle as well, to them? King Malcolm had promised them some moneys, and Sir Ernulf would probably lend them some. Sufficient, they hoped, at least to purchase some of the stock there . . .

Olifard eyed them, rubbing his chin. "No," he said, "I will *not* sell you one animal. Not one!" He paused. "But I will *give* you them, all of them! Yes, give them. See you, I have thought on this. That I was insufficiently grateful to you for killing that boar which was plaguing this property. All the folk hereabouts sing your praises now. And I did nothing but commend you. So this I would, and can, do. I have other flocks and herds. You shall have these. You can use the King's siller to add to them, if so you wish. But the stock there is yours, I say."

Looking from the older man to each other and back again, the brothers wagged their heads, scarcely believing what they heard. Hugh tried to find words but produced only incoherencies. Duncan did rather better.

"We thank you, sir. You are kind. We will never forget it."

"It is something well earned. And costs me but little. You will help your brother with these lands, boy?"

"I have given him Redheugh, sir. For himself," Hugh exclaimed. "He will make a good laird for that very special place. I . . . we thank you with all our hearts!"

"Say no more. But . . . . I would urge that you keep my folk there in your service. They have served me well, and will do so with you, I have no doubt."

"We have already told them that they remain, Sir Walter. We like them very well."

"That is good. So be it. My debt is paid. And I wish you well in what you have earned . . ."

They left Smailholm Tower on its crag conceiving themselves to be the most fortunate of young men.

10

They were heading north again, but by east this time, for Aldcambus and the coast, to commence the labours necessary to bring the two houses into a state for their occupancy, before heading westwards over the hills to lead the Swinton sheep flocks back to their winter grazings – this when Duncan made his announcement.

"Now that I have a house of my own, and the wherewithal to keep a wife, I intend to ask Meg Cockburn to marry me." That was abruptly, almost defiantly said. "I have long wanted her. Now, I have something to offer her."

Hugh took moments to digest that, as they rode along. "I . . . I see."

"You will not say me nay?"

"No-o-o. I have no call to, have I?"

"I judge not. She would make a good wife for me."

"Yes. No doubt. She has . . . attractions."

"Think you that she will accept me?"

"Who knows? Women have their own notions as to men and marriage. But now that you are a laird in your own right, I would think that she would see much to, to commend it."

"And *you*?"

"Me? I like Meg well, yes." That was the best that he could think of to say. He did not add that he foresaw complications.

"A shepherd's daughter, and strong on her feet, she will take well, I say, to Redheugh."

"No doubt. But, now that you are a laird, if a small one, you *could* aspire higher, Duncan. Than a shepherd's daughter."

"I seek no higher. And I am still a bastard!"

They left it at that.

At Aldcambus they enlisted the help of Dod Lumsden's wife Eupham, and a couple of other local women, in the process of cleaning, tidying and rearranging the quite large house for residence. Not that Hugh was fussy about this, and he did not see himself using many of the rooms anyway; but after years of not being occupied, considerable refurbishing was called for. Redheugh would be different, for the Robsons had dwelt therein for long, it seemed.

Actually there was not a great deal that the young men could usefully do in this housework, apart from moving furniture, beds and chests around; so before long they left the women to it, and proceeded over to Redheugh, Duncan's eagerness to be there undisguised. They found that Tam Robson was away servicing his lobster creels, according to Jeanie his wife, but he should be back shortly for he had been gone since breakfast. They decided to go and meet him, those cliffs drawing them on, their fascination compelling, for he would be using that little boat they had seen down at the one corner of beach available.

In fact they saw the boat before ever they reached the steep winding track down to the shore, the man rowing it landwards thereto, the craft stacked with the wickerwork creels. They waved, and won a wave back, whether Robson recognised who they were at that range or not.

"That cave," Duncan said. "While he has his boat out, can we ask him to take us in it to see the cave below the tower?"

"Why not? He is your man now. You are master here."

They reached the head of the path and started their careful descent as the boat came in to the shingle.

Tam Robson was unloading still-clawing, pink lobsters into a lidded basket as they arrived, and greeted them in friendly fashion, not casual but anything but subservient. He announced that it would not be much longer before he would have to take in his creels, anchored to floats out there, as the winter seas would make lobster-fishing impossible, indeed would drag away any creels left in place. Did they like lobster meat?

The brothers confessed that they had never tasted it, such being unavailable to Swinton.

"While we are here, at the boat, we would wish you to take us to see this cave you spoke of, under the Fastness tower," Duncan said. "Would you do that?"

"If you wish it, yes sirs."

"My brother, Duncan Swinton, is now laird here," Hugh mentioned. "Redheugh is handed over to him, with its sheep and beasts. So you will be seeing much of him. And he likes it well, here."

"And you remain my shepherd and friend, Tam. And stay on in the house, if you will. I shall require only a chamber or two."

"Och, do you say that, now? That is right guid o' you. Jeanie was wondering what was to be the way o' it. That'll suit us fine, just." He pointed. "See you, gie's a hand wi' some o' these creels, and there'll be room for us a' in the boatie. Aye, and watch your fingers! These critturs can gie a right bite!"

Wary indeed of the lobsters, which appeared to go on living when removed from the sea, their great claws waving menacingly, they got the boat unloaded, and managed to climb aboard without getting bitten or even their feet wet. Clamping the lid down on the crawling creatures, Tam pushed off with an oar and then sat to row, refusing their offers to assist – as well, probably, for neither of them was expert at the exercise.

They were rowed round the threatening cliff-foots, these seeming even more daunting from below, keeping well out to avoid the litter of reefs and skerries projecting seawards, over which the tide surged and broke whitely, the craft heaving somewhat alarmingly since it had to go broadside-on to the rollers. Above them the sea-birds wheeled and planed and screamed, some diving into the water quite close at hand, and coming up with small silvery fish gleaming in their beaks.

They had to go well over a mile before they saw the thrusting tower-topped stack soaring ahead. But no sign of a cave. Tam told them that this was part of it all, the secret entry to it, sharply round the stack-foot, and the opening thus also protected from the full force of the prevailing easterly tide-combers. Protected also by its barrier of reefs, save for the by no means obvious passage through.

Sure enough, navigating round what amounted to a small headland, and between the rocks, at an acute angle they saw the dark cave mouth, narrow and high, yawning before them, the tide surging inside. Expertly Tam steered the boat in; but once inside he could no longer row, for there was insufficient width for the oars. There was a sort of shelf along the left side, which narrowed the space, weed-hung, but which could be walked upon. Tam had to use one oar to pole them onward, pushing against this shelf.

The sharp bend in the cave he had reported had the effect of reducing the sea's swell and creating a practical landing-place against the ledge; but also, of course, it much reduced the light which came from the cave mouth, so that it became very dark in the furthest recesses. The roof being high, this meant that they could not actually see where the shaft had been cut in the living rock up to the tower. Tam said that if he had known that they were coming here, he would have brought a torch to light. But he pointed up to where the hole was, and explained how a rope ladder could be let down from above, and whatever was to be brought in or sent out raised or lowered thus. They had a somewhat fruitless discussion as to what such cargoes could have been, to have made all this work and planning necessary or profitable.

One day, to be sure, Duncan would explore that shaft.

They were rowed back to the little beach, whereafter they helped Tam to carry his lobsters up the cliff and on to the house.

There they explained to Jeanie that Duncan wanted them to remain in Redheugh House, Jeanie to act as housekeeper for himself meantime. He would require only a couple of rooms at present, but probably more later. The couple seemed happy with this arrangement, although it transpired that they had a cottage up at Dowlaw, which really was the shepherd's house and where their son and his wife and bairns now lived, the son, Rab, acting as under-shepherd. They could retire there when necessary.

126

A meal of lobsters, with the Robsons, proved to be to their taste, before they returned to Aldcambus.

The brothers spent a week at their properties getting all in order for more or less permanent residence, with October colours beginning to replace the green, the heather still blooming richly contrasting with the russet bracken and the golden birches. Then they set off westwards again for Cranshaws, picking up one of their flocks in the Monynut area on the way.

The assembling of great numbers of sheep for the autumn move was always a major task, for that spring's lambs, after five months of growing up in the freedom of the hills, were ever unruly and demanded much herding. But it was reunion for the shepherds, who inevitably had known much isolation in the interim.

Meg Cockburn, as always, was delighted to see the brothers, and showed it vehemently. She was going to be faced with a decision on this occasion, Hugh recognised, but he could hardly warn her.

He did not get a chance to do so, anyway, for very soon after they had arrived, Duncan took the opportunity, while her father was talking to Hugh, to take her arm commandingly and lead her off alone. They seemed to be heading for the nearby woodland.

It was some time before they returned, indeed the evening meal had commenced in the old roomy kitchen. Hugh saw Meg eyeing him almost apprehensively, but nothing was said.

After they had eaten, and the talk eased off a little, it was Meg's turn to do the leading-away. She came to take Hugh's arm and drew him to the door, and out. She peered up at him in the October dusk.

"You know of this?" she demanded urgently. "He has told you – Duncan?"

"Er . . . yes. You mean, about, about you and himself?"

"Yes. He has asked that I wed him. Wed! Me!" She shook his arm. "I am only a shepherd's daughter, see you. What, what should I do?"

He searched her face. "What do you *want* to do, Meg? Your wish in this?"

"I do not know – I do not! You see, I . . . I . . ." She did not finish that.

"It would be a good marriage," he said slowly. "For you both. Duncan is now something of a laird. With a fine house. He owns sheep and beasts. And he is very fond of you, lass."

"Aye. And I am fond of him, mind. But . . . I prefer you, Hugh!" That came out in a rush, and she gripped that arm so hard that it hurt.

He wagged his head, wordless. What *could* he say to that?

"I know, I know! That you canna wed me. But . . . to wed your own brother, even half-brother! It will be . . . right difficult."

He knew it. They were walking on, towards those trees again. Suddenly she turned and threw herself into his arms.

"Och, what am I to do, to say, Hugh? What am I to do?"

"You will wed one day. *Some* day, one day, lass. Nothing more sure, no? And you will not do better than Duncan Swinton, I think. He is a good man. And has always wanted you, I know. And . . . you would make him very happy."

"But, you . . . ?"

"I . . . we would have to be, to be loyal to him, Meg. We must understand that. Loyal. No more . . . of this!" But still he held her close.

"That is it! *Can* we do it? After all, after all we have done together! Can we?"

"We must. If you wed him. But, if you do not – what then? Duncan would be in despair, I think. And would blame *me*! Nothing more sure. Me, his own brother!"

"You would have me to do it, then? Wed him." Again she all but shook him.

"I think . . . yes." That took a deal of saying, brief as it was.

They were silent for a while. Then she turned up her face to his, lips eager. "One . . . last . . . kiss!" she whispered.

That was a long and passionate embrace.

"Then . . . you will do it?" Hugh said, when he was able.

"It seems that I must, does it not?"

Hand in hand they went back to the house.

Later, when they sought their room, Meg escorted them to their door, as ever. But this time Hugh embraced her first, and only briefly, before all but hurrying within.

It was some time before Duncan joined him. He came over to look down at his brother on the bed, in the flickering candlelight. "Would Abbot William wed us, think you?" he asked.

Hugh sat up and grasped his brother's wrist. "She will do it, then? Wed you?"

"She will, yes. I think . . . I think that you told her to!"

"How could I do that? She is her own woman, that one! And now she is yours, it seems!"

"Mine, yes – when we are wed!" Levelly he said it.

"Then I am glad for you, Duncan. You have won a fine woman."

"Won . . . ?"

They left it at that.

In the morning, they started on the southwards herding. But it would not be long before they were back, they assured.

11

Their flocks delivered safely at Swinton, and distributed, the brothers paid a visit to Melrose Abbey. They were received kindly by the abbot, who did not hesitate when he was asked, diffidently, if he would conduct Duncan's marriage service. He would indeed, and gladly. Where? Here at the abbey?

Duncan cleared his throat. "I thank you, but no, my lord Abbot. That would scarcely be suitable. This great and splendid sanctuary. See you, I am a bastard, although now I own lands, thanks to Hugh here. And my woman is but a shepherd's daughter, excellent as she is. No, if we could prevail on you to come to Redheugh, on the coast? There is a little chapel there, dedicated to a Saint Helen. It is now seldom used. Most fairly placed. Looking out to the cliffs and sea. If I could wed there . . . ?"

"St Helen's! I know it not. St Helena was famed for the discovery of Christ's true cross. She was married to the Roman Emperor Constantius, but renounced by him, mother of Constantine. When her son built his great church on Golgotha at Jerusalem, she is said to have found the buried cross. Part of it now is owned by King Malcolm, his great-grandmother, Queen Margaret, bringing it to Scotland. So – yes, if you would have your marriage there, so be it. I will come. When is it to be?"

"At your convenience, Abbot William. You honour us . . ."

It was arranged that the ceremony should be held soon, for with November nearly on them and the celebrations of All Hallows and the saints, Margaret herself, Fergus and Andrew making that a busy month indeed for the clergy. So the sooner the better. Ten days hence, then? Duncan would hasten up to Cranshaws, to ensure that this would be suitable for Meg

130

Cockburn, then return, and they would escort the abbot up to Aldcambus for the service. Hugh realised that he himself would have to take the road also, to see that his house was duly prepared for visitors and a wedding feast.

So the day following the brothers took their different ways, north-westwards and north-eastwards. They hoped that the golden October weather would last.

At Aldcambus, Eupham Lumsden, when told what was expected of her, was somewhat overwhelmed by it all, especially to be having an abbot to cater for, but eventually agreed that, with Jeanie Robson helping her, she would prepare no banquet but an adequate meal for the wedding party. How many would there be?

Hugh reckoned a dozen at most, Duncan certainly wanting no large affair. The sheriff and brother Alan; Meg's father and brother; the abbot and possibly an acolyte; the bride and groom and himself. There might be one or two more. Soup, fish, lobsters, meat, wildfowl, as she suggested, would be more than sufficient. He ordered an additional table in the hall for the Lumsdens themselves, the Robsons and other local folk.

Then he went over to Redheugh and informed Tam and his wife of the situation, and that they would be having *two* new occupants of the house there. They immediately offered to move out to their son's cottage at Dowlaw, but Hugh said no. Stay where they were meantime; Duncan and Meg might well prefer to have them there, for help in the house, and company. If it was otherwise they would be informed.

All arranged, he returned to Swinton Parva, where Duncan joined him that same evening. All was well. Meg would be at Aldcambus one week from that day, with father and brother. They could go on the morrow and tell Abbot William.

In the event, it was quite a party which set out for Melrose to collect and escort the abbot, for sundry kinsmen of the Swintons had elected to attend, although no women. And the abbot brought along his prior as assistant, the latter, having been trained at Durham, being interested to see this St Helen's

131

chapel, they learned. Hugh hoped that Eupham Lumsden's catering would be able to cope.

Melrose to Aldcambus was very much a cross-country journey, and not all there were as hardy horsemen as the abbot and the Swinton brothers, so it took them most of the day to cover the ground. Eupham's hospitality was therefore much in demand well in advance of the wedding feast.

There was still sufficient evening light for the brothers to be able to take the two clerics down to inspect the chapel, prior to the morrow's ceremony – not that, in its simplicity and size, there was much scope for planning and arrangement. Abbot and prior agreed that it was basically just a small Celtic shrine, little altered in the transition to the Roman Catholic faith, which had more elaborate church plenishings and details. But it much pleased them, nevertheless. They also conceded that it was most happily placed, and the prospects seawards spectacular. Duncan told them to wait until tomorrow when, if they were so inclined, after the wedding at noon and feast thereafter, they could be taken to view the Redheugh cliffs in daylight. He did not seem to imply that he would be otherwise preoccupied.

In the morning, the Cockburn family arrived in good time – which meant that they must have set off on their garrons well before sunrise, Meg looking the most confident, whatever the turmoil of her emotions. She sought a room to change into her wedding gown, which she had sewn with her own fingers. When she reappeared, Duncan viewed her with pride indeed, almost wonderment.

All was ready well before the planned noonday, and since there was no point in hanging about and waiting, they all set off early down to the chapel, quite a procession. Nor was there any point in seeking to keep the two bridal parties separate in the circumstances, as was the custom, since it would only have tended to emphasise the difference in background, this the Swintons concerned not to evidence. They all went down together, bride and groom actually arm in arm.

The Lumsdens and Robsons proved also to have been up early. They had been down to deck the chapel with heather, pine branches and holly against its red stone walling. Hugh wondered whether the place had ever been used for a wedding before.

Although they formed no large gathering, the little sanctuary was almost crowded. There was no distinct chancel and nave, only the simple, plain rectangle, stone-flagged floor, and the quite solid altar at the east end. All there must needs stand.

The service that followed was as simple, and acceptably so, despite the lofty status of the officiating clergy. They had noticed a holy-water stoup in the walling, to the right of the altar, the previous evening; and the abbot had brought a bottle of water down with him. This he emptied in. Then, with the bride and groom standing nearby, he commenced the service with a brief prayer, and then a blessing of this water. He handed a small phial of oil to the prior, and turned to the happy couple.

He told them that they had, of their free will, decided and elected to enter together into the estate of holy matrimony, which was good and proper but not to be embarked upon without due care and consideration. He took it that this man Duncan and this woman Margaret had so considered and cared? Also that they knew of no valid reason why they should not take each other as husband and wife?

The pair nodded, wordless.

Abbot William went on, not unkindly, to the effect that he was assured that they were both baptised persons, members therefore of Christ's Holy Church. Baptism was for the washing away of sins. But, however effective that had been, undoubtedly this man and this woman would have committed many a sin since then, as indeed had all present. Therefore, before coming to enter this holy estate which they sought, in the presence of Almighty God and of these witnesses, it was good that they should have a second baptism, so that they should commence their union without any and all past sins and follies to hamper it. Did they so agree?

More nods. They were beckoned over to the water stoup in the walling, there to be sprinkled with the blest water, and told that their sins were forgiven, and the sign of

133

Christ's cross marked on their foreheads with a wet finger.

Thus prepared, the actual joining together was effected with marked brevity but warm sincerity, and little feeling of ritual, the taking of each other as man and wife seeming to develop therefrom most naturally, almost inevitably.

Then it was the prior's turn. He came over to them to anoint them again from the phial of oil, on their heads and in the Name of the Holy Trinity, declaring that this was the Oil of Gladness and that it would, by Christ's grace, bring all gladness to the marriage thus effected and celebrated.

And that was it, save for the final benediction upon them all, the couple hardly able to believe that they were now joined together as one, indissolubly, in the sight of God and man.

It took the exchange of felicitations thereafter to convince them that it was true, at least as far as the man was concerned.

When Hugh bestowed a brotherly kiss upon the bride, she gripped his arm tensely for a moment before turning hastily away.

The little chapel of St Helen, whoever she was, was left with the holly and pine branches and the heather, and one more memory to add to its ancient cartulary, as the company headed back to the House of Aldcambus.

Hugh need not have worried about the provisioning, for Eupham Lumsden and her assistants proved themselves more than adequate to the occasion, whatever the night before's depletions, with nothing seeming in short supply, no complaints and all very satisfied. The speech-making, like the wedding ceremony, was brief but sincere.

Thereafter, still only mid-afternoon, no sort of celebratory entertainment seeming apt, Hugh proposed taking Abbot William and any others who might wish to join them, to see Redheugh and its cliff-girt coast, as promised. His father and brother Alan accepted the invitation, and rather to the surprise of all, Duncan announced that he would come also, to show his wife of what she had become the mistress, unusual after-marriage preoccupation as this might be. Meg seemed nowise off-put.

They went mounted to Redheugh, Meg riding pillion behind her husband, all there much impressed by what they saw looming ahead. While interest was shown in the house of the property, especially by the young woman whose home it was to be, there was no suggestion that they should inspect it forthwith, all attention being irresistibly drawn to the extraordinary background of vivid red precipices, soaring headlands, and heights beyond. There was certainly no disappointment amongst the viewers, all exclaiming, Meg not least vocal. She was clearly beginning to dispense with any preoccupation that she was but a shepherd's daughter amongst lairdly folk.

They did not go all the way to the Fastness tower, with daylight beginning to fail, but saw enough to have them all asking why they had never before heard of this place, a wonder as it was. Duncan and his bride were left at Redheugh House to celebrate their wedding night, and the others returned to Aldcambus.

That evening, marital affairs off their minds, the sheriff, abbot and prior turned to national matters. Something of major importance to the realm had apparently developed. The great Somerled, self-styled King of the Isles, had won a dramatic victory, on sea and land, against the Norseman Godfrey Olafsson, King of Man, who had also called himself King of the Isles. Somerled now held Man as well as all the Hebrides, Nordreys and Sudreys, and dominated all the West Highland seaboard, so perhaps he was entitled to give himself that style and title, although King Malcolm, needless to say, did not relish having two kings in Scotland. But since Malcolm MacEth had been freed and given back his earldom of Ross, he being married to Somerled's sister, the Islesman had announced his desire to come to some sort of agreement and possible alliance with the King of Scots, where up till now they had been mutually inimical if not actually at war. This would be beneficial to the realm, and King Malcolm was anxious to confirm and establish the situation, prepared to enter into some sort of treaty which would accept the Isles kingship provided Somerled acknowledged himself as sovereign and overlord.

None there condemned this as weakness, for all knew that Somerled was no real threat to mainland Scotland, whereas King Hakon of Norway was. The Norsemen were ever a menace. They had long possessed the Orkney and Shetland Isles and now held much of northern Ireland. Somerled had driven them out of the Hebrides, and now taken the Isle of Man from this lesser Viking. The danger was that Hakon and his barbarian hordes, having lost the West Highland seaboard, might turn to Scotland's east coast, for they were inveterate and determined invaders. So an alliance with Somerled would not only protect the Highland west but, with the earldom of Ross covering much of the north-east, would help protect that side also, much aiding the royal forces. Moreover it would help to anchor those formerly rebellious earls of the north more firmly to Malcolm.

Sheriff Pate said that the Earl Cospatrick had told him that King Malcolm was planning a meeting with Somerled. He had thought to spend the Christmas and Yuletide season at Scone and Perth, where he had been crowned and had taken his oaths of kingship. It would be an apt place to see the Islesman, and at the same time demonstrate the hoped-for alliance to the earls who had so recently assembled against him there. So he wanted a show of strength, and would be calling upon Cospatrick and the other south-country lords to support him there, not this time with armies but with their knightly and lairdly vassals – which in fact did represent armed strength. So they must all be prepared for a royal summons to Perth for Christmastide. Even senior clergy would be expected to attend, it was understood, not only to show Holy Church's support, but because Somerled had founded an abbey at Saddell in Kintyre, the first such on the north-west seaboard, and it was important that this foundation should be recognised, and used as a unifying factor.

Abbot William declared that he would be there, if this was desired, the others likewise.

In the morning, the visitors departed southwards, the sheriff and Alan saying that they would escort the clerics back to Melrose. Hugh would settle down to being laird at Aldcambus.

12

In the weeks that followed, prior to the Earl Cospatrick's summons to join his entourage for Perth, Hugh inevitably saw a great deal of his new sister-in-law. And, in fact, after the first two or three occasions, when there was some strain and reserve, they managed to settle down to a fairly satisfactory relationship, accepting the situation, not pretending that they were not fond of each other but accepting that feelings should not be shown too openly. And it was evident that Meg was by no means unhappy with Duncan, which greatly helped. She might not be in love with him, as he was with her, but their physical association clearly did not offend her, she having a lusty nature anyway. If Duncan himself was apt to be watchful at first, that soon wore off. It was all a deal better than had been feared.

Meg, of course, was very busy in getting the house to her taste, and his. But she did not ask the Robsons to leave. They were allotted the lesser wing of the establishment, which they had used anyway. They provided good company as well as aid. For his part, Hugh knew a certain loneliness at the House of Aldcambus. Redheugh saw the more of him.

The brothers were busy also, with much to learn about managing very different kinds of properties from fertile lands in the Merse. Here, on this all but savage coastal area of steep slopes and heather moorland above the cliffs, both the farming and stock-raising methods varied considerably. The animals did not have to be moved to summer and winter pastures, but much more winter feed in the form of hay and oats was required. And the soil being less productive, and cultivation areas scattered wide, much more labour was necessary in ploughing the rigs and feeding the ground with manure and fertilising aids. They learned that seaweed was a most effective treatment, strange as this seemed to them, and much labour and time was expended on gathering the weed along the coast. There was no lack of it on the rocks and skerries, but it had to be loaded into Tam's boat and then carried up that cliff-path, and then carted on slypes, horse-drawn sleds, for spreading on the selected ground.

Hugh and Duncan, after much prospecting, decided that their lands could benefit from considerable simple drainage, artificial drainage. Nothing of this appeared to have been attempted hitherto, and there were many areas, slopes, shelves, and hollows which were waterlogged and reed-filled, sour, which if drained off would provide possible tilth. So, enrolling assistants and hiring some more local men – this with the moneys which had duly arrived from King Malcolm – they set about aligning and digging drains and ditches to carry off the water, a hard and lengthy task, but one which they were assured would prove valuable in increasing the growing capacities of their upheaved lands.

Then there was the cattle situation. They judged that Aldcambus could carry a much greater head of stock than it had at present. Where to get the beasts? They had heard of trysts, so-called, along the Highland Line, at Crieff, Perth itself, Blair-in-Gowrie, even Falkirk, where the Highlandmen brought their surplus beasts to be sold each autumn, vast numbers of them, at low prices, for those mountains could not support large stocks in the winter when the high grazings were barren and often snow-covered, so that in fact only the breeding stock was retained and the rest taken south to sell off. But for the brothers to get away up there, buy and then herd the beasts all the long way back was an off-putting conception.

It was Meg who solved this problem for them. She told them that in November, even early December, drovers went up to these trysts and bought cattle cheaply, then herded them southwards to the Lowland markets, even as far away as Carlisle and Newcastle-upon-Tyne, there to sell them at considerable profit. Hugh and Duncan knew about the drovers, and often used their drove-roads of course; but they had not realised that one such, which passed not far from Cranshaws to the west, by Longformacus and over to Greenlaw and the borderline, was frequently used in November; always they and their own sheep flocks had moved homeward before that. She said that, if some of these drovers learned that they could make a sale comparatively nearby, here at Aldcambus, they would be well pleased, she was sure, to save themselves a long further journey, and come over to sell. It would be a matter for bargaining. These Highland cattle were hardy and should do well on their kind of ground.

Duncan and Meg rode westwards the very next day, to tell her father and brother to inform the Longformacus shepherd that there was a market for drovers' herds a deal nearer than over the border, where an honest price would be given.

In the event they did not have to wait long, for only eight days after the pair returned, the weary lowing of cattle on the west wind heralded the approach of about one hundred and fifty beasts and their drovers.

This was rather more than the brothers wanted. They had invited Dod Lumsden and Tam Robson over to do the necessary chaffering for them, as more likely to win realistic pricing than would seeming gentry; and these presently came up with the interesting proposal that if they would buy *all* the animals, the drovers would let them have them at a still more advantageous price than they had agreed upon, to save them going on further with only some two score to sell. These were the smallish black cattle of the mountains, not perhaps the biggest beef-producers, but strong, sturdy creatures which would thrive well in the winter storms of this coast. This deal was concluded appreciatively, and all concerned expressed themselves as happy. The royal bounty was being well spent, and the two estates all but overstocked. Indeed the brothers began to wonder whether, in a year or two, they might be able to purchase more land, up there on Coldinghame Muir, from the priory monks. Abbot William might put in a good word for them.

*   *   *

In mid-December the expected summons arrived from the Earl Cospatrick, all his northern vassals to present themselves at his castle of Dunbar, in Lothian, on St Drostan's Day, to ride for Perth, at the King's command. It seemed that Christmas would be spent there, or at Scone nearby.

It seemed a strange place to go to pass the festive season, and winter hardly the best time for travel, even though the hardest of the weather would probably be yet to come. But royal commands were not to be ignored. Meg would go home to Cranshaws for her Yuletide.

Hugh wondered whether he and Duncan were indeed vassals of the earl, since the monarch himself held sokage or superiority over these lands, and had been able to order Olifard to hand them over, with no reference to Cospatrick. But they were of the earl's far-out kin; and it might be claimed that their lands here lay within the earldom of Dunbar, the castle and town of which were only a dozen miles away. They would go there, anyway.

The ride up the coast in thin, chill rain was no auspicious start to this curious mission. Dunbar Castle was itself hardly the place for an assembly, for it consisted of a number of towers projecting out of the sea on upthrusting rock-stacks, these linked by covered-in bridges, under one of which was the entrance to the fishing harbour of the fair-sized township, a device which enabled the castle keepers to close or open the haven at will by merely lowering or raising a sort of great portcullis of iron which could block all access, and so enforce the payment to the lord of one-tenth of all fish caught. But however useful thus, and for defence purposes, it was scarcely suitable for the gathering of a horsed contingent. So this had to be effected in the town itself, where the earl maintained a large house for his own convenience. Here the brothers found the company assembled, including their father and Alan and many others whom they knew.

About seventy of them rode next morning on the long journey to Perth. After fording the Tyne at the East Lynn of Preston, well back from the coast now, they headed up the Vale of Peffer to the great bay of Aberlady, at the Peffer mouth, and then on along the shore of what was now the Firth of Forth, by Seton, Salt Preston and Musselburgh, to reach Edinburgh by early nightfall. It was not actually raining, but the cold grey skies were threatening. There were mutterings about the royal choice of timing and venue for this confrontation with the Islesman.

Next day, still following the Forth westwards, they reached Stirling, where they could make the first possible crossing of what had now become a river. Here they met up with other lords and their lairdly supporters coming from south and west.

It was wet again in the morning, and the remaining thirty-odd miles to the Tay at Perth made less than pleasing going. Yet, despite the conditions large numbers were on the road northwards. And as Tay was neared, slower-moving but splendidly attired groups of clerics, coming westwards from St Andrews in Fife, were encountered. It appeared that Malcolm had, as it were, killed two birds with one stone, and had arranged the official installation of Abbot Arnold of Kelsaugh as Bishop of St Andrews and Primate of Scotland a few days previously, at which all the senior clergy of the land had been present; and now they were available to attend this Scone meeting.

At Scone Abbey itself, comparatively small however ancient and prestigious, accommodation was limited; but St John's Town of Perth had room for all, for apart from the town-houses of the Earls of Strathearn, Menteith, Atholl and Angus, and those of lesser lords, practically every religious foundation had an establishment here, Benedictines, Augustinians, Cistercians, and the rest, and the churchmen were throwing them open to all, in token of their great indebtedness to the King's grandsire, David of blessed memory. Sheriff Pate and his sons sought out the monastery of the Cistercians, where they found Abbot William installed, who welcomed them warmly and had them provided for.

They learned that Somerled, with his sons and not a few of his curious-looking clan chiefs and captains, was already in residence at the abbey, with the King and his most senior lords temporal and spiritual. All appeared to have gone well with negotiations, and so far a congenial atmosphere prevailed. All the former rebel earls were present, save for Ross, who had a long way to come through snow-bound mountains – but he was expected at any time.

On the morrow, they all crossed Tay and trooped up to Scone Abbey for the ceremonial signing and sealing of an accord. It was hardly a treaty, between the two principals – not the final one, which had to await Ross's arrival, but dealing with the position of the Isle of Man, which was situated not in the Hebrides at all but off the English and Irish coasts, and the holding of which might cause friction with the kings of England. So an agreement was necessary confirming that neither Somerled nor Malcolm had any inimical intentions towards neighbours east or west, the Islesman promising indeed to protect adjacent coasts from any Norse invaders. The English envoy to the Scots court was present to receive and then transmit this assurance.

The ceremony was held in the abbey-church itself as the only place large enough to contain all the company. When they entered, with the sanctuary ablaze with candles, and the atmosphere somewhat smoky from the many braziers alight to counter the winter chill, despite the faint haze Hugh's eyes fastened at once on what stood above the chancel-step and before the high altar. Four throne-like chairs were there, facing the congregation and flanking a very different item of furnishing. This was a great block of polished and carved black stone, of seat height, hollowed on top and with rounded handles, volutes, at each side to lift it by, Scotland's renowned talisman, the Merble Chair. With something like awe the young man gazed at it, the fabled and famous Stone of Destiny, on which scores of Kings of Scots had been crowned. Many were the legends as to its origin, one being even that it was Jacob's Pillow, from the Book of Genesis, which an Egyptian princess had brought to Ireland with her husband, an Irish princeling, her name Scota, which produced the style Scots – although probably the stone was St Columba's portable altar from Iona, brought here by Kenneth mac Alpin who had

142

united Picts and Scots, the hollow at the seat being usable as a font for baptism. Tradition said that he, and only he who was crowned on this stone could be undoubted King of Scots. That it was sitting there today was silent testimony to the importance of the occasion, its sacred aura being as binding on Somerled of the Isles as on any, it having come from his Isles.

A ululation of horns heralded the appearance of the High Sennachie who, thudding with his staff-of-office for silence, announced the entry of Malcolm mac Henry mac David mac Malcolm mac Duncan, High King of Scots, with Somerled mac Gillebride mac Gilladamnan mac Fergus, King of the Isles. Also the earls of Scotia, along with the Abbot of Scone and the Primate of Holy Church, the Bishop Arnold of St Andrews.

In they filed, Malcolm leading, but at his side although half a pace behind, a fair-haired, smiling giant of a man, simply clad in calfskin waistcoat over silken shirt and saffron kilt, but radiating a natural power and authority, a figure indeed to cause others to seem somewhat ordinary, however splendid their attire. Next came the Princes William and David, then the Earls of Strathearn, Menteith, Fife, Atholl, Angus, Moray and Cospatrick of March and Dunbar. Bringing up the rear were the Bishop Arnold and the old Abbot of Scone.

A choir of boys provided a sung accompaniment.

Malcolm went to seat himself on the Stone of Destiny, waving Somerled to the chair on his right and his two brothers to those on the left, leaving the fourth seat for the abbot. Bishop Arnold went to stand behind the Stone, as indicating the backing of Holy Church, while the earls stood in flanking position at either side, all a symbolic representation of what claimed to be the most ancient enduring realm in Christendom. The Sennachie thumped for silence again.

"Hear all!" he cried. "The *Ard Righ*, High King of Scots, in the presence of the *ri*, and the lesser kings or earls, and with the blessing of Christ's Church, hereby declares his favour and friendship for Somerled, *Ri* and King of the Isles and of Man, here present, accepting him and his as part of the kingdom while recognising all the said Somerled's rights and rule over the Isles and his mainland domains, this

for their mutual upholding and support, now and hereafter."
He paused. "In token of which His Grace Malcolm now offers,
as seal and promise, the Kiss of Verity on Christ's own cross –
of which there can be no more true and enduring covenant."
And from under his tabard-like robe, the Sennachie produced
a fist-sized and lidded silver casket, which he opened, and
bowing, handed to Malcolm.

If Hugh had been in awe before, now he was still more
so. For here was enclosed, enshrined, a fragment of the true
Cross of Calvary on which their saviour had been crucified
eleven hundred years before, brought from Hungary by the
King's great-grandmother, the blessed Queen Margaret, part
of the larger piece held by her own grandfather King and
Saint Stephen of Hungary, the Holy Rood, after which
King David's abbey of Edinburgh had been named. So here,
before their very eyes, were both of Scotland's most ancient,
treasured and prestigious symbols, the Stone of Destiny and
the Holy Rood.

Malcolm took the casket, rose and, raising it to his lips,
kissed the wood contained therein, and then turned to hand
it to Somerled Norse-Slayer.

That man gazed at what he held for long moments before,
not rising but sinking forward off his chair on to his knees,
there kissed the relic reverently, lingeringly, before standing up. Thus he spoke, his voice strangely soft, sibilant,
almost musical to come from so commanding and impressive
a figure.

"For this, my lord King, I thank you, from my heart, this
of the cross." He paused, holding the casket high, and looking
around him. "As to the other, our compact, we shall see. And
hope! *I* will keep it, the compact, while you do! This I swear."
That was said in a different tone, even though his voice still
held its lilting Highland intonation. He looked from the rows
of earls in the chancel to the front ranks in the crowded nave
where the Norman nobles stood in line, the High Steward,
the High Constable, the Knight Marischal, the Doorward,
the Dempster and the rest, none eyeing him lovingly. "Your
advisers, King Malcolm – heed it!" That was warning enough

for anyone, indicating that Somerled knew well who were his enemies, and of the Norman and Flemish opposition to the ancient Celtic polity. He sat down.

In the distinctly uneasy silence which followed only the single bark of approval from the Earl Cospatrick sounded.

Malcolm looked about him nervously, until the Sennachie came to his aid, taking the casket for the King to touch again, and then hiding it under his robe as before.

"So the compact is made and resolved, as all here are witness," he said. "His Grace Malcolm asks the blessing of Holy Church upon it."

The Primate turned to the altar, to go behind it and raise his hand, to pronounce a resounding benediction upon what had been done, what was intended, and upon all present. Then the Abbot of Scone gestured to his choristers, in an aisle, to strike up, to the beat of cymbals.

Thus all made to appear and sound suitably ordered and dignified, Malcolm rose, to lead the procession out, this time with Somerled a full pace behind and now smiling genially, even though not all he passed did the like.

Hugh eyed Duncan and their father. The latter shook his head, wordless.

That evening, they discussed that strange ceremony with Abbot William. He agreed with the sheriff that the auguries for a successful alliance between their realm and the Isles lordship did not look good. The Normans had been hostile to any close accord from the beginning; and Malcolm was not really a strong monarch. If it suited his advisers to change policy, he was unlikely to resist them for long. Those Normans all had kinsmen in England, many of them also owning subsidiary estates there. King Henry Plantagenet was becoming aggressive, talking of claiming paramountcy over Scotland, based on the pretensions of King Knud of Denmark, or Canute. who had called himself Emperor. The Scots-Norman nobles were unlikely to stand fast against Henry, whatever Malcolm said, and this Somerled knew it. How would the Church react, in trouble? Abbot William was less than confident. Bishop Arnold was of part-Norman blood.

145

They all went to bed in uneasy frames of mind.

Nevertheless, next day spirits rose, with the arrival of the other Malcolm, Earl of Ross. Not that he was a particularly strong nor inspiring figure either, elderly, stooping, and tending to show signs of his long years of captivity. But he completed the roll of the *ri*, the Celtic team of earls, was married to Somerled's sister Bethoc, and was of the royal line, son of Eth or Ethelred, an elder brother of King David, who had been passed over for the throne because he had offended his father and mother by adhering to the old Celtic instead of the new Catholic Church – hence his son's period of captivity, lest he aspire to lead an attempt to gain the crown.

Malcolm greeted him in friendly enough fashion, although he had been his gaoler, for now the kingdom needed the earldom of Ross's men and resources in the north-east, against King Hakon. Kingship and statecraft were very much a matter of balancing priorities; and the threat from Hakon was more immediate than from Henry, even the Normans recognising this. So at least some pretence of amity prevailed.

Moreover, next day was Christmas Eve, and celebrations were in order, the churchmen tending to take over. Not that they had it entirely their own way, for the Celtic contingent had alternative ideas as to how Yuletide should be commemorated, which made for something of a clash. For instance, Log Even, the ceremony of selecting, dragging and burning the Yule Log, competed with the very different atmosphere of the Holy Night; and other largely pagan-inspired traditions such as the Mistletoe Bough saturnalia and the Animal Carnival, with young people dressing up as beasts and birds, and apt to behave consequentially, scarcely helped the Blessed Nativity processional and other messianic observances. However, a general atmosphere of celebration was generated, and matters of state, government and alliance were relegated to the background meantime.

Largely because of the Earl Cospatrick's sympathies with Somerled and the Celtic polity, the Swintons saw quite a lot of the Islesmen and the other earls, and, on the whole, found them good company, the former especially hearty and uninhibited. Some of Somerled's lieutenants were highly interesting, not to say challenging; Saor Sleat MacNeil, his foster-brother and chamberlain, Conn Ironhand MacMahon and Dermot Flatnose Maguire, Ulstermen and captains of gallowglasses, being particularly prominent, all but dramatic. Hugh found that there were few dull moments when in their company. These obviously all but worshipped Somerled, although in far from subservient fashion, and in consequence the Swintons came to look upon the Islesman king in a new light, and liked what they learned.

A parallel development was Abbot William's interest in the Celtic Church and its traditions – not that these characters were particularly religiously inclined, nor Somerled's entourage including a Columban cleric. But questioned, they were able to give him much information which instructed and intrigued him. He himself was, to be sure, of purely Scots descent, and could feel a stirring at his roots for the long centuries of the national faith. After all, it was less than a century since all this land had worshipped in the tradition established by St Columba, from Iona and before that from Ireland, not from Rome.

Hugh wondered whether the great Melrose Abbey might thereafter demonstrate slightly different aspects of worship.

So that Christmas was variously celebrated at Perth and Scone, along with the winter solstice, and on Twelfth Night itself the final accord was concluded and affirmed between the two kings, in another and more congenial ceremony than the previous one, with Malcolm, Earl of Ross appending his declaration that he had no intention of seeking the Scots throne for himself or his successors, so long as this agreement was adhered to. And Somerled would allow his great fleet of over one hundred and sixty vessels of war, longships, galleys and birlinns, to aid King Malcolm in his efforts at resisting the aggressive monarchs of Denmark and of England.

A banquet that night marked the conclusion of a successful endeavour for all concerned, even though Somerled was now being referred to, somewhat slightingly, by Norman nobles as Sit-by-the-King.

On the morrow it was departure for all, in every direction, and St John's Town of Perth was left to reflect upon the ups and downs of the making of history.

13

Back at Aldcambus and Redheugh, Hugh and Duncan found no lack of tasks to occupy their winter months, for these properties demanded much more activity at such time than did the Merse pasturelands inland. Being so close to the sea, they got little or no snow and not much frost either; but the ground, being less fertile and very stony, required much more cultivation to grow the necessary winter feed for next year for their rather overstocked farm. Without deliberately so choosing, the brothers had become farmers in quite a large way, and were having to learn their craft speedily. Winter ploughing and manuring was essential here, and constant draining to keep the scattered cultivation areas from becoming waterlogged in the frequent storms.

These storms, although foretold and warned about, were nevertheless an astonishment to the new lairds, especially when the gales, as often, were easterly. The force these generated was almost unbelievable, so that it was frequently impossible to stand upright along the crag-tops and some way inland. The wind off the sea hit the cliffs with hammer blows and was deflected upwards, so that it could lift sheep, and men, right off their feet. The waves, although over two hundred feet below, struck the walls of rock with sufficient fury to send spray and spume in white, drifting blizzards well up into the heather, seaweed and even shells amongst it. For days on end these storms could rage, and hardy indeed had to be the stock to survive them. As well that it was those small, sturdy Highland cattle which they had invested in, shaggy, short-legged. The sheep huddled together wherever they could find shelter of a sort, packed close. In these conditions men could work only indoors, in barns and byres, stables and mills where, however, there was always much to be done, in threshing, parcelling hay in bundles which would not be blown away when taken out for the beasts, packing wool into bales, grinding corn and repairing and sharpening implements.

Yet not infrequently, after these storms, there were days of cold, clear calm, when nothing could seem more peaceful and serene, recent angry flourish of wind and sea scarcely to be credited.

So that year of 1161's first months were passed, the Swintons accepting, even enjoying, the challenge.

Then, in breezy March, with preparations for the lambing about to begin, a messenger arrived from King Malcolm at Roxburgh. The brothers were requested to join Abbot William at Melrose, to proceed further with the Soutra hospital endeavour. They had thought of this often and wondered how, if at all, the project went.

They were off to Melrose next day, leaving Meg, Dod Lumsden and Tam Robson to look after everything.

Abbot William had been to see the King, and had received his instructions. No actual work, it seemed, had been begun on the project, only a survey carried out. Sundry locations on the chosen area had been marked out; and now decisions had to be come to as to the actual siting of the various buildings and establishments, so that these were most conveniently placed for their distinctive purposes. Malcolm had expended much thought on this; but with a realm to rule he could hardly do as he would have wished, to go himself to spend the necessary time examining and comparing the sites and their suitability for the requirements envisaged. For much more was to be considered than the mere general positioning of the hospital as a whole, as had been their previous remit. It seemed that there were to be a number of different departments and units, each with its own preferred placing, both as to the ground itself and its relation to the others. Only the church or chapel of the establishment had had its placing decided, where that magnificent view had burst upon the travellers. Now they were to seek out the best and most appropriate sites for all the other buildings and enclosures – no light task, it seemed.

There were to be two distinct hospitals, one for infectious diseases, fevers and pestilences, well apart from the rest; one for ordinary sick and injured; a chirurgery and bleeding-house; a workshop for the distillation and preparation of medicinal plants, also a garden to grow them; even a mortuary and graveyard. These for the hospitals alone. But there were also to be hospices for travellers and for the aged; monastic quarters and dormitories; a farm; wood and fuel stores and stabling, byres and storehouses.

Scarcely able to take in all this, the brothers could only wag their heads in wonderment. How could they possibly make such decisions?

The abbot said that he had, and had been given, fairly clear ideas as to what was required. They would go and see what they could do — by royal command.

In the morning the trio were off up Lauderdale, with a couple of the abbey's lay brothers and two pack-horses, for nothing was more sure than that their survey would take days, and there was nowhere in the Soutra area where they could lodge overnight, so they must encamp. This did not trouble the Swintons, only March though it was, campaigning conditions having inured them to worse; but they were interested that the abbot seemed quite prepared for it.

On the subject of campaigning, they were told that there might well be more of that ahead of them, before long. The Earl Fergus of Galloway had died at Holyrood Abbey, and his two sons had returned from exile in England to take over the earldom, this with King Henry's agreement, the elder of the two half-brothers, Uhtred, being related to him. There might be trouble, it was feared.

It took them three hours' riding, at the pace of the pack-horses, to reach Oxton and then Glen Gelt, where they struck up off the highway westwards on to the high plateau area of their choice. It was triangular and measured, the abbot estimated, over two miles in width with three-mile sides, these bounded by the Gelt and Armet Waters, possibly four or five square miles of territory to cover. Most of it, of course, would be quite unsuitable for any of their purposes, inaccessible or

151

peat-hags and bogs. Much of what they looked for must be reasonably near the highway, although roadways up and in would almost certainly have to be constructed. So they should plan routes for these also.

Where to begin, in their strange and rather daunting task? Abbot William, perhaps naturally, thought of the monastic quarters first, which should surely be somewhere near the church site, that is at the very apex of the triangle, the northern tip, looking out over Lothian to the Forth, Fife and the Highland mountains. But Hugh suggested that, since this could be more or less taken for granted, would it not be sensible to try to seek out the sites for the hospitals beforehand, with these the reason for the entire project? That was accepted.

What, then, were the requirements for the two hospitals? These did not have to be very near the highway, as would be best for the travellers' hospices; indeed the fever one should probably be well distant. The King – who seemed to be very well versed in all this, no doubt having inspected the hospital in France which had sown the seed in his mind – said that certain conditions were essential. The hospitals had to be built on dry, well-drained but level ground, the higher within reason the better, for clean air. Also, for this reason, it was advised that they should be raised off the ground, that air might circulate freely and noxious discharges and exudations from the sick should not linger and contaminate the floorings, to be able to drain away, and all to be kept very clean. The sites, although not very near the highway, must be reachable by not difficult roads or tracks, for many of the sick would have to be brought on litters, no doubt. So they were looking for firm, high, level ground, and not too far from the monastic quarters, for the monks and lay brother nurses ought not to have to walk great lengths in hard weather to their duties, up on this high moorland; and they would have their spiritual duties to perform also.

So the party proceeded northwards, over the heather, with the Lammermuir heights around, eyeing all keenly, but not turning aside for detailed inspection until they were well on towards the point of it all.

Duncan it was who spotted the first possible site, soon after they had crossed the still discernible Roman Dere Street track, on a shelf of one of the three modest summit ridges which rose out of the plateau. They rode over to inspect this. It proved to be a small crescent-shaped terrace, perhaps one hundred yards wide, twice that length, and fairly level, with underlying rock and no boggy patches. Would this be big enough for a hospital building? They reckoned it to be about half a mile from the probable church site. Their uncertainties as to detailed requirements now became very evident to them. They thought that it might serve, this for the fever department, but there might be conditions against it.

Moving on, what they did see was the little valley, not much more than a groove, of a small burn leading down eastwards towards the highway. This ought to provide an access road, for as far as they could see it had no steep sections nor sharp bends, and the stream was too minor to produce flooding. It would help to recommend Duncan's site.

As the triangle of high ground narrowed, they were able to see the highway ever drawing nearer on their right, and to perceive that another stream formed a larger valley beyond it. This, although in the same approximate line as the Gelt, was in fact beginning to descend in the other direction, northwards. So they had crossed the watershed and were now in Lothian. Not that this affected their quest; the monarch could take over whichever land he desired, even though most of eastern Lothian was the Earl Cospatrick's property.

They saw one other possible place for a hospital, where a Pictish stone circle had been located, although most of its monoliths were now fallen. But the fact that it was there meant that the position would be firm, dry and airy, for these sun-worship sites were always so chosen. And it was more extensive than Duncan's shelf.

They decided to go on to the proposed chapel area to make camp, for the March days were short still and they wanted to select a sheltered spot where there was water and wood for a fire.

At the ultimate tip of their ground they exclaimed again at

the far-flung prospect, even though the weather and cloudy skies shrouded the distant mountains from sight, and the Scotwater or Forth estuary looked grey instead of blue. They still thought that the church should be built here, on the very lip, as it were.

Duncan led them off south by west and downhill into the wide valley of the Armet Water, which he had explored on the previous occasion, and where he thought that they should encamp, for there were scattered thorn trees and scrub oak there.

So down at the waterside they pitched their two tents and tethered the seven horses on the greensward, gathered fallen wood for the fire, and the lay brothers prepared a simple meal. Duncan wandered off. Presently he came back and, declaring that the food would keep whilst the light would not, urged them to come with him to the crest of a little sloping ridge nearby. There he waved a pointing hand. Where another smaller stream came in to join the Armet was a broad, shelving, basin-like spread of green land, green with grasses not mire, reeds or bog-cotton, with a few stunted trees growing out of it, perhaps half a mile across.

"There is your farm," he asserted. "Dig a few drainage ditches down to the burns and you will grow better crops there than we can do at Redheugh and Aldcambus. There may be others, but here is one farmery at the least." A few months ago he would not have been thus knowledgeable.

Well pleased, they went back for their meal. They would examine that tract more fully in the morning.

It was pleasant sitting round the camp-fire as night fell, listening to the abbot's fund of stories, not all of them churchmanly by any means, Hugh pressed to describe his boar-slaying exploit and Duncan expatiating on clifftop experiences and storms. Finally the three abbey men chanted a tuneful compline before, horses watered, they all bedded down in their blankets for the night. They had feared that it was going to rain – but perhaps that compline had kept it off?

In the morning, dull but dry, they explored the farmery area and decided that it was all more than might have been hoped for, in such a wilderness situation. Not only that, but they identified possible sites nearby for two other necessary establishments, a laundry and a mill, both of which would need a lot of water, of course, this to be supplied by the Armet, which after its junction with the lesser stream produced a small waterfall which could be deepened, enlarged and harnessed. This all within a half-mile of the chapel site.

Leaving the lay brothers with the horses at the tents, the trio went prospecting on foot, considering this as likely to be more rewarding as to detail than when mounted. And they did find it so, for afoot they gained a better impression of the ground, learned of wet and undrained spots, followed deer-paths which they could have missed and which led to interesting hollows and corners, and generally gave them the closer information which they required.

But it was all much slower, of course, and with their large area to cover, they were only perhaps half finished by dusk, when they returned to the camp. However, by that time they had discovered possible sites for the larger hospital, two of them, each with water available, and an alternative for the fever one; also another access route, and springs which could supply the freshest of drinking and cleansing water.

Discussing their findings that evening, they decided that there was not a great deal more that they could do. They could prospect somewhere near the proposed church where the soil was deep enough to make a graveyard, a mortuary to be erected close by. Where the best place for a chirurgery and bleeding unit would be they just had no notion. They could select various other possible situations for hospice buildings. But that would be sufficient, they thought, for the King's purposes. They would complete the unfinished survey on the morrow, and then return to Melrose, and there draw up on paper, as best they could, a plan of the whole area with their findings marked thereon. They had seen no other terrain to rival Duncan's suggested farmery.

They slept, reasonably satisfied.

*   *   *

Back at the abbey the following evening, Abbot William produced large sheets of paper used for inscribing decorative scriptural texts and psalms, quill-pens and coloured inks, and they set about each mapping out their impressions and remembered details of the entire Soutra territory, marking in the various locations in different colours. Undoubtedly Duncan's was the best, most accurate, and he was allotted the task of preparing the final version, incorporating all details of the other two. This they would take to the King.

So on the morrow it was down Tweed to Roxburgh, in the rain. This weather at least made it probable that Malcolm would not be out hunting or hawking.

They found the King in his personal tower, and were admitted to audience with little delay, thanks to Abbot William's name. They were greeted with what amounted to enthusiasm; obviously this Soutra project was close to the royal heart. The King's personal chaplain, Richard, was the only other present.

Plied with questions, the Swintons let the abbot do most of the answering; and he was able to satisfy in practically all respects. But when their map or chart was produced, Malcolm's approval was all but ecstatic, and Duncan came in for much praise. Locations were pointed out, advantages listed, alternatives offered, the King nodding, pointing, cross-questioning.

"You have done most notably well, my good friends," he declared. "Have they not, Richard? Here is a most excellent plan for action. And action there shall be, and forthwith. Richard, send for my master-builder, the man Elliot. Have him here at the soonest. And see to our friends' refreshment. I will send for them when Elliot comes."

The trio were led off to another tower, to eat and wait. They gathered that the master-builder lived in Roxburgh town, a bare mile to the west.

They had over an hour to wait and then were summoned back. They found a great hulk of a man with the King and chaplain, Gibbie Elliot, of late middle years, built like a bear and a hairy one, but with shrewd eyes and no seeming awe of the company he was in.

He was shown the paper chart and had all the requirements explained to him, the King going into great detail. Timber buildings at this stage would be best, for speedy erection, although the church should be of stone from the first. Obviously a great deal of wood was going to be required, seasoned wood; but Elliot would have large supplies of such at his yards no doubt. Other and special materials such as thatch, slates, tiles, piping, hangings and the like would be made available. A start at the earliest.

The master-builder did not seem in any way overwhelmed by it all; but he did say that before he began to draw up plans and assemble supplies he would require to make a survey of the ground to assess all needs, access over difficult ground, numbers of men to be employed and the like. This was accepted, and Malcolm said that the Swinton brothers would take him to Soutra and show him all. How soon could they go?

Elliot declared that he was at His Grace's disposal; and Hugh said the sooner the better. They could escort the builder up there, demonstrate all, and then leave him to return alone while they made their way across the hills to Aldcambus. Let them go on the morrow? There was no need for the abbot to accompany them.

So all was agreed, the monarch assuring them that he would by no means forget all the good work being done by his so loyal friends. No doubt the Almighty also would bless them, since all this was being done in Christ's name and in the cause of Christian love. Meanwhile he would have a copy of their map made for them, to guide Elliot, for he wished to keep the original.

Another night, therefore, in the castle-palace, with Elliot to come for them in the morning.

The large builder duly arrived at sun-up on a suitably large horse, which meant fairly slow going for the others. On their way, they dropped Abbot William at Melrose, he wishing them well and suggesting that it might not be long before they were called upon again over this ambitious project. They borrowed one of his tents for, at this pace, they did not expect to be able

157

to show Elliot all before nightfall. Food also they collected. Then on for the River Leader and up Lauderdale.

Gibbie Elliot proved to be quite a good companion, with many anecdotes to recount about King David's reign, especially in the great abbey-building process. He had served his apprenticeship in that extraordinary endeavour, and had been involved in the latter stages of Jedburgh, Kelshaugh, Dryburgh, Melrose and Holyrood Abbeys. Admittedly he had never tackled anything like this hospital project previously, most of his work being with stone, masonry, for castles and tower-houses as well as churches; but he did not foresee major problems other than that of access for the carting of heavy timbering and the like.

In the event, this was Elliot's main preoccupation that day, the plotting of routes up from the road for his heavy and massive building materials. Carting could be done only as far as the highway edge, whereafter horse-drawn sleds or slypes, such as the Swintons used for transporting seaweed and manure, could be used to some of the sites they pointed out to him. But more remote places would probably require pack-horses, a difficult and slow procedure, for timber beams and planking.

That day they covered only a bare half of the chosen places before going to camp at the same spot as previously. They found the builder only moderately concerned, at this stage, with the actual sites – that would come later. Nor was he much interested in the farmery, pasturage and milling side of it all. Others could see to that.

No compline was chanted that night before the campfire.

By noon next day their companion had seen enough and, with the map, could put preliminary plans and costs before the King. It would be an expensive exercise, but nothing like that of building stone abbeys, with all the elaborate masonry and decorative work. And King David had left his grandson an ample fortune of the late Queen Matilda's moneys.

They took their farewells of Gibbie Elliot at Oxton then, and

headed off eastwards by Carfrae and Longformacus through
the Lammermuirs, glad to be riding free and fast again. They
had been gone only six nights, but it seemed a long time. Back
to lambing – and Meg.

14

They made a busy spring of it, there on the cliff-girt coast, but well enjoying most of it, the lambing, the calving, the tilling, the draining, the repairing of shelters and the rest. Also the fishing in Tam Robson's boat and the tending of the lobster creels.

A major development was Meg's announcement, in early May, that she believed that she was pregnant, to Duncan's delight. He immediately assumed that she had to be nurtured and coddled as though she was in dire danger of miscarriage or other disaster – to her amused dismissal, proclaiming that she was no feeble, fragile female such as perhaps he had grown up amongst, and well able to fulfil all her customary chores and duties for months yet. He remained anxious, watchful, attentive.

They heard little of affairs of the realm in their windy corner of the land, save a rumour that the King was sick, details unspecified. That is, until June, when Sheriff Pate paid them a visit. He had grave news for them.

"Malcolm has been gravely ill," he told them. "Vomiting blood, eating nothing, losing weight. He is something better now, but his physicians were much alarmed for him. Indeed, some were saying that he might well become the first to enter this new hospital which he is so eager to build in these hills! His brother, Brawny Will, has declared that it was this of the hospital which had kept him alive, so anxious was he to see it completed, to seal his compact with God before he died, for he has shown little interest in anything else."

Saddened, the brothers heard this. They had come to approve of and like their unusual liege-lord, no warrior-king as he was and too gentle for being monarch over such as

Scotland. He had never been robust, like his brothers, but they had not anticipated any dire breakdown such as this. Hugh wondered whether in fact some awareness of his impending physical trouble was responsible for his preoccupation with the building of a place for the sick, in the first place.

Their father admitted that it might be so. But he was otherwise concerned. The trouble was that grievous problems of state had arisen, and Malcolm was showing little interest in these.

"There is a double threat to our realm – triple, if we consider Hakon of Norway's danger to us, although Somerled of the Isles and Malcolm of Ross are looking to that," he said. "Henry of England is demanding that the counties of Durham and Northumberland and Cumberland, at present held by Scotland, be yielded up to him. And the Archbishop of York, one Roger, has petitioned the Pope in Rome to declare him superior of the Scottish Church, as the nearest Metropolitan, the which could much support Henry's false claim to paramountcy over our kingdom. It is damnable. Bishop Arnold of St Andrews is advising Malcolm to ask the Pope to raise *him* to the status of archbishop, Metropolitan, thus making the York claim of none effect. But the King is delaying, showing real interest only in his hospital. We need a strong monarch at this dire juncture, not a saintly weakling!"

His sons shook their heads.

"Nor is that all," Sheriff Pate went on. "Henry is using Galloway to bring pressure on Malcolm. The half-brothers Uhtred and Gilbert, sons of Earl Fergus, are at odds, seeking to divide the province between them, actually fighting. Henry supports Uhtred, his kinsman, calling him earl, and is threatening to send an English army across Solway to aid him if Malcolm does not himself do so. It is but an excuse, a device, of course, to put an English force into Scotland – and once in, they would be hard indeed to get out! Our kinsman, Cospatrick, is much concerned for, as you know, he claims Galloway for himself. He is urging the King to let him take a host there, to show the boar flag, keep the brothers in check and give answer to Henry Plantagenet. If he does do this, no

161

doubt you two will be sent for to aid in leading the Swinton and Merse bands."

They did not greatly like the sound of that. Presumably this warning was part-reason for their father's visit.

Away from gloomy forebodings, they asked if he had heard whether a start had yet been made on the Soutra project's building operations, to be told that indeed it had, this the one matter on which Malcolm was showing determination. Much work was in progress. Their sire had not been up to look, but he had heard that scores of men were employed under the builder Elliot's supervision.

Hugh suggested that if he would like to see what went on for himself, he could take a round-about return route to Swinton Parva and they would escort him so far and show him what was intended. This was agreed.

Next morning, then, all three took the hilly road westwards for that score of rough miles, quite eager to inspect. And they were not disappointed. Before ever they reached Glen Gelt they could see long lines of wagons trundling up the highway beyond, stacks of timber deposited here and there, and horse-drawn sleds disappearing from these on to the plateau. The King might be flagging in statecraft but not in good works.

Up on the high ground it was already a transformation, with buildings being erected, more stacks of timbering, ditches and drains being dug, work-horses and men everywhere. Approaching as they did, one of the first items that they saw was that shelf of the little summit where Duncan had proposed the first site, for the fever hospital, now with scaffolding part hiding wooden walling but not the rafters of the roof which were already in place. On going over to examine this, they found the structure to be about one hundred and fifty feet in length by a third of that in width, single-storeyed, its flooring joists in place and raised some three feet above the levelled ground.

Duncan was much pleased.

One other smaller building was even further on in construction, presumably one of the hospices. And foundations were being dug at the site of the former stone circle, which they took to be for the larger hospital, although the sweating diggers were unable to inform them. It was all most heartening.

Up at the apex of their triangle they were surprised to find the stone walls of the church already a couple of feet high, this not large but bigger than St Helen's Chapel at Aldcambus. Here was Gibbie Elliot superintending his masons, but also working with his own hands and trowel, doing what he knew best. He was glad to see the visitors, and did not attempt to hide his pride in what he had managed to achieve in less than three months. Finding a quarry near enough, for suitable building stone, had been his biggest problem, he revealed. The King's Grace was right pleased with progress, he averred, although, such as he was in health, he had not been able to come and see it all; but he hoped to do so soon, even if he had to be brought in a horse-litter.

Loud in their praise, the Swintons left the builders to it, for they had long riding to get them to their respective homes even by the June nightfall. Father and sons, parting at Oxton, agreed that it had been well worth coming. It was a pity that their approval and appreciation were marred by worry about the King's health and the national situation.

The unwelcome but anticipated summons from the Earl Cospatrick duly arrived a week later. All the earldom's vassals to assemble at the Earlstoun of Ersildoune at the soonest, with fullest manpower and horsed, armed. Hugh and Duncan had no spare men they could take with them, and did not consider themselves now vassals of the earl anyway, but would support him personally. To Meg's lack of enthusiasm they rode off, with their helmets and chain-mail tunics.

It was all very much as before. They went to Swinton first, but found Sir Ernulf's contribution to the host already gone, under their father and Alan; so it was on to Lauderdale for the muster. Ersildoune was again thronged with men and horses, come from all over the east Borders and Lothian. It appeared that they were awaiting the Dunbar contingent before moving off westwards.

Next day, eighteen hundred strong, and all mounted, they started on their long journey. Cospatrick hoped to pick up almost as many again on the way, in the King's name, especially from Bruce of Annandale, the most closely threatened by Galloway troubles. The brothers rode, as before, with Learmonth of Ersildoune. With no foot and few lordly Normans with their heavy, slow destriers, they made good time of it up Tweed and over the heights of Tweedsmuir into upper Annandale, reaching Lochmaben in the afternoon of the second day. There its lord welcomed them, with eight hundred men, and the information that the Fergus-sons were reported to be basing themselves in two of the far south-western peninsulas of the great province, Uhtred in the Kirkcudbright–Borgue one, where he could look for English aid to come across Solway from the Carlisle area of Cumbria, and Gilbert in the Machars of Wigtown, where apparently he had the greatest support, this together with the third long peninsula, known as the Rhinns. Both were allegedly assembling large forces for a major confrontation.

This struggle between the half-brothers did present the royal polity, and therefore Cospatrick, with something of a problem. Actually, he had no desire to come to blows with either, at this stage. If one of them triumphed and proclaimed himself Earl of Galloway, it would be different. Meantime they posed no threat to the King. This expedition was, therefore, not in fact against them but against Henry Plantagenet, to answer his challenge and prevent him from sending an army ostensibly to support Uhtred but really to bring pressure on Malcolm. So Cospatrick's task was to wave the King's banner over much of Galloway sufficiently to leave Henry in no doubt as to the Scots' independent action, and not necessarily to do any fighting. Somerled of the Isles had been urged to send his fleet to patrol off the Galloway coasts and Solway, also to inhibit the increasingly aggressive English. It was this anti-Henry bias which was largely preventing the Norman nobles from taking part in the expedition; with their English estates and kinsmen, they did not want to offer the Plantagenet offence – a grievous weakness in the present Scottish situation, which King David presumably had not foreseen when he brought them or their fathers up to help him establish his shaky throne after the feeble reigns of his royal brothers Alexander and Edgar.

Bruce advised that an armed tour of most of Galloway, without actually approaching the positions of the warring brothers, should meet the case, avoiding confrontation and battle if possible, so long as their presence was made entirely evident to the English borderers in north Cumbria. No doubt these would be well informed as to what went on on the Scots side.

They would go again over Nith to Dunscore and across to the Urr and Kenmure. Then through the Rhinns of Kells to Bargrennan, down the Cree to Creetown, and so east to the Fleet and Haugh of Urr again, thus avoiding entry to either of the two trouble-spot peninsulas. Finally, on due eastwards, by Crocketford and Dumfries, to cross the lower Annan and reach the Cumbrian border at Canonbie – this well back from seeming to challenge Carlisle itself, even though in theory this last was under Scots dominion. Such a progress, assuming no fighting, ought to take them ten or twelve days, without undue haste, since it represented some two hundred miles. Another forty miles back to Lochmaben, and they would, it was hoped, consider their task accomplished.

Cospatrick and Waldeve satisfied with this programme, they moved off westwards.

It was good for the Swinton brothers to be riding with Rob Bruce again, a cheerful, lively companion. As anticipated, the trio were sent off in advance as scouts, in their accustomed role. It seemed but little time since they were hereabouts doing exactly this before, but so much had transpired in the interim. They recounted some of it as they went.

Their scouting, on this occasion, was more or less nominal, for no attack by the Galwegians was really anticipated. No doubt their presence and advance would be observed and word sent to the Fergus-sons; but in their feud with each other, neither was likely to want to take on the power of the realm, and from all accounts it was improbable that they would unite to counter it. Also it was well possible that both would be preoccupied with the offshore presence of the Islesmen's fleet and its threat. So the scouts were a deal less anxiously vigilant than formerly.

And there was no hurry, the mounted host behind deliberately only covering some score of miles each day, mere dawdle for mosstroopers. It is to be feared that some of the communities passed in the process suffered the more inevitable depredations, whatever the leadership ordered.

It took them two days to reach Kenmure Castle, where they remained for a spell, sending parties down both sides of long Loch Ken, flag-showing, but not meeting with any opposition. Then on by Clatteringshaws into the Rhinns of Kells, high country but not inhospitable in these summer conditions. A night in the hills between the Lochs Dee and Trool and they came down to the township of Bargrennan. They found few of its menfolk there, these having left to join the Lord Gilbert down in the Wigtown area. The army spent a couple of days thereabouts, making their presence felt, the womenfolk in especial made very much aware of it. Then on down Cree to salt water at Creetown, at the head of great Wigtown bay.

This was as near as they wanted to get to Gilbert's array, some ten miles off it was assumed.

They saw no signs of Somerled's galley fleet in the bay.

Eastwards now for the River Fleet and the root of the other, Borgue, peninsula, to pass another couple of days at the familiar location of Haugh of Urr, where that castle keeper made Cospatrick and his lieutenants a doubtful but careful host. He was an Uhtred man but did not flaunt the fact.

Their onwards progress, still eastwards, very much emphasised the great extent of this Galloway, almost a small kingdom on its own – as it had been once, the Brythonic sub-kingdom of Rheged in High King Arthur's time; for they had still almost fifty miles to ride before reaching the Cumbrian march at Canonbie, crossing the great rivers of Nith and Lochar, Annan and Kirtle, Ewes and Esk. There was surely enough here for these warring brothers to share without fighting each other to win it all?

The availability of suitable fords for an army to cross did

166

entail far from direct journeying and took longer than Bruce of Annandale had assessed. It was four more days before they could finally turn and head westwards again for Lochmaben, the boar banner shown and duty done. They had not had to draw sword or dirk throughout – save to cut the throats of purloined cattle-beasts and sheep – no casualties inflicted, apart perhaps from sundry female ones in some degree. They hoped that King Henry was duly informed and given pause, and that the Fergus-sons had taken the required message to heart.

Home to the Merse and the so different east coast, then.

15

The remainder of the summer of 1161, and well into the autumn, was mercifully free of extraneous demands on the Swinton brothers, despite ominous tidings reaching them of the realm's affairs, for they were discovering the farming year to be sufficiently demanding. Sheep-shearing was a major activity, and the sending off of the bales of wool to the Flemish merchants at Berwick-upon-Tweed, by pack-horse train. Then harvest was upon them, no simple task with their small scattered rigs to be cut, stacked and then the grain gathered into barns. Their increased stock demanding more winter feed to be grown, meant new cultivation sites and rigs to be established, which required much stone-clearing and drainage, also extra seaweed-collecting and carting, to feed the soil. So there was no lack of work for lairdlings who had not the moneys to employ any great number of paid toilers.

The word of activities on a different scale, of the monarchs and great ones, which filtered through to them, was not encouraging, even though they heard that King Malcolm was recovering in health. Henry Plantagenet had not invaded Galloway, but he was bringing ever-increasing pressure to bear on Malcolm in pursuit of his paramountcy ambitions, demanding all sorts of tokens and submissions, as though the King of Scots was indeed some kind of vassal. For instance, he was asking that the two Scots princesses, Ada and Margaret, youngsters whom Hugh and Duncan had never even seen, and who lived with their widowed mother at Haddington, should be given in marriage to Floris, Count of Holland and Conan, Duke of Brittany respectively; this because he had no suitable sisters of his own, and he was anxious to have as allies these two influential continental princes in his efforts to secure fullest possession of the French properties he had inherited from his mother and gained by his marriage to Eleanor of Aquitaine. These marriages would further tend to link Scotland to his empire-building.

Henry, as well as requiring the return of the northern counties of Durham, Northumberland and Cumberland, ceded to Scotland by his predecessor King Stephen, was now also demanding that Malcolm should come south to England to pay homage to him for the English earldom of Huntingdon, which had come to the late David with his heiress wife, Matilda, this on pain of forfeiting it if there was refusal. And, if that was not enough, the Plantagenet had received at his court Godfrey Olafsson, and was hailing him as still King of Man – which would ensure Somerled's fury and complicate relations with Malcolm.

All this the brothers heard, from various sources, over the months, and recognised that the consequences could well be serious. How the King's Norman-Flemish courtiers were reacting and advising, they could only guess. A clash between them and Somerled of the Isles looked almost inevitable now.

But forebodings were at least temporarily relegated to abeyance when a courier arrived at Aldcambus, in October, from Roxburgh, commanding that the Swinton brothers attend on the King's Grace for his opening of the Soutra hospital project in four days' time. So Malcolm was presumably sufficiently well to make the journey, they were glad to learn.

They were uncertain, however, whether this call meant that they were to go to Roxburgh to join the royal train, which seemed rather unnecessary. But another messenger came next morning, from Abbot William, saying that he would meet them at Oxton on the due day at noon, to await the King's arrival. That was better.

Meg wished that she could have accompanied them to see this great occasion, but she was now in no state for the rough ride through the hills, with her baby due in some six weeks' time, Duncan averred.

Three days later they found the abbot awaiting them at Oxton, with the information that the royal party was on its

169

way – he had seen it from Lauder Common. Malcolm was less than fit, still, and taking the journey by easy stages, but his state was much improved.

They had fully an hour to wait. When they saw the King, at the head of no very large company, the brothers were almost shocked at the difference in his appearance from heretofore. He had never been large in stature nor of solid build like his brothers; but now he was thin, emaciated, gaunt and stooping, looking a deal older than his twenty-two years. But he greeted them warmly, hailing the trio as his very good friends and allies in this great venture of the hospital now come to blessed fruition. It was noticeable that neither of his brothers had come with him for the occasion; presumably they were not interested in such endeavours.

Malcolm had them to ride at his side now. Clearly he was much exercised, indeed excited, over the day's programme and what he was going to see; for although he had been kept informed of all developments, this was his first visit to Soutra since his illness, and he was more than eager to see all that had been achieved on his directions, the fulfilment of all his plans.

Following the now accustomed route up on to the plateau from Glen Gelt, they came first to a white-plastered timber and thatched building which they had not seen before, long and low, with two doors and with tethering-posts for horses at the back. This the King declared was one of three hospices or night-shelters for travellers, deliberately sited within sight of the highway. Food and bunks would be provided here.

Up on the higher ground, the transformation was extraordinary. Constructions had sprung up near and far, of varying sizes but all single-storeyed – for winds up here in winter would be strong – some plastered, some not, nearly all thatched-roof, stabling and outworks attached to some. Malcolm, who had had their map enlarged and marked in with details, explained the uses of all. The first at which they actually halted and dismounted to examine was the fever hospital on the shelf, which was now completed, a well and drains dug around it, steps up to its raised flooring, windows with lower shutters to open and fixed glass tops, rows of timber beds, piles of blankets, a kitchen off at one end and a nurses' room at the other. All were duly impressed.

They glanced briefly at other buildings, but Malcolm was anxious to see the church, the crown of the establishment, which Elliot had assured him was now finished on the outside but not internally. The King was already looking tired.

He was revived, however, by the sight of the little chapel on the brow of the quite steep downward slope, modest as it was compared with all the magnificent shrines his builder had worked on. There had been no attempt to make it cruciform in shape, but it had good, decorative windows at the east end, smaller ones at the sides and rear, two doors, and a slated roof crowned by a cross-topped belfry.

Exclaiming, they all dismounted, and the King led the way in, with Gibbie Elliot awaiting them in the main doorway. Within, there were as yet no furnishings, but there was a raised chancel, with a solid stone altar, and a carved wood pulpitum just below the chancel-step. Eyeing it all, Malcolm congratulated Elliot on his efforts, and then went to stand in the chancel, facing the company and raising his hand.

"Hear me, my lords and friends all," he said, his voice urgent but not strong. "Today we see the outcome of long planning, much thought, a deal of prayer, and no little application. Here we have contrived something that I believe to be of much worth in the sight of Almighty God and Jesus Christ His Son. God requires us to worship Him, yes. And my grandsire and some amongst you have done so in more than just words, in building great abbeys and churches to His glory. And well done so. But Christ also said, 'Feed my lambs.' Meaning His flock, all His flock, the poor, the hungry, the weak and the sick. And said this three times, to emphasise His command, His pleas. Feed His lambs. Until now, we in this realm have perhaps failed in some measure to fulfil His plea. Now, now . . ." He fell silent, as though overcome with emotion.

Embarrassed, throats were cleared.

Straightening up drooping shoulders, Malcolm found voice again. "Now, we seek to show, belatedly, that we have heard.

171

In France I saw what could, what should, be done to feed at least some of Christ's lambs. A great hospital for the sick and needy, for the aged, and shelter and provision for travellers. I saw there my duty and privilege, and have sought to emulate. Here is the answer to my prayers."

For most listening, this clerkly sort of talk was distinctly off-putting coming from a monarch. Stances were shifted and feet shuffled.

The King went on. "I have been greatly aided in this great endeavour by others, my master-builder Elliot and his toilers who have achieved so much in short time, at my so constant urging. But in especial I have to thank three who have surveyed and planned and established all for me, found this Soutra area as suitable, covered all the ground, plotted the sites and positions, even found the necessary farming-place, which I have yet to see, a labour of love indeed. These three are here present," and he gestured. "My lord William, mitred Abbot of Melrose. My good and loyal Hugh de Swinton. And his foster-brother, Duncan. Without these, this project would not have come about. I thank them, from my heart."

Again the panting pause while men murmured. Hugh wished that there had been a chair in the place for Malcolm at least to sit.

But the King was not finished yet. He pointed. "Gratitude should be expressed in more than words," he declared. "It is my pleasure to grant to the abbey of Melrose my lands of Lessudden with all its pertinents in perpetuum; also those of Maxpoffle, Woodfordhouse and Ilefestone, these with the mills, multures, fisheries and all other hereditaments. Also to appoint the Abbot William as Vice-Chancellor of my realm, depute to the Bishop Edward of Aberdeen. This by my royal command."

The abbot started to speak, but as comments arose all around him, changed his mind and bowed deeply.

"Sir Hugh de Morville, my High Constable, step forward."

Hugh de Swinton, for one, was surprised at this order, for so far as he knew, de Morville, a Norman, had had no hand in this entire concept.

He was to be more surprised still. "Hugh de Swinton, come to me here," was the next command.

He moved forward to the chancel-step, but the King motioned him on closer.

"Now kneel," he was instructed, when just before the monarch. "Constable, your sword."

Now Hugh understood. The High Constable was the only man who was allowed to keep his sword in the presence of the monarch, save in war service. Mind in a whirl, he knelt before his liege-lord.

Malcolm took the sword and raised it high. Then he brought it down, gently, first on Hugh's left shoulder, then on his right, tapping. "Hugh de Swinton," he intoned, "I hereby dub and create thee knight, in the sight of God and in the presence of all here. Be thou good, faithful and true knight until thy life's end. Arise, Sir Hugh!"

Gulping, Hugh got to his feet. He looked at the King, shaking his head, scarcely believing what was thus done, wordless, and so stood. Then the exclamations from behind brought him to his senses and he bowed and backed away, only just in time remembering that awkward chancel-step.

Abbot William's hand was out to congratulate the new knight when Malcolm's voice resumed.

"Duncan Swinton of Redheugh, in recognition of your notable services in this matter, I hereby give and grant to you the lands of Lumsdaine, Oatlee and Brown Rigg, contiguous to your property of Redheugh, hitherto pertaining to the Priory of Coldinghame, and now exchanged with the said priory for other of my royal lands, these to you with all buildings, pertinents and pendicles thereof, to be held direct of the crown. And I also declare that you be Macer of my sheriffdom of Berwick, in succession to John de Rayton, resigned. This also by my royal command."

This announcement also drew murmured comment, for it represented preferential treatment indeed for the bastard son of a milkmaid, whoever his father, for the office of Macer was one of little profit but some distinction. The fact that the recipient's father was himself Sheriff of Berwickshire

173

was the more significant. What would Sheriff Pate say to this?

To conclude the inauguration and celebration, the King, stepping down, now asked Abbot William to consecrate this building as a house of God, and as spiritual centre for the great community herewith founded, and to be established for all time. This the abbot did, moving up before the altar, with sincerity and suitable fervour, although at no great length, seeking the Almighty's blessing on their endeavours, on His Grace's person and on all present.

The thing done, all trooped outside, Malcolm himself leading the congratulations towards his helpers, weary as he now seemed to be.

The said helpers were in a state of almost stupor – at least two of them were, the abbot less astonished, being the experienced and prominent man he was, although even he had never expected to be appointed Vice-Chancellor, assistant to the King's chief minister of state, a position which would inevitably make great demands on his time and encroach on his activities at Melrose.

Hugh was too astonished really to appreciate fully that he had now been raised to the so-coveted status of knighthood, something which had never so much as crossed his mind. To be a knight was almost the ultimate pinnacle of the ambitious, for although a man could inherit other titles, a barony, a lordship, even an earldom, and work towards such as thane, sheriff, coroner or crowner, chamberlain, provost, even prior, abbot and bishop, none could inherit or achieve knighthood; even Malcolm himself had had to journey to France, and fight for King Henry there, to attain to the coveted position, one of the elect, the chosen. Sir Hugh de Swinton – now he was that! And all because he had helped, in some measure, the King to attain his desire. What would his father say, who himself was not a knight?

As for Duncan, he was almost equally bewildered, not so much on account of the extra properties granted to him, enlarging his Redheugh estate to quite an impressive lairdship, but of this appointment as Macer to his father's sheriffdom.

174

What did it mean, imply, involve him in? Station, standing, repute, it would give him, the bastard, yes. But what were his duties, to fulfil it? And he also wondered what Sheriff Pate would say to it.

Some disappointment for Duncan followed, however, for he had been hoping to show the King the faraway land which he had surveyed and selected; but now Malcolm, obviously tired, declared that he was for off. Another time he would inspect it all more fully.

Hugh had assumed that the royal party would be returning to Roxburgh, but it seemed not. The King was now to head for Haddington, in Lothian, a much shorter journey, not more than ten miles to the north-east. He was, it transpired, going to visit his mother and sisters there. And the new knight discovered also that he was commanded to accompany the monarch thither, himself and the abbot, but not Duncan.

So there was a parting and dispersal, most of the company turning southward for the Tweed, Duncan heading eastwards for Redheugh, and a small group with the monarch north by east, for Haddington on the Lothian Tyne.

Abbot William explained to Hugh as they rode. Haddington, a fair-sized town and large estate, was the dower property of the King's mother, Ada, Countess of Huntingdon, who had been a daughter of the English Earl Warenne of Surrey. She had never been queen, for her husband Henry had died before his father, King David. She had chosen in her widowhood to live on her own dower lands rather than at Roxburgh, and when her three sons had grown up and departed to David's royal castle, she had remained at Haddington with her two daughters, where she was setting up a large nunnery and almost abbey-like church. Now the King was going to see her and his sisters, and on no joyful mission. For the Countess was to be told that the elder of her daughters, another Ada, was to be given in marriage to Floris, Count of Holland, in accordance with Henry Plantagenet's overture. The other demand, that her sister Margaret was to wed the Duke of Brittany, Malcolm was bypassing meantime, claiming that she was too young. Why Hugh, and the abbot, were involved in this, was because they

175

had been chosen to escort the princess to the Low Countries shortly, and they were to meet and make arrangements with her and her mother now.

So the second astonishment of the day came to Hugh. He was to travel overseas with this royal bride, he who had never been furth of Scotland before. Was this partly why he had been knighted?

To reach Haddington, at the foot of the hills below Soutra, they had to turn eastwards along the northern foothills of the Lammermuirs, by Hunmanbie and Ystrad – where one of the party, the Norman de Gifford, had his seat – and thence by Lethington to the Tyne valley and the town. The October dusk was falling by the time that they reached their destination, and the King, slumped in his saddle, was looking exhausted.

His countess-mother did not live within the burgh itself but outside to the east another mile, on the north bank of the river. Reaching there, ahead Hugh saw, in the gloaming, a vast, isolated mass of hill rising leviathan-like out of the river's plain. Abbot William told him that this was Traprain Law, a place of notable history and legend.

The Countess Ada's house was no castle or palace but a long, two-storeyed hallhouse, unpretentious but commodious, well supplied with outbuildings, stabling and the like, even its own mill by the waterside. But it was the many other buildings in process of erection all around which took the attention, these to form what was to be the largest nunnery, seminary and place of learning in the land. King David had left his emulators.

The visitors met the countess and her daughters for the evening meal, in the great hall, a handsome and comfortable apartment suffering none of the restrictions imposed by defensive construction, such as small windows and arrow-slits, stone vaulting, thick walling and narrow doorways. It had colourful hangings and tapestries on the walls, much ornament, two great fireplaces at either end, and a minstrels' gallery where a group of nun singers and instrumentalists made them entertainment. The chamber was lit by a host of candles.

The countess was still only in her early forties, a good-looking woman, of slender build to have been the mother of

176

her five children, especially of Brawny Will. She greeted her guests kindly, whatever their mission, showing great interest in the progress of the Soutra development, and therefore being particularly attentive to the abbot and Hugh. She declared that she could have done with their services here at her nunnery site.

The two princesses were very different from their mother and from each other: Ada, aged fifteen, big-built, almost clumsy, but of an outgoing nature, hearty, laughter-loving; Margaret, three years younger, small, petite, shy. The thought of her being sent to be bride for a continental duke was off-putting.

The meal given them was the best which Hugh could remember, much superior to anything served at Roxburgh or by the Earl Cospatrick: fish soup and oysters from Aberlady Bay nearby, salmon from the Tyne, roe venison, wild-goose, also from Aberlady's saltings, oatcakes and honey, with wines and ale to wash it all down. Meanwhile the choristers sang for them.

The King retired immediately the repast was over, and in the circumstances the others were not long in seeking their couches, again in well-appointed and comfortable quarters. These nuns knew how to look after their guests.

In the morning, after a breakfast brought to them in their rooms, the abbot was telling Hugh about the story of that great hill just to the east, rearing majestically in the early autumn sunlight, when they were sent for to attend on the King and his mother. Malcolm was looking the better for his night's rest, but clearly unhappy over his discussion, Countess Ada likewise. She it was who spoke first.

"This of my daughter's marriage is scarcely to my liking, but who am I to question the needs of kings and kingdoms?" she said. "I would have hoped that Ada would have had a few years yet before being wed. And not to be sent to another land. But, such is the fate of princesses! At least, I find, she will have good and kind guardians and companions until she is handed over to this Netherlander, old enough to be her father!"

What was there to say to that? They bowed.

"We have decided that the journey must be made soon," Malcolm declared. "Before the winter storms set in and the seas rough. Within two weeks, shall we say? To sail from Berwick-upon-Tweed, where there are many ships sailing to the Low Countries, ships of the Flemish wool merchants and the like. I will make orders for this. So you will come here, to Haddington, in two weeks' time, and collect my sister, to escort her to The Hague, Count Floris's capital-messuage. Is that understood?" He sounded stiff, more formal, than usual.

"Yes, Sire and Highness," the abbot said. "We shall take good care of the Princess Ada. This Floris of Holland is well spoken of. We will pray for her good reception and happiness."

"Do that," the mother agreed. "At least she is of stout heart and cheerful spirit. She will make the best of it all. I will have her ready for you in two weeks' time, my lord Abbot and Sir Hugh. How long, think you, the voyage will take?"

Hugh was not knowledgeable about seafaring, but at least he knew about the Norse Sea winds. "In early winter, Highness, the winds blow largely from the east and north-east, seldom from the south. So the ship should not meet head-winds, and so avoid overmuch of tacking." That was as far as he could go.

Abbot William went a little further. "I went to Rome once, and by the Low Countries. But it was in summer. I think that it was about five hundred miles and took us six days. We came home faster . . ."

"That would be with the summer's south-west winds . . ."

"I will see that you have a good ship and shipmaster," the King said. "Two weeks, then; that should be enough time for all to be in readiness and for you to put your affairs in order. I thank you." And he waved their dismissal, an uncomfortable son with his mother.

Outside, the abbot pointed to that strange hog's-back hill again. "That, Traprain Law, tells the story of another princess to be married against her will," he said. "Thanea, daughter of King Loth, who gave name to this Lothian. And of much the same age. Only, she rebelled and would

178

have none of it, a young fighter indeed. And she won her battle."

"When was this? And what king was this Loth?"

"A southern Pictish sub-king. Under the British High King, Arthur, not under Pictish Alba. Indeed, Arthur's sister was Thanea's dead mother. Loth was pagan but Thanea, like her mother, was Christian. Her father would have her to marry another pagan princeling, but she refused. So he sent her to be some sort of slave to his chief shepherd in your Lammermuirs. There this Prince Owen sought her out and raped her. When she became with child, unwed, her father, an angry man, ordered her death, the pagan penalty for a high-born woman in such state. And he cast her over yonder south cliff-like face of Traprain, in his spleen. But she survived. So Loth decided that her strange Christian God was looking after her, and he handed her over to his own preferred deity, the sea-god Manannan, this by casting her adrift in a coracle without any paddle, in Aberlady Bay. The outgoing tide took her as far as the Isle of May, when it turned, and the coracle drifted up-Forth, to ground at Culross in Fife, where St Serf, a Celtic missionary, had a monastery. He took Thanea in, and there her son was born. Serf christened him Kentigern but called him Mungo, or mannikin – St Mungo, to be, who was later to go west and found Glasgow."

"Lord, what a tale! St Mungo. Him I have heard of. Serf also. But never this Thanea."

"The Glasgow folk, for some reason, call her St Enoch. A strange story. I cannot think that we should tell it to this Princess Ada! Although she may know of it."

"No, it would scarcely enhearten her! I do not greatly look to enjoy this task the King has laid on us!"

"It may be none so ill. It may be that we can make it somewhat less of an ordeal for the girl."

"That we shall see in two weeks' time . . ."

16

Hugh was fortunate in having Duncan to leave to look after all at Aldcambus for the uncertain period of his absence abroad. With Dod Lumsden and Tam Robson as experienced helpers all should be well – although he would miss the birth of Meg's child. He hoped that Duncan's new duties as Macer would not take him away from Redheugh overmuch.

Abbot William duly arrived at Aldcambus the day before they were expected at Haddington, with a young lay brother named Michael to act as their servitor and a pack-horse to carry the necessary gear and clothing. They set off for Haddington next morning on the twenty-five-mile ride. It was not quite farewell yet, for they ought to be back for the night, this being as good a halfway halt as any on their way to Berwick.

They found all ready for them at the hallhouse, the young Ada reasonably cheerful, her sister tearful and their mother maintaining a determinedly calm and supportive behaviour. She had sundry instructions for the abbot and Hugh, gifts to take for the Count Floris, with a letter; and they collected another pack-horse laden with clothing and baggage.

There were choked-back tears at the actual parting, for who knew whether the countess would ever see her daughter again, the men promising to come on their return and tell the mother about the journey and the reception in Holland.

Young Ada quickly recovered her spirits as they rode east by south again. She proved to be a good horsewoman and by no means delayed them. Clearly, apart from the parting, she was looking on this episode as quite an exciting adventure.

Back by the gloaming, at Aldcambus, the very pregnant Meg took the princess in hand, installing her for the night at

Redheugh, the girl fascinated by the red cliffs and spectacular scenery. For a king's sister she was easy to deal with.

Next day it was another parting, with much well-wishing all round, especially for Meg's safe delivery due in three or four weeks, Duncan's anxiety pronounced. Then, with Michael in attendance, it was onwards for Berwick-upon-Tweed, twenty-two miles or so due south now over Coldinghame Muir.

Hugh had been at Coldinghame Priory once or twice, for the prior and his monks were his neighbouring landlords; but this was no occasion for paying respects, and the princess and abbot would inevitably have created a major impact and delay. So they skirted the monastic establishment and headed on round the coast, which suddenly here changed from high precipices to lower little headlands, bays and beaches, by Eyemouth and Burnmouth, fishing villages, until they could see the towering Berwick Castle, a royal stronghold, ahead of them.

Berwick, where Tweed entered the sea, was the greatest port in Scotland, its walled town a centre for innumerable merchants and shippers, mainly Flemings, who had come here to pursue the wool trade, most important for the Low Countries, which were cattle rather than sheep terrain. This was where the wool from all the Lammermuir shearings was sent, to be shipped overseas. Hugh had been here with a pack-train in June.

The abbot's instructions from the King were to seek out a ship called the *Nicolaas*, under a shipmaster named Borgmann, which would take them to Scheveningen, the port of The Hague.

So, within the great gate of the town walling, they threaded the narrow streets lined with tall houses – for space was precious here – booths and warehouses, making for the harbour, young Ada agog.

The haven was full of ships of all sorts and sizes, with much loading and unloading going on, foreign voices predominating, for the vessels which took back the wool to the Continent, the bales stacked all around, also brought here the nation's imports of wines, cloths, paper, weapons and household plenishings.

Finding the right vessel in all this plethora of shipping

181

proved less difficult than might have been expected, for they were in fact accosted by a rough-looking individual who demanded to know if they were the King's party? No doubt well-dressed young women like the princess were seldom seen in the harbour area. He declared that he had been looking for them since the day before, Maister Borgmann right impatient to be off. Presumably there had been some misunderstanding about dates and times.

They were led to one of the larger craft, moored to the outermost of the wharves, a two-masted vessel of high sides and clumsy appearance, but which no doubt was well built for its task of transporting wool bales.

They dismounted and began to unload the pack-horses, their sentinel assuring them that he had been ordered to take charge of the beasts. They would be stabled here at Berwick until they were required again, thus relieving the travellers of the task of making necessary arrangements.

A gangplank took them up and aboard, where they were met by a stocky, bearded and unsmiling man, who eyed them carefully as though checking their authenticity, barked the name Borgmann, and turning, took them promptly aft to the stern quarters under the poop. They rather got the feeling that they were in disgrace for being late and holding up sailing time. The smell of fleeces was all but overpowering.

The shipmaster handed them over to a subordinate and left them, without further communication. Down a steep stairway they were shown their cabins, two small apartments, each with four bunks, and another, slightly larger, with a fixed table and its attached forms. Their guide at least smiled at them, although he did not say much; probably he had little of their language.

The abbot and Hugh eyed each other. Not the most auspicious start to their journey; and the accommodation scarcely princely, abbatial or even knightly. They would make the best of it; but the princess . . . ?

Ada, surveying her cabin and bunks, laughed out loud, evidently far from upset. She flung her baggage on to one of the beds, and asked who was going to keep her company here?

Hurriedly the abbot assured her that it was all hers – the three men would share the other. She looked almost disappointed.

It was not long before, unpacking their gear, they realised by the shouting and bustle aloft that the *Nicolaas* was in fact moving. They hastened to the deck, and found one sail being hoisted and two rowing-boats towing the ship's prow out from the wharf and the warps being cast off.

Interested in the procedure, they watched, the shipmaster shouting instructions, much activity. They saw how the small towing-boats pulled the large, heavy vessel gradually round, not so much drawing its weight after them as changing its bows' direction so that the wind could fill the single sail and thus produce the power to surge ahead. Soon these tow-ropes were cast off, and a larger sail was run up. The craft began to move due southwards across the wide outer harbour area, almost a bay, not eastwards for the open mouth of it, this because of the east wind, and tacking necessary. Presently, with much sail-flapping and shouting of orders, the required turn-around was effected, and heading northwards now, they drew that much closer to the harbour mouth. Still another tack, and they made it, into the open sea, and they were able to turn southwards again, this time for good, the wind abeam, only very minor tacking now required. The shipmaster Borgmann handed over to his steersman and came to speak to his passengers, still abrupt but less seemingly sour. Probably that was just his manner.

"Food," he declared. "One hour. In cabin. Good." And he strode off.

They decided that they would get used to Meinheer Borgmann.

The men went below again, but Ada remained on deck, enthralled by this new experience.

In due course the promised food was brought to their cabin by two grinning crewmen, and good it was and plentiful, soup and stewed mutton, buttered bread and brandy-wine. If this was typical fare, they were not going to make a hungry voyage of it.

The swaying of the ship in mainly broadside-on seas rather

spoiled the man Michael's enjoyment of his meal, and he fairly promptly took to his bunk. Fortunately the other three were not thus affected. But, with night falling and only a single flickering candle to each cabin, they were not long in turning in. The princess was the least eager to retire.

The creaking and groaning of straining timbers at first kept Hugh awake, but the ship's motion did not trouble him, although it continued to send poor Michael out to the bucket provided for their convenience.

That voyage began to develop a strange unreal atmosphere, for Hugh de Swinton at least. He had not realised that he was such a physically active character, and aboard ship activity was minimal, walking round and round the deck and climbing the poop and fore platforms not really meeting his needs. The hours at first seemed slow to pass indeed, with little or nothing to be done in them. The weather was not bad, but windy and chilly for just sitting on deck. The abbot seemed to be able to contemplate his own far horizons satisfactorily enough, and held morning and evening prayers for them all, which no doubt was good for their souls. Hugh found himself unduly looking forward to meal-times, and in consequence ate too much for his comfort.

Unexpectedly, it was Ada who came to his rescue. Energetic herself, she devised a game they could play, which consisted of trying to throw hoops over pegs from varying distances, the upright pegs being their candlesticks and the hoops made out of twisted strands of rope, this in itself occupying some of their time. The object was to toss their circlets accurately enough over the candlesticks so as not to knock them over, a difficult task indeed, especially on a swaying deck. Sometimes crewmen came to try their hands at it, and once even Borgmann himself deigned to make the attempt, but quickly stamped off disgusted. Ada was the clear winner.

She invented another pastime for them when ring-and-peg palled. She found two empty wine-barrels which could be rolled along the deck, in races, using a spar to guide them. Shaped as they were, with a bulge in the middle, they did not

184

roll straight, and a constant and delicate pushing, tapping and guiding was necessary to steer any sort of course. So the King of Scots' sister, the mitred Abbot of Melrose and Scotland's newest knight were to be seen daily herding undisciplined barrels over the tipping, heaving planking, to the amusement of the Dutch seamen. The unfortunate Michael, no seafarer, spent most of his time between bunk and bucket.

With the winds set easterly, only a touch of north now and again, despite the sideways seas they made good time, seldom out of sight of the English shoreline until they reached the wide mouth of the Channel, on the fourth day. Having to tack much more thereafter, as they headed more into the wind and into rougher, shallower seas, they took another day and a half to finish their voyage. Even so, the passengers were not aware of their approach to land, until it was pointed out to them, so low-lying was the coast, the Low Countries indeed.

How their navigator knew where, along that all but invisible shore, to turn in was a mystery, for because of the shallows they kept fairly far out. And even when they did swing landwards, all that they could see was an apparently endless line of yellow sand-dunes, all that kept the waves, it seemed, from surging in to flood the flat polders behind, much of which, they were told, was below sea-level.

It was in fact an extraordinary and obviously man-made gap in the dunes, far from wide, into which they headed, straight as to sides, cut through the sand-hills for about half a mile, so broad was the dune area. As the *Nicolaas* threaded this they passed another ship, outward bound, and a couple of fishing-boats. Then abruptly the passage ended and they emerged into a wide lake or lagoon, again clearly artificial, oblong and open, its south shore lined with docks and buildings: Scheveningen, the port of The Hague, or Den Haag as they were informed they must now call it, their vessel's destination. They made for a quayside at the western end of what appeared to be a township consisting mainly of warehouses, and there tied up at what was evidently an accustomed berth.

Preparing to disembark, shipmaster Borgmann came to

them, and, in his usual jerky fashion, informed that since he himself lived in Den Haag, if they would wait a while and he saw to the various duties involved in harbourage and unloading cargo for different destinations, he would personally take them to the city, only two miles away, and also arrange the hiring of the necessary horses. Glad to avail themselves of this offer, they landed, and went to wander the streets and alleys of this busy port, with its tall, gabled buildings of dark red brick, with brightly painted shuttered windows and crane-like hoists for raising cargoes, largely wool it seemed, to upper-storey storage, its canals and bridges; four of these they crossed, high and hump-backed to allow barges to sail beneath; and its folk, clumping about the brick-paved streets in wooden clogs, men, women and children seeming to find this apparently clumsy footwear comfortable enough. It was all so very different from the port they had sailed from, Berwick, with its stone buildings climbing the slopes of a hill above Tweed's mouth, its narrower lanes and wynds, its sea breezes gusting up streets and terraces. Princess Ada never stopped exclaiming at what she saw.

After an hour or so they returned to the quayside, to find Borgmann awaiting them. He had a man with five riding-horses and two pack-animals hired for them, which the abbot paid for, and loading the last with their gear they all mounted, four men and the girl. It was still only mid-afternoon.

Once clear of Scheveningen, the visitors were still more struck by the scene, unlike anything that they could see at home. It was the flatness of the landscape which astonished them, the vistas both endless, boundless, yet somehow limited, in that there were no heights or even rises, much less hills, to show distances and form horizons. The highest ground was in fact formed by the dykes on which the roads ran, straight with the low, green, cattle-dotted polders stretching to seeming infinity on every side, all reclaimed from the shallow sea, they were told. The only features projecting above all this level expanse were windmills, each with its four great sails slowly revolving, many of them indeed, for according to Borgmann these were necessary to provide the power not only to grind corn and the like but for pumping water out of the polders and along canals, in a terrain dominated by water, seeping everywhere. Also, on that skyline, to the south-west, were the towers and steeples and pinnacles of the city, their destination.

On land, and away from his shipboard responsibilities, Borgmann had become quite vocal, informative. He told them that Den Haag should really be Den Gravenhaag, which could be translated as the graf's, or count's hedge or enclosed property, the city having grown up round the Count of Holland's palace. Count Floris the Third, the present ruler, was, it seemed, a kindly enough man and no tyrant – which was comforting news for young Ada. Holland, they learned, was only one part of the Netherlands, consisting of North and South Holland itself, Friesland further north and Brabant to the south. Other countships and provinces were Groningen, Drenthe, Overijssel, Gelderland and Zeeland. The listeners were suitably impressed.

They passed few other horsemen on their raised roadway, although some walkers, most travel apparently being done by barge and boat on the canals which outnumbered the roads. Two of these canals led directly into Den Haag, and some of the barges they saw were obviously laden with bales of wool, for the city was a major centre of the woollen trade and the manufacture of cloth, blankets, drapery and apparel. Hugh wondered how many, if any, of his Lammermuir sheep's fleeces ended up here.

The palace was not difficult to find, standing out tall and many-towered, these with conical, tiled roofs, and a profusion of timber balconies and galleries projecting from the ubiquitous brick walling.

Passing the fine town hall, they came to the splendid gateway in the courtyard walling of the palace, which Borgmann named the Gevangen Poort, and where he said that he would leave them, palaces not being for such as himself. The abbot asked him what was the procedure for getting a ship back to Scotland, and was told that no doubt Count Floris would see to that. But he himself would be sailing again for Berwick in about ten days' time, on his final voyage before winter set in; and if they were ready to leave by then, they could have their former cabins. They had not expected to be electing to sail again with this somewhat unforthcoming mariner. But they had come to recognise him as better than on first impressions, and an excellent seaman. They could do much worse than travel back with him.

So it was farewell meantime, and informing the gatehouse guards that here was the Princess Ada from Scotland come to the court of Count Floris, the visitors were allowed to proceed into the courtyard, while a man was sent to apprise the count of their arrival.

They could have made no complaints as to their reception, at any rate, unexpected as it must have been. Floris, a slightly built, fair-headed man in his early forties, came to greet them in person, with half a dozen of his court, two of them ladies, which, in the circumstances, was a thoughtful touch. He was of genial, open-faced appearance, and although he scanned his bride-to-be keenly enough as he approached them, it was without any aspect of judgment or criticism. For her part, Ada showed her interest more frankly, gazing at him with tongue tipping her lip assessingly. Her companions hoped that she was not distressed by what she saw.

If she was, she gave no sign of it, smiling and dipping a curtsy, as no doubt she had been instructed by her mother. This produced a bow from the count, who then stepped forward to take her hand and raise it to his lips in a courtly gesture. So far, so good.

Then he turned to her companions, and they introduced themselves, the count declaring them to be very welcome to his poor house. Gesturing for servitors to deal with the horses and baggage, he took the girl's arm and led the way inside.

Poor house he may have named it, but the Gravenhoos was finer than anything that the visitors had ever seen, larger, more decorative and richly furnished, almost overmuch so by Scots standards. Whatever Ada's life was to be hereafter, lack of this world's goods was obviously not to be a handicap.

A chamberlain of a sort took the men away, to conduct them

188

to their rooms in a wing of the palace, while the count led the
girl off elsewhere. From now on, they realised, their escorting
duties and guardianship were over. They had both become
fond of Ada.

Compared with the spartan cabin quarters they had occupied on the *Nicolaas*, the apartments they were now to use
seemed indecently rich, in size, style and plenishings. They
were informed that they would be taken to Count Floris's table
in due course.

Used to sharing quarters with Abbot William, Hugh found
himself at something of a loss alone in his grand chamber,
as he changed out of his travelling clothes and into the
not particularly fine gear which was the best that he could
bring. As a knight, now, ought he to be investing in better
garb? Such seemed unimportant in Scotland, but here . . . ?
This was a city where clothing was made; perhaps he could
purchase something in Den Haag, and possibly charge it to
the funds which King Malcolm had entrusted to the abbot for
expenses? After all, Scotland's standing and credit might thus
be enhanced. He went in search of his friend.

The abbot, in a similar chamber nearby, thought that while
this was not really necessary, there would be no harm in so
buying, there being ample moneys in his purse, and so far
they had spent only on hiring the horses. But he asserted
that Hugh looked perfectly well turned-out as he was, and
over-dressing nowise to be sought. His own monastic garb
was modest compared with that of some senior clerics.

Before long the chamberlain came to conduct them, along
corridors and through anterooms, to what was no great hall
although a fine and spacious apartment ablaze from hanging
chandeliers reflected in many mirrors. Here was a single table,
lengthy enough and with chairs, not forms, flanking it, not the
T-shaped arrangement normal in the houses of the great ones
at home, with no raised dais and top table for the lord and his
especial guests, and long, lower seating for the less important
and retainers. This appeared to be a room for private dining
of the count and those close to him. Half a dozen people,
including the two ladies seen at the first meeting, were standing

189

about, and greeted the newcomers civilly, all very richly clad, the women showing considerably more bosom than was usual in Scotland. There was no sign of the count and Ada. From a room off came the sound of soft music. Servitors in handsome uniform waited around the mirrored walling.

Then the music changed and became louder, and in from the anteroom came Floris, in blue velvet bedecked with gold, the girl on his arm and in her best gown, smiling widely at this ceremonial, catching the eyes of the abbot and Hugh, and somehow looking very young. All bowed, as Floris led his bride-to-be to the head of the table and sat her down with a flourish, then gestured for the two Scots to come and sit on either side, before taking his own throne-like chair.

The music changed to soft again, as all sat.

The count made a short speech then, naturally in Dutch, but turning frequently to incline his fair head towards Ada, so presumably it all referred to her, she meantime making faces at not being able to understand a word of it. Another wave of the hand right and left towards her late escorts, and he finished by patting the girl's head, to murmurs of approval.

The meal which followed was a notable spread considering that the palace cooks had had no prior notice of the arrival of the Scots party. Presumably lay brother Michael was being entertained elsewhere. Ada did ample justice to it all, as did the others, shipboard fare having been plentiful but lacking in variety. The girl was clearly taking all this, as it were, in her stride, and even enjoying all the attentions paid to her.

The repast, all but a banquet, over, they moved out of what was clearly only a dining-chamber into a larger apartment which might have been termed a withdrawing-room, equally well lit and with two large fireplaces burning not logs but peat, the walls tapestry-hung, the tessellated floor strewn with woven rugs. The musicians had preceded them here, to a sort of minstrels' gallery at one end, where they now entertained with lute and pipe and harp, singers male and female coming to make their contributions.

This went on for some time. Ada was soon yawning, the language problem not helping to keep her lively. Presently she rose and came across to her friends, to whisper. She said that she had been given a great bedroom and no fewer than three maids to attend her, this with a giggle, and that the count was kindly but that she did not understand most of what he said. Also she thought that she had eaten too much. Did they think that she might go to bed?

The abbot suggested that she waited until the present elaborate and rather lengthy duet was finished, and then he would go over with her to Floris and indicate that retiral was sought, after a long day and much journeying. To make it all seem the more natural, he and Sir Hugh would seek permission to retire also.

This design presently was carried out, and all accepted graciously, the count rising to escort the girl personally to her suite of rooms. Probably the company was well enough pleased to be left on its own.

The two Scots, finding more food and wine awaiting them in their rooms, discussed the language problem. They both knew a certain amount of French which was much spoken at court at Roxburgh, and some Latin, especially the abbot, naturally, that being the language of Holy Church. Would these Netherlanders know either, or both? Ada, reared amongst nuns, would probably have some Latin, possibly French also, since her mother was the daughter of an Anglo-Norman earl. They would try it out in the morning. This was a problem which they ought to have anticipated.

In the event, next day Count Floris proved to be a fluent French-speaker, having Latin also, so communication was much improved all round, Ada herself reasonably well versed.

The programme for the day was to make a tour round Den Haag and its environs, on foot in the city and horsed in the afternoon. There was apparently much to show the visitors, in especial St Janskerk, the cathedral where in one week's time the marriage would be celebrated, thus enabling the Scots to return to their own country before winter voyaging became difficult and hazardous.

So a party of about a dozen set out, cloaked, including the two ladies, one of whom proved to be the count's sister Ursula; the other's identity was not clear, although she was called Anna, but the abbot guessed that she might well be Floris's mistress, from the glances which they occasionally exchanged. Also included was the Bishop of Zuid-Holland, who would conduct the wedding service and would now show them his Domkerk.

This, not far from the palace, was a magnificent structure to be built wholly of timber, with two spired towers and innumerable pinnacled buttresses and niched and canopied statues, its great windows of stained-glass much impressing Abbot William. Internally it seemed vast, loftier than any Scots abbey, with many aisles and side-chapels, recumbent effigies covering the tombs of Floris's ancestors. The high altar was much more elaborate than the Scots had seen at home, even the chapel altars, plainer but still more decorative and ornate, their more austere Celtic Church tradition having moderated their own ideas as to worshipful adornment. But they could not deny the flourish of it all.

The bishop demonstrated and informed, advisedly in French; also indicated something of the forthcoming marriage ceremonial and order, inviting the abbot to assist if so he desired. Ada was suitably attentive.

Thereafter, leaving the prelate, they visited the town hall, this again lofty but built of the usual red brick, the burgomaster hastily summoned from his merchanting. Then a series of calls on workshops, manufactories, mills and forges, which interested Ada more, seeing wool spun and woven, the cloth cut and made into a great variety of garments, blankets being produced, carpentry worked, beer brewed, even chain-mail being forged. It became obvious to the visitors how all the count's so evident wealth was generated, and they realised how comparatively lacking in such commercial initiative they were in Scotland.

Returning to the palace for refreshment, a smaller party was provided with splendid Flanders horses and led by the count on a circuit of inspection of the adjacent countryside. This

192

was anything but straightforward, or for that matter circular, since it had to be ridden by dyke tops which, in the nature of things, tended to be in straight lines and vast quadrangles, enclosing the green, low-lying polders and reclaimed ground. It was possible to ride across some of these, but there were of course boggy areas, and there were canals to complicate matters. So it was often a very square-about progress to reach features of interest seemingly quite near at hand, villages, large houses, lakes and meres for hawking and wildfowling, small woodland tracts and sacred shrines. It was all so very different from any horse-riding and visiting done in Scotland, that exclamations were constant from the newcomers, all but disbelief expressed.

A still more splendid banquet was served that evening, the purveyors and cooks evidently meeting their master's challenge, with meats ranging from swans' breasts and peacocks with tails displayed to raw herrings and strange shellfish, and even roasted wild boar ribs, Hugh was interested to note. Stomachs distinctly overloaded, they retired for the night.

The next day was wet and blustery and was spent indoors, playing at games, some of them new to the visitors, examining pictures, illustrated documents and manuscripts, with dancing in the evening, at which the Scots demonstrated some of their own special reels and foursomes, the man Michael being summoned from the servants' quarters to make up the set, bashful as the lay brother was over it all. Some of the Dutch attempts to emulate, however extraordinary, at least produced much laughter.

By the following morning the weather had improved, and Floris had an especial trip for the guests. They would go to see the house and property which was to be the princess's dower, one of his apparently innumerable estates which he had carefully chosen because of its situation, called Leidschendam, eight miles due east of Den Haag. This was on a long stretch of higher ground, he said, formed out of ancient sand-dunes, where there was some scrub forest and actually heather grew and sheep pastured, all but unique in his Holland. So it would be like home to

Ada, he believed. It was a thoughtful touch, they appreciated.

Although it was only eight miles, they had to ride almost as far again in order to reach it, because of the dykes and the need to cross canals by bridges. And in the end, when the count pointed to woods ahead as this Leidschendam, they were still looking for the high ground, to be told that they were on it, to their astonishment. Admittedly they saw heather growing, past its best now in late October, and a few sheep of a long-tailed sort grazing on it, but they had not been aware of any significant rise in the land-level, so slight and gradual had been the approach. And here they observed men digging and stacking peats. This peat-burning in the palace had puzzled Hugh, who hitherto had seen nowhere that could produce the right sort of turf for fires. So this was where it came from, presumably centuries of heather-growth laying it down.

The dowery house, with its steading, farmery, fields, barns and windmill, proved to be a pleasing and quite large establishment, and represented a notable asset for Ada, whether she fully recognised the fact or not. For an arranged royal marriage she was doing none so badly, thanks to Floris's forethought.

Next day, being Sunday, after a private service in the palace chapel, quite a large company went out to the cathedral for a rehearsal of the wedding ceremony, bishop and count in collaboration. This took some considerable time, with much arranging of entrances, positioning, seating-precedence, choirs and the like. Female attendants for Ada, under the count's sister, were instructed, and Abbot William given his part to play. Two more days to go.

They went hawking round the polders and lakes the following morning. There was no lack of wildfowl for their sport, mallard, widgeon, teal, golden-eye, herons or cranes, and a kind of goose they did not have in Scotland which seemed to be called snaegans. Ada was used to falconry, and quite distinguished herself, doing better than many, so much so that she asked that they might repeat the programme the day following, this being granted, even though the weather deteriorated again and curtailed things. Prayers were said for improved conditions for the next and great day, for the sun to shine on the bride.

Shine it did not, but at least it was not wet nor windy, and in mid-forenoon the two processions set out from the palace to approach the cathedral by different routes, behind instrumentalists, the streets thronged with waving, cheering citizenry, Ada on Hugh's arm – for the abbot had gone on ahead to be part of the clergy's reception. Two laughing girls, nobles' daughters, had been enrolled to hold up the long train which had been produced to help Ada's best gown towards wedding standards.

The timing was excellent, the bridegroom's procession, with the shorter route to follow, arriving sufficiently beforehand to be all properly positioned when the bridal group appeared, the count, with his attendants, standing at the chancel-steps before the bishop, Abbot William and other clergy, while the vast crowded building all but shook to the blare of trumpets and horns.

Ada, clutching Hugh's arm tightly now, showed her first signs of tension, the grandeur of the place, the great numbers all watching her, the challenging noise, all having effect, as well, possibly, as the realization that here was the crux, finality, that hereafter she would be for the rest of her life attached to this waiting man, in the sight of God and the world. At fifteen years it was an occasion to test indeed.

When she reached the chancel-steps, the bishop raised an arm and the noise died away. There was a moment's silence and then a single voice, clear and high, rose in lovely song, hauntingly, until it was lost in the triumphant praise of a full choir, the prelude to marriage.

The ceremony thereafter proceeded more or less as it would have done in Scotland, with Hugh handing over the bride, the celebrant's address, the taking of vows, the exchange of rings and the pronouncing of man and wife, Abbot William finally proclaiming the benediction of married persons, this in Latin of course.

So the thing was done, accomplished. The Princess Ada was now Countess of Holland, a married woman, Hugh's arm no longer required. She was led down through the great congregation on her husband's arm now, to pealing music and sung praise, and out into the streets of vociferous crowds. Henry Plantagenet of England would be satisfied. Would Floris, and Ada, hereafter? That was for time to tell.

The feasting that followed was not confined to the palace. All Den Haag was to celebrate, with cattle in their scores, their hundreds sacrificed, roasting-fires in every square and open space, barrels of beer likewise, great cheeses, casks of butter and mountains of bread stacked high, bands of minstrels, jugglers and performers roaming. All for a fifteen-year-old girl from far-away Scotland. Such are the consequences of statecraft.

That evening, after not too prolonged an entertainment, husband and wife retired, to the plaudits of the company, Ada casting somewhat anxious glances in the direction of the abbot and Hugh. Their part played, there was nothing that they could do save to smile reassuringly, and perhaps pray. But they judged that, by what they had seen of him, Floris would be a fairly kind initiator to marital bliss.

They sought their own couches soon thereafter, their late charge's well-being very much on their minds.

It was mid-forenoon on another wet day before they saw Ada again, although the count, looking perfectly normal, was out and about betraying no hint of anything untoward. When the princess-countess did appear, she at first kept her eyes downcast, but seemed otherwise reasonably self-possessed. Unsure of the propriety of asking how matters fared with her, her former escorts did not actually approach her, after a formal good morning.She it was, therefore, who fairly soon came to them and ventured a shy smile, but unspeaking.

"My dear daughter-in-God," the abbot said, carefully, "we greet you warmly, most warmly. We hope that you are well? And . . . happy? After your . . . great day."

She nodded, still wordless.

"We have been wishing you very well," Hugh added, a trifle lamely.

"I thank you," she answered. "It, it is none so ill."

196

"H'mm. Your husband, I think, is a kind man."

"Yes."

Floris himself came up. "My wife will miss you when you are gone," he declared. "But I will seek her happiness. And my own." Was that reassurance and dismissal both?

They bowed.

The count led her off.

Since this seemed to be implied, they rode down to Scheveningen that day to enquire of Borgmann and the *Nicolaas*. They found the shipmaster at the docks superintending the loading of his final export cargo of the year, barrels of beer, bales of cloth, casks of cheese and unwieldy crates of pots and pans. He said that he had seen them in the processions of the previous day and had partaken of the street-feasting. He was sailing in two days, on the early morning tide. Would they require their cabins?

Both now feeling that the sooner they got back to Scotland the better, they said yes. All being agreeable to the count, they would come aboard the evening before. They hoped that the weather might improve.

It was, in fact, fine enough for hawking at least on their last full day in Holland, this no doubt Ada's choice; and she seemed well enough content thereat and afterwards. No doubt she would miss them, but she clearly had an ability to adapt herself to circumstances, and an optimistic outlook. They felt that they could leave her without undue qualms.

The final parting next afternoon was less trying than it might have been, and in no way dramatic, Ada and the count saying farewell at the palace gate, with no tears and clutchings, the girl thanking them dutifully for their kindly escort and care and asking them to tell her mother and sister that all was well with her; obviously a prepared little speech. She did not mention King Malcolm nor her other brothers. For their part, the abbot and Hugh wished her growing happiness, enduring content and fulfilment, with God's blessing, the abbot signing the cross over her. At the last moment, as they were bowing themselves off, she stepped forward to touch both their arms and shake her head, with her lip-biting gesture. That was as far as the drama went.

They made their way down to the ship, thoughtful.

The voyage home, although somewhat delayed by contrary winds and roughening seas, was less than comfortable but uneventful. The eventual sight of the Cheviot Hills behind Berwick-upon-Tweed was welcome indeed, duty done. They had been away for barely a month, but it seemed longer.

17

All was well at Aldcambus and Redheugh, very well, for Meg had produced a daughter, small in size but unique apparently in character, and already the source of enormous pride for Duncan, his former anxieties now transformed to self-congratulation. She was to be named Lara and was clearly going to play a major part in life hereafter.

Lesser matters, such as the well-being of the two, and now extended, properties, the health of the monarch, and national affairs, seemed to call for little comment.

Two days after his return, Hugh rode north to Haddington to inform the Countess Ada as to her daughter's state, conditions of life and marriage. He was thankful to be able to give a good account, and the countess was appreciative and grateful, relieved to learn that the Count Floris was kindly natured, and interested to hear of the dowery house gesture at Leidschendam, which she saw as an excellent augury for the future. Nothing was said about the proposed marriage of her other daughter to the Duke of Brittany.

Thereafter there was much work for Hugh in making up for lost time on his properties, the winter months demanding quite the most attention on this seaboard terrain. His Netherlands experiences consequently tended to be not forgotten but to attain an almost dreamlike quality.

They saw nothing of Abbot William that winter; he was now Vice-Chancellor of course, as well as Abbot of Melrose, and would be a busy man. Hugh and Duncan did manage to pay a visit to Soutra and to discover the hospital already functioning in some degree, and building work proceeding despite the hard weather conditions. They heard that the King was still frail, but much concerned with the progress of this his great venture. Apparently some of his advisers considered that he ought to be more interested in the running of his kingdom than of hospitals. However, he did not seem to be requiring the Swinton brothers' services meantime, in this or other respects.

Strangely, after so much activity on the King's behalf, it was months, running into years indeed, before a request came for action from Hugh, and from an unexpected source. A messenger arrived from Aldcambus's original owner, Walter Olifard, Justiciar of Lothian, declaring that he would be holding justice-eyres at Haddington in a few days' time and he would be grateful if Sir Hugh would meet him there, for he had a matter to put to him, a personal matter.

Hugh wondered what this could be; but duly made his way the sixteen miles to Haddington. He called first on the Countess Ada to pay his respects, and there learned that Olifard was actually lodging in the countess's house for the few days, and so awaited him there when the day's proceedings at the Tolbooth should be finished.

Over a meal at the royal table, then, Olifard explained. Hugh's reputation as a boar-slayer was behind this summons. Olifard's brother Osbert held the lofty office and style of Thane of Arbuthnott, up in the Mearns, a northern county not far from Aberdeen. And the area near his house of Arbuthnott was being terrorised by a particularly ferocious bear. Many attempts had been made to dispose of it, without success; indeed it was the boar which did the slaying. The Swintons were renowned for their abilities in this matter, Hugh in especial. The plea was, would he go north and attempt to deal with this brute? He would gain the gratitude and esteem of more than the Thane of Arbuthnott if he would be so good.

As Hugh blinked at this extraordinary proposal, the Countess Ada actually clapped her hands.

"Sir Hugh the boar-slayer!" she exclaimed. "Here is a knightly challenge indeed. Much more noble than any battle-field feat of arms. You will do it, Sir Hugh? Save these good

200

people from hurt, and add another rose to your chaplet, my friend?"

What could he say to that? He could not refuse. And he owed the justiciar something, he supposed. But the Mearns was a long way off.

"My brother has himself sought to do it," Olifard said. "He has led hunts. But the horses always shy and turn, will not face the creature. And afoot . . . ! It is very large and fierce. *You* know boars, have proved yourself. He, and all up there, would be much in your debt if you could rid them of this curse."

Hugh nodded. "Very well, I will try. When?"

"So soon as you may. The brute ranges wide, and kills frequently. It savaged two children just days before my brother left there to call on me."

"I will go then, before the lambing . . ."

"Bless you!" the countess said.

Hugh had never been further north than Perth, and was unsure indeed just where the Mearns might be. Olifard told him where, and how to get there. It would be simplest to go by ship to Inverbervie, a harbour south of Stanehive; but that would require a sea-going vessel, no mere fishing-boat. He might have to wait long enough to find one sailing north from Berwick or one of the Forth ports, for Aberdeen. He probably would ride it in four days or five. By Stirling and Perth, Strathmore and Brechin to Montrose, and then on up the coast. Near to two hundred miles. It was long since Olifard himself had done it, but he recollected no major hurdles, no mountain passes to cross . . .

On his way home, Hugh called in at Dunbar, the largest haven north of Berwick before Leith, and learned there that it was seldom that any vessels from there, or calling there, voyaged up to Aberdeen. Dundee, perhaps, and a change to another craft there, but . . . ?

He decided that it was his horse for him.

Duncan and Meg, when they heard, declared him daft to have agreed to go on this crazy and dangerous venture, all no concern of his. If he did this, and indeed did manage to slay the boar and remain alive, he could be called upon

201

to traipse all over the realm to rid the land of such creatures. Folly!

But his word given, there was no turning back for Hugh de
Swinton. Two days later, armed with two different lengths
of spear, a short, wide-bladed sword, a dirk and hawking
gauntlets, he was on his way.

He reckoned that his sturdy garron, best for this task, could
probably average fifty miles each day, so four days ought to
see him at this Arbuthnott. Edinburgh the first night, halfway
between Stirling and Perth the second. After Perth he would
be on unknown territory for him. Having got that far he would
not waste time trying Dundee, at the mouth of Tay, for a ship,
when two more days' riding ought to serve.

The March weather was blustery but not wet, and the ride
to Edinburgh easy, with no problems there as to overnight
accommodation, for he called at the justiciar's town-house in
the Canongate, and although Olifard himself was not present,
his son Walter was there, and made Hugh welcome. He proved
to be a solemn young man of the studious sort, but friendly
enough. He looked after his father's great Lanarkshire estate
of Bothwell, where he was superintending the building of a
large new castle, the architectural details and problems of
which he explained at length to his visitor who tried to seem
interested.

Away betimes in the morning Hugh made Stirling soon after
noon and was able to proceed on across Forth and up the Allan
Water as far as Auchterarder before dark, knowing his way as far
as Perth. Arriving there by mid-afternoon the next day, he had no
difficulty, once across Tay, in finding the route into Strathmore's
great and wide valley, between the Sidlaw Hills to the south and
all the mighty rampart of the Highland mountains to the north,
the going complicated by the many large rivers flowing out of
the latter and having to be crossed by fords, the Isla, the Dean,
the Prosen, the Clova, the South Esk, the Westwater and the
North Esk, apart from lesser streams. Because of the need for
fords, the road was anything but straightforward, and Hugh did
not get further than Forfar that day.

There he learned that he need not go on down Strathmore to

Brechin, but by following the Lunan Water, from Restenneth Abbey nearby, he could eventually reach the sea at Lunan Bay, south of Montrose, a considerable saving in miles. Doing so, he was able to spend the next night at the oddly named fishers' village of Ulysseshaven, locally pronounced Usan, after having admired the cliff-girt horns of Lunan Bay, especially Red Head, rivalling his own coastline at home. He was at Inverbervie by next midday, and there turned up the valley of the Bervie Water for the four or five miles, allegedly, to Arbuthnott.

This Mearns county he found to be a green land of low hills and long grassy ridges, largely bare of trees but always backed by the great barrier of the Highland Line, typical cattle country and more prosperous-seeming than he had expected, his assumption having been that these northern parts would be all but hazardous, with wild, kilted inhabitants. What he now saw of the folk, they were none so very different from his own.

The Bervie valley, never wide, narrowed in suddenly where there was a major S-shaped bend of the river, and here was a smallish castle, within the loop. He was assuming this to be Arbuthnott, but a man herding cattle up the steep bank told him that it was Allardyce, Arbuthnott a couple of miles on, beyond St Ternan's Kirk; at least, that is what he thought the herd said, but his accent was such as to leave names in doubt. Further, soon he was passing a church, small and of red stone, on a shelf above the waterside. No village here, although up on the higher ground he could see the thatches of cottages half hidden by bushes and new leafage, for there were trees in this valley.

After another mile or so, he came to a still steeper section, with the red sandstone rock showing, all reminding him of Aldcambus and Redheugh, although the stone was not nearly so vividly scarlet. And rounding a sharp crutch of what was now almost a ravine, he found a small subsidiary burn coming in on the left, in its own gorge, to join Bervie. Here on the high and rugged little peninsula formed between, rose the V-sided walling of another castle, how large it was difficult to judge from below but clearly in a strong defensive position. This could only be Arbuthnott. There was no sign, from here, of any castleton or village.

Working his way up the right-hand side of this, well below the walling to begin with, he found the ground beginning to rise and the river cascading. Thereafter he came to a wide grassy terrace, with further hilly ground beyond, and here was the frontage of the castle, barred off by a deep moat and drawbridge; and northwards, a little way off, a clachan of small houses, barns and sheds, the castleton.

Presumably Hugh's approach had been observed from the castle, for, although the drawbridge was down and the portcullis up, three men stood on guard at the entry, eyeing him, spears in hand.

He rode up to them. "The Thane of Arbuthnott, Sir Osbert Olifard – is he here?" he asked.

"Och aye," he was told, in a voice with a very different accent from those he was used to. "Fae asks?" Fae presumably meant who.

"Sir Hugh de Swinton. From far-away Berwickshire. Sir Osbert, I think, will know the name."

"Aye? Och weel, Ken'll awa' ben and find oot. Bide you there."

Hugh dismounted and waited, as one man went off inside. The other two eyed him, without hostility but assessingly in a sort of humorous inspection.

It took some time for the individual called Ken to return, accompanied by a massively built man of late middle years, greying, with strong features but inclining to stoutness. There was no resemblance to the Justiciar Olifard. He stared at Hugh.

"You, sir – can it be?" he exclaimed. "Do I hear aright? Swinton? Can it possibly be he whom I sought? Hugh the Fair? Sir Hugh de Swinton from the Merse? Of the boars?"

"I am Hugh de Swinton, yes. Asked to come here by the Justiciar of Lothian. Are you his brother, Sir Osbert Olifard, Thane of Arbuthnott?"

204

"I am, yes, and I rejoice to see you. Speedily you have come, indeed. And a long way."

"The need was urgent, I was told."

"Urgent indeed. But — come, sir. I need not say how welcome you are to my house." He gestured to one of the men to take the horse and unstrap the baggage behind the saddle. He led Hugh in under the gatehouse archway. "I rejoice to see you. We are in dire trouble here with this boar, as you will have heard."

"Do not rejoice too soon, Sir Osbert. I may be no match for the brute. I but come to try."

"We all have done that. Pray that you, more experienced, practised, will be more successful."

They crossed a cobbled yard to the doorway of what was not so much a keep as a long stone hallhouse of three storeys surmounted by a parapet for defence, which formed the base of the triangle of walling which he had seen from below, an unusually shaped fortalice indeed, adapted to the peculiar site, strong but commodious.

Within, they mounted to the great hall, where Hugh was surprised to see no fewer than five women bending over a table, busy on what was clearly a large and colourful tapestry, being threaded and stitched.

"My daughter, Margaret. And her helpers," Olifard said. "Here is Sir Hugh de Swinton, come to aid us in the grievous matter of the boar," he declared. "He has come without delay, ridden far and fast. Refreshment for Sir Hugh."

Straightening up, the women gazed at the newcomer thus announced, before four of them thought to bob their heads and tuck away their needles and threads.

But Hugh was also staring, and as obviously. For although the three younger women were well enough worth looking at, one of them was quite the most striking creature that the man had ever set eyes upon, not exactly beautiful, tall, splendidly shaped, raven-haired, with long, fairly narrow features finely chiselled, a wide and generous mouth and dark eyes as large as they were lustrous and deep. She carried herself with such confident but natural grace that there could be no doubt that this was the thane's daughter. As the others hurried off, she came forward and, smiling, dipped just the hint of a curtsy.

"The hero himself!" she exclaimed, but with a touch of laughter which took away any note of exaggeration in her voice. "I scarcely thought that you would come, Sir Hugh. Indeed, doubted our right to call on you. To do what we ought to be able to do for ourselves! I told my father so."

"Margaret is . . . outspoken!" Olifard said. "I fear that I have not raised her aright! Since her mother died. Heed her not."

The gurgle of mirth which greeted that was sufficient comment – and warning perhaps?

Hugh actually stammered, so struck was he, so affected by what he saw and heard. "I . . . I am no hero, lady," he got out. "Just, just a Merse laird's son. Of no especial worth or deeds . . ."

"Yet you are knighted, sir. At as young an age as myself, I think? Which is scarcely usual, no?"

"That was but for aiding King Malcolm with his Soutra hospital endeavour – nothing more notable."

"You slew my uncle's boar at Smailholm, did you not? And others, we have heard. Forby, took the King's sister to the Low Countries. Do not feign too much modesty, Sir Hugh!"

The man realised that he would have to watch his step with this one.

"Enough, Margaret, enough!" her father ordered. "Fetch Sir Hugh some wine, until his provision arrives. What chamber will we give him . . . ?"

"The one above my own, in the round tower, will be best," she said, going over to a dresser beyond the great central table, where flagons, beakers and tankers were ranged. "Your baggage, Sir Hugh? The men will have brought it in from your horses?"

"One horse, lady," he told her. "I travel light and with but little. And do not call me sir, I pray you – I am unused to it!"

"Very well, so long as you do not name *me* lady! As though I was my mother or grandmother! Here is wine from Flanders – will that suit your so-travelled knightship?"

Her father shook his head helplessly. He might be thane and ruler of large territories, but clearly his daughter ruled herself. "How long have you been on the road, my friend?" he asked. "How did you come here?"

"This my fourth day. By Edinburgh and Stirling, Perth and Forfar, Lunan Bay and Inverbervie. The justiciar told me . . ."

"Four, only? Long days' riding. And Inverbervie, not Fordoun? Then, you came up the Bervie Water. Unharmed! You saw no sign of the boar?"

"No. Should I have done so?"

"The brute lives there. In the valley. Not far from here, indeed. There is a dean called Pitcarles, where it has its lair . . ."

The daughter brought Hugh his wine. "One sight of our boar-slayer and the creature hid in its den!" she asserted. "See you, I will look to your baggage and then take you to your chamber." And dipping that mock curtsy again, she left them.

"Young women . . . !" the thane ejaculated. He shrugged. "Provision will be up shortly. Sit you. You occupy what were my brother's lands of Aldcambus in Berwickshire, I understand. I never visited them. I know Smailholm . . ."

"The justiciar has such great lands. On my way, I spent a night with your nephew, sir – William, from Bothwell. He was in the Edinburgh house. Bothwell seems to be a notable place. And he told me that he is building a mighty castle."

"Aye. Will has his ambitions, clerkly as he is! One of which is to wed Margaret here, and so inherit Arbuthnott, to add to the rest he will succeed to! For I have no son. But . . . she has other suitors!"

Silent, Hugh nodded.

"Sir Ernulf de Swinton is your uncle, is he not? A great man under King David. And your father the sheriff? I met him once . . ."

They spoke in such fashion until Margaret Olifard arrived back, to tell Hugh that his baggage, so little of it, had been taken to his chamber, and she would now conduct

207

him there. Whereafter a repast would be ready for him, to sustain him until they had their modest evening meal. If he was ready . . . ?

She led him out, and through a small inner courtyard, this flanked by lean-to outbuildings against the walling he had seen from below, kitchens, brewhouse, stabling and the like, to a round tower which formed the apex of the triangle. Here they climbed a narrow twisting stairway to the first floor's single, circular chamber.

"This is my own room," she said. "I like it here, away from the noise and to-do of the main house. And looking down into the two deep clefts of the Bervie and the Neithe, and their woods and waterfalls. I have a maid in the attic at the top, one of those helping me with my tapestry. You can have the centre chamber – secure between us two women! It is not large, but it will serve, I think."

"I thank you. I require no fine quarters, only a bed and a blanket . . ."

"We can do a mite better than that, I judge. And you may be here for some time, boar-hunting."

"You say so? I had not so judged . . . ?"

"The evil brute does not always show itself. If it has feasted well on cattle or other, it can lie up for days. And you may not be successful on your first foray – even you!"

"That is true. I am less sure of myself than is your father. I have killed boars, yes – but there are boars and boars! This of yours sounds especially ill to deal with. Others, you say, have tried and failed. Do not build over-high hopes . . ."

"The failing could be costly, Hugh de Swinton. Your life!"

"I know it."

"Yet you hazard that life for strangers! Why?"

"I was besought. And strangers can be as worthy as known folk. Particularly when, when like the Olifards! Or . . . one of them!"

"Ha! There speaks a hunter of more than boars, I think!"

"No, no. I . . ." He shrugged. "Have it as you will."

Smiling, she led him up the further stair.

Opening the door above, she took him in. A fire had been lit in this other circular chamber, blankets were laid out on the bed, and his baggage on a chest, with a great tub of steaming water awaiting his ablutions. In entirely practical fashion she spread the bed for him, and told him that after long days' riding he would benefit by a wash-down. Gelis the maid would be available if he rang the bell there. He could find his way back to the hall's withdrawing-room when ready?

He thanked her, decided that he was being rather too effusive, and changed to an apology for interrupting the tapestry-working. Was this a pursuit of hers?

"I endeavour decently to cover bare walls," she told him lightly. "I am none so good at it. My mother, now, she did better. But I try. I can draw the cartoons, the designs, on the webbing, passably, in charcoal. But for the stitching of high and low warp I lack due patience. So I plague Gelis and the others to do much of the duller needlework, the backgrounds and the like, while I stitch what interests me. Unkind of me, no? But then, I can be unkind – as my father never ceases to tell me! But heed me not! Women's talk!"

"No, you interest me. I saw many handsome tapestries in Den Haag – that is, The Hague, in the Netherlands. And wondered how they were made."

"To be sure. The Flemings and such folk are masters of tapestry. Do not look for the like here! I but pass the time with it. The notion of it all is good, a temptation to me. But the work can be a labour for such as myself, other than the drawing."

"You make your own designs? Draw them with charcoal, you say. As what?"

"Oh, ancient saints. Sinners also, if there is a story to them. Birds, animals, flowers, coat-armour, anything with colour and form to hold the attention. You will see some of my poor efforts. Indeed, there are two in my chamber below, see you. Come, I will show you."

Hugh flattered himself that he was doing none so badly now.

Downstairs, entering the room below, he was not displeased to find it almost as untidy as his own was apt to

209

be at Aldcambus, women's clothing and gear strewn around. Margaret did not apologise for it, nor did she seem to see anything inappropriate in leading a man into her bedchamber.

"There!" she pointed. "And there."

Dutifully Hugh looked where she directed instead of elsewhere, for there were two wall-hangings, one behind the bed and a smaller one above the fireplace, both very colourful. The larger one showed a man and a woman, both wearing only loin-cloths suitably draped, with an animal, a great cat apparently, peering from behind a tree, the man with a dagger in his hand.

"Pyramus and Thisbe," she explained. "You will know the tale? From Ovid. Lovers refused permission to wed. They fled, not together. Thisbe came to this mulberry tree. There a lioness threatened her. It snatched her veil. It had just slain an ox, and there was blood on its mouth, and so on the veil. Thisbe ran. Then Pyramus came up, saw the bloodstained veil and deemed Thisbe to be slain. So he stabbed himself. When Thisbe came back, and found his body, she hanged herself on the tree. Before that, mulberry fruit was white. It became black, in mourning, and has remained so."

"I had not heard that," he admitted. "A grievous tale. But you have stitched it well."

"None so well as I would have wished. Is Thisbe not too fat, above and below? How think you?"

He cleared his throat. "I . . . ah . . . I am scarce competent to judge. But it all seems to me most excellently pictured, contrived – how do you say it?"

"Limned, worked and stitched. *He* is better – but men are always easier to deal with than women, no?" She pointed again. "The other is a scene from our own doorstep, here. I think that I have given the cattle too great horns. And the mountains are too lofty."

"I am lost in admiration!" he declared, but he was looking more at the speaker than at her handiwork.

"There speaks one who may lack judgment!" she said, tapping his arm. "Now, your water up there will be cooling.

And victuals will be awaiting you. Aloft with you, our saviour-to-be!"

Escorting him to the door, she paused. "From what you have seen, so far, we stranger-Olifards whom you have come so far to aid will have to prove the worthiness you spoke of, I think?" she offered, as a parting-shot, and tripped off down the stairs.

Hugh foresaw that he was going to require more than the spears and sword he had brought, at this Arbuthnott.

That evening they discussed the boar problem. Sir Osbert asked whether it would be advantageous to arrange for numbers of helping hunters to assemble, in order to distract and possibly confuse the creature, thus assisting Hugh in his attempt; but Hugh thought not. No point in endangering others, to little or any benefit. Only he should seek to get close enough actually to stab the brute; and in these circumstances it would almost certainly ignore others anyway, concentrating on the man close by. So nothing was to be gained by others being present; indeed Hugh would prefer to be alone at it.

Once he was shown the location of the animal's den then, he would make his plans. The terrain on which the encounter would have to take place was important, the state of the ground. Boars preferred marshy wet land, their wide-spreading four-toed feet, all but webbed, enabling them to move swiftly through bog and swamp, despite their weight – and such terrain was not for horses, the hooves of which sank in. So, although a horse could be an advantage in the hunt, as far as speed and height were concerned, it would be necessary to lure the boar on to firm ground if possible.

Hugh's experience with the Smailholm beast had taught him a lesson. Some sort of barrier, of stones or bushes, narrow enough for a horse to jump or otherwise get through, could be a great help, so long as the boar followed on through, and did not manage to avoid and get round it, slowing up and confusing the creature and rendering its charge less dangerous, and subsequent attacks on it more feasible. So, if such an obstacle could be contrived on ground firm enough for a horse to cover at speed, and jump, it might be very useful.

But the boar might not so commit itself, preferring to lurk on soft ground. In which case an on-foot encounter would be necessary. Here, a prior exploration of the terrain would be almost essential, for on wet boggy land he, the man, would be at major disadvantage, himself sinking in, his movements cramped, when swift reaction was vital. So what would be looked for was some firm tract amidst the marshy area, where he could base himself against the boar's assault – not the easiest thing to find, perhaps. Some fairly close and careful examination of the ground, therefore, would be advisable. If the boar would permit this!

It was agreed that this should be attempted in the morning, with some of their men to help.

Margaret, who had listened to all this heedfully, now announced that she would accompany them on this first inspection. Hugh declared that to be unwise, her father knowing better than to do more than nod. She ignored both.

When it was bedtime, the young woman said that she was for off, and Hugh promptly added that it had been a long day and his own couch beckoned. So they left Sir Osbert to his own company.

As they climbed the round-tower stairs, the maid Gelis, a sonsy, bold-eyed, buxom creature, came down to inform Sir Hugh that his bed was prepared, more water was awaiting him, and a bite and a sup was there also. If he required anything more she was at his call, above.

Margaret smiled, halting at her own doorway. "Gelis is ever attentive," she informed. "Who knows how much care she might afford you, if you besought her! For myself, goodnight, Hugh – and dream of better game than boars!"

He was glad that she was naming him Hugh now, although a little disappointed, with the maid there, that he could hardly make any lingering leave-taking before she closed her door.

At the next landing, Gelis solicitously wondered whether there was anything else that he required of her? And when he said that he could think of nothing, she shrugged, laughing, and said that she would be down at sun-up, with more hot water. If he needed anything meantime, just to ring that bell and she would hear it above. He said his third goodnight and went within, very much aware of feminine presence below and aloft, this tending both to preoccupy and tantalise him, for he was an entirely normally made young man.

If he dreamed thereafter of such matters, it was not enough to awaken him, nor to be recollected in the morning.

18

In the morning, indeed, his awaking was such as to arouse its own reactions, finding his head being patted and stroked, and the division between a very adequate pair of female breasts presented to his opening eyes as Gelis, leaning over his bed, had her gown gaping somewhat. She declared that he slept soundly, and she had heard no call for her services overnight; that she had brought in the hot washing water, and here was a drink of warm honey wine to take the sleep out of him. Anything else that he could desire at this hour? She could light the fire for him if he wished, for warmth while he was bathing himself?

He mumbled that this would be unnecessary and that the room was warm enough; indeed, saying this, he realised that because of it he must have pushed the blankets down, and that therefore much of his nakedness was uncovered. He reached to pull them up, then thought better of it. Why so do? The young woman would not be averse to what she might see. Was it his imagination that Gelis almost reluctantly took herself off?

Washed and clad, he was downstairs and crossing the courtyard when a call from behind turned him. Margaret came, waving, to declare that she had slept later than usual. Had he had a good night? And survived Gelis's attentions?

Yawning, he told her that all had been very well and, greatly daring, that she looked too sparkling-eyed and lovely for this hour in the morning – at which she asserted that clearly he was still bemused by sleep.

Sir Osbert had already finished his breakfast, and left them to theirs, saying that he would go down and arrange for some of his men to have horses ready to accompany them in a preliminary and advisedly cautious inspection of the boar's area; that is, if de Swinton felt prepared to make a start on their project thus early?

"Hugh is barely awake," his daughter told him. "Aberrant! He is comparing my looks with beauty!"

The thane made his escape.

Over porridge, cream, smoked fish and honey, in an anteroom of the hall, hung with more tapestries, Hugh, none so sleepy, learned more of the art, being shown how, allegedly, Margaret's own efforts, displayed on one wall, did not compare with her mother's on another, although the man could see little difference in excellence. He suggested that, after all this, she might think to stitch one of a boar – that is, if the subject had not become too painful! He was duly reproved for the levity.

When it was their turn to go down to the cobbled yard – for Margaret was still determined to accompany this expedition – they found horses and half a dozen men assembled, Hugh's garron amongst them. He ensured that his spears and sword were there, although it was unlikely, it was thought, that he would require them this day.

Sir Osbert explained the programme. They would all ride down, on the higher ground of the east side of the Bervie Water, to above the Pitcarles Den, where they would survey the boar's accustomed terrain from well above. Assuming that the creature was not to be seen, Hugh and himself would go down on foot, but leading their horses lest a quick escape was called for, there to examine the ground more closely, whilst those above kept vigilant watch. They would look for the desired firm patches amongst the wet, riverside haughland and meadow, and see what could be done about creating the barrier of bushes Hugh had spoken of. He could then plan his tactics for the confrontation. Of course, if the boar emerged in the meantime, this all might not be possible, and they would have to adapt to circumstances as best they might. He had sent one mounted man down there already, to keep watch. But who could tell – the brute could already be ranging abroad, and this planning impracticable.

The party of nine rode off, and in no light-hearted fashion. It was apparent that the entire boar situation was very much

215

on all minds hereabouts, and a dread prevailing such as Hugh had never come across previously. This animal's ferocity was sufficient to intimidate an entire community. It must be a huge and particularly aggressive specimen.

It did not take them long to reach the specified area, approximately midway between the castle and the little church dedicated it seemed to St Ternan, one of the Columban brethren. There, on an eminence of the winding braeside bank, they found their scout waiting. He had nothing to report. There had been no sign of the boar, so at least the valley was clear, so far, for their inspection.

Sir Osbert pointed out to Hugh the area where the animal had its lair, down at a sharp bend in the river where there were not exactly cliffs but high banks of considerable naked red rock, scrub trees and bushes about the foot. Amongst all this were crannies, scarcely caves but inlets and re-entrants of the rock, in one of which the creature dwelt, exactly which no one had risked investigating. One brave herdsman had declared that he had got near enough to hear it snoring – but few took that as gospel.

All dismounted and the two knights armed themselves with Hugh's spears and swords – just in case. Margaret, warned beforehand that on no account was she to suggest coming with them, now announced that she would go halfway down, and so be in a position to see further up- and downstream than the pair could in the floor of the valley, and closer to them than the others above. The boar *could* be out hunting elsewhere, and might return while they were down there. So long as this was the limit of her involvement, her father relented.

The remainder of the party had their instructions. If the boar appeared while he and Sir Hugh were unprepared for it, they were to make diversionary moves, mounted, to try to distract and confuse the brute, to prevent it from attacking the two principals, if possible. Half a dozen horsemen weaving around, even though well out of harm's way, ought to have some effect.

Leading their mounts, the trio descended, very much on the alert. Part-way down, further so than they would have wished, the men found a sort of grassy terrace, on which they left the young woman.

The valley floor was fairly typical for a minor river close to the hills in upland country, winding and with many reedy water-meadows within the various bends. There was here a sufficiency of marshy ground for any boar, no lack of bushes of elder and thorn, but firm patches of any size would be less readily found. It was still only late March, and melting snows remained on the mountains where these streams' headwaters rose, so that the river was fairly full, and the overflowing less than dried out.

Picking their way, they commenced their search. Hugh was looking for somewhere reasonably close to the creature's den – for if there was to be a confrontation the boar must be made aware of his presence; but not too near, or he would have no room and time for manoeuvre. And a stretch of firmish ground, long enough for the garron at least to work up to a canter, was desirable. They recognised that these requirements would have been more easily met in high summer.

The valley floor widened and narrowed erratically, and the narrows were usually where the firmer ground was to be found. They came across one such quite quickly, but it was round a sharpish bend, and so was out of sight of the den area. Leading the horses and seeking to avoid the boggiest parts, they moved nearer. Keen as their searchings were, they were still more urgent in their glancings forward for the possible appearance of their quarry; also upwards, for signals from Margaret and the people higher, who might be able to see down for details which they could miss.

When Hugh felt that they were getting rather close to the lair vicinity, he began to wonder whether the other side of the river might prove better for their purposes. Boars would cross water, he knew, if they had to. He had never heard of one actually swimming, but they might do so. The question was, would this brute choose to cross if it saw him on the other side, or ignore him, put off by the water? There was a risk of this; and since in the end they had to come to close quarters, he decided that it was not worth trying, unless all else failed.

Olifard was clearly becoming apprehensive about this too-near approach. He pointed, as it were inland, to where a re-entrant of the valley probed rather deeper than did some. It would not matter if the battleground was well back from the river, would it? The animal would see him as well there as anywhere. And being slightly higher ground, it would be apt to be the firmer. Moreover, there were bushes up there.

Hugh agreed. With still no sign of the boar, they turned thitherwards. In fact a very small burnlet came down here, draining the re-entrant.

About one hundred yards up, they found a stretch which would serve, grass and turf rather than reeds and tussocks, solid enough for the garron's hooves, and enough of it to allow a cantering pace. This would do, then, still within easy sight of the den area.

Now the barrier. Sir Osbert hallooed and waved his men down, Hugh keeping his attention in the other direction. That halloo might well rouse and bring out a sleeping boar.

No doubt the summoned retainers were thinking the same thing as they rode down. But no boar appeared. Arriving, however watchfully, they were set to cut and dig up and heap bushes and brushwood, and gather stones, to form a crescent-shaped barricade, quite lengthy so that the quarry might not be tempted, it was hoped, to dodge or avoid it but to charge right on through; yet narrow enough for the horse to be able to leap it without disaster.

This took some time, and with still no emergence of the boar, Margaret came along to join them.

Something of a council of war followed. The animal might not be there at all, today, hunting far afield. It possibly could have another lair elsewhere, though no one had ever suggested such a thing. There could be a female boar, a sow, which it might visit on occasion – the creatures never, as it were, cohabited. Was there any point, therefore, in waiting here now?

Hugh decided that he must at least attempt something, make some closer investigation, possibly tempting the creature out, if it was indeed there. He told the others to wait, to be ready to ride off if the animal appeared, leaving him to deal with it. When Margaret objected that this would be shameful, craven, he pointed out that it was best for him, as for them. He wanted no distraction, at this stage, for the brute, his aim to lure it after him alone, and towards this barrier, not possibly dashing off after other prey. Doubtfully that was accepted.

So, leading the garron, he moved off down to the riverside again, and there turned upstream. He went cautiously now, needless to say, wary indeed. How close dare he go? And with the horse? Around the lair area pointed out to him was much fallen rock, boulders, with stunted hawthorns. He did not want to get caught in that, with the garron, and an angry boar on its own ground.

He did get nearer and nearer, with no developments. Unfortunately he did not know, any more than anyone else, the exact location of the den in possibly ten score yards of rugged braefoot here. It would not do to go *past* the place, and possibly be trapped.

He risked going about halfway along amongst the tumbled rocks, the horse's hooves clinking and scraping on the stone, enough noise to arouse the most well-fed boar surely. If it emerged behind him, would the river be his best escape route . . . ?

But nothing happened – and he certainly heard no swinish snorting. Not knowing whether to be relieved or disappointed, he turned back. There was to be no confrontation this day.

A return was made to the castle, reactions varied. Sir Osbert ordered his men to go around telling the local folk that any sighting of the boar was to be reported to him without delay.

Margaret suggested that their guest might like to see that they had more than unforthcoming swine to show at Arbuthnott and neighbourhood. It was a notable area for Pictish relics and monuments. And the Highland foothills were spectacular, the coastline also. So that afternoon the three of them went riding again, this time in the other direction, northwards into the higher country. The young woman appeared to be something of an authority on the mysterious Picts, or Cruithne, as she declared that they should really be called, pict or pictori being merely a name the Roman invaders had given them because they had a pictorial rather than a written language, using symbols instead of letters. Cruithne meant wheat-growers, which was significant, she asserted, in that it revealed that they were a settled, land-cultivating people, not barbaric nomads as many assumed – and their cultivation in more than the soil. All Scots ought to know a great deal more about their ancestors, she claimed.

Hugh was suitably humble on the subject.

As they rode, he also learned about Sir Osbert's position, he being unsure just what thanedom represented. He was told that it was a very ancient title and office, royally bestowed, and often hereditary. Under the early Celtic, indeed Pictish, mormaors or sub-kings, who had developed into earls, thanes were deputies, more or less combining the offices of governor of provinces and justiciars. To some extent that still applied, although the justiciary side of it was the more important now, he having all the Mearns in which to see justice done, a large area. But he still had non-justiciar functions to perform. For instance, if the King required armed forces to be raised here, it was the thane's task to muster them, and either lead them himself or appoint a lieutenant. And if any man was forfeited by the crown or outlawed, it fell to the thane to apprehend him, if possible. Duties of that sort. They held their appointment directly of the monarch, as heritors under the crown. He was Baron of Arbuthnott as well, of course, and to some extent the two responsibilities intermeshed.

His daughter declared that he sounded like the terror of all wrong-doers; whereas in fact he was far too soft with most of them.

However, she was more concerned that their visitor should be informed as to their Pictish heritage, for they all, even Mersemen, had some Cruithne blood in their veins, for was not King Loth, St Mungo's grandsire who gave name to Lothian, a Southern Pict, and his rule extended down to the Merse? Did they have no stone circles and standing-stones down there?

Hugh admitted that he had seen a few monoliths in the

Lammermuirs, and near Haddington, supposedly all that was left of stone circles. There was a hill called Nine Stanes Rig where they summer-pastured their Swinton sheep, where there was a circle. And they had a broch, which he understood to be a Pictish, circular refuge-tower and fort, on Cockburn Law near the Whiteadder.

This last much interested Margaret, for she had never seen a broch although she had heard of them. There was none that she or her father knew of in this area. She demanded details.

Hugh's description of a great round stone tower, like some mighty beehive, with walls say fifteen feet thick but honeycombed to provide little mural chambers within, and stairs winding up to a parapet, was interrupted by their arrival at their first relic, not a circle this one but an isolated, free-standing monolith on a little mound, possibly a gravestone, splendidly carved with peculiar but artistic symbols and figures. There was an odd, prancing animal, with a curling tail instead of hind legs and a sort of trunk coming out of its forehead. Below that a crescent moon pierced by an arrow broken in three parts, like a Z. Then two linked breast-like circles, with another broken arrow in the form of a V. And finally the figure of a man in some sort of armour, with a very pointed beard, holding a sword and shield. On the other side of the stone was typical Celtic interlaced decoration.

They examined this and debated what it all might possibly mean, for obviously it must have some significance, the symbols themselves and possibly the order of placing, for much careful work had gone into the carving of it all. Olifard thought that it probably represented the grave of some clan chieftain, and these strange devices identification. But the young woman objected that these same symbols appeared on other stones she knew of, and so must have a wider application.

They pressed on, to climb to the grass-grown ramparts of a hill-fort, this enclosing quite a wide area, four defensive rings with ditches between. Margaret said that there would have been a timber stockade, probably, within the central space where they were able to distinguish the stony foundations of huts. The all-round view from this fort was magnificent,

221

to the blue of the Highland mountains on one side, and the equally blue sea on the other.

But the young woman was pointing to much nearer at hand where, crowning a lesser eminence not far off, were the upright columns of a stone circle, eleven of these standing although one or two reeled somewhat: the sun-worship temple of the community which this fort had defended, she asserted.

They went down to inspect this, and discussed the alignment of the stones relative to the solstices, the notions of the sun-worshipping druids, and St Columba's contention that they were in fact only paying homage to the Unknown God through the sun which warmed and produced fertility, with their curious harvest, procreative, Yuletide and other rites, not forgetting grim human sacrifice.

They visited other reminders of the distant past before the sinking sun sent them back to Arbuthnott, with Hugh taking the opportunity to suggest that, if they wanted to see a broch, the Olifards should pay a visit to his house at Aldcambus, where they would be more than welcome, and he would take them to Edin's Hall, as it had come to be named.

They arrived back at the castle to learn that the boar had indeed been seen, down near St Ternan's Church, by a gravedigger, who had promptly fled. So the morrow might prove more productive of events.

That evening, after a worthy repast they enjoyed a relaxing spell before the hall fire, with Margaret playing the lute and the clarsach, and singing to it, Hugh even venturing on a couple of Border ballads, to tentative but helpful accompaniment.

When he mentioned his couch, she said that Gelis ought to have all in readiness for him; but she would accompany him so far. Her father wished his guest a good night's sleep, since he might need it in the morning!

"How do you think of this struggle with the boar?" the young woman asked as they crossed the courtyard in the dark. "It is a challenge, I can perceive. But do you have to summon up all your resolution? Dread it? Or seek to put it all from your mind? If you can?"

That was hard to answer. "I do not dread it, I think. But I

do not take it lightly either. I am well aware of the dangers, but believe that I ought to be able to deal with this creature. It has brute-strength, yes, cunning and fierceness. But a man's wits it has not got. Nor . . . a little faith perhaps!"

"Other men have not outwitted it."

"I have had some training and experience. Say that I am hopeful, but not over-confident."

"That could be said of us all, I think. I, I fear for you, Hugh."

"You are kind. But do not let it trouble you. I can always flee if the pace gets too hot!"

"Can you? *Would* you?" She gripped his arm, shook it. "Am I to believe that?"

He wagged his head, silent.

At her room's door she paused. "Upstairs, Gelis will be awaiting you. That one can offer more than hot water and bedside provision! You have but to give the sign."

"You judge that I would? Or should?"

"I judge you a lusty man, for more than boar-fighting."

"And . . . ?"

"And men interest me, yes. As well as tapestry and Picts!"

"Aye. Your father says that you have many suitors."

"Does he? Not suitors, I say. That takes the matter too far. But not a few men could consider wedding the thane's daughter and heiress!"

"M'mm. I, I am warned!"

"A woman learns about men, and needs to. Goodnight, Hugh de Swinton. I shall not be listening to hear sounds from your chamber above!"

"I hope that I do not snore!" he said, in an attempt to show that two could play this game.

She laughed as she closed her door on him.

Upstairs, Gelis was indeed there. "Ha, sir – you didna see yon boar, then? Och, you'll be right disjaskit. But mind, there's mair to 'Buthnott than boars!" She gestured within, and preceded him in. "The bed's made, the fire's lit, and the can'les. Your tankard's yonder. And the water's hot. You'll want a wash-doon after a' yon riding?"

"You are very kind, Gelis."

"Och, it's easier to be kind to some folk than others, just! A man, even if he hasna killt yon boar, needs a bit hand noo and then! Unable to wash your back, no? It's no' easy to wash your ain back, is it?"

He eyed her with a twisted smile. "You would *wish* to wash my back for me?"

"Why for no'? You canna dae it yoursel'."

"Very well, since you are so kind. I can judge that you will be good at it!"

Her chuckle was throaty as she moved over to the steaming tub.

Hugh was quite prepared for her to come and assist him to undress, but she seemed to be content to watch, while throwing another log on the fire.

Unclad, he made for the tub, not embarrassed but aware that he was being assessed if not necessarily admired. But no harm in giving a little pleasure, if this was indeed the case. He tested the water, and stepped in.

She came promptly, solicitous that the water was not too hot for him. "You wouldna want to get scauded," she declared, stooping down to her task, and not precisely at the rear.

Helpfully he turned round. "I can serve the front very well," he assured, rather concerned that her forward-leaning posture and wide-necked bodice did not produce reaction from him which might affect the washing process behind.

Gurgling, Gelis went to work with cloth, expertise and enthusiasm, generous in her interpretation of back-washing. Hugh, accordingly, had to adjust his stance not infrequently.

That ablution seemed to take quite some time. Was he so begrimed? After all, he had had a wash the night before. Not on his back, of course.

Then he had to be dried, and thoroughly, involving more handiwork. When at length he might step out of the tub, before making for the bed he thought to snuff out the candles, although whether that would be rightly interpreted he was unsure.

"Och, there's plenties o' licht frae the fire," Gelis commented.

He lay down and carefully covered himself with the blankets, as she came to look down on him.

"My thanks. And a very goodnight to you," he said, with what he hoped was a note of finality.

She raised her brows at him, leaning forward. "Is there nae mair I can dae for you, then?"

"I thank you, no, Gelis. I, I am weary. And tomorrow will be a big day for me, belike. Off with you."

"I wouldna hae thocht you were *that* weary!" she told him, with a shrugging of more than just shoulders. "Och, weel – I'm just upbye if you canna sleep and need a bit help at it." And rearranging his blankets carefully as he had done himself, which brought her warm feminine aura and invitation notably close to his face and nose, she smiled and left him.

As the door slammed behind her, he wondered what Margaret was thinking of it downstairs, for she, listening or not, could not have failed to hear that exit. He had heard, of course, of Highland hospitality . . .

It took him a little while to sleep; but at least it was not boar-slaying that was on his mind.

In the morning, wakened as before to helpful ministrations and enquiries as to well-being and weariness, Hugh found Margaret and her father at the breakfast table. His eye was caught semi-humorously, with one uplifted brow, by the young woman, he declaring firmly that he had had a good night and was ready for the fray. Sir Osbert took him up on that, even if the daughter did not.

"How would you have it today?" he asked. "The same as before? Men mounted on the higher ground, ready to make diversion if need be? Assistance? Efforts to coax out the boar, perhaps?"

"Could that be done, sir, without endangering the coaxers?"

"I think that it could. Using the ground to advantage. The braeside above the brute's den. It is steep, all but a cliff. Two men, up there, shouting, throwing down rocks. It would be roused, hear, scent them. Come out. If it *is* there today. It could not climb up to them, so they would be safe. But if you were down at the riverside, waiting, it would see you. And so probably seek to attack you. As you would have it."

"That is a good device, yes. Well thought on. And if the men kept on shouting . . ."

"Yes, that might distract the boar somewhat and make it less determined," Margaret suggested.

"No-o-o. I think not. I *want* the creature to be intent on me. So that I can lure it to my barrier. Once it is out, no distractions. Unless . . ."

"Unless you are endangered. Your plan failing. Then you might be glad of it."

"Perhaps, yes. Whether shouting, behind, would serve, who knows . . . ?"

Presently, the men assembled again below, the party moved down as before to the den area. Would the animal be in residence today?

They followed the same procedure, Margaret going down to her halfway terrace and Sir Osbert accompanying Hugh further, but not quite to the waterside. No sign of the boar as yet.

Leaving Olifard well behind the barrier they had made, Hugh, leading his garron, moved forward, perhaps most of the way to the lair vicinity, cautiously, on softish ground here, ready for instant action. After waiting a short while, he turned and waved to Sir Osbert, who in turn hallooed to the men waiting higher. Two of these dismounted and moved some little way downhill to the head of the rocky bank above the den. Soon they were lost to sight, but after an interval their shouting rang out, followed by the thud and crash of falling rocks.

Spear in hand, sword at side, Hugh stood.

The men's shouting continued — until abruptly it was drowned out by another sound, a great, snuffling roaring. Out from the bushes below the bank surged their quarry, at last, in angry reaction.

Hugh, prepared as he was for this, was shaken by what

226

confronted him. Never had he seen so large a boar as this, almost black save for white gleaming tusks, massive of shoulder, long of snout, solid as a Highland bull. Here was challenge indeed.

The brute, at the waterside, cast about, obviously seeking the source of the noise and disturbance and falling stones. Summoning all his hardihood, Hugh raised his own voice, to add to the din.

That had its results. The boar turned, saw him, and without any delay lowered its head to come charging, bellowing its loudest. And the garron, seeing also, reared in fright and would have swung round and back had not Hugh urgently restrained it. Normally an amenable although quite spirited animal, so chosen for the task, it was as alarmed as its master by what it saw.

Hastily Hugh mounted. He did not have to rein his mount round, his task to hold it back from dashing off too soon and fast. He had to let the boar get reasonably close so that it would not have time and inclination to swerve and encircle that barrier to which he was leading it.

That proved to be the least of his problems, for the boar advanced on them at an extraordinary speed considering its size, weight and short legs, and quickly it was in fact all too close, snarling as it came.

Swinging slightly uphill to reach the firmer ground, Hugh glanced back over his shoulder. The creature was about fifty yards behind. He could let his mount canter, then. The barrier was around three times that distance ahead.

Now the trouble was that the garron in its alarm was heading to avoid the said barrier and had to have its head forcefully reined round to keep it on the right line. The ground was still soft enough to limit its speed, and another glance behind showed the boar catching up. This was going to be a race indeed.

With only one hundred and fifty yards to go mere seconds were involved. Quickly he ensured that there was no chance of his mount avoiding the bush barrier; and knowing it, the animal increased its pace to the fastest possible, not far off a gallop, with the need for the long, high jump, and the growling behind spurring it on.

Hugh, spear firm in his right hand, loosened his sword with the left, holding his breath.

That barricade loomed up, and at the first crackle of sticks and twigs beneath its hooves, the garron took off. With the speed reached, it made a good, long leap, landing heavily amongst the last layer of brushwood. There it stumbled on the obstruction, but recovered itself, and plunged on.

Now the crux – or the beginning of it. To wrench the fleeing horse round to face the oncoming peril. Savagely Hugh jerked and pulled. The garron only part turned, to plunge on. Desperately he tugged, shouting his commands. Still only partially his mount responded, against all its will and instinct. But the man kept up the pressure, dragging and heeling. He got the animal far enough round to see the boar crashing its way through the brushwood, pace duly, inevitably, slowed but its course nowise diverted.

Stabbing-spear poised, ready, Hugh sought to control his sidling, dancing, terrified horse, to urge it forward now, directly at the boar, twenty yards away.

Perhaps it was too much to expect of any horse, even this one which had faced the Smailholm boar. But this brute was half as large again, and more ferociously noisy, snarling threat. The garron reared high on its hind legs, forefeet pawing the air, determined to turn back. Seeking to impose his will on it and at the same time watching the boar and couching his spear, Hugh rose in his saddle, tense; and as he did so, his mount did what it had never done before: it brought down its forelegs and bucked with its hind, throwing its rider. The man, unbalanced, fell heavily to the ground. The garron wheeled round and fled.

Landing with a numbing crash, Hugh desperately summoned every sense in him. The boar had burst out of the bushes now and was heading straight for him. What to do? Get up and run? He would not outrun that creature. Stand and face it, with the spear? Rushing him, its weight would knock him over, for sure. Down on the ground, as he was, better? Flat, less of a target for the brute. On his back, spear ready to strike? He would be trampled on, but . . . ? Those tusks! Flat, left arm over face, spear up. Sword no use. Could not draw it in time, wield it. Spear only . . .

All this flashed through his mind in the instants left to him. Then the boar was on him, roaring, head down, tusks menacing.

Probably it was Hugh's good fortune that the brute, incensed by the delays of the bushes, had sought to regain its fast rush, and so hurtled on the recumbent man at major force and speed. So that, in fact, it could by no means stop at him, but plunged on over him, those curious claw-feet striking, stamping on him. A blessing, too, that its tusks thrust upwards from its lower jaw, not downwards, and at that pace could not make contact with the man lying flat. The arm over his face protected Hugh from the sharp feet, and he was barely aware, at the time, of the trampling weight on his body, swiftly over as it was. He tried an upward thrust of the spear, but if it grazed the brute's hide, that was all.

But now? It would be only moments before it would be back to rend him, for it was surely unlikely that it would choose to pursue the fleeing horse when it had a stationary victim available. And this time it could come in less of a rush, be more effective. How best to receive it? To save himself, if scarcely actively to assail the brute? Remain lying? Or kneel? On his feet he would be knocked over, for sure. Lying flat had seemed to show him the beast at its least effective. On his stomach, then? For better use of the spear? Could he . . . ?

That was as much debate with himself as he was given time for. The boar had checked its rush, turned, and was coming back at him. The urge was to get up and run. But that would be folly. The animal, outrunning him, would throw him down from behind and savage him. Best this way, flat, ready.

In snorting, snoring rage the boar bore down on him. He was aware of the little, gleaming pig's eyes, its working snout, the stiff bristles of its mighty shoulders, even the stench of it – but most of all, its wide-open jaws, sharp dog-teeth and those tusks.

As it came at him in sheerest fury, Hugh raised himself on one elbow only sufficiently to give maximum thrust to his spear, and then hurled it directly at those gaping jaws. And he heard the clatter of it striking home, even above the grunting snarl, as he flung himself flat again, both arms now above head and neck.

Then the creature was trampling over him, sharp claws on his back. But even in the state he was in, Hugh realised that this trampling was different, not only in that it was slower but that it was to one side, somehow twisted, direction less sure. He hardly felt the pains in his back as he recognised that he had survived this charge also, that the brute now plunged on part-sideways. Had his spear indeed saved him, then?

Twisting round to peer over his shoulder, still flat, he saw the spear. The boar was dragging it, from one of its humped shoulders, its shaft trailing along the ground. It had missed the open mouth, struck a tusk perhaps, and plunged on into the hide thus. And changed in some measure the line of the creature's assault.

But even as he looked the brute shook itself and the spear fell out on to the grass.

So, now? The boar was obviously not seriously wounded and it would be but further enraged. And he had no spear. Could he draw his sword from its sheath then, in time, lying as he was? And wield it? He would need to stand. One sword-slash would not serve to disable an animal with that leathery, bristle-protected hide. The spear-point had penetrated, but not gone in deeply.

The boar was stationary now, shaking itself, as though it still had the spear in it, like some mere irritant. Then, snorting horribly, it turned back to face him again. Hugh uttered a silent prayer.

The creature lowered its head to charge once more, then raised it again, turning it. And with reason. An alternative target had appeared, a horseman riding down towards it – Sir Osbert. Indeterminate for moments, the animal stood, swaying. Then, roaring, it chose to transfer its fury to this new challenge. It commenced another charge.

230

Kneeling now, Hugh blessed Olifard, and at the same time called him a fool. If his own tough garron would not face this menace, what hope was there for a blood-bred horse? This was crazy-mad . . .

Clearly that horse thought the same. As the boar came on, it did the same as Hugh's mount had done, reared, skidding not to a halt but a swerve, and sought to turn, all but unseating its rider. Flail and tug as Sir Osbert would, his mount knew better. It plunged off at right angles, the other animal in pursuit.

Hugh got to his feet and stared, shaking his head. Then the thud of more hooves, approaching ones not departing, jerked his head round. And there was the other Olifard, the female one, riding down on him, hair streaming, beating fist on her horse's rump. He gulped, in further astonishment, horror indeed.

"Hugh – up! Up behind me!" Margaret yelled, while still some score of yards off. "Quick! Up!"

"No! No!" he yelled back. "Go! Get away!"

"Dolt! Mount! Quick!" She pulled up her all but panicking horse, reining it round and leaning down, hand out to assist him.

Hugh recognised that he would be dolt indeed not to do as she ordered, this stage reached. He threw a swift glance left-handed, and saw that the boar was still chasing Sir Osbert, but with the ground rising the horse was increasing its distance. It would be only moments before the brute changed course, to return to softer, more favourable terrain and easier quarry – himself, and now Margaret. Nodding, he shouted.

"Yes. But my spear!"

"Leave it! Leave it!"

But he had run to pick up the weapon – for well might they need it. Then he turned, to find the horse alongside again and all but dancing in its agitation. He reached up to grasp Margaret's outstretched hand and, hampered as he was by the spear, somehow managed to grip the back of the saddle, and with a mighty effort hoisted himself awkwardly up. The horse plunged off, the man clinging to the young woman's person.

Margaret did not have to urge her overloaded mount to hasten, and as far away from the boar as it could go, without getting bogged down in the soft ground. Racing, it headed for Margaret's terrace-stance. Both the Olifards' horses had a strong instinct for self-protection, whatever their owners'.

Panting, Hugh clutched his rescuer, protested that she ought not to have come, endangering herself – to back-thrown comments as to his sanity if he thought that she could have sat there and allowed him to be savaged by the animal. He was grateful, of course, but also humiliated – he, the boar-slayer! It was difficult, in the circumstances, especially with her long blown hair in his face and mouth, to justify his position.

Giving up the trying, it came to him that here he was, arms round the waist of this attractive female, something well beyond his hopes of an hour or so before.

They rode on up to where the group of men waited, watching, Sir Osbert and Hugh's garron already there. All pointed down towards the river, where the boar could be seen rooting around, the chase abandoned. Almost reluctantly now, Hugh exchanged Margaret's saddle for his own, however much he frowned at his garron. Without discussion all turned back, for castle and castleton, drama sufficient for one day.

Subsequent discussion there was, in the castle, and it did not lack averment, detail, question and explanation, with averment foremost; on the Olifard side that this must end their visitor's boar-baiting, and on Hugh's that it must not, quite heated becoming the altercation. Hugh, under the pressure of so spectacular failure, was determined, and the young woman in especial vehement. He asserted that he had learned much of value from his day's experiences; she that he seemed to have learned only little if he insisted on going on with this folly. For his part, her father declared that, as it were hand-to-hand combat was obviously hopeless, in the circumstances, it seemed to him that the bow and arrow was the only solution. This had been tried, of course, more than once, but the archers always too far off, for their safety's sake but also for the arrows to penetrate the boar's tough hide.

However, the bush barrier contrivance of Hugh's had given him the notion that it might be possible, if they could erect a very different kind of barrier, of stout timbers, high enough for the archers to hide behind and the boar unable to get over. Then they could shoot arrows at the close range required, near enough to penetrate. It would have to be a fairly lengthy barrier, admittedly, for the boar not to get round it . . .

Hugh asked how this construction was to be put in place? It would have to be built somewhere that the boar could be expected to approach, or there would be no point in it. That meant down on the low ground near the river. Was that feasible? To be effective, it would have to demand quite a deal of building. And what would the boar be doing while the timber was being brought down and the barrier erected? What would the builders think of that? Yet to construct it anywhere up on the high ground, they might well find the brute never came near it.

Sir Osbert had no ready answer to that, and his daughter agreed that it was impracticable. But, apart from his declared folly of making another single-handed attempt at it, had Hugh any better proposal?

He said that he had various thoughts on the matter, not yet fully thrashed out. But he would be a match for that brute yet, God willing!

She shook her head over him. Then, pointing, she declared that he was bending forward in his chair, not leaning back. Was he hurt? In pain?

Nothing grievous, he assured. Just the boar's hooves, or claws. A bruise or two, possibly . . .

"We shall see about that!" she asserted.

Sure enough, when it came to bed-time, and they crossed to the rear tower as before, Margaret had not forgotten. At the first-floor landing, she did not pause but proceeded on higher.

"Tonight I am not leaving Gelis to attend on you," she announced. "This of your back, I say, may call on some caring."

"It will be well enough," he declared, man-like – and was ignored.

Gelis was waiting at his own open door, and raised eyebrows at the sight of her mistress.

"Sir Hugh has a hurt back," she was told. "Go you down to my chamber, Gelis, and fetch me up the unguent and salve which I keep in the little kist by my bed. And bring some clean cloth also." And to the man, leading him into the candle- and fire-lit room: "Now, have off your doublet and shirt, my so-stalwart friend, and we shall see what the enemy has done to you!"

Hugh wagged his head, but began to do as he was told. His doublet was of soft tanned leather – which probably had saved him from much worse injury. But he winced as he got down to the silken shirt, the fabric of it sticking to his back at first.

"So-o-o! A bruise or two! Hugh, the skin is broken. You have been bleeding. This should have been looked to . . ."

"It is nothing . . ."

"Come over to the light."

With a mixture of protest at the fuss, and male satisfaction at the concern and intimate attention for his person displayed by this particular young woman, Hugh allowed himself to be examined, and, when Gelis returned with the ointment and salves, ministered to, the abrasions washed from the steaming water of the tub and then sponged and anointed. He drew the line, however, at permitting a cloth to be wrapped around his torso as bandaging for mere scratches as he termed them – although he could not see them for himself. If the unguents rubbed off on his blankets, so be it.

Gelis stood by the tub, obviously anticipating another comprehensive washing process. But somehow the man was not prepared to accept that, to appear quite naked in front of this Margaret. Just why, he could not have said. Was that ridiculous? For the servitor-woman, it had not mattered. But the thane's daughter, to whom he was much drawn, and whose own person he would have found delectable indeed to survey – that was somehow different. Hypocrite he might be, but that was how he felt.

"I will forgo the bathing tonight," he announced, taking the cloth from Margaret and making a demonstration of

234

dipping it in the water and washing his face and hands with it.

Gelis all but hooted a laugh, but her mistress nodded, seemingly understandingly.

"Then we will leave you to bed yourself and snuff out your own candles," Margaret said. "I hope that your back does not keep you from sleep. And that in the morning you will have wiser thoughts about that boar! A goodnight to you, Hugh." And she touched his arm lightly. "Come, Gelis."

He saw them out, only half naked, with thanks.

Thereafter, taking off his breeches, he discovered no more abrasions, although of course he could not see his buttocks; he could feel no broken skin there. There was blue bruising on his right thigh in two places. He hoped that it would not stiffen up for the morning.

It was quite some time before he slept.

19

Hugh's legs and back were actually sorer when he arose than they had been the night before, but the pain was quite bearable and certainly insufficient to prevent him from attempting his determined duel with the boar. He made that clear as soon as he arrived at the breakfast-table.

"This day we shall seek to come to a conclusion with our swinish foe!" he declared, lightly but decidedly.

"You are sure, man?" Sir Osbert said. "You are concerned to try again? And feel able to make the attempt? In your person."

"I do . . ."

"I say that it is not only foolhardy but wrong!" Margaret declared. "Tempting God, who spared you yesterday. Forby, you are holding yourself a trifle bent, Hugh. You are in pain?"

"Only a little stiff. That will wear off. And perhaps the boar will also be a little stiff this morning! From my spear-thrust at its shoulder."

"How think you to go about it, this time . . . ?"

"Do not encourage him, Father! It is a madness. It could cost him his life!"

"So could many another matter, such as we all essay at times!" Hugh asserted. "But I have thought well on this. After yesterday. See you, the creature charges open-mouthed, roaring. There is possibility in that. I brought my sleeve-gauntlets. If I could use one, on my left arm, toughened, wrapped in further leather, for the brute's jaws to clamp on, then I could stab in deeply with the short spear, stab and stab!"

"But the creature's weight, man!"

"Aye, there's the trouble. I would be knocked over, quite.

And I need to be standing, to gain fullest force of the spear. I learned that yesterday, lying flat. I do not think the sword to be of any use. So, I will require a support. Behind me. Not a man, no, but some firm buttress, stay, which I can lean against. A tree-trunk. Or better, a rock, a great stone. Otherwise I will go down. This came to me in my bed, last night."

"My barricade, which I suggested? For hiding archers? Of timber . . ."

"The brute would not stand idle while that was put up. No, something already there. A hawthorn tree, perhaps? There are some on the low ground. One large enough to lean back against. Or an upstanding rock. There are fallen rocks near the creature's lair. If I could get to one there, before it charged to attack me, using the gauntlet and then the spear, I think that I might win this battle!"

"Or be crushed to death against your rock!" Margaret countered.

"Not if I could strew smaller stones just in front. A rickle of them. Enough to make the boar stumble, lessen its charge somewhat. Such might already be there, below that brae. I judge now that I made a mistake before in seeking to achieve it mounted and out on open ground. Better near the lair itself, amongst the rocks and bushes. And with no horse to bolt."

Olifard looked doubtful. "This would mean you getting very close. Gain no warning when it came out at you. If you could get there unseen, in the first place. Little time to find a rock to serve you. And stones to gather."

"I know it. But I could make a first view from above, from the brae-head. Without the brute knowing. Then move on down, quietly. Gain a fair position before it heard or scented me. If that was possible, I would be ready for it."

"Let us hope that the wretched animal is away, as it must have been two days ago," the girl said.

"I think probably not. Slightly wounded as it is, it will be apt to keep to its den."

"What help can we give you in this?" her father asked.

237

"Little, I think, sir – if any. Indeed, I would want no folk about, to disturb the brute. Silence is best."

"You think that we will allow you to go alone down there, possibly to be slain, and not so much as come to try to rescue you, at the least!" Margaret exclaimed.

"So long as no one disturbs the boar . . ."

"See you," Sir Osbert said. "If some of us were at the other side of the Bervie. On the higher ground there, wooded ground. Out of sight. And the noise of the waterfalls would prevent the boar hearing us. Then, if you were in trouble, we could ride down, and across the river. It is not deep, for horses."

"Very well. And can you supply me with some leather strapping? To toughen my gauntlet."

"That at least I can do – if you are so set on this folly," Margaret said. "You can show me what you need . . ."

So, presently, preparations made, the company parted, Hugh to go on alone, afoot, with his spear, dirk and gauntlet, down the north side of the Bervie Water valley, the Olifards and some of their men to ride round, cross the ravine of the Neithe Burn, and so reach the south side. The leave-taking was inevitably somewhat fraught, with many injunctions as to care, not to continue with it one moment longer than was necessary if matters went awry, as they probably would, to throw himself into the river as an escape, and so on, Margaret, in her concern, leaving him in a state of something like anger.

With very mixed emotions himself, Hugh strode off.

He found his way down to the head of the knoll with its all but cliff-like side, above the river, treading cautiously now, anxious not to make a sound, to crack a twig, using his spear to clear his way amongst the undergrowth. As near the edge as he dared go, he peered over and down.

With the bushes and scrub hawthorn down there, it was difficult to make out what might be suitable rocks, upright or otherwise. What was evident from up here was that there *were* a lot of rock-falls, and so probably many smaller stones also. And there was no sign of movement, boar or other. So far, so good.

Something else Hugh perceived. He did not know exactly where to look for the boar's lair in that stretch of perhaps two hundred yards; but it might be better to go down and approach from the other side from heretofore, from the west, not the east. There appeared to be more trees and cover in that direction; and if the brute did hear or sense his presence, it would not be so apt to see him so soon as it would by his approach over the open ground. He would try that. So far, he could see no glimpse of the Olifard party opposite.

So moving along, gingerly he began his descent. Picking his way with extreme care, since any slip, fall or noise might ruin everything, he crept down, thankful for the spear as prod and support. Every few feet he paused, to listen. He heard only the noise of the cascading water.

He reached the foot. The hawthorns were, of course, not yet in leaf, but they provided a sufficiency of cover, with their closeness and the thicket of their branches. As to the rocks, there was a profusion, of all sizes and shapes. Quickly he perceived that the trees would not serve in the supporting role: he should have realised that hawthorns sprouted branches and twigs much too near the ground to allow him to back up against one, with any useful effect, save by cutting and trimming, which was scarcely possible here and now. So it must be a rock.

Now, where was the lair? No sounds came to guide him. He would just have to move slowly, quietly forward, looking, listening – and hoping to find a rock suitable for his purpose. Actually, he judged, the nearer he was to the den itself, the better probably, for that would give the beast less time to make its own decisions and to work up a charge. And the creature must be able to *see* him, in all this cover . . .

He did discover a lump of rock which might suit, almost as high as himself and reasonably flat to rest his back against. Casting about, he saw that there were many stones of different sizes lying about nearby. Still as silent as he could be, he stooped to gather as many of these as he could, to litter a few feet in front of his chosen rock, in a sort of semicircle. Thus far he seemed to be entirely on his own.

He was at least being given time to create his stumbling-block protection.

But with no developments, he began to wonder whether the boar was indeed there this day? He decided that mere waiting would serve him nothing, indeed possibly produce doubts, agitation in him. So, taking a deep breath, he raised his voice and uttered a loud and long halloo.

He was surprised at the immediacy of the reaction. Almost before he had finished, a rumbling growl sounded, and continued, and from very near at hand. Had the animal been waiting, ready? Was he so close to its den? At least the noise was not coming from behind him, which had been a fear.

With a trampling rush the brute appeared from his half-left, not thirty yards away, having perceived him at once. It came, head down, jaws wide, snarling and grunting. Hugh gripped his spear tightly, well down the shaft, and raised his thickly gauntleted left arm, as ready as he was able to be.

The beast accelerated remarkably in the short distance it had to cover. But quickly it was into Hugh's stones, and they had their effect, causing it to slip and stumble and lose pace. But it came on, anger in every bristling inch of it. The man crouched, tense, left arm out.

Stones barrier notwithstanding, the eventual contact was shocking, the impact literally breathtaking, hurling Hugh back against his rock. He would have been bowled right over without the solid support, however much it pained his already sore back. But pain, just then, was not on his mind; action was.

The boar had reared up at him. With its wide-open mouth puffing stench at him, he thrust that gauntleted arm down, with all his strength, to get past the creature's upwards-pointing tusks, half winded as he was by the collision. He felt the jaws snap down on the leather in vice-like grip, and hold there, those little eyes so near his own, gleaming menace. And, panting for air, he drove in his spear, with utmost thrust, as nearly as he could gauge just behind the massive shoulder, where the heart should be, the spearhead duly sharpened for this moment. It penetrated, and thankfully he felt it go

240

deep. Also he felt the animal convulse, wilt, and slide a little sideways.

Desperately he sought to drag out the weapon for a second plunge, pulled over as he was by the sagging weight of the boar. Not entirely successful because of the toughness of the brute's hide which caught on the metal of the blade, he had merely to drive it in again at what he hoped was a different angle, drive in deeper still.

Then he realised that he was falling, toppling over, unable to sustain the weight on his left side, his arm still clamped tightly in those jaws. Down he crashed, dizzy with pain and lack of breath, in sprawling collapse, only just aware of what was happening, the spear jerked out of his grip by the fall.

Awareness, when it came, brought with it a surge of hope. He realised that there were two collapses, the boar's as well as his own – and that he was on top. The creature, partly beneath him, was jerking its legs and heaving, making snorting noises, but these were different, more throaty, more gasps than menace. And then the man felt his left arm freed, all but numb as it was within the gauntlet.

Somehow he rolled over and staggered to his feet.

The boar did not, but lay, thrashing those short legs.

In a flood of emotion, relief, thankfulness, almost disbelief, Hugh stared down at his foe. The boar was by no means dead. It was convulsing, its breathing gulps and gasps, but it was not rising, nor seeming to try to do so.

The man stooped, to draw out the spear, which itself was waving and jerking. He got it free, and with swift calculation drove it down once more, exactly to where he judged the animal's heart to be.

Whether or not his previous thrusts had indeed made the vital penetration he did not know, although they had clearly had major effect. But this fierce and potent stab most evidently found its mark. The great beast seemed all but to lift off the ground, shuddering and choking, and then sank back and lay still.

Leaning over on the shaft of his spear to support him,

241

panting, Hugh de Swinton knew that he had done it. The Arbuthnott boar was dead.

It took some little time for the man to recover himself, emotionally as well as physically drained. He sat down there beside his quarry, leaning forward, head in hands, while his breathing returned to normal and he gathered his wits.

Then he bethought him of those waiting up there on the high ground across the Bervie, unable to see what went on because of the trees and bushes. They would be anxious. They would have heard his halloo probably, although the water's noise might have muffled it at a distance. They must be informed. How? Just to halloo again they would assume to be a second challenge to the boar. If he shouted differently? Went to the water's edge? They might see him there . . .

Rising, he went down to the river-bank. And there, through a gap in the trees on the other side, he saw them, sitting their horses up on the heights. If he could see them, they could see him. He waved and shouted, and shouted again. Would they think that he was calling for help?

Whatever they thought, there were answering waves and cries, and he could see the riders starting forward.

He waited there. Margaret and her father were well in the lead. Reassuringly he waved again, and saw the girl wave back. At least they would realise that he was in no grave trouble.

Margaret reached the river first, and splashed across the comparative shallows without a moment's hesitation, heeling her mount's sides. He went to meet her.

"The boar, Hugh?" she cried. "Has it not appeared again?"

"Aye, it appeared," he assured her. "It is there."

"Where? You mean . . . ? It is back in its lair? Did not assail you?"

"No, no. It came. It is there." He pointed back.

Her father came over, asking the same questions.

"Come," Hugh told them, and turning, led the way.

He clearly heard the gasps behind him as they reached the scene of the conflict. There lay the menace, outstretched, the spear still sticking out of its side, the leather gauntlet nearby.

"It is done," he said, somewhat at a loss for words now, his voice anyway drowned in exclamations from behind.

Margaret threw herself down from her horse and came running. "Hugh! Hugh!" she cried, and hurled herself into his arms, all but sobbing, unlike herself as this might be.

He was no more eloquent than she was, as he clutched her to him – and this not on account of the pain in his back.

It was Sir Osbert who found speech, dismounted and coming to stare down at the boar. "Soul of God, you have done it!" he exclaimed. "You have done it, man! Slain the brute. Done it! Dead! Here is a wonder to behold. The boar no more!"

Hugh, reluctant to release the young woman, felt that he had to move over to the animal, taking her with him. "The gauntlet did it," he averred. "And the rock at my back. The stones slowed its pace so that I could stab."

"And you? You are unhurt?" Margaret hardly glanced at the boar.

"It winded me. That is all. You wrapped the gauntlet well, for me."

"The size of it!" Sir Osbert said. He drew out the spear, as his men rode up, loud in comment. "Even larger than I had thought. The weight! How you did it, Swinton, I do not know. Speared through the heart?"

"So I endeavoured. Behind the shoulder."

Margaret shook his arm, and the man realised that it was painful, the left arm, the one which had been within the gauntlet. So the brute's tusks and teeth must have achieved something.

"Do not cozen us!" she told him. "Making little of it. Here was a deed to shout over! Not to belittle."

"Once I had thought of the gauntlet. The open mouth. And the support . . ."

"Still you question our wits! We are not babes. We . . ."

Her father intervened. "The deed is done, and will not be forgotten. Ever. Many, many, will give thanks for it." He turned to his watching men. "Take this boar up. Bring it to my house. Tonight, we will all feast. To celebrate. And in honour of Sir Hugh. If the brute is eatable, we will all devour what would have devoured us, if it could! But there will be much else to eat! So see you to it." And he moved to his horse.

Margaret looked at Hugh, and smiled now, patting not shaking his arm. "You have no mount, so it seems that you must ride behind me again. As last time you left the scene of battle! Or, would you rather that *you* rode, with me behind?"

"I would not." That was definite. "In front, I could not hold on to you!"

"Ah! And you wish to do so, boar-slayer?"

"I am a man!" he said simply.

"Oh, yes, you are that. Then aid a woman up, sir!"

So they rode back to the castle, the boar, slung between two horsemen, bringing up the rear, Hugh holding on securely to his second support.

Short notice as it was, the cooks did not fail the company that day, having presumably raided the ice-house below the round tower for venison, beef, fowl and salmon. The boar had been skinned and cut up, its head placed on a platter to decorate the top table, with candles to light it and Hugh's gauntlet stuck back in its jaws, its flesh roasted. This proved tough and stringy to eat, but rejected by none nevertheless in the crowded great hall, the local folk, women as well as men, being present in large numbers, the castle servitors much to the fore, Gelis in especial making her presence felt. Hugh of course came in for much acclaim, this developing in frankness and heartiness as the evening wore on and wines loosened tongues not usually so eloquent in the presence of their lord and master. Sir Osbert made a speech about the hero of the day, to the latter's embarrassment, Hugh's reply being brief indeed, and even so such as to have Margaret's head ashake in exasperation. The entertainment thereafter went on for rather long for the principal guest, whose person was now a fairly comprehensive ache; but the other guests were in no hurry to depart, and the Olifards reluctant to turn them out on this so special occasion. In the end Margaret, with an eye on Hugh's features and bearing, had a word with her father, and Sir Osbert rose, announced that festivities might continue for some time yet, but that Sir Hugh was bruised and in some pain from his encounter with the boar, and would be best in bed. To cheers from the company, he led the other two out, Gelis following them solicitously.

Margaret now took charge. Hugh was for *her* chamber meantime, where she had her medicinal ointments and salves. She would inspect what state he was in and what could be done to better it. Gelis to get Sir Hugh's room prepared. Sir Osbert said that he was content to leave their knight errant in good hands.

So this time, escorted to the round tower, he was led into the first-floor chamber, while Gelis, smirking, went on higher. Margaret's smouldering fire was replenished, candles lit, and Hugh ordered to remove his clothing. He did so without comment this time. He was told to come over to the light.

Examined carefully, he was informed that he seemed to have no more skin broken, but that his back and arms were comprehensively bruised. She had two ointments, one made of goose grease with angelica and elder leaves, the other with viper's bugloss and marshmallows, the first for inflammations, the second for poisons. Both rubbed in should help. In her close inspection, she probed at the belt of his breeches.

"See you, the bruising goes down further," she declared. "I fear that you will have to remove these also." And, anticipating objections, she added, "Trouble naught, I have not reached one-score-and-two years without seeing men naked!"

He nodded. "*You*, I do not care. It was different with Gelis."

"So." That was all the comment she made, as he lowered his breeches and stepped out of them.

Stooping to peer, she shook her head. "As I feared, the bruising goes on. Your buttocks and thighs have not escaped. That boar has trampled all over you."

"Fortunately only the back of me," he informed, glancing down.

"If you say so! Now, over to my bed. Lie on it. And we shall see what can be done for this manly if foolhardy person!"

"You are kind . . ."

"Wait you until I start hurting you!" she counselled. "Come."

Nothing loth now, he moved over, to lie face down, she removing some female clothing cast thereon. He settled himself comfortably.

"I never thought to be occupying *this* bed!" he observed, boldly.

"Nor will you for long, friend!" she returned, bringing the candles closer, and then the pots of her ointments. "See you, turn this way a little, for the light. I will be as gentle as may be."

"I can stand a deal, placed thus!" he asserted.

And that was the truth. Lying there, in the mellow candlelight, with that young woman sitting down beside him, and first anointing him with the embrocations, then stroking and rubbing these on his skin, fingertips gentle, searching but heedfully, kindly, from shoulders to calves, on and on, was a joy, bliss, soothing yes but arousing also to be sure. Hugh recognised that it was perhaps as well that he was lying on his stomach.

"These salves require to be well rubbed in." Margaret told him. "Tell me if I hurt you."

"You may do this as long as you will!" he said. "Perhaps heaven will be like this?"

"You are so sure that you are bound for there?"

"Who knows? But meantime, this will serve. For *me*. But – for you?"

"I do not find it an affliction. And it is the least that I can do for our benefactor."

"The *least* . . . ?"

"Ah, best that you be content with your lot meantime, Hugh de Swinton!"

When at length the young woman was satisfied with her ministrations, whatever the man felt, she rose. "I hope that will ease your pains somewhat," she said.

246

He hoisted himself off the bed at the other side, very much aware of his masculinity, even though she had turned away. "I thank you, Margaret. I, I shall never forget that. Your kindness, and . . ." He left the rest unsaid, gathering up his breeches. "Perhaps I should don these again? Gelis will be awaiting . . ."

"No doubt. The solicitous Gelis! You find her attentions acceptable?"

"H'mm. Yes, and no. She is very helpful. But I do not call for *all* her . . . diligence."

"No? You select, then? Off to your own bed with you, now. And lie kindly, sleeping well."

She led him to her door, but before opening it turned to eye him, half naked and clutching his clothing in a bundle. Smiling, she wagged her dark head. Then, stepping forward, she put her arms round him, nowise throwing them but carefully, heedfully, over person and gear, and raised her face to kiss him.

Taken by surprise, he would have exclaimed, but thought better of it as he felt her warm lips stir briefly under his, slightly open. Then she released him, drawing back and opening the door.

"Goodnight, Hugh," she said. "That is my thank-you. Anointing *not* the least! Do not dream of boars!"

"I, I shall dream of *you*. Aye, you I swear!"

"That I cannot prevent!" she conceded, and closed the door behind him.

Upstairs, wits in some disarray, Hugh was scarcely in a state fully to appreciate Gelis's considerations, although he did declare that he would not require back-washing this night, owing to the unguents applied thereto.

"Yon crittur gien you your paiks, sir?" she asked. "Och, but *you* gien it mair! We're a' richt beholden to you, mind. Aucht that any o' us can dae for you we'll dae, you ken!"

"You are kind, always. But I know of naught, meantime."

"If your back's sair, I'll help you off wi' your breeks . . ."

This manoeuvre heedfully accomplished, Hugh got into bed and was tucked in, a process involving close contacts

247

and judicious handling. He endeavoured to be appreciative and dismissive both, before, laughing, she was gone.

It had been an eventful day, he told himself. But, in fact, it was the last half-hour or so of it which filled his mind before sleep took over, rather than his earlier exertions.

In the morning he was stiff but not otherwise much incommoded, and at breakfast, his task at Arbuthnott accomplished, he felt bound to propose departure more or less forthwith. This was vehemently rejected by father and daughter both, not to be considered. He must have time for recovery of fitness and strength, if naught else. And was there any reason for him to betake himself off in haste?

He pointed out that it would take at least three days to get home, and he had been away now for over a week. His establishment at Aldcambus demanded much attention, especially at this season of lambing, calving, tillage and repairing the winter's damage. For he was no rich baron, but merely a working small laird, a farmer indeed, his knighthood an odd gesture on King Malcolm's part, scarcely suitable in the circumstances.

This averment clearly interested Sir Osbert, who pressed for details, although Margaret was more concerned that their visitor should see more of their Mearns countryside while he was here. Their coastline, in particular, was worth seeing, even if it did not have such great cliffs as he told of down on his own lands. She had been thinking to take him this day thereabouts – if he was fit to ride?

He could not say that he was not, when he had just been proposing to set off on a three-day journey; and without a great deal of coaxing he allowed himself to be persuaded to put off his departure until the morrow. Then he answered Sir Osbert's enquiries as to Aldcambus and Redheugh.

So, before long, he found himself on horseback again, his own back not grievously distressing him, and being led by Margaret down the Bervie Water again, past all the scenes of conflict and on beyond St Ternan's Church to Inverbervie village and the sea. Asking who St Ternan was, Hugh was informed that the name was probably a corruption of St Ethernan, who was one of Columba's missionary brethren, he who was best known for founding the first beacon lighthouse in all Scotland, this on the Isle of May at the mouth of the Firth of Forth or Scotwater, to warn ships of danger of rocks and reefs. Hugh would know of that?

He told her, laughing, that if the Mearns folk had corrupted the name from Ethernan to Ternan, they had not done so badly as had the blessed saint and queen, Margaret, the present monarch's great-grandmother; for she, in her chosen task of changing the nation's Columban Church to the Roman Catholic one they had now, had also changed the name of the Isle of May's saint from Ethernan to Adrian – which just happened to be the name of the Pope at Rome of the time! No doubt in an exchange of favours.

Reaching the shore they turned northwards, to start ascending cliffs at once, at what was called Bervie Brow. These were less high than at Redheugh and Fastness and St Ebba's, but they were sufficiently spectacular, pierced by caves, and deep and quite steep coves and chasms, which had to be circumnavigated, some indeed narrow valleys of incoming streams which the riders had to descend into, ford, and climb out of again. Other burns cascaded over the precipices as waterfalls; and all along these cliffs sea-fowl roosted and wheeled and screamed. Margaret said that certain sorts of eggs were in demand at Inverbervie, and the youths of the village were adept at climbing down to the ledges and crevices, not always safely. There had been deaths. Indeed the younger brother of a friend and neighbour of theirs, Allardyce of that Ilk, had been killed by falling, not a twelve-month past, a lad of sixteen years – a dire tragedy.

Owing to the up-and-down and round-about nature of their progress, it took a long time to cover even a few miles of this coastline. Not that Hugh was complaining; he was much enjoying the company he was keeping, whatever the scenery. Admittedly they had to ride in single-file almost all the way, he behind, but Margaret pointed out all that was to be seen and noted, and not infrequently dismounted to show him details

249

of the cliff-face and the like – which gave him opportunity to go and help her up and down from the saddle, and even to take her arm when he judged that she ventured too near to the edge of the precipices and yawning depths, contact which she accepted without comment as natural, apparently.

After perhaps a couple of hours of it, they saw ahead of them a clifftop castle, smallish but dramatically sited, with its subsidiary outbuildings, quite large in proportion, stretching inland on a sort of plateau between two ravines.

"That is Kinneff," Margaret said. "Its baron, David Dallas, is a good friend. We shall call on him. He has large lands, and other houses than this hawk's-nest of a place. He may not be at home."

When they reached the castle they were told that, although the laird was not present they could in fact see him, a boat being pointed out to them as it was rowed in towards a small haven in a narrow, deep bay just to the north. He had been out fishing for flukies, a favourite pastime, and was now returning. So the pair rode down the steep track to the boatstrand to meet the incoming three men.

Dallas of Kinneff proved to be a good-looking, tall young man, of open countenance and friendly manner, and obviously delighted to see Margaret Olifard, whatever company she might be in. He complained that he had not seen her for too long, having been away up at his Deeside properties and only back two days. He had been intending to repair that omission very shortly. This came out in something of a spate; but all the time he was eyeing Hugh assessingly.

The young woman told him that he would be most welcome, as always, whenever he could find time to come to Arbuthnott. But now she suggested that he hailed Sir Hugh Boar-Slayer, the hero who had managed to rid them of the Pitcarles menace at last, at the third attempt and at great danger to himself, and some consequent pains. Whereafter Dallas eyed Hugh still more thoughtfully, his congratulations correct but only moderate.

They were offered hospitality up at Kinneff Castle, but Margaret declined, saying that they would go as far as

250

Whistleberry and then turn inland and return to Arbuthnott by the Muir of Auchendreigh and Montgoldrum, where she wanted to show her visitor Pictish relics, and that would take them most of the remainder of the day.

So they left the fishermen, to go northwards, up to the clifftops again.

Hugh, when they could ride side by side for a little way, remarked, "That David Dallas admires you not a little, I think! As is not to be wondered at!"

"Oh, David is an old friend. I have known him all my life. We are of an age."

"Yes. And he is a man of substance. He is one of the suitors which your father mentioned?"

"You might call him that," she replied lightly. "Others might outbid him!"

"M'mm. You will have your own . . . preferences?"

"To be sure. Some I would not consider, however much my good sire might see their suits as advantageous."

"Advantageous? You mean for you? Or for himself and his thanedom?"

"Oh, both. But he is concerned that he has no male heir. Only myself. Whoever weds me could, if the King agrees, become Thane of Arbuthnott and the Mearns one day, a notable office and responsibility. So, he has to consider carefully. But, heigho – so have I!" She smiled. "See, yonder is Whistleberry. It belongs to David also. Still more of a hawk's-nest, or eagle's, this one, than Kinneff itself. He says that, if I would wed him, that could be my dowery house!"

She pointed ahead, where a single stone tower soared on a thrusting pinnacle of rock above the waves, reminding Hugh somewhat of Fastness, on his own coast, although this was on the clifftop not halfway down. He made no comment.

They did not halt at the strangely named Whistleberry Tower, merely eyeing it from a nearby height, Hugh declaring that in an easterly winter gale it would be an ill place to live, the girl contesting that, saying that should it not be an exciting challenge?

251

They turned inland then over high moorland, due west-wards, the ground rising all the time. Soon they were amongst sizeable hills, modest compared with the blue mountains which formed the background but worthy heights and ridges nevertheless. To one of these higher parts Margaret pointed.

"Largie Law," she said. "On top there is a great cairn and circle. A burial-place it is thought. Some chieftain."

They climbed to this, and found a great mound of stones within its ring of monoliths. Dismounting, the young woman led Hugh round to the back, where there was an opening, and roofed passage lined with flat slabs of stone. Hitching up her skirts in frankest fashion, she got down on her hands and knees and proceeded to crawl inside. The man could not but follow, admiring more than merely her enterprise and the stonework.

Not that he could see much as they progressed, for naturally it became completely dark, their persons blocking any light which might filter into that low entry – so dark indeed that presently he bumped into her, and realised that it was not her bottom he had collided with but that she was kneeling upright now. Gingerly he did the same.

"This may not be the best treatment for your back!" she said. "We are in a central chamber. I should have thought to bring flint, steel, tinder and candle. It is well made. Outside it seems but a loose pile of stones. In here it is lined with large flat slabs. The roof also. I think that we ought to be able to stand. Just."

He sensed her rising carefully and then felt a hand groping down for his own. Hand in hand then they fumbled around that dark cell, feeling their way with outstretched fingers, an intimate proceeding indeed, even though they found nothing save a loose stone or two. Margaret said that no doubt the tomb, if such it was, had been robbed long ere this.

In no hurry to emerge from this close and linked proximity, Hugh remarked on the young woman's especial interest in the Picts, asking what had led her to this? She told him that it was probably their mysterious symbols on their stones which first drew her to the Picts. But they all ought to know more about them, should they not? Most of them had some Pictish blood in their veins, so surely they ought to be better aware of their ancestors.

Creeping out was not difficult, for now there was daylight ahead of them. Margaret, out first, Hugh found scrubbing her muddy knees with handfuls of damp grass, entirely unabashed. She admitted that it was a pity that they had found nothing in there, but he assured that he had enjoyed the unusual experience, but hoped that it was not every man she would risk taking into that darkness! She raised one eyebrow at him, at that, and asked if he considered her devoid of judgment? That silenced him, as he assisted her up to her saddle again.

They rode down, and then across the mossy Muir of Audendreich, to where a single standing-stone, without symbols, reared beside a tiny lochan. Close by, the girl again dismounted, to point out a souterrain or earth-house, a sort of underground tunnel, again well built and stone-slabbed. This was high enough for them to be able to walk through, although stooping, which caused Hugh to wonder whether these Picts had been a small people, in that they had not made it just a little higher. The same in that cairn they had left. Margaret did not know, but suggested that it might merely be a defensive feature, as so many doorways in castles and towers were made low to force enemies and invaders to have to stoop awkwardly to enter and so put themselves at a disadvantage with their weapons.

A mile or so on they came to another cairn on the rising ground of Montgoldrum; but this one's entrance passage was fallen in, so they could not enter. However, one of its circle of monoliths had a crescent-and-V-rod device carved on it, and some other design which had weathered too much for them to distinguish details. Again they debated the possible meaning, without reaching any solution. The young woman said that there were innumerable such features all around this area, which must have been a very populous part of the Mar mormaordom.

They headed back southwards for Arbuthnott, well ready for a meal.

That evening, at bedtime, Hugh was told that another back-anointing would be beneficial – to which he made no least protest. The same procedure as before developed, the patient more than patient, and becoming bold enough to announce that, without wishing her ill, he could desire that Margaret's own back required attention and soothing likewise, whereat he would be delighted to oblige. That earned him a slap on a so-far unbruised part of his anatomy nearby.

All too soon, for him, the treatment was over and he donned his breeches. At the door, despite the fact that she was carrying a lit candle, he looked hopefully at her. Wrinkling her nose at him, she outstretched sideways the arm which held the candlestick, and curled the other round in an enclosing gesture. He of course moved promptly to be enclosed, and received the hoped-for kiss, perhaps just slightly more prolonged than the previous night's, before being pushed downwards under the threat of the candle flame.

Upstairs, again of course, Gelis had to be dealt with. He was not unkind in his reactions, with so much to be grateful for.

Next morning, he felt that he had to be off, despite urgings to stay longer all but persuading him, and resolution having to be summoned. The actual farewells were scarcely what he would have wished, in that he did not manage to see the young woman alone. Sir Osbert reiterated the heartfelt thanks of all at Arbuthnott for such notable services rendered, and said how welcome Hugh would be to return. For his part, Hugh urged a visit to Aldcambus of father and daughter, and before too long.

"This of the Edin's Hall broch," he said. "Margaret, with her interest in the Picts, must see that. There has been so much of the Picts here, but no brochs. The thing is huge and strange."

"I would wish to see that, yes," she nodded.

"And there is King Loth's capital, at Traprain, nearer still to my house. He of the Southern Picts. A hilltop city of sorts." And in case Olifard was less enticed by Pictish remains, "And you, sir, might like to see the King's great new hospital of Soutra, a most notable project? And visit your brother at Smailholm. Come in the summer months."

"We shall do that, I hope?" That was a question, as she looked at her father.

Sir Osbert inclined his greying head.

"I would take that as a promise," Hugh declared. He reached out to shake the older man's hand. "I thank you for all your kindness to me, sir." He turned to the girl. "And you." He managed to put considerable fervour into those two words.

"My kindnesses have been modest," she said smiling – and did he detect some emphasis on that last word? "But then, I am a modest young female! See, here is some of my unguent and lotion," and she held out a leather bag with two little pots in it. "Find you some kind woman to rub them on for you. That will not be too difficult, I think?"

He would have answered that suitably – but not in front of Sir Osbert. He reached out to take the bag, and she came close and raised her face towards his. But as her eyes met his they carried a message; and it was very much her cheek which she offered to him for a chaste kiss.

He bestowed it, as required. But he would treasure that eloquent look nevertheless. There were more ways than one of expressing kindness.

Hugh turned to his horse, and mounted. "I salute you," he said. "Both. And shall always do so." And he reined his garron round and was off, spear and sword in place but that gauntlet left behind as keepsake.

He did not look back.

20

Hugh found all well at Aldcambus and Redheugh, with his small niece seeming to have developed in even so short an interval, and to have the latter establishment all but geared to her every need and wish. The lambing had started, and that and all other farmery matters appeared to have gone on perfectly well without the laird's attentions – which was perhaps a humbling thought.

He had been away for only two weeks, but the realm's affairs evidently had not stood still in the interim; and although Hugh was not personally in a position of any responsibility in these, he was concerned. Duncan told him that the word going around was that King Henry of England had returned from his French wars triumphant, having gained practically all the lands which he had long been claiming, through his mother and his wife, and was said to be in aggressive mood. And, being the monarch that he was, Scotland might well feel the effects of this.

In fact, only a week after Hugh's return, some hint of this reached Aldcambus, in the form of a monkish messenger from Melrose Abbey. The Abbot William besought Sir Hugh's company there, if he could arrange it, and at his earliest convenience, this in King Malcolm's service. No details were given, but the monk said that it was to do with English demands on Scotland.

So next day Hugh was ahorse again, for Tweeddale.

It was good to see the abbot again, even though the news was less so. Henry Plantagenet, in victorious frame of mind, was making demands on Malcolm, the old story of Northumberland and Cumberland and overlordship; and these claims were being given immediacy by that other long-standing fallacious assertion, of the hegemony of the Church of England over the Church of Scotland, the allegation that, since the Scots Primate, the Bishop of St Andrews, was not Metropolitan or archbishop, then the Archbishop of York, the most northerly Metropolitan, had jurisdiction over Scotland in ecclesiastical affairs. And that, to order this important matter forthwith, Archbishop Roger himself was coming north and would meet King Malcolm at the border, at Norham, in two days' time. The arrogant folly of it, according to Abbot William.

That man was involved, as an adviser of the King and Vice-Chancellor; but the more so in that Bishop Arnold of St Andrews was grievously ill and could not be present to confront the Englishman. The Chancellor, the Bishop of Aberdeen, it was hoped could be brought down in time, but this was not assured. So William might well be the senior cleric present on the Scots side, and Malcolm was relying on him. Hugh, of course, was not ecclesiastically knowledgeable; but the King, who was summoning a large company of his lords, barons and knights to accompany him to the meeting, had personally asked for his attendance, looking on him apparently as very much a useful supporter after the Soutra developments.

That man did not see that he could contribute anything of value to the situation, but could not refuse to go along, especially as the abbot clearly would value his company also.

The following morning, then, they rode down Tweed to Roxburgh, Hugh recounting his adventures in the Mearns, although not expanding on his feelings for Margaret Olifard.

At Roxburgh Castle, between the two rivers, he found his father and brother amongst the gathering of notables, with the Earl Cospatrick, the Lords Waldeve and Home and many another, including Walter Olifard the justiciar – the last especially interested in the boar-slaying episode needless to say. Indeed it did not take long for this to get round the assembled company, and Hugh found himself hailed as some sort of hero, Prince William being particularly interested, and declaring his abhorrence of the brutes always and his astonishment that they should have been adopted as the symbol of the royal house of Scotland.

King Malcolm's preoccupations were otherwise. He was much concerned over the forthcoming confrontations with the archbishop, and how effectively to rebuff his claims and assertions to spiritual overlordship, as a step towards national overlordship, without grievously offending King Henry whom, unlike Brawny Will, he held in high regard, the prince who had knighted him. He was not going to give way in this matter, to be sure; but it was important that the Plantagenet's ire should not be overmuch aroused, and retaliation moves produced. The King's Huntingdon earldom, inherited from his grandmother, David's wife, could be at stake, with its great revenues and manors in eleven English counties. It was a difficult situation. The Chancellor had not yet arrived from Aberdeen, and Abbot William was closeted with the monarch and his advisers for most of the evening.

It was on down Tweed in the morning, a great and distinguished company. Norham, only a dozen miles from Berwick and the sea, was almost double that from Roxburgh, going by Kelshaugh, Edenmouth, Birgham and Coldstream; and considerably before they reached their destination the King was showing signs of fatigue and weakness. Malcolm had never fully recovered from his serious illness, a matter of concern for all, with a realm to be ruled.

The Tweed made major windings in the last score of miles of its lengthy course, unusual in so wide a river as it had become. From opposite Birgham its south side was Northumberland; and thereafter fords and crossings were few and far between, with no bridges until Berwick itself, emphasising that Northumberland had never been part of Scotland proper, although ceded to it, with Cumberland and Durham, by King Stephen thirty years before, source of much friction between the nations. Norham's situation typified this. The only ford thereto was a mile west of the village, its castle a mile east of it although on the river's bank. Where would the archbishop choose to meet the King of Scots? The message had merely said Norham, which implied Northumberland soil, with King Henry claiming that country back as having been given away unlawfully by his predecessor Stephen.

In the event, they saw a large company, with pavilions erected and horse-lines established, in the haughland just across that Norham ford – a subtly arrogant touch which meant that the Scots would have to file and splash across the fairly narrow shallows to reach the waiting English, and so look the more like suppliants. Prince William and the Earl Cospatrick said that they should wait on their own side, and let the wretched clerks come across to them; but Malcolm saw no advantage in that, and ordered the crossing to be made.

Fully as large a party as their own was drawn up awaiting them as they arrived in twos and threes, and by no means all clerics, Archbishop Roger, in full canonicals, in the centre. He was a tall but stooping hawk-faced man, unsmiling, the reverse of benevolent, even though he raised a hand high in sketchy benediction, which however proved to be not on the newcomers but for the success of their meeting. None would doubt whose success was being invoked.

The Scots dismounting, introductions were minimal, the Prince-Bishop of Durham and de Clare, Earl of Gloucester, notably a friend of King Henry's, making themselves known. Clearly this was going to be no social and amicable exchange of views. Malcolm, less stiffly, indicated his brothers, Prince William and David, Earl of Huntingdon; also the mitred Abbot of Melrose – minus his mitre. He said that he had come at his good cousin of England's request, to discuss any relevant matters relating to Holy Church in their two realms.

"No, my lord King, not to discuss! To inform and state," the archbishop declared, with no preamble or courtesies. "We have not come all this way from York for profitless debate. The situation is clear and undoubted. All must be rectified."

"Mostly it is clear to us, yes, my lord Archbishop. We are unsure of what you would wish to be rectified?"

"Why, Sire, merely the essence of it all. That your Scots Church, not having the Pall, having no archbishop nor Metropolitan, cannot be independent of the nearest Metropolitan – myself. It is simple indeed, and should require no debate.

Under His Holiness the Pope, Metropolitans hold supreme authority."

"We cannot accept that," the King said, his weariness in his voice. Then he shrugged, and turned to Abbot William. "My Vice-Chancellor, Lord Abbot of Melrose, is more schooled in Church matters than I am, sir. He will better answer you."

William bowed. "My lord Archbishop, in this matter, strangely, you have answered your own question. You said – "

"No question, sir! I do not question. I state. And on highest authority."

"State, yes, my lord. And the authority you quote unquestionable – His Holiness in Rome! You have just said it. Under the Pope you hold your authority, but he is supreme. And Pope Calixtus the Second gave fullest assurance to the late King David, grandsire of His Grace here, that the Church of Scotland was wholly independent, under himself."

There was a momentary silence while the other digested that. "This is mere hearsay!" he got out.

"It is on record, my lord. Dated 1120. Forty-five years ago."

Frowning, the archbishop conferred with the Bishop of Durham, whilst the Scots chuckled, some of them.

"So-called records can be forged," they were told, at length. "This assertion rings false. It is contrary to all custom and precedent."

"The letter bears the papal seal and signature . . ."

"These too could be forged!"

"Not two Popes' seals and signatures! For there is, at St Andrews, another letter from the next Pontiff, Honorius the Second, who assures King David that all the sees of the Scottish Church are, as he declares, 'special daughters of Rome, and exempt from all jurisdiction save that of the Pope'. I have seen this letter."

"The sees of Galloway and Glasgow have always been subordinate to York!" the archbishop exclaimed.

"You say so, my lord – but His Holiness does not!"

Another voice spoke up, that of Malcolm's personal chaplain and close friend, the Prior Richard. "King Alexander the First obtained the full agreement of your superior, my lord, the Archbishop of Canterbury, back at the commencement of this century, that our Scots Church was in no way subject to York. And this was accepted by your then monarch, King Henry the First. What could have changed that? Forby, the Blessed Queen Margaret, his mother, and His Grace here's great-grandmother, who turned Scotland to Rome from the Columban faith, received especial praise and commendation from Pope Urban the Second, who assured her that her Church would ever remain in the Vatican's especial care."

"Times and conditions change!" the archbishop jerked. "It is canon law, precept and prescription of Holy Church that the Metropolitan, and only the Metropolitan, has the duty to enforce due Church discipline, to dispense indulgences, to preside over provincial synods, and much else. Here in Scotland you have none who may lawfully do this, none who wears the pallium. I do. I claim the right."

"And we deny it!" Abbot William declared.

There was a pause, as men stared, glared at each other.

"We regret that our meeting is thus fruitless, my lord Archbishop," the King said, then. And he sounded it. "But now the situation is clear to us all, no room for any doubt. It is as well that we forgathered and settled it. My lord of Gloucester, will you convey my very real respects and goodwill to my royal cousin, King Henry, with my congratulations on his great attainments in France?" And, with the required royal touch, "So, this audience is closed." And he reined his horse around.

All the Scots followed suit, watched in silence by grim-faced English, as they headed back to the riverside and recrossed the ford.

Abbot William had replaced Hugh de Swinton as the hero of the hour as they returned to Roxburgh. But however cheered, even gleeful, were most of the company, Malcolm himself was not. Fifty miles of riding was overmuch for him in his present state of health; but it was more than that which was oppressing him. He admitted to the abbot, while expressing his appreciation of the service rendered, that he was worried as to the effect of this day's work on Henry Plantagenet. He feared that the archbishop would not have made this attempt without Henry's blessing, possibly indeed at his urging. What would result? He feared, he greatly feared retaliation in some form. The Plantagenet was a powerful friend but an ill man to cross.

The King was barely able to sit his saddle by the time that they reached Roxburgh Castle, and retired at once to his bedchamber. His court, under his brothers, celebrated his victory for him, that evening, the abbot's and Hugh's very different and contrasting triumphs not overlooked.

On the way back to Melrose next day, the pair discussed the position as regards King Malcolm, his health and his character, and their effects on his abilities as monarch. They both much liked him as a man, recognised his virtues and applauded his good works, especially of course the Soutra undertaking. But Scotland always needed a strong king, and Malcolm was scarcely that. If, as he so evidently feared, the Plantagenet was angry over the previous day's failure at Norham, and made further demands, how would Malcolm react? The English threat was never far from the minds of Scotsmen, for there were ten men south of the border for every one north. Would and could Malcolm rally the Scots nation to withstand assault, if it came to that? They both doubted it.

The abbot told Hugh that he had heard rumours that there was a faction at court murmuring about seeking Malcolm's abdication, on grounds of ill-health, and the elevation of Brawny Will to the throne. He did not think that this was a serious proposal at this stage, or with any major backing; but if the King's state did not improve and there was major trouble with England, it might receive more powerful backing. Malcolm himself might even welcome it. He had no son to think of, and clearly did not particularly enjoy his position and power.

In that case, Hugh wondered, what sort of a monarch would William make? He was certainly more forceful than his brother, but less mature, headstrong indeed. Would a headstrong king be any better for Scotland than a diffident one? If only their father had not died young. He had been a sound and able man . . .

In a state not exactly of foreboding the friends parted at Melrose, the abbot promising to keep Hugh informed as to any major developments on the national scene, Aldcambus being scarcely the sort of place news reached readily. Perhaps that had its advantages, in the present state of affairs?

21

Scotland did not have to wait long for word of the reaction of Henry of England to the Norham situation. Even before the abbot sent a messenger to Aldcambus with details, stories had reached there of dire trouble. When, in May, the monkish courier did arrive, Hugh was more or less prepared for bad news.

Nevertheless, he was astonished at what he then heard. Their King was no longer in Scotland. Henry had summoned him south to Woodstock in Oxfordshire, and he had gone – this on threat of being deprived of the valuable Huntingdon English earldom, richer than all the royal possessions at home. He was to go and do homage for that, under feudal law. Not only so, but he had to take the nominal Earl of Huntingdon with him, David his youngest brother, and the sons of sundry of other Scots nobles, as hostages for Scotland's submissive behaviour after the shameful rejection of his hand of friendship in Church affairs at Norham – this on threat of armed invasion. And, against the judgment of most of his advisers, Malcolm had done this, unable to stomach the thought of warfare-experienced English armies marching over the border and plunging his realm into bloodshed. So now their monarch was on this humiliating journey southwards, David of Huntingdon and the other hostages with him, leaving behind a nation in a state of shame and turmoil, Prince William making angry noises and declaring that *he* would never have acted so, and swearing that if a single English company came up to cross into Scotland, he would send them back with bloodied escutcheons, or such of them as survived.

Hugh and Duncan were, of course, appalled, and fearful of further developments. But there was nothing that they, or others like them, could do about it, save be ready for any call to arms.

Life at Aldcambus and Redheugh had to go on, as before, whatever the trauma of the nation.

It was almost a month later, with no hard news emanating from the King in England, but rumours aplenty, that news of a very different sort reached Hugh de Swinton, from the north, not the south – at least from Edinburgh. The Justiciar Olifard based there sent a messenger to announce that his brother, the Thane of Arbuthnott, was about to pay him a visit connected with the troublous affairs of the kingdom, and had asked him to inform Sir Hugh that he would give himself the pleasure of calling upon him at Aldcambus while he was in the area. Just when that would be he had not said, but presumably within the next few days.

This, needless to say, exercised Hugh's mind, tending to drive other concerns out therefrom meantime. He would be glad to see Sir Osbert, of course; but the question was – would he be accompanied by his daughter? The message gave no hint of that.

For the next two days, then, Hugh was in a state of some preoccupation. Would he be seeing Margaret or would he not? So much did this question prey upon his mind that he seldom ventured far from Aldcambus House in case he was not nearby when the Olifard visitation materialised.

In the event, three afternoons later, he was helping Dod Lumsden to dip sheep when he saw three riders appear over a swell of the grassland from the direction of the deep Pease Dean. He could not be certain that one of them was a woman, but something about the carriage in the saddle seemed to indicate it. He hurried off to meet them, anyway.

Soon there was no doubt about it, two men and a woman. The chances of it being anyone else . . . ? He all but ran, waving.

He got a wave in answer, too.

Coming up with the trio, he schooled himself to salute Sir Osbert respectfully, and recognising that the second man was one of the boar-hunters of those weeks ago, now acting groom.

But his eyes were seldom off Margaret, looking very lovely, hair blowing in the breeze off the sea.

"I see your red cliffs, yonder," she called. "A wonder! So vivid!"

"And you! You all. A joy to see."

"We visit you sooner than we had expected," her father said. "But events required that we come south, grievous events."

"Not so grievous that we cannot enjoy our visit," the young woman asserted. She pointed. "What numbers of sheep!"

"This is sheep country. The knuckle-end of the Lammermuirs. Cattle also, to be sure, but sheep are the main stock. I got your message, sir. Have you ridden from Edinburgh today?"

"We have. And go on to Roxburgh tomorrow."

"Roxburgh! So soon? Surely not. There is much to see here . . ."

"The realm's needs take precedence, I fear . . ."

Hugh took them to the house amid much talk, Margaret especially interested in all that she saw.

Oppressed by the thought that this was going to be such a very brief visit, Hugh detailed all that he wanted to show his guests, particularly of course Edin's Hall broch, which was almost a dozen miles away, and wondering how it was all going to be fitted in. He declared that, if they were not too wearied by their riding here, they should go and inspect the Redheugh and Fastness cliffs area after they had had some refreshment. Sir Osbert's mind was not on viewing scenery, obviously, and it was his daughter who came up with the proposal.

"You do not need *me*, Father, at this Roxburgh, to give your tidings. Leave me here then, tomorrow, while you go on, and collect me on your way back. Then Hugh can show me what he will, and you can see what time you still have on your return."

Their host all but held his breath as he awaited the thane's answer to that.

Olifard looked doubtful. "I could be gone two days or more . . ."

"There appears to be no lack of doings here to keep us busy!"

266

"I could have Meg, my brother's wife, to come from Redheugh to, to keep Margaret company, sir," Hugh said reassuringly, the decencies to be upheld. "If go you must, so soon?"

"It is important that I do, my friend. There is dire trouble afoot, for the King's Grace and for the nation. Somerled, Lord of the Isles, or King thereof as he names himself, has decided that Malcolm is no fit occupant of the throne. He intends to unseat him, and set his brother-in-law Malcolm MacEth, Earl of Ross, in his place – he who is the son of the late King David's elder brother Ethelred. To that end Somerled is raising not only the Isles but many of the Highland clans, even so far down as my own country. The Mearns rings with it all. He is gathering his great fleets of longships and galleys to bring his armies down, in the west, no doubt to the Clyde. To invade our Lowlands. With King Malcolm away in England, Prince William and the others must be warned. It is a grievous threat. The Islesmen are great warriors. They defeated the Norsemen, the Vikings. The Lowlands must be roused to withstand them. Or we may have a new king, a *Highland* king! And Somerled leading the realm!"

Hugh wagged his head, recognising of course the seriousness of it all, but at the back of his mind unable to help wondering whether this would be so ill a development. When he had seen Somerled at Perth and Scone, he had struck him as an able, strong and honest man. Malcolm MacEth was scarcely of the same stature, but under Somerled's guidance he might make as good a monarch as either their present one or Brawny Will. And with the Islesman's fleets and clan armies, the English would find Scotland a much harder nut to crack.

"I see why you have to go warn them at Roxburgh," he said. "But, in fact, this Malcolm MacEth of Ross has greater right to the crown, has he not, than has Prince William, if it becomes vacant? He is the son of King David's *elder* brother, Ethelred, no?"

"Yes. But there are doubts as to his legitimacy. It is a difficult matter. He is not of *David*'s line, whereas William is."

"Who would make the better king?" Margaret asked practically.

"Who can say?"

"The Earl of Ross, with Somerled, could at least unite Highlands and Lowlands," Hugh suggested.

They left it at that, and went to prepare for their visit to the cliffs.

At Redheugh, Hugh introduced Duncan, Meg and little Lara. Meg, asked to come over to Aldcambus in the morning, to ensure the comfort of the thane's daughter, eyed that young woman keenly, assessingly, and then Hugh, whilst agreeing to co-operate.

Leaving the horses, for the clifftop track was scarcely for riding, Hugh led his guests along the so scenic walk, to constant exclamations from Margaret, Hugh's urgings not to go too close to the edge, and occasional physical restraints, and Sir Osbert's remarks on heather growing so near to the sea, the extraordinary positions sheep got themselves into part-way down the precipices, and the dangerous nature of the shoreline, all reefs, rocks and skerries, yet with the floats of lobster creels clearly to be seen dotted there amongst it all. Explanations followed, and Tam Robson's boat pointed out in its cove.

Fastness, on its thrusting stack, produced the usual astonishment, and the young woman had to admit that neither Kinneff Castle nor Whistleberry could rival this in sheer, dramatic siting and inaccessibility. Below the stack Margaret saw a pair of seals, and had to be very heedfully held secure lest her peerings for more endangered her.

The June evening was calm, even though the sinking sun did put the east-facing cliffs in shadow. Hugh enlarged upon conditions here in winter gales, and pointed out the scraps of dried seaweed and even quite large shells cast up these two hundred feet above the tide.

Back at Aldcambus, Eupham Lumsden had the rooms duly prepared for the visitors, although perhaps not quite in the manner of Gelis at Arbuthnott. Unfortunately there was no detached tower here to convey selected guests to, and with father and daughter both heading bedwards at the same time, there was no opportunity for lingering goodnights. Hugh did obtain a squeeze of the arm, however, at one door, and Sir Osbert's nod at the next.

But it was good, at least, to lie thereafter in the room directly above and think of his love just below – for Hugh was now admitting to himself that he was in love with Margaret Olifard, however improbable it seemed that he would ever win a thane's daughter and heiress for himself.

In the morning, with Sir Osbert's anxiety to be off, apparently reconciled to leaving his daughter at Aldcambus until his return but requiring instructions as to how to get to Roxburgh from there, Hugh proposed escorting him part-way and putting him on the right road. Edin's Hall broch, on Cockburn Law, was in the general direction. They could all go that far together – which Hugh felt was something of a noble gesture on his part.

So the four of them rode off due southwards, over the hill to the Eye Water valley and then over further ridges to that of the Whiteadder, the peak of Cockburn Law now prominent before them. At a sharp right-angled bend amongst craggy rocks, in what was here quite a major stream, with an ancient ford just above waterfalls, the thane was directed to follow the river down to Bonkyl and then over the ridge to Duns town, and thence by Polwarth and across the Merse by Hume to Kelshaugh and Roxburgh, another thirty miles, but fairly easy riding.

They parted there, Sir Osbert agreeing that he and his man could find their way back, if not on the morrow then the next day. Hugh refrained from declaring that there was no hurry, Margaret wishing him well with the prince and the others, but urging him not to get involved in any warlike plans for circumventing Somerled of the Isles.

Alone at last, Hugh took the young woman to admire the cascades and little waterfalls in their twisting chasm below the scattered ancient pines. Then back to the horses, to point higher, westwards. They could not see their destination from here, a shoulder of the hill intervening; he declared that it was quite possible to ride up to it, no steeper than some of the Mearns hills they had surmounted. They debated why there should be a broch here and not in the Arbuthnott area where Pictish remains were so frequent, and came to no conclusion.

Up on the higher ground of the law, presently Hugh was able to point out the tall, beehive-shaped structure up there on a green shelf of the hillside, well below the summit, with the river curling deep in its valley far beneath. As they climbed, away to south and east the Merse spread, mile upon mile, to the blue plain of the sea and to the far line of the Cheviot Hills and the Northumberland border. Hugh endeavoured to show his companion approximately where in it all lay Swinton and his calf-country.

Margaret said that she had not realised that this Lowland country would be so hilly, the name misleading.

When they reached the broch, and dismounted, she was enthralled. It was much larger than she had anticipated, a circular tower, tapering as it rose, but even so reaching a parapet-crowned wallhead sixty or so feet high, the walls of dry, unmortared stone still wide enough up there to form a walkway, although now broken down much in ruin. Below they were up to seventeen feet in thickness, enclosing quite a large open area, grass-grown and perhaps forty feet across, which Hugh suggested could be for driving in cattle and sheep for protection from raiders. This was, to be sure, the purpose of this notably major structure, a defensive refuge for the folk to roost secure in when invaders were about. All around it were the foundations of houses and hutments, usually round in shape, indicating quite a population up here on this lofty hillside.

"Why they should have such a tower here, when they relied on rampart-guarded forts elsewhere, as in your Mearns, I know not," Hugh said. "They say that there are brochs in the far north of our land, I understand. There must be some reason behind it. Perhaps it was the Norsemen, the Viking raiders, who called for especial protective measures, fortlets insufficient? Those barbarous invaders never ventured far from their longships at the coast. It could be that. And yet there is a broch near to Peebles, which is far enough inland."

He led the girl into the grassy court, showing her the easily guarded doorway, and then across to the entrance to the walls themselves, these indeed the main feature of the establishment. Helping her up steps, past a ground-floor chamber which in a castle would be called a guard-room or porter's lodge, he took her hand to conduct her up the narrow mural stairway. It was pleasingly dark in there, which called for close contact and due guidance.

"I see why you like brochs!" the young woman observed, but did not shrink away from him.

The stair was not a turnpike, but wound round the walling in no very steep spiral, with numerous little mural chambers off, to left and right, those on the inner side having slit windows to the yard, those on the other without, so that there were no openings to offer weakness on the outer walling. Hand in hand they explored. Not that there was anything to see, or feel, except each other.

Up at parapet level, where more care was required owing to its broken-down state, they sat to eat the honeyed scones Eupham had provided, and to sip honey wine, well content to survey the far-flung scene.

"I have looked forward to this," Margaret admitted presently.

"You mean the scene? Or, or the company!"

She raised that single uplifted eyebrow of hers. "Does it signify? Anyway, I am grateful to Somerled the Islesman for making it possible."

"Would your father not have come, otherwise?"

"I am not sure. He said neither yea nor nay each time that I spoke of it."

"Ah! So you did remind him."

"To be sure. I wanted to see this broch!"

"M'mm. And you are not disappointed?"

"Not so far, friend Hugh."

"I must watch how I tread, then," he declared.

"Do that."

He was watchful indeed as he conducted her down those dark stairs, going first and proceeding backwards lest she should trip and stumble, so that he would catch her. She seemed to be entirely sure-footed, however, in this as in so much else.

Remounted, he took her back by a round-about route through the Lammermuirs, to show her the stone circles of Nine Stanes Rig and the Craw Stones, on to the Pictish forts of Black and Green Castles, then back over Snawdoun and the Papana Water to the still finer White Castle, these foolishly named by later generations, this last with its magnificent views northwards over the Lothian plain to the Scotwater and to Fife beyond. Margaret had to concede that the Lowlands were not devoid of interest.

They were ready for the fine meal that Meg had contrived for them, on their return, even though she refused to share it with them, but waited on them like any maid.

Eating over, Margaret went off to her room, and came back with quite a sizeable bundle, which had evidently been part of her baggage. Before the withdrawing-room fire, she presented this to the man, declaring that he must not be too critical.

Surprised, he took the fairly heavy bundle. Tied up with cord, he unwrapped it, to find and unfold a colourful tapestry, perhaps six feet square, and on it depicted a man, spear in hand, confronting a wild boar, head down, tusks gleaming white, all against a background of trees and rocks.

"Guidsakes!" he exclaimed. "Here, here's a wonder! Lord – look at it! The boar! So like the brute. The boar . . . !"

"If scarcely like yourself! But the spear is well enough! For you to hang on your wall."

"You mean . . . ? It is for *me*?"

"Who else? None other has the right to it."

"But you did it all! Stitched all this. For me!" He stepped forward to throw his arms around her, to hug her, all but shake her. "All that work, that time! For *me*!"

"Not forgetting . . . the boar!" she got out, gaspingly.

Loth to let go of her so enticing person, he allowed his hands to linger until she backed away. "I shall treasure it always. The tapestry of the boar. Kind, kind." He turned, to consider it again, examining it more closely. "Those tusks! The snout! The hunched shoulders. How you do it, I do not know."

"I have made *your* shoulders over narrow, I fear. They are wide. As they needed to be! For fending off boars . . . and set upon women!"

"I, I was carried away."

"As, almost, was I!" She shook her head at him, in case he took it wrongly. "Where will you hang it? The tapestry."

"In my bedchamber, to be sure. Where I can admire it, always. Before I sleep. And, and admire the one who made it." It came to him to strike while the iron was hot. "See you, come and help me choose where to put it." And gathering up the woven hanging, he held out his hand.

She followed him out, even though she did not grasp that hand.

Upstairs, Margaret eyed Hugh's bedroom with frank interest. It was scarcely tidy – but then, her own had not been either, he recollected. She went to straighten up the unmade bed.

"You could do with a Gelis here, I think," she said.

"Or a you!" He laid the tapestry down on the blankets. "Where, then?"

"Above the bed, here?"

"No. I could not eye it there. As I lay."

"Then over the fire?"

"I would have to turn my head to see it. Best over there, I think. Near the window. Where I can lie, and think of Margaret Olifard!"

"You will not dream of boars attacking you?"

"I will dream otherwise, I warrant. Of her who made *that* boar. Of the kind hands that stitched it. And, and . . ."

"Dreamer! You who are so much of a doer! They do not always go together."

"I can dream by day, as well as by night, see you. Can dreams ever come true?"

"That, I think, depends on the dreamer. Now, can I help you to hang this thing? It has loops at both top and bottom."

"It will require pegs. I can find some downstairs. Wait you . . ." And he left her there.

When Hugh came back, with sharp-pointed yew pegs to hammer into the white clay-plastered walling, and a mallet, he found her sitting on his bed. Almost he made the obvious comment, but restrained himself. He was not helped by her own remark.

"Almost, had I lain back, I would have slept!" she declared. "All the riding through your hills. The wind. And the great repast your brother's wife gave us." She pointed a finger at him. "She has a liking for you, that one, you know!"

He thought it best not to reply to either of these statements. "Here are the pegs. Now, to get it up."

Hanging that tapestry entailed quite a performance. First of all a chest, which contained clothing, had to be dragged over to below the chosen position, for them to stand on. Then, Hugh up first, with the material, helped Margaret to get up beside him. There was not much room for the two of them on that chest-top – which produced no complaint from the man. Then there had to be judging and measuring as to just where the hanging was to hang, and the pegs to go. Hugh had left the mallet on the bed, so the young woman had to get down and fetch it and be hoisted up again to hold the tapestry while her companion hammered in the pegs above, near the ceiling, at arm's length, difficult, he being glad to use her support. Then the quite heavy worked material had to be lifted up, to hang, requiring both sets of arms. It was found that one of the pegs was not quite rightly placed, so that the tapestry would be hanging slightly askew and bunched. So that peg had to be extracted, no easy task at that height, repositioned, and hammered firmly in, Margaret holding up her handiwork meanwhile, much physical contact inevitably involved. But with the thing hanging straight at length, they got down, to admire it. Even in the fading sunset light it looked very fine, its features and colours outstanding.

"Good!" the man said. "I thank you. There it shall give me much pleasure. And not forgetting the hanging of it, either!"

They moved the chest back to its proper place.

"So, now I make for my own chamber," she told him. "Unless you are very different from me, I think that you will not admire your boar for very long this night!"

"I say that I will. And admire much else." He sighed. "I only wish that I had a sore back tonight, which required your ministering attention!"

"You cannot have everything!" she told him lightly, and headed for the door.

Escorting her down to her room, when she paused at that door, he searched her features in the dim light. "This has been a good day," he said. "For me, at least. Alone with you, in the main. And now . . ."

"And now we say our goodnights. But . . . gratefully."

"Myself, yes. But you?"

"Oh, yes. I have much to be grateful for." And she touched his wrist.

That was invitation enough for him. He reached out to take her in his arms. She was tall, and did not have to upturn her face much to his; but upturned it was. He bent to kiss her on those moist warm lips, and felt them stir beneath his. It was quite a prolonged embrace before she gently withdrew.

"They say that . . . enough is as good . . . as a feast!" she told him, smiling.

"Enough?" he said, spreading his hands. That was sufficiently eloquent.

"Be patient, Hugh," she advised, and went within, closing the door only slowly, unhurriedly, behind her.

Climbing the stairs again, he savoured that word. Patient? He felt urgent, not patient. But patience implied something to wait for, did it not? Would she have used the word casually? Or meaningfully? She was not a casual young woman. Could he hope . . . ?

He did eye his tapestry for some considerable time before he slept.

In the morning, with the possibility that Sir Osbert could be back that evening, Hugh decided that he must make the most of it, and his opportunities with Margaret. Due consideration convinced him that, the weather being good and with little wind, the cliffs were indicated. Right along them, as far as St Ebba's Head and nunnery. That would be a long walk along the tops. But what about their foots? View the cliffs from below, in a boat? Tam's boat. A change, it would be. And suitably close proximity for the viewers. Something new for the young woman.

Margaret, apprised of this at breakfast, declared herself happy with the notion – if she could trust herself in a boat with him? Uncertain just how to take this, he assured that he was now quite a practised oarsman, and the sea would be calm. She accepted that with a wrinkling of her nose.

So they set off for Redheugh, where both Duncan and Tam Robson offered to accompany them, and were politely told that that would not be necessary. They would, however, check on some of Tam's lobster creels on their way.

Hugh conducted the girl along the precipice crests for roughly the mile necessary to reach the steep track down to the only tiny cove where a boat might be beached. The descent thereafter involved much handholding and lifting of skirts. Safely at the foot, Margaret rather breathlessly exclaimed at the smallness of the craft there drawn up, and the largeness of the white-capped waves, but was informed that it was a seaworthy boat and once beyond the reefs and skerries which broke the combers, they would find the swell moderate. Whether or not reassured, she helped him push the boat down into the water, and was assisted inboard, careless at least over the display of much white leg.

Taking the oars, with Margaret only a couple of feet away facing him from the stern, Hugh dipped, and started to pull. At first, weaving in and out amongst the weed-hung rocks, it did prove to be a rocking and swaying process, with the girl very much aware of the nearness of the water to her hands as she gripped the sides, especially when splashes came aboard from breakers, which her companion declared to be modest and harmless. However, once out beyond the skerries, the water was unbroken, and the Norse Sea swell regular but not unpleasant, even when they turned sideways-on, to head southwards down the coast. Hugh hoped that he had not misjudged, and that Margaret was not inclined to seasickness.

Soon thereafter the young woman's attention was fully occupied. The cliffs looked still more dramatic from this level, soaring and fierce-seeming, the stacks, buttresses, crevasses and chimneys thereof much more apparent than from above. And their denizens, the thousands of birds, roosting on every ledge, crack and shelf, wheeling in the air, diving into the sea, with splashes around them, screaming and wheepling and croaking, held her spellbound, exclaiming when she saw the divers coming up again with gleaming, wriggling, small silver fish in their beaks, sometimes close enough for the shaking of their wings to scatter water on the pair in the boat. Hugh named the fowl as various breeds of gull, terns, razorbills, guillemots, kittiwakes, shearwaters, petrels, fulmars, even the occasional puffin, whilst admitting that there were some he could not identify.

Presently he was able to point out what Margaret had assumed to be two small rocks but which proved to be the heads of a couple of seals, watching them from the water, like round-eyed old men with down-turning moustaches. They quietly sank away as the boat drew close, but in a few moments reappeared on the other side, clearly intrigued.

Hugh rowed into the cave beneath the Fastness tower, and round its bends was able to point upwards to where he said the shaft opened to give access to the building; that is, if some sort of long rope ladder was lowered, no ascent possible without one. The girl could see nothing in the gloom however much guidance was given. The man would have liked to linger, close together in that dark place and gently rocking on the tide, but could think of no good excuse to do so.

They had passed a number of coloured floats marking the positions of sunken lobster creels, but Hugh said that these would best be investigated on their way back.

Beyond Fastness there was almost five miles before they came to the mighty headland of St Ebba, the loftiest and most challenging feature of all that coast, quite a lengthy row for

277

the man. Passing configurations which he named as Souter, Brander, Hurker, Mawcarr and Heathery Carr, he told the girl about St Ebba. She was a Northumbrian princess, daughter of King Ethelfrith, in the seventh century, a strong Christian who, having been saved from shipwreck here, saw it as the place to establish a nunnery free from the pagan assaults of the Norse raiders who terrorised this coast; but as added precaution, having her own and her nuns' noses cut off, some say their breasts, to make them less attractive to the Danes. The nunnery was now deserted, but its ruins were still to be seen on the clifftop, three hundred feet above the waves. They would visit them presently.

St Ebba's Head was different from the rest of that cliff-girt coastline not only in being higher but by being more cut into with great water-filled chasms, yawning, sheer-sided craters like vast quarries gouged out of the solid rock. These were the haunt of seals, also cormorants and shags, the girl was told; and the thrusting whitened stacks guarding them, like vast, jagged teeth, tusks indeed, the unlikely homes for myriads of shrieking fowl. Margaret did not know whether to be fascinated or repelled.

There was nowhere to land here and Hugh had to row on for almost another mile before he could put in at a small haven and fishing village, the name of which had got corrupted to St Abbs. Here they landed, the man thankful enough to stop rowing, for he had been at it for almost three hours. It was good to stretch legs instead of arms.

They had to start climbing almost at once, northwards, over grassy hummocks and shoulders, to reach the clifftops from the rear, as it were, a long ascent, their route taking them up on to what developed into a spine or ridge, which on the landward side flanked a strange, deep valley cradling a long, narrow loch, an unusual feature to find in such a position. But then, this entire locality was unusual indeed.

At length, panting somewhat from their climbing – which drew the man's attention the more to his companion's heaving bosom – they reached the lofty summit area of the great headland, not at all like the normal clifftop scene, more

278

of a minor range of hills on which sheep pastured. But seaward, after the grassy downward slopes, these dropped away suddenly to the dire rock-lined gashes and chasms which they had stared at from below, terrifying drops to the surging waters; terrifying, that is, to Hugh, not himself a sufferer from vertigo but whose stomach lurched when he saw Margaret go close to the edge to peer downwards, she obviously untroubled by it, only enthralled by the dizzy drops and gaping voids. The man, of course, found it incumbent on him to hold her safe.

He led her to the furthermost projecting peninsula of it all, the grassy apex of which was cut off by a partly artificial ditch, which he declared might well have been there before the nunnery, for almost certainly this would have been the site of a Pictish strong-point centuries earlier. Near this he pointed out the fallen remains of masonry, mortared not dry-stone, and said that he had been told that this was where, at a later date, the nuns had set up a male establishment for lay brothers, no doubt partly a protective measure and also to supply manual labour, but which in time probably had assisted in the corruption of what had started out so chastely religious, and led to the eventual dissolution. Some distance seaward of these remains they came on more, similar, which were presumably the nuns' own premises, much broken down and scattered. But further still, almost on the cliff's edge, plainly to be seen, was the oblong outline of the chapel's foundations, an extraordinary spot indeed to set a church. Service therein must frequently have been drowned out in howling, battering gales, and in fact literally in spray and spume.

Having exclaimed and wondered over all this, Hugh led the young woman over to the very lip of the yawning gulf where, just a few feet below the cornice, projected a tiny grassy shelf, where wild thyme grew.

"Here," he said. "Here we can sit and eat our scones, and view it all. That is, if you are not daunted? I have sat here many times."

"Daunted? Of what?" she enquired. "Should I be?" And she raised her brows at him. "At the heights? Or the birds? Or the company I keep? Other women have no doubt sat here, the noseless, breastless ones. Or, perhaps, other friends of your own?"

"No, no. I have sat here alone, hitherto. You, I think, are not a fearful woman!" Crouching down, he lowered himself to the ledge, and reached up to aid her down to it, holding her securely for, admittedly, a slip here could have been fatal. She descended safely and without fuss.

Turning, they sat amongst the wild thyme, its scent countering that of the bird-droppings on the cliff-sides. They faced the ocean, backs against the rock.

"This is . . . joy!" the man said, simply, and his arm slipped round between her and the stone, protectively. She did not shake him off.

Silent they sat for a while, watching the wheeling fowl and the surging tides and all the empty plain of the sea, Hugh very much aware of the rise and fall of female breathing.

"I love you, Margaret," he announced, quite quietly, factually, after a while.

She made no comment.

He held her still closer, if that was possible, and the hand of the arm around her cupped her right breast, and shared the rising and falling with it.

"You are all in all to me," he went on, almost as though he was explaining it all to himself. "Have been since first I knew you. The woman of my heart."

Still she did not speak.

"Here, in this place, I have to say it. You understand?"

She nodded. "I understand," she told him gravely.

"I love you, I want you, I need you." His calm speech was changing. "But – that is not enough, I know."

"No? Do I seem so demanding?"

"You seem . . . out of my reach!"

"Hardly that, Hugh!" She smiled, as she moved her person a little within his arm.

"Out of my reach," he repeated. "I feel that."

"I am sorry."

"Are you? You, lass – you? How do *you* feel? Can you feel anything for me?" He all but shook her. "Can you? Do you?"

280

"You ask it, Hugh? Think you that I would be sitting here, on this edge of eternity, far from all others, with you holding my bosom, if I did not care?"

He drew a quick breath and withdrew the hand a little – to have it gently but firmly reached for and restored to where it had been.

That spoke louder than any words. Hugh clutched her with an ardour which was next to dangerous in their position. "My dear! My dear! My heart! My love! Can it be true? That you *love* me, also. You?"

"Can you doubt it, still? Would I have done what I have, allowed what I have, treated you as I have, had I not cared for you?"

"Cared, yes. But . . ."

"Cared, and deeply. You are hard to convince, my love. Yes, I love you, Hugh de Swinton. Have done from early on, I think. Before ever you slew the boar. It took me a small while to recognise it. When I had to come for you, on my horse that time, when the boar might have had you, I knew . . ."

She got no further, as he turned her to him to be kissed and hugged and kissed again, and nowise discouraged by any lack of response. It was as well, in the circumstances, that they both had good heads for heights.

When she could, she freed an arm to point downwards, before using it to ruffle his hair. "It would be a pity . . . to end it all amongst the seals!" she said.

He was heedless. "You never told me. How you felt."

"It is not a woman's part to declare love first! And you have not mentioned the word until now, in this place."

"But, but – you must have known! I, I . . ."

Another bout of kissing and fondling.

"Those nuns must be turning in their graves!" she got out.

In time, the inevitable question came. "What will your father say?" Hugh asked, in different voice.

"Ah! Well may you ask." Margaret sounded different also.

"Would he allow that I wed you?"

"I do not know. Oh, I wish that he had had a son. That I was not his only heir."

"Aye, heir to the thanedom of Arbuthnott and the Mearns. And I but a second son, a small laird of barren clifftop acres. He will want a better match for you than that, I fear."

"He admires you greatly, I know. And he is grateful. Your courage. And you are a knight. But . . ."

"But, yes. Great ones have their own needs and demands."

"I will do what I can. Seek to persuade him . . ."

"Then you *would* marry me? If it was left to you?"

"Need you ask? Think you I would be content to play mistress to the man I loved, while wedding another?"

That set his mind in a whirl. "M'mm."

"We must hope," she said. "My father is fond of me. Will not wish to hurt me. We have that."

"But will that be enough? What of Dallas of Kinneff? And Allardyce of that Ilk? Others, who would better serve? And who want you."

She pressed his arm, but said nothing.

"If there was anything that I could *do*! To make him favour me."

"You killed the boar. None other did that."

"But that is not what he needs, for you. He will be looking for position, power, lands . . ."

She shook her head. "Do not let us spoil this moment, Hugh, by such worries. That is for the future. Here we have proclaimed ourselves, our love. That is for sure, for always. Here, as you said, is joy . . ."

He was prompt in demonstrating his agreement with that.

In time, they remembered the scones. Also the fact that Hugh had to row back, a long way for any single oarsman. And there were lobster creels to service. Reluctantly they rose, climbed, and set off, eating as they went, but frequently hand in hand.

Down at the boat, Margaret offered to assist at the oars – if she would be of any use. But, on her admission that she had never tried the rowing, Hugh declared that the Norse Sea was hardly the place to start learning. That he would be better on his own, with the sideways swell to counter.

They headed northwards, and soon were peering upwards,

282

to try to discern the exact ledge, amongst hundreds, where they had not exactly plighted their troth but opened their hearts to each other.

Tam Robson did not set his creels further south than Fastness, and so they had quite a way to go before their first red float appeared, although they had passed others, differently coloured, no doubt belonging to the St Abbs fishermen. Margaret had never experienced lobster-creeling before, and she was not greatly enamoured of it now, for the first one hoisted up did contain a large, claw-waving creature which looked fearsome indeed, and which Hugh had to extract from the wickerwork cage through a net funnel, which took some doing if hands were not to be nipped, a rearward hold, and in a certain position on the lobster essential. Then the catch had to be deposited in a large lidded basket, and bait, in the form of old fish-heads which had been making a smell throughout the voyage, taken from a basket, placed in the creel, and this lowered again on the end of its rope and float. This all took time, needless to say, and Hugh decided that only a token servicing would do, in the circumstances, or they would be late indeed in getting back to Aldcambus. Three lobsters and two empty creels sufficed, and they made for the cove, Hugh's shoulders, wide as they might be, aching. He had never rowed so far before.

An excellent thought occurred to him as they rode homewards, and as he kept straightening up the said shoulders and flexing his back muscles. Embrocation, carefully applied, might be advantageous, in more ways than one. He suggested the same to his companion.

She had expressive eyebrows, that young woman, and knew how to use them. "As bad as that, is it?" she wondered. "I did not bring any ointments nor lotions with me, I fear!"

"Oh, I should think that Eupham Lumsden will have something that would serve," he said. "Some mixture of herbs."

"Is this why you took me to St Ebba's Head?"

The man was concerned over more than the contents of Eupham's cupboard as they neared his house. Would Sir Osbert have returned from Roxburgh? There was no sign of the extra horses when he saw the paddock, to his satisfaction. It was dusk now, and unlikely for the travellers to appear that night.

The Lumsden cupboard did contain home-mixed lotions of sorts; and appropriating these, Hugh ordered plenty of hot water for night-time washing.

The pair had a good meal, late as it was, and it was not long thereafter before their couches called, the man producing the lotions, and Margaret doubting whether anointing would help tired back muscles. But she did not refuse to accompany him upstairs to his own room.

There he was prompt in stripping off his clothing and heading for the wash-tub, the young woman watching him amusedly. When he had washed his frontal parts, and still she sat on the bed, he asked if she was not going to come and bathe his back for him?

"Am I your hand-maiden now?" she enquired.

"Ah, well, lacking Gelis, should I send for Eupham? Or Meg?"

"Men!" she declared, head ashake, but came over.

She was not as thorough in the matter as Gelis would have been, but he thought better of complaining. He dried himself, and went to lie on the bed, on his stomach as required, the girl asserting that she did not know which of the two pots of ointment to use. He advised both, to be safe, and awaited her ministrations.

"I have a notion that this is all something of a play-acting!" she told him, but started to apply one of the mixtures, her fingers gently smoothing, soothing, more stroking than rubbing. It was a very pleasant sensation, to be lying there in the half-dark room, her hands on him, especially when she started to hum a little melody, repetitious and in time with her massaging. Presumably Margaret did not find it too unpleasant and wearisome either, for she continued the process and the humming for quite some time.

Even so, the man was greedy, urging that she tried the other lotion also. She slapped his back at that, but did as he urged.

He wondered, of course, just how far he could go at this,

now? Could he turn over on his back? He could hardly claim that his chest muscles required the anointing.

"I could wish," he announced, "that I had allowed you to assist at the rowing, as you offered. Then *your* fair person might have needed embrocation, also, and I could have repaid your kind attention!"

"So, think what I have been spared!" She rose. "That will serve, I think, oarsman!"

He turned and sat up. He held out his arms.

Smiling, she stooped to be kissed goodnight, and was enfolded, pulled down upon him and held fast, his lips on her hair, her brow, her eyes, her mouth, her neck and lower, hands not inactive either.

"Your back . . . is clearly better!" she managed to say.

"I wish . . ."

"To be sure you do! Almost, I could say the same! But . . . not yet, my dear. Not yet. We must be patient, no? Until we see our course more clearly before us. Can see the way ahead. We love each other . . ."

"Yes, that is it. We *love* each other."

"But our love will not fade, for a little patience. And be the better when we can take each other with no reserves, I think."

"When will that be?"

"Let us hope not too far hence. It is no wish of mine to disappoint nor thwart and irk you. See." His busy hands had been stroking, feeling at her bodice; and now she opened it for him, so that he might touch and kiss those warm, rounded breasts; which he did with murmurs of bliss, incoherent, out of such busy lips.

"Something of a promise," she said, kissing his downbent head, and nodding at his so apparent masculinity. "It has been a good, a joyful day. Let us end it so, saving for still better to come, we hope and pray. Now, before we confound fine resolutions – goodnight, my heart!" And she turned his head up from her chest, to kiss his lips almost fiercely. Then rose, and practically ran for the door, and out.

She left the man in turmoil.

*   *   *

The next day he took her northwards to visit Dunbar, with its great castle of Cospatrick's on its series of rock-stacks; and then inland into the hills to where the Swinton sheep were pastured, where they saw and were given entertainment by Meg's father and brother. When they got back, it was to see the Olifard horses grazing in the Aldcambus paddock. There would be no temptations to fight that night; but they had at least enjoyed some moderate collusion up on the high heathery slopes.

Sir Osbert was scarcely concerned as to how his daughter had passed her time in his absence, his mind preoccupied with the national affairs. Somerled of the Isles had struck, it seemed, invaded the mainland. A great fleet of longships, birlinns and galleys had come up the Firth of Clyde, to disgorge its thousands at Dumbarton. These were being carried across the narrows into Renfrewshire and eastwards, to seek to put Malcolm MacEth of Ross on the throne while King Malcolm was sick in England, a dire situation for Scotland. The northern earls were said to be rising again, in favour of Ross, mustering to march southwards, probably at Perth. It was war, civil war, and the English threat never far distant.

Walter fitz Alan, the High Steward, whose lands of Renfrew and Cunninghame were in the direct path of Somerled's invasion, had gone to lead the immediate opposition, with his Norman knights. Cospatrick of Dunbar and March was gathering the Mersemen and border mosstroopers to defend Roxburgh and the south-east. Keith the Marischal and de Morville the High Constable were to march north, to attempt to hold the narrows of Forth at Stirling against the earls, and defend Edinburgh against the Islesmen if they swung that way. And Bruce of Annandale was to see that the Galloway brothers did not join Somerled or give help to any English move in the south-west. All this had been hastily put in hand in these last two days, he, Olifard, having arrived at Roxburgh at the height of the reaction to the alarm.

Listening, Hugh felt almost guilty that in those two days of the realm's need, he and Margaret had been enjoying themselves. And yet, would Somerled be so ill an influence on Scotland . . . ?

It seemed that Sir Osbert had been given his own orders by Prince William, who was now representing his brother's crown. He was to return at once to the Mearns, and seek to raise a force from the lairds and barons of that area and Deeside, to separate the earldoms of Mar to the north and Angus to the south, even that of Fife if possible, to prevent these from combining to join the other Celtic earls and aid the Islesmen and Ross. This charge had put the thane to great concern, for he had had no experience of warfare and armed leadership, his thanedom having been comfortably remote from battle, invasion and major conflict, save for having to deal with Highland caterans and minor clan feuds. When he had sought, from Prince William, the loan of experienced fighters to assist him in this task, it had been made clear to him that none could be spared, with all being fully occupied, most already away with their own lords and leaders. When the Earl Cospatrick complained that the so-useful Swinton brothers, his advanced-party skirmishers, were amissing, the prince's answer had come up: let Sir Hugh and if possible his brother go to the thane's aid.

Needless to say, Hugh was nowise averse. The more he was with Margaret the happier he would be. The campaigning part of it might be less to his taste, but he could not refuse that in the realm's service. What Duncan would say, remained to be seen.

That young husband and father was reluctant to leave Redheugh, but also felt that he had to go. And there was to be no delay, for Olifard was for off first thing in the morning on their lengthy journey northwards.

Clearly then, this was not the moment to approach Sir Osbert over the matter of his daughter's affections and future. That must await a more favourable occasion. But, was there a possibility that this new involvement for Hugh might present him with some support for his personal cause?

It was with some surprise that the Swintons learned that the Roxburgh authorities had been sufficiently concerned over this move to prevent the Earls of Mar and Angus from joining the others that it had been decided the delay in riding the long road

287

to the Mearns could be avoided by the thane's party going by sea. Accordingly, a ship would be ordered to take them northwards from Berwick-on-Tweed to Inverbervie. This would entail an approximately one-hundred-mile voyage; and unless the wind changed into the north from the south-west, unlikely in late June, they ought to cover that in a twenty-four-hours' sailing.

That night there could be no intimate partings.

Next morning the five of them rode off southwards the twenty-two miles to Berwick, where they found a vessel awaiting them, a comparatively small craft which unfortunately had no accommodation for horses. This was a complication which they could have done without. It meant that they had to leave Sir Osbert's groom behind, with the beasts, to bring them on northwards at his own time, that long ride, picking up one of the Aldcambus men to assist him, while the principals would need to obtain mounts at Inverbervie to get them to Arbuthnott. Somebody at Roxburgh should have thought of this.

It was midday before they sailed, a new experience for Margaret. She had been out on a fishing-craft from Inverbervie, but never on what could be termed a voyage. Fortunately the weather was fine and the sea calm. Their skipper said that he would have them up to Inverbervie well before noon on the morrow.

Accommodation on the vessel was modest and very limited, and even with the crew crammed into one smallish cabin, the three male passengers into the other, there was only a sail-locker available for the young woman. However, she made no fuss about putting up with that for one short night.

So Hugh had proximity to his beloved that afternoon and evening, but no privacy, conditions not apt either for broaching the subject of marriage to her father. The talk was all of the crisis in the realm and how Sir Osbert was to play his required part, who he could approach for armed men, whether the Earl of Fife was likely to join the other Celtic earls, and if so what could be done about that. Hugh and Duncan could not be a great deal of help to him at this stage.

Most of the time they seemed to be in sight of the land, even when off the wide mouths of the estuaries of Forth and Tay. The wind, warm but fitful, was consistently from the south-west and sent them northwards in good time. It is never really dark at this time of the year in these latitudes; but by the time that the dusk had hidden the shoreline and sleep beckoned the passengers after a plain but adequate meal, the skipper estimated that they would be not far south of Arbroath.

Hugh was concerned about Margaret's comfort in her sail-locker. When travelling any distance, wise folk always carried their own blankets strapped behind their saddles, and the young woman had hers; but by no stretch of the imagination could her quarters here be named comfortable, nor the buckets for sanitation other than elementary. But she asserted that the sail-cloth would make a reasonable mattress, and that she would do very well, rocked to sleep by the waves. Crouching together in that dark, low-ceilinged cockpit, they did achieve a brief embrace of sorts, and whispered endearments, before Hugh returned to the others.

All slept remarkably well thereafter, considering the conditions.

Their skipper was very pleased with himself when they appeared in the morning, able to point out Red Head far astern and Montrose coming up ahead. He would have them at Inverbervie in two to three hours. Then he would go back to Arbroath and ship a cargo of smoked fish to take to Berwick.

Much appreciative of time saved by this voyage, the passengers disembarked at the fishing haven. The thane had no difficulty in collecting four horses to take them the four miles or so to Arbuthnott, even though these were not of the highest quality. They were at the castle by midday.

Sir Osbert lost no time now. Men were sent out to all the local barons and magnates requiring them to attend on him at the castle without delay, leaving behind orders for their maximum manpower to assemble as quickly as possible, armed and horsed. He despatched other messengers up to Deeside, some twenty-five miles north, to raise the lairds thereabouts. Then he turned to Hugh.

"You and your brother, my friend, have experienced warfare, are versed in its demands, as we are not. You must be my eyes and wits, in this. I want to know whether the Earls of Mar and Angus are on the march, where they are if so, and where it might be possible to halt them. I recognise that this is no light charge to put upon you, for you do not know the land. But you do know the ways of armed hosts and fighting men. I will give you a guide who does know the area to the north and the Dee valley. Will you do this? Find out in especial what Mar is doing. Whether he marches. Or has already marched? And whether we can stop him."

"We can try, sir. But, that is north. What of Angus? That is *south* of here. Is not the Earl of Angus's seat at Arbroath?"

"Yes. But I think that Gillebride of Angus may be less eager to join the other earls. As you will know, he is married to your Earl Cospatrick's sister, and has other links with the Lowlands and the present royal line. I will send men south to discover what he does. *You* head north towards Mar. And get me word back as soon as may be."

"As you will, my lord Thane. When do we go?"

"Now. So soon as you may. Mar may be already on the way to join the others. At Perth perhaps. So, all haste. You will need messengers to send back to me . . ."

So it was farewells almost at once, Margaret concerned that her love did not run into any kind of danger. Their parting embrace ought to have informed Sir Osbert if he did not realise it already, that his daughter was more than a little involved with Hugh de Swinton.

22

The brothers rode off, with four companions, their guide a
stocky individual in his late thirties named Hamish, who
seemed to come from Strachan, none so far from Deeside,
and three others to act as couriers. They headed at first
almost due westwards along the upper Bervie Water some
six miles, and over the watershed to the Luther Water, where
they made for Auchenblae, a village renowned for its links
with the early saint Palladius. Here they made their first
enquiries. Had the villagers heard anything of a large force
heading southwards down the Cairn o' Mount drove-road, or
through Strath Finella? No such word had reached them.

Still westwards, through the narrow wooded strath itself,
so oddly named, for strath meant a wide vale and this was
anything but that; and called after the Lady Finella, wife
of the mormaor of the Mearns, who had been responsible
for the death of Kenneth the Second hereabouts. It was a
picturesque locality however grim its story of murder and
betrayal. At the far end of this, where the valley opened
into the true Highland mountains, were the few houses of
Glen Saugh, here because of the ancient royal hunting-forest
of the Celtic kings, whose deer-dyke, for the driving of the
game to the strategically placed archers, was still a feature
of the landscape. They again asked their questions, in the
name of the thane – for the great north–south drove-road
passed nearby. No large company of men had passed this
way recently, they were told.

So that was good news. Mar, if making for Perth, could
have chosen to follow the much further west pass through the
mountains, out of Deeside, by the Cairnwell and Spittal of
Glenshee; but this, much steeper and more difficult, seemed

less likely for a sizeable host. So the probability was that, if he was marching, he had not yet started, or at least had not got thus far. A dozen miles from Arbuthnott, they decided to halt for the night here, before heading due northwards now into the high mountains, haste less vital. Hamish said that there were ten more very rough miles over empty country, by the Cairn o' Mount pass, before the next shelter could be reached, at Glen Dye.

With Sir Osbert's authority, they had no difficulty in obtaining accommodation and food for the night. It seemed a long day to Hugh and Duncan, after awakening at sea, off Lunan Bay, now to be facing one of the loftiest pass routes in all Scotland and possible confrontation with an army on the march.

They discussed with Hamish the extraordinary tale of Lady Finella's hatred; and the other royal story, told of this selfsame area, where Queen Ingeborg, Malcolm Canmore's first wife, had been sent, all but exiled, to his hunting-seat of Kincardine Castle nearby, when he became infatuated with Margaret Atheling, and where Ingeborg died shortly afterwards 'not without suspicion of poison', so that he could marry Margaret the Saint, the present monarch's great-grandmother. Ingeborg's two small sons had survived, and the elder was the ancestor of Earl Cospatrick.

Off early in the morning, they started to climb into the heathery wastes, keeping a careful look-out ahead, only deer very much in evidence all around them. Up and up they rode, but saw nothing but stags and hinds. Hamish said that this drove-road was frequently quite impassable in winter snows, and they could well believe it. No trees grew, no shelter of any sort offered itself, only endless miles of steep heather slopes, rocks and peat-bog.

Hugh had looked for some sort of narrow pass through the crags, but nothing of the sort developed, the highest point being just the summit of Cairn o' Mount itself, with their track passing near the Pictish burial-cairn which gave the mountain its name. No place here for any possible ambush of an army.

The view northwards, over more heights, was still empty

of aught but deer. Here Hugh sent one of the couriers back, to inform Sir Osbert that so far there was no sign of any force from Mar and Aberdeenshire. Then they pressed on.

After some more miles they found a deep valley opening before them, Glen Dye they were told, the Water of Dye threading it and running northwards. This interested Hugh, for down in it the quite sizeable river took a sharp right-angled bend round a steepish bluff. Here was the first possible location they had seen for an ambush. Let an unsuspecting army, strung out, get halfway round this, and it could be cut into sections and made ineffective by a much smaller force.

Their road followed the Dye Water down another three miles, in its twisting valley, until quite suddenly all opened out and a great spread of lower country lay before them. This was Feughside, Hamish informed, the wide strath of the Feugh Water, and Strachan, pronounced Strawn, where he had been reared, the centre of it, where the two rivers joined. They would be there in a mile or so. Deeside lay only another five miles beyond.

At Strachan, Hamish took them to his brother's small farmhouse, where they were well received and fed. No word of any force coming southwards had reached here as yet – indeed they had not heard anything of Somerled's invasion and the earls' rising in support of it. Here Hugh and Duncan held a debate with Hamish and his brother as to their further progress. They knew nothing of Deeside save that it was a major strath, more or less dividing the Mearns area from Mar and Aberdeenshire, populous as it was lengthy, and fertile. If they found no signs of a host therein, or word of one heading westwards for the other Cairnwell–Glen Shee pass, could they assume that the Earl of Mar was not in fact intending to join the other Celtic earls? Hamish said no. Mar was a huge earldom, and its lord could call on support from all over Aberdeenshire, a vast area. He could summon thousands to his banner. It would take a considerable time for all to assemble, presumably at Kildrummy Castle, Mar's main seat. The muster could still be going on. It was too soon to say that there would be no Mar involvement in this warfare.

What, then, should the Swinton brothers do now? Move on, to see if there was any news of an assembly in Deeside? And if not, probe further north still towards Mar itself?

The Strachan brothers said yes to the first but saw no point in the second. If Mar was already gone westwards they would know of it in Deeside. Also they would know if he was still assembling at Kildrummy, for the Earl Morgund had sundry vassals in the great valley, and would have called on them to join his array. No need to risk heading on northwards into Mar itself.

So it was on the further few miles, through lower hills, by Finzean and Ballogie, to the Dee itself, in a magnificent wide strath with much cultivated land and many villages and hamlets, more of these on the north side of the broad river than on the south. They crossed it by a ford near Birse, to reach the township of Aboyne.

As it transpired, they learned all that they required to know at this Aboyne, a thriving place with a well-doing inn. Yes, the Earl Morgund was mustering his people, but had not yet started southwards in force. He was going to come this way, no doubt to head over the Cairn o' Mount, for he had ordered his south Deeside vassals to assemble at Clune, on the lower Feugh, and he would pick them up there. Had he been intending to use the Cairnwell pass, he would have arranged another meeting place on the north side and further west. Just when he would reach and cross Dee none could say. How many would adhere to Mar's summons, as against Sir Osbert's, remained to be seen; but that was not Hugh's and Duncan's responsibility.

What *was* their duty now was to turn southwards again at speed, to inform the thane of the situation. There was nothing that they could usefully do here; earlier messengers would have brought Sir Osbert's orders. It was now evening, and the Cairn o' Mount pass was no place to cross by night. They would return to Strachan, snatch a few hours of rest there, and be off at first light.

This they did, weary but reasonably satisfied.

* * *

They were back at Arbuthnott next day by mid-afternoon, to find it a hive of activity, its proximity alive with men and horses, Margaret busy indeed arranging catering for the numerous local barons and lairds who had answered their thane's call, including Dallas of Kinneff, Allardyce of that Ilk and Ogilvie of Barras, all of whom seemed to be showing more interest in the young woman than in her father's plans and problems. Sir Osbert was greatly relieved to see Hugh back so soon, and with his news. He said that the response to his call so far had been most heartening – he reckoned that not far off twelve hundred men would be at his disposal by the morrow, better than he had anticipated, and that not counting any from Deeside. The Earl of Angus did not appear to be mustering, which was a blessing. But how many men Mar would produce was another matter, two or three thousand, perhaps. If so, what could the Mearnsmen do against such a host, untrained for war as they were?

Hugh had his own ideas as to that. He told the thane about the sharp bend in the Water of Dye, in its narrow ravine, and its possibilities for an ambush. If Mar came over the Cairn o' Mount, as seemed likely, then he would have to negotiate that hazard. There was opportunity.

The older man did not seem to appreciate the full significance of this, still seeing numbers as all-important. Hugh and Duncan sought to explain. It was doubtful whether they succeeded in informing him of the niceties of using the land to fight for them; but what they did achieve was the other's acceptance that *they* knew what they were talking about, and could take the weight of decision off his hands. If this was the way to deal with Mar, then let them try it. Neither he, nor any of his supporters here, had any better, or other suggestions. So let Sir Hugh and his brother take charge.

Extraordinary as it might seem, then, Hugh found himself more or less in command of a small army. If some of the other lairds were doubtful about this young stranger taking charge, the thane's authority prevailed, his assertions that the Swintons had much experience in warfare, in Galloway and elsewhere, assisting, and the fact that Hugh had been knighted a help.

So that evening there was little opportunity for any dalliance with Margaret, the castle full of strangers anyway. Hugh spent most of the time explaining his proposals to the leaders of the Mearnsmen, how discipline, timing and secrecy were the essence of it all, and the lie of the land notably important. Also in assessing the numbers of men who would be available, and deciding who would be in charge of groups and sections.

Sir Osbert, preoccupied still over numbers, was for waiting until he could amass maximum totals. But Hugh was more concerned with speed, timing. Mar might march at any time, might indeed be on his way now. In an ambush, being on the spot and prepared was much more important than the size of the force. He urged a move just as soon as possible, first thing in the morning indeed, so that they might reach the chosen area in ample time to make their dispositions. He was uncertain how long it would take for a force of this size, made up of levies, unused to travelling as a host, possibly many of the men indifferent riders, to cover the score or so miles to Glen Dye. There was much else he was uncertain of also, to be sure, more particularly what might happen if they came face to face with Mar's array before they reached their destination.

That night Hugh and Duncan shared a room with four other guests, so there was only the briefest of goodnights with Margaret. She did manage to convey to him, however, her concern for him on the morrow and her urgings as to not thrusting himself forward into danger, despite her pride in his new leadership role.

There were some eight hundred men assembled at Arbuthnott in the morning, of all types and ages, with some fifteen lairds to lead them. Others would be arriving in due course, but Hugh would not wait for them; these could come on later, with Allardyce left to bring them to the Dye. Before they made a start the thane addressed the leadership, emphasising the importance of their mission, their good fortune in having Sir Hugh de Swinton and his brother to take command, and the

296

need for obedience to his orders – for he would be acting in the name, not only of himself but of King Malcolm. They would be almost certainly confronting a much greater force than their own; but Sir Hugh had confidence in their ability to halt and overcome the rebel earl's host. They would ride in four troops. There must be no straggling, no diversions, no questioning of orders, for theirs would be a formidable and critical operation, demanding exact timing and action. Was it understood?

Mounting, and with a wave to Margaret – unfortunately remaining in the company of Allardyce – Hugh led off, Sir Osbert at his side. Duncan had gone on ahead, with Hamish and two others, to act as scouts.

They followed the same route as on two days before, only much more slowly, and inevitably considerably strung out, up Bervie and over to Strath Finella and Glen Saugh. Duncan would send back word if Mar's force was sighted ahead on the high ground. If it was, reaction would depend on conditions arising, but Hugh at least prayed that this would not happen. Reaching the deer-dykes, they turned to face the mountains, a long climb for a lengthy company.

Hugh was seeking to remember in detail the exact layout of the land in the Dye valley, for this was all-important. He had looked at it carefully on his way back, the day before, but memorising how, to be able to plan it all, and to hide eight hundred men, was a thought indeed. If they got that far . . .

One of Duncan's trio came back to them when halfway up to Cairn o' Mount – and the sight of him riding down to them had Hugh biting his lip. However, the message was to say that there was no sign of any host from the summit, and that deer at furthest viewing were undisturbed, which implied that there was nothing ahead to affect them for some considerable distance. This produced sighs of relief.

The drove-road varied in width as it did in surface and conditions, on the open heather, so that the company could spread itself somewhat and not require to ride three or four abreast as had been necessary down in Strath Finella;

therefore the force was not so greatly strung out. Even so, they made no very tidy and regimented advance, and glancing back frequently, Hugh shook his head over these Mearnsmen's ideas as to discipline. They were, of course, mainly farm-workers, cattlemen, wood-cutters, millers and the like.

At the Cairn o' Mount summit there were still no tidings sent back by Duncan, and the long and undulating descent to the Dye was begun. It was well past midday.

In the valley itself, Duncan awaited them. He pointed ahead, and up. There, on the high ground beyond, Hamish was placed in a position to see far northwards. At first glimpse of any company heading towards them he would send word, which ought to give them ample time to ready themselves.

That was heartening, but Hugh wasted no time. He took the leaders forward to the chosen sharp right-angled bend round that rocky bluff, to point out the features and the dispositions demanded. The bluff itself was all but sheer, and no assault could be made down that; but its top would make an excellent command-post, with views down both sides. Also, the bare, stony summit would provide them with plenty of rocks to hurl down upon the riders below and help to create confusion and some casualties. The grassy slopes on either side were steep, but not so much so that men, dismounted, could not rush down upon the strung-out foe. The problem here was that the waiting ambushers must not be seen by the advancing enemy as they came over the heights northwards. What Hugh proposed, if they were given time, was that their folk should be set to work cutting down whin bushes and scrub birch and hawthorn, fairly plentiful in the valley, and out of it erecting barriers on the higher ground, to hide behind. This would not be noticeable as strange and unnatural from any distance. Then, further back, in sundry folds of the hill flanks on both sides, the mounted men would wait until signalled to charge down upon the confused and disorganised force below, cutting them up into sections – for almost certainly its leaders would be riding at the front of the lengthy line. Hopefully, they would drive some substantial proportion into the river.

His hearers were duly impressed although, from their

questions, not all were sure of the role they were expected to play. There would have to be considerable further instruction, demonstration and repetition – if there was time for such.

So it was back to the main body and duties allocated, a slow process, the bush-cutting started and the dragging up to the higher ground put in hand. Hugh went prospecting hollows and folds for mounted men to hide in – and all the time keeping an eye on the vantage-point where Hamish was stationed, watching the north. No signal nor message came therefrom.

By dusk he was reasonably satisfied. How this nondescript force would behave when and if it came to action he could not tell; but he had done what he could. No camp-fires were to be lit that night, although it was surely unlikely that any major host would attempt this mountain-crossing in darkness.

Sentries were posted, just in case. Men slept as best they could, horses tethered, the narrow floor of the valley making for a very lengthy camp. Hugh dozed and awoke, dozed and awoke throughout the short June night, responsibility heavy upon him. These hundreds of men were relying on him to lead them, their lives all but in his hands, something he had never envisaged, never sought. He envied Duncan, who seemed to take it all in his stride, even Olifard who had handed over responsibility to him. He doubted if he was a born commander!

There were no overnight alarms.

In the morning, less than well fed, Hugh revisited all positions, and satisfied himself that all was in readiness, at least as far as was possible. He spoke with all the leaders. There was still no word from Hamish. Hugh sent Duncan to check all was in order there.

They waited.

In mid-afternoon Allardyce arrived with almost another five hundred men, to add to the congestion in that valley. Fortunately he brought further supplies of food with them, largely oatmeal to be eaten raw, which, washed down with burn-water, would swell in men's stomachs and stifle the pangs of hunger. The newcomers had to have the situation explained to them, to be shown the ground and given their instructions.

There was no sign of any host coming from Deeside, or anywhere else, by nightfall. Morgund of Mar was certainly taking his time about going to the aid and support of his fellow Celtic earls. No addition to their own numbers came from Deeside either. The Mearnsmen fretted, and squabbled amongst themselves. Hugh found the commanding of an idle array almost as taxing as undoubtedly would be the actual warfare.

They settled for another night. It started to rain, which did not help. There did not seem to be anything for it but to wait, with what patience they could muster.

Wait they all did, with varying reactions and no sign of any approach from Deeside. The only approach was, in fact, from the other direction when, in the early afternoon of the next day, three riders appeared from the south, and one of them a woman – Margaret Olifard. Not only her father and Hugh were astonished.

Their astonishment grew and developed as she explained what had brought her. The invasion, rising, and threat to the throne was over, no more. Somerled of the Isles was dead, and his son with him – not in battle but by assassination. Somewhere near Renfrew Castle, the High Steward's seat, the deed had been done, by night, in the midst of the Islesmen's sleeping army. Alleged envoys had come under a white flag, to bring terms to Somerled; and gaining access to his tent, had stabbed him and his son. Whether the Steward had had anything to do with it was unclear, although the deaths greatly benefited him. For the Islesmen, lacking the great leader whom they all but worshipped, had seen nothing to be gained by going on with the campaign, had returned, mourning, to their ships and sailed back to the Hebrides in a state of utter and chaotic grief. What had happened to Malcolm of Ross and the other Celtic earls was unclear, their whereabouts unknown; possibly they had never left Perth – and were unlikely to do so once they heard this news. The word had been sent to Arbuthnott by Bishop William of

Melrose, for Hugh. Possibly the tidings had already reached the Earl of Mar, which would account for the lack of any southwards advance.

The attempt on King Malcolm's throne had vanished in that tent near Renfrew.

Astounded, the Mearns array heard all this, scarcely able to believe the young woman's story. It seemed all so utterly unreal, there in their hidden mountain glen. There was relief, of course, no fighting and danger ahead of them now. But there was a kind of revulsion also, shame that their cause should have been won this way. Anticlimax also prevailed, of course.

Sending for Hamish and his scouts, all made ready to turn and head back for Arbuthnott, Hugh finding that all seemed to look upon himself as still in charge, to marshal the four sections and produce a fairly disciplined withdrawal, although he would have handed over command to Sir Osbert. When all was in progress, on their way up to Cairn o' Mount again, in some sort of order, he was able to ride beside Margaret and her father.

"You came yourself to inform us, not just sending a messenger," he commented. "That was like you, I think. Few women would have so done. You could not have known that there would be no fighting."

"The abbot's long message would have been difficult to entrust to just any man. And the friar who brought it had ridden on. Besides, I wanted to tell you myself. That you were out of danger. All your responsibilities behind you. That is, if battle had not already begun. I was anxious. Can you wonder? And I was not sure where you would be, where I would find you."

"Hugh had us all prepared to ambush any advancing host, in that dog's-leg of a valley," Sir Osbert said. "He knew how we should do it, placed and arranged all, up on the heights and down in the glen. Using the bend to screen us. And bushes. It was good, very shrewd thinking, using the ground to aid us. *I* would never have thought of it. This of the ambush."

"It was a very simple strategy, sir."

"None here but you would have thought and planned it, I swear. None would have *been* here."

"My brother would have done it. In Galloway we did the like . . ."

"But you had the command. You were able to order and control the men, all men. And they did your bidding. Their lairds also. Your knowledge and will was accepted. You inspired all. I was impressed."

"Hugh is a leader, Father," Margaret asserted. "However much he seeks to hide it! He . . . he even seeks to lead me, at times!"

"Me? Never! I do not, could not!"

They were riding side by side, close enough for her to rein still closer and, leaning a little, to nudge Hugh with an elbow.

"No? Not even . . . to the altar?" she asked, a little breathlessly.

He swallowed, so unexpected was this urging, this signal. Possibly Sir Osbert had to swallow also. Presumably the young woman assessed this as a hopeful and opportune moment to take the plunge.

"I . . . ah . . . I am greatly fond, enamoured, of your daughter, sir," he got out. "I have been, for long. From, from the first. I would be daring, sufficiently daring, to seek her hand in marriage, my lord. If you, if you would so agree."

The thane did not reply for long moments, turning in the saddle to stare, then seeming to concentrate on guiding his mount past a black stretch of peat-hag. Certainly it was an unusual and unlikely moment and situation for a declaration, a request, of this sort, riding at the head of a retiring army over one of the loftiest passes in the land.

"*I* would wish it so," Margaret observed, helpfully.

Her father was frowning. "This is . . . difficult," he said at length. "There is much to be considered, considered well. You are my heir, Margaret. I hold a thanedom. Much hangs on any decision of mine, of this sort. You must understand it, both of you. Whoever weds you, girl, could become Thane of

302

Arbuthnott and the Mearns, if the King concedes, governor of an entire province, justiciar of it all likewise. And there are many lords, barons and lairds in it, some of them riding behind us now. They have to be heeded, thought of."

"I would wish to wed none of them."

"*Your* wishes, Margaret, are not all that have to be considered."

"Surely they merit some consideration? From my father! And, have you not just said that Hugh has command? The ability to order and control men – and *these* men, these powerful ones behind us. Is that not important in this matter?"

"They have great lands, many men. He has not."

"I do not seek any thanedom, sir. Or power and position. It is Margaret's hand in marriage that I seek. Another could be thane, surely? Without wedding her?"

"It should be kept in my line. Blood tells. The Olifards are Thanes of Arbuthnott."

"None I wed could be an Olifard," his daughter said.

"No. But . . ." Sir Osbert waved a dismissive hand. "Leave it, now. I have to consider . . ." He reined back, to speak with some immediately behind.

"At least he will consider," the young woman murmured. "It is not outright rejection. And I will seek to work on him."

They left it at that.

It was night before they won back to Arbuthnott, which meant that it was too late for most of the house-guests to leave for their own homes. So there was no opportunity for the would-be spouses to exchange confidences, much less embrace. The talk in the great hall, and later in the crowded bedchamber, was all of Somerled's murder and the difference this dastardly act would make, not only to the Isles and the Highlands but to all Scotland. A sense of shame reigned, even if tinged with relief, not only for King Malcolm's throne but also for themselves, that no battling had been demanded of them.

In the morning, with all of the others departing, Duncan

303

was for setting off southwards, for, there being no ship for them now, it would take three or four days more of riding, on borrowed horses, and he was anxious to get back to his busy life at Redheugh and to Meg and the child. But Margaret persuaded Hugh to stay for one day more – not that that took a deal of doing – and Duncan had to accede.

She took the brothers on a tour of country to the south-west which Hugh had not seen before, riding by Fordoun, or Fotherdun, formerly Dunfothir, where the earthworks of the great Pictish castle or fortress still remained, this their ancestors' guard over the entrance to the Cairn o' Mount pass, which was the key to the north-east. Then on to Kincardine Castle, the royal hunting-seat, which nowadays, the girl said, was seldom used, where Canmore's Queen Ingeborg had been banished and died; and back by the three notable hilltop cairns of Sheils, Phills and Kenshot. It was all very pleasant but, shamefully, Hugh would have wished that Duncan had not been there. The same applied even more so that night when, after an evening of music and story, the brothers contributing border ballads, bedtime came, and Duncan was of course still sharing the chamber with Hugh, and that man could scarcely request that his brother should be given a separate room. So again goodnights had to be fairly formal, although later, Gelis did her best to cope with the situation, to Duncan's distinctly doubtful reactions.

Next day they were for off. Margaret did manage a brief quick word with Hugh when her father was offering Duncan a choice of horses, saying that they were to be a gift, the least that he could do by way of thanks for the brothers coming all this way to assist in their endeavours. His daughter, in the interim, advised Hugh not to reopen the subject of marriage meantime. She would use every opportunity and wile to persuade her father, but heedfully, tactfully, choosing her moments. She had hopes that her determination might prove stronger than his. So leave the pleading and the pressure to her, no?

She rode with them down to Inverbervie, on the north-south road, where the parting was such as to have Duncan eyeing his half-brother, and declaring thereafter that he believed that Meg was right in saying that there was something between Hugh and the Lady Margaret, something on both sides. Hugh admitted that there might be, only might, and promptly changed the subject.

The long journey to Berwickshire, down the coast and around the estuaries of Tay and Forth, commenced.

23

Fairly soon after his return home, Hugh made the much more modest journey to Melrose to see Abbot William, to learn of the national situation after the collapse of Somerled's invasion. Also to say thank-you for the monkish messenger sent to Arbuthnott to inform of what had happened at Renfrew, and its consequences.

He found his friend still gravely concerned about the state of the realm. The King was on his way home from Doncaster, where he had been laid low, but was still desperately weak, and only able to travel, in a litter, a few miles in each day. It was the belief of most in high positions that Malcolm was a dying man, although of only twenty-six years. And the word was that he had been forced to give Henry of England, under grievous threat, almost all that he had demanded, all Scots claims to Durham, Northumberland and Cumberland surrendered, and much else, including the retention of hostages – to the fury of Prince William, who was now openly acting regent, he saying, with some reason, that his royal brother was no longer in any fit state to rule a nation. The failure of Somerled's invasion was a great relief, of course, however disgracefully achieved, but there could well be more trouble ahead. For Henry Plantagenet had now received Godfrey Olafsson at his court, as King of Man, and promised the Norseman English aid in retaking the island kingdom from Somerled's son. This would almost certainly produce war in the Western Sea, for the Islesmen would fight, and with English fleets now able to use Cumbrian harbours, so close to Scotland's border, and the Galloway brothers not to be trusted, Henry could well find it convenient to invade Scotland in the south-west – which might well, indeed, be the object of his championing of Olafsson. The Plantagenet would gain his desired paramountcy over Scotland by any means open to him, an utterly ruthless monarch. So further military service might well be required of the Swintons in the not too distant future, since summer-time, of course, was the best for sea-fighting, and they were now into July.

The abbot thought that Hugh ought to go on to Roxburgh to see Prince William and his advisers, to tell him of what had transpired in the north, and that a sizeable and fairly effective contingent could hereafter be raised in the Mearns, hitherto scarcely considered to be a recruiting-ground. Also it would do his name and reputation no harm to reveal this, and that he had been given command of this force by the thane. It looked as though Brawny Will would soon be King of Scots, so it would be sensible for Hugh to bring himself to the prince's notice. When the younger man protested that he had no desire to push himself forward, his friend declared that this was part of his duty to the realm, for he could be as useful to the crown in the future as he had been in the past; it was not mere self-seeking.

They talked of Soutra and developments there, how the hospital and its various hospices, now established, were being recognised as a useful and admirable institution, something at least to enhance the reputation of the unfortunate King Malcolm.

Hugh spent the night at the abbey, and in the morning rode on down Tweed the extra fifteen miles to Roxburgh, unsure of how he should approach Prince William, and why.

In the event, at that castle, he all but turned and left again when he discovered that Brawny Will was away hawking somewhere and none knew when he would return. However, the sight of a familiar and friendly face restrained him, that of young Rob Bruce of Annandale who, it transpired, had also just arrived from the west, with news from his father for the prince. It seemed that the Bruces were keeping careful eyes on the Galloway brothers, whose loyalty was more than suspect, and every so often Rob was sent to court with a report. Actually, it seemed that the two sons of Earl Fergus were even more estranged than ever, all but at each other's throats; so they were less of a menace if Henry Plantagenet decided to call on them to help with an invasion, too busy fighting each other.

Rob was interested to hear of Hugh's and Duncan's involvement in the Mearns, where he had never been and about which he knew nothing. After all, it was two hundred miles away from Annandale.

When at length the prince's party arrived back from their hawking, the problem of Hugh's approaching him was solved, for Rob's report had to be presented and he took Hugh with him.

Oddly, thereafter, Brawny Will showed more interest in the episode of the Arbuthnott boar-slaying than in the abortive attempt to assail the Earl of Mar's force. He applauded Hugh for getting rid of his boars, and urged him to continue the good work. He went so far as to declare that when he was king, *he* would get rid of the wild boar as regal symbol, from those barbarous Pictish times, and adopt the king of beasts, the lion, as his emblem and standard. This announcement, although interesting, Hugh thought showed a marked lack of concern for Malcolm's condition and well-being; but William had always been a notably down-to-earth and outspoken character. What sort of a monarch he would make remained to be seen.

Hugh raised more interest in the Mearns situation amongst some of the prince's advisers, particularly Keith the Marischal and de Morville the High Constable. He forbore to ask whether their fellow-Anglo-Norman, the High Steward, had had a hand in the so-convenient assassination of Somerled of the Isles.

The very separate towers of the elongated Roxburgh Castle ensured that its residents could be suitably isolated into their various ranks and importance overnight, preserving the royal family and their officers of state from over-close association with lesser folk. Hugh and Rob Bruce were relegated to a very much middle-rank towerlet; but they passed an amiable evening together, before going their different ways in the morning, duties accomplished.

That summer was one of waiting, for Hugh, waiting for word from Arbuthnott. July passed into a wet August, and still nothing came. Other word reached him however. The King was home from Roxburgh at last, but in a very weak state, indeed failing. The physicians believed that there could be no recovery. Prince William was in effect ruling the land, or such of it as would accept rule from him or anyone else save their own chiefs. So far the English monarch had made no move, having his troubles nearer home, quarrelling with his barons and earls, and more direly with the Archbishop of Canterbury, Thomas à Becket, all but civil war looming; also French preoccupations were never far off. So Scotland had a breathing-space, although few expected this to last, the Plantagenet being who and what he was.

Then, at length, in early September, a peripatetic Augustinian friar from Soutra brought to Aldcambus the relayed message Hugh had been awaiting, from Margaret Olifard. She thought that it might be worth his while to come to Arbuthnott. Not unnaturally, no details were entrusted to the monks.

Belated harvest-time as it was, Hugh left that to Duncan, and was off northwards the very next morning, a man striving to keep his hopes moderate.

Instead of crossing Forth at Stirling Bridge, as formerly, he followed the friar's advice and took the Queen Margaret Ferry over to Fife, some nine miles west of Edinburgh, and thereafter headed due north from Dunfermline through the Fothrif and Cleish Hills to Abernethy and Perth, thus saving fully fifty miles. Unfortunately there was no similar regular ferry across the Tay estuary, or many more miles could have been cut from the journey. The King's great-grandmother had established the one at Queensferry in order to bring pilgrims over to her great new abbey at Dunfermline, where was her husband's main palace, the first stone abbey of the Roman Catholic faith to be established in Scotland, and her torch of enlightenment for the new religious system.

Thus, and with no delaying factors and reasonable weather conditions, Hugh arrived at Arbuthnott by noon on the third day, good going, and no doubt also representing his urgency of mind. What was he going to discover at his destination?

It was distinctly frustrating, when he got there, to find that neither Margaret nor her father was at home. They could not have expected him quite so soon, of course. Gelis, bustling around making the visitor welcome and feeding and patting him, informed that they had gone to call upon Ogilvie of Barras, some miles to the north, but should be back before nightfall. Did Hugh mishear, or did that young woman announce this last rather regretfully?

So the urgent guest had to wait, again, with what patience he could muster, Gelis managing to find reasons for ensuring that he was not left for too long alone.

At length, father and daughter arrived – and on this occasion, at sight of him, Margaret threw herself into Hugh's arms – which he took to be a hopeful sign, Sir Osbert not commenting.

Then there had to be a meal, of course. Hugh could scarcely follow the young woman to her room while she changed out of her riding-clothes and washed, so he had to summon up more patience, he who was not the most patient of men.

When they got down at table, however, after grace-before-meat and Gelis had left them, Margaret was not long in getting to the point.

"Father has been considering the matter of your proposal of marriage, Hugh, and has certain proposals of his own to put to you, in turn. It is my hope . . ." She left the rest unsaid.

Sir Osbert cleared his throat. Was that a good sign, or the reverse? "My daughter's wishes mean much to me, Sir Hugh," he began. He did not usually say *Sir* Hugh. "I have been thinking on the position. You know the difficulties. I naturally would wish my thanedom to remain with the Olifard blood, and name. But . . ." He paused.

Biting lip, Hugh waited.

"It is important that the Mearns baronage and leaders accept the thane without question and demur," he went on.

"Even with the King's assent that is a major consideration. A complete stranger imposed upon them would not be welcome and the necessary co-operation might be withheld. Coming from another part of the realm. And no great lord. We are that way, in the Mearns. Clannish, if you like. But you are now known to most of them. They accepted your command in the field, even though no fighting developed. That is some advantage. But the name remains a problem."

Aware of Hugh's tension, Margaret, eyeing him, spoke. "Father has a suggestion."

"Yes. The name is important, for acceptance. De Swinton is old and honourable, possibly as old as Olifard, or Oliphant as some call it. But . . . it is foreign to the Mearns. I cannot ask that you change it to Olifard. That would offend my nephew of Bothwell, and other members of the family. But Arbuthnott is different. It belongs here. If you could change your name to de Arbuthnott? Then, if you and Margaret had a son, or sons, they would be Arbuthnotts, accepted. How say you to that? I could not ask an elder son to change his name, of good family. But you are a second son, and as we understand it, will inherit no lands nor style from your father, the sheriff. How say you to becoming Sir Hugh de Arbuthnott?"

Hugh stared. Change his name? He found no words.

Sir Osbert went on. "And, for due acceptance, you would have to come to dwell here, to live. Not all the time, but some of it, much of it. That the Mearns might come to know you. And you to learn, one day, if the crown approved of it, to become thane in my place. So that your son, by Margaret, would follow on. You understand? It is a great thing to ask of you. But . . ."

Hugh looked at the young woman. Her lovely face was a study, gazing at him, hope, question, concern, writ large. And seeing it he all but laughed. What was she fearing, his beloved? That he would refuse? This small thing? This tiny price to pay for gaining her? The greatest need and joy of his life. This thanedom meant little to him, although perhaps it should. To live at Arbuthnott would be no burden, so long as he had Margaret to love and live with. He was not so

311

greatly attached to Aldcambus as all that; Duncan could see to Aldcambus. These were minor matters. And here was this man talking about him having a son by Margaret! The very thought of it turned him all but dizzy. Margaret, his . . . !

He found her father eyeing him almost as anxiously. Were they both crazed? He shook his head.

"My name is of small matter," he got out. "What signifies is Margaret, my need of her, my love for her. Give me Margaret – and ask what you will!"

"Oh, Hugh, Hugh!" she exclaimed, almost choking.

"You will do it, then? Take the name. Come to dwell here. All but act my son. You will?"

"Think you I would say other?" It was of the girl that he had asked that.

"I am glad," Sir Osbert said.

His daughter did not require to say anything, her eyes and expression sufficient.

Her father went on, in a somewhat different tone of voice. "This night you have lifted a load from my mind. Something that has troubled me for long years. As a young man I did a great wrong, committed a sin, the guilt of which has afflicted me over the years. I repented of it, yes, but have done naught to pay the debt I owe to my Maker. I wish to do so. I vowed to go on a crusade to the Holy Land, to seek to recover Our Lord's birthplace from the infidels. But, my duties as thane here have kept me from it. Having no son . . ." He shrugged. "I am not so young as once I was. But not so old for it to be beyond me, even now. So, this night, I can see it as possible. You understand? One day, before overlong, my ancient debt may yet be paid."

"Father . . . !" Margaret exclaimed.

"I never told you, lass. Why burden you with my guilt? This is why I have been so concerned over your marriage. Do not ask me what I did, all those years ago. It is a matter between me and my Creator. But, pray God, my vow will be fulfilled. One day . . ."

This curious confession and assertion altered the entire tone and tenor of their exchange, introducing a new sensation and admixture of emotions. Further talk was contra-indicated, somehow inhibited. Indeed, almost at once thereafter Sir Osbert rose from the table, and went over to the door to let out one of the hounds which was whimpering there.

The other two exchanged long and eloquent looks.

Now, Hugh at least could scarcely wait for the remainder of the evening to pass until he could claim weariness from long riding and his bed calling. After all, he had *had* long riding.

Sir Osbert, preoccupied, made no protest at the eventual announcement. The pair headed off across the courtyard, arms linked.

"Joy! Joy!" Hugh exclaimed, all but unbalancing his companion in his enthusiastic hugging. "We can wed. You are mine! Mine! My love, my heart, my all!"

"At a price! The price of your name, Hugh. It is not too much to ask, my dear?"

"What is a name? I am the same man. And a better man for having *you* to love and guide me. No, no, that is little price. I would have paid a deal more to win you."

"You had already won *me*. It was only my hand in marriage that you had to win . . ."

Up the round-tower stairs they climbed, to halt at her bedroom doorway. They could hear Gelis's murmur of singing up above.

"Someone awaiting you!" Margaret said, pointing higher. "Ever attentive, ever hopeful Gelis!"

"Aye," he nodded. "So, we had better say our goodnights here, no?" And he pushed open her door.

Eyeing him, brows raised, she smiled. "Dare I? Dare I let you into my chamber, this night of all nights, Hugh Arbuthnott-to-be?"

He swallowed. "You . . . you have my word!"

"Ah, your word of what?" But she preceded him into the room and indeed shut the door behind them.

"Word that I shall behave . . . as *you* would wish!"

"M'mm. There speaks a man of cunning, I think! I do not know whether I should feel reassured?"

"And *that* could mean – what?"

313

"Only that women can be weak, at times. So, my husband-to-be must help me to be strong. Your word on that?"

"Cunning, did you say? Me! I know who is the cunning one."

"Your word, sirrah?"

"Very well. But do not be too strong, my love. For we could call this our betrothal night, I say."

"Betrothal is not marriage! Not yet. But – oh yes, we can celebrate. In . . . some measure."

He looked over to the small fire and the steaming tub which Gelis had prepared for her mistress, as no doubt she had done upstairs for the visitor.

"There is one celebration that I would ask of you – and feel that I have the right to ask it this night, my love. Yonder!" And he pointed. "I have voiced this before, I think. But now I claim the right. You have seen *me* unclad, and washed my back. Above, in the other room. Now, it would be to my bliss to do the same by you! Wash your back, *you* unclad. Would that not be fair dealing?"

She wagged her head at him. "I might have guessed, in letting you herein! Naked, I would be . . . defenceless! Who knows how far you would seek to go thereafter?"

"Not if I had given my word. As I do."

"Would you call this helping me to be strong?"

"We will help each other. If we must!"

"I hold you to that!" she declared.

She moved over to the steaming tub, tested the heat of the water and then went to stand by the fire, to poke it into brightness.

"Thoughtful," he commented boldly. "So that I can see the better! May I aid you?"

"You see yourself as lady's maid?"

"I see myself as the most fortunate man in Scotland!"

"Be not so sure, braggart! How know you that I am not . . . grievously misshapen, blemished?" And she began to unfasten her bodice.

Promptly he stepped close, to assist, removing it heedfully. She wore a shift beneath, fairly scanty as to its upper portion, revealing fine white shoulders and the deep cleft between firmly swelling breasts. He stooped to kiss each of the shoulders, and then moved his busy lips down further to the bust.

"It was my back, was it not, which you were concerned over? To wash it," she mentioned.

He was too preoccupied to answer, not only kissing but seeking to pull down the shift at the same time.

"Too hasty!" she reproved. "You are being unschooled, are you not? The skirt comes off first, before the shift."

"M'mm." He changed his stance. "This girdle? Do I untie it?"

"See you, my man, much better that I do this myself. Fetch you a towel over from that chest. The small chest. We are going to require that. You will find towels therein."

He did as he was bid, if reluctantly, went to the wrong chest and had to be redirected. By the time that he had raised the lid, abstracted a towel, and turned back to the fireside, Margaret had discarded her clothing altogether and was standing, her back to him, naked as when she was born.

He drew a long quivering breath at the sight of her, drinking in the vision of delight, before going to enfold her in his arms, hands cupping those lovely breasts from the rear.

They stood thus for long moments, and those hands distinctly rose and fell, not only with his own deep breathing. At length she spoke.

"You have, have hard protrusions!" she objected, and then gasped a little laugh. "I mean . . . on your doublet and belt," she hastened to add. "And my poor flesh is unprotected quite, sir!"

Hugh drew back and turned her round to face him, stepping further away to absorb all that he saw, head shaking, no words forthcoming.

She was indeed delectably made, from her long graceful neck, hair shaken loose to frame it, her bosom full without being heavy, the nipples dark and pointed, the belly below gently rounded down to the dark triangle between the sculptured thighs of long shapely legs, feet still within the heap

315

of her discarded skirt and shift. She did not shrink from his gaze, long as he stared; but nor did she flaunt herself, standing there almost as though wondering whether she came up to his expectations.

Revel as he would in what his eyes showed him, the man strode forward to take all that beauty and voluptuous promise in his arms, forgetting all about protrusions of one sort or another against tender skin, hands busy as lips, however few words were enunciated.

It was the woman who had to do the speaking. "Remember . . . your word!" she panted, but not pushing him away. "Be strong, Hugh . . . in case . . . I am weak! Weaker than . . . this!"

He straightened up at that, gazing into her eyes. Then he nodded, almost grimly, practically shaking her. And he showed her his strength in an alternative fashion, stooping to pick her up bodily, and carried her over to the tub, to set her standing therein, she who was no slight sylph.

"This, this has never happened to me before!" she got out.

"You have never been promised in marriage before!" That was next to roughly said.

"No-o-o. Is this normal behaviour, think you?"

"Only where the man is sufficiently strong!"

"Aye, dear Hugh. Am I hard on you? On your resolution. And, yes, on myself! But – we must save something for the wedding-night, must we not?"

Whether or not he agreed with that, he began the washing process.

Thereafter he did not confine his attentions to her back. Nor did she seek to have him do so, stroking his head as he comprehensively bathed her.

Neither found words necessary.

When he could no longer find parts of her unwashed, he reached for the towel and commenced the drying. This completed to his satisfaction, save for her lower legs and feet, which of course were in the water, she told him to lay the towel on the floor and she would step out on to it for the final drying.

316

Helping her out of the tub, he got down on his knees to finish his task, Margaret lifting up one foot and then the other, and he taking the opportunity to kiss her toes, to her laughter – until, beginning to go higher, she rapped knuckles on his hair warningly. Sighing, he rose and picked her up again, boldly, to carry her to her bed.

"I wondered when it would come to this!" she said, when he set her down. She remained sitting, not lying.

He sat beside her, still holding her. "Must I still be strong?" he demanded.

"Perhaps it is my turn?" she conceded. "Sharing the burden. A kiss, no more?" That was scarcely a command, not even a plea, more of a tentative suggestion.

"You would wish it so?"

"Wish? No. But think it best, my dear. Best. And pray that we will not have to wait overlong for . . . the rest."

Searching her face, he nodded. "No doubt you are right. Sore trial as it is."

"It will be the sweeter, no? More . . . honest. And this is not all sore? Meantime, a kiss."

That was one way of describing what followed. If Hugh had been thorough in his washing and drying, he was still more so in his kissing, and with a clearly loving and naked woman in his arms the scope was wide indeed, especially when she did some kissing in return, and no mere polite acknowledgment. In the end it was the man who called a halt, suddenly sitting back, all but pushing her from him, and getting to his feet.

"No more . . . of this!" he got out hoarsely. "I cannot. It is too much for me. I cannot, I say . . . !" Shaking his head, he turned, and strode off, calling a choking goodnight over his shoulder.

But at the door he turned, stood for a moment and then went back to her, as she still sat upright on her bed watching him, wordless. He bent then, to kiss her a deal more gently, on hair and brow and lips.

"My love, goodnight! That was no way to leave you, my heart's darling. I thank you for this night. Bless you, my woman. Thank you!"

317

She gripped his arm, nodding, as he left her again.

This time, as he paused, opening the door, it was to call back. "That was harder than slaying any boar!" he told her, and left her.

Upstairs, thankfully he found that Gelis had departed, no doubt presuming after the long delay that any more waiting would be unrewarding. The washing water barely steaming any more, he forbore to bathe himself. Perhaps it was cold water that he needed then? Bed for him, lonesome bed, even if sleep seemed unlikely, whatever he had said to Sir Osbert about being tired.

In time he slept, nevertheless.

The next two days Sir Osbert thought it wise to take Hugh on a round of visits to various Mearns magnates and landowners, to introduce him to those who had not already met him on the expedition to counter the Earl of Mar, and to inform of the proposed developments, the change of name, the marriage, and the heirship to the thanedom. On the whole all this was well enough received, the Merseman's renown over leadership and boar-killing standing him in good stead, his knighthood also, although one or two of the loftier ones did purse lips somewhat over the thane destination. Hugh left his future father-in-law to do the talking, maintaining a modest demeanour, hoping to make a reasonably good impression. At least there were no actual protests voiced.

The two evenings involved, by mutual consent, the loving couple restrained themselves from overmuch testing of their resolutions, their goodnight partings advisedly moderate however otherwise they might feel. Gelis at least approved of this, and sought in her own way to compensate, towards the man at any rate, although Margaret warned him that there were limits to her forbearance on this issue.

The vital matter of the proposed wedding date was, of course, much discussed and debated. Hugh naturally was for it at the earliest, Margaret far from contesting that. But Sir Osbert had to point out that some time must be given him to make the necessary arrangements, not so much for the ceremony as for what was involved in the consequences, especially in this of the thanedom. Although more or less hereditary, these were in fact royal appointments, and the succession had to be confirmed by the monarch. And with King Malcolm so ill, possibly dying, approaching him in the matter would be difficult. Indeed it was probable that it should be Prince William who would have to give, or withhold, permission. It was not the best moment for such negotiations. When Margaret suggested that they might marry first and negotiate afterwards, her father, without actually saying so, more or less indicated that he would prefer it otherwise. Clearly he desired that the thanedom should remain with the Olifard bloodline, this all-important to him; and the inference was that if the crown rejected Hugh as thane-to-be, then Margaret might have to look elsewhere for a husband. This was not stated, but the possibility was there – which much concerned the couple involved. Privately Margaret told Hugh that she would rebel over this. While applauding that, Hugh wondered whether rebellion would succeed? She was of full age, yes; but *could* she refuse to marry where her father ordered, as his sole heiress and only child? Could he not insist, and prevail? Many an of-age daughter had been married against her wishes, by the simple expedient of having Holy Church annul any other union on the request of the crown. However, it had not come to that, and they must pray that it would not.

So, on the third morning, it was off for the would-be bridegroom, with hopes that he would be back soon and in nuptial readiness. Even Sir Osbert wished him well in this, a man torn by conflicting needs and desires.

24

Hugh was not going to rely wholly on Sir Osbert's perhaps less than determined efforts at convincing the crown that he, Hugh de Swinton, would make a worthy and effective heir to the thanedom of the Mearns; he must see what might be achieved, if not by himself, then at least at his own instigation. And Abbot William seemed to be the obvious adviser.

So it was not long after his return to Aldcambus that he was off again to Melrose. The abbot, as ever, welcomed him warmly and listened understandingly to his account of the situation, to his hopes and fears.

"My friend, you must go and see Prince William yourself. I will come with you, if that will be of any help," the abbot said. "Do not leave it all to Olifard. The King, I think, is on his death-bed. It could be any day that his brother will succeed him and mount the throne, a sad situation. But, who knows, perhaps as well for the country and nation. For Malcolm has not been the man to govern Scotland, whatever his virtues. A much stronger hand is required at the helm. William *may* provide this – if he will be guided, take advice. For he is stronger, but also headstrong, lacking in judgment perhaps. We must hope and pray that he will heed wise counsellors. In this matter of *your* future role, it is unfortunate that the need for decision should arise at this stage. For King Malcolm likes you well, and I think would agree to you being raised eventually to the thanedom. You have served him well, especially over Soutra, and he has knighted you. But he may die any day, and you can scarcely go to put it to him, in his present case. So it must be to William."

"I see it. And the prince has no especial regard for me, I fear. I have campaigned with him, yes – but only as one of many, a leader of scouts. And *he* is not greatly concerned with the Soutra hospital, I think."

"No. That is not the direction in which William's interests lie. But he will have naught *against* you, I judge."

"He may consider my knighthood unearned, misdirected. Scarcely on the field of battle!"

"He knows of what you sought to do in the Mearns, against Mar . . ."

Next morning, the pair set off for Roxburgh, in driving rain.

Uncomfortable travelling as it made, at least the weather had prevented Brawny Will from pursuing his passion for hawking and hunting, and so was in the castle. And while Hugh might have had difficulty in gaining his presence, Abbot William, as Vice-Chancellor, was in a different position and could request audience, and did.

Even so they had to wait some time before being ushered into the royal tower, where the prince was in noisy and boisterous game-playing with his boon Anglo-Norman companions, unsuitable as this might seem, with a dying brother in a chamber just above. He did not eye the abbot with any especial favour but, oddly enough, when he caught sight of Hugh behind, his expression changed.

"Ha – Swinton, the killer of boars!" he exclaimed. "Here is a man who knows how to deal with the brutes." He was panting from his sportive exercise, and was obviously somewhat drink-taken. "Come, Sir Hugh, show us how to slay the pest . . . pestiferous creatures!" He had a little difficulty in enunciating that.

Abbot William glanced at his companion, eyebrows raised.

"I, I can scarcely do that, Highness," Hugh protested. "What may I show you, with no animal, no spear . . . ?"

"Come, man, you have a tongue in your head! Tell us how. See you, Hervey here will act the boar. He is the right shape, I swear! Down on your knees, Hervey! And growl! Tusks you have none, but your snout is none so ill! Down, I say!"

To shouts of laughter Hervey de Keith, son of the Marischal, went down on all fours, grinning, to emit grunts and howls.

Much embarrassed, Hugh shook his head. "Highness, I can tell you but little. There are boars and boars, some larger, more savage than others. These great ones should not be hunted on horseback. The horses will not face them. Rear and bolt." He had to shout, to make himself heard above the din of Keith's snortings and the urgings-on of the other young men.

"Hear you that, Hervey? You would make any mount bolt!" the prince cried.

Hugh looked at the abbot who, expressionless, nodded.

Taking that as guidance to continue with this crazy exchange, he went on. "Dismounted, I used a gauntlet. Stout padded leather, on the left arm, and a dirk in that hand. A short stabbing-spear in the right. Seek a barrier, bushes or the like, which the boar has to come through, to get at you, to slow it down. So that it does not knock you over. Your back against some firm support. Then, as it comes, thrust bent arm and gauntlet between its open jaws. And stab, stab. You would be over, without the support, with its weight. I can tell Your Highness no better than that."

"Heigh-ho!" Brawny Will acknowledged. "We have no gauntlet for Hervey! So this boar remains unslain. You are spared, Hervey!"

There was much shouting and horseplay.

Hugh went to murmur to the abbot. "Shall we retire? There is no profit in this. They have all been drinking. Here is but folly. I cannot speak with the prince now."

His friend gripped his arm. "Speak, yes. It is perhaps your opportunity. No harm, at least. He is in the mood to favour you. He will heed you in some measure, I think. Perhaps more kindly than when more sober! Try him, Hugh."

Doubtfully, Hugh approached the unprincely prince. "Highness, may I have a word with you? A brief word," he besought. "Why I am here. Of your goodness."

"Word? More boars?"

"No, Highness. This is of more import. To me." He had to raise his voice to be heard, but he could hardly pull the heir to the throne over to a corner of the hall to speak

322

more privately. "It is a difficult matter. Of my marriage. It is . . ."

"Ha! Marriage, you say? The boar-slayer is to wed! Save us, after boars, women should be easy meat!"

"It is not that. She, the woman, is . . . fond of me. As I of her. Margaret Olifard of Arbuthnott. It is her father, Sir Osbert. The thane. He has no son, no heir, other than this one daughter. And he is eager that the thanedom remains with his line, his Olifard blood. So it must go through his daughter's husband. And, and he is not assured that I might be acceptable to the crown, as thane, or heir to a thanedom. Even though I took the name, not of Olifard but of Arbuthnott. As I would do."

"What ails him at you, man?"

"It is not that. He is well enough disposed. It is the question of me as next thane. He is not assured that I would be acceptable. Not only to the barons of the Mearns but to the crown. That I am not of sufficiently high degree."

"Olifard? Olifard? How high is *his* degree? They came up here with my grandsire David, from England, did they not? Of no great birth. Married well here, belike. But no great nobles. Themselves they must have won the thanedom through marriage."

"Yes, so I understand. And are the more proud of it, belike. But . . . the crown, Highness? Would it be . . . would you . . . would the King consider me as possible? To heir it? Not that I am eager to be thane. Only eager to wed Margaret Olifard."

"So she is that sort, is she? A hot wench? You want her – but she seeks marriage first!"

"No, no, Highness, not that. Leastways . . ." He shook his head. "We are fond, both of us. Sir Osbert would agree. But must be assured that the thanedom will remain in his line. So . . ."

"What ails him, I asked you, man? *You* will make as good a thane as he does, I would say. Or any of his Hieland chiefs."

"They are scarcely Hieland, Highness. The Mearns. I, I . . ." Hugh's voice died away as he realised just what the prince had said and implied.

323

"Near enough to the Hielands. I have been at yon Kincardine. A great place for the deer. But the folk wild-like. You would find that when you were trying to lead them against Mar and *his* Hielandmen, did you not?"

"I got on well enough with them." But Hugh's thoughts were now very much elsewhere. He looked at the abbot again, who had been listening to all this, and again he got a nod and the flicker of a smile. He dared hardly put thoughts into spoken words, but had to. "Your Highness would accept me? As heir to a thanedom? Through the daughter. Accept?"

Brawny Will was seemingly tiring of this conversation, for he was looking and grinning at some of the horseplay going on across the hall, obviously about to move over thereto.

"You would be as good as any," he declared, shrugging. "None of them could deal with that boar, could they? Deal with our enemies up north as you dealt with the brute and you will make none so ill a thane." And he was on his way across the chamber as he ended that.

Scarcely believing the almost casual acceptance of it all, Hugh gazed after him.

"You see," Abbot William said. "You need not have feared."

"He would have me! As a thane! Just . . . like that!"

"To be sure. As would the King, I think, if he was able to say it."

"All over this of the boar!"

"William has this strange hatred of boars. None love the creatures, but he appears to have some especial mislike. To *your* advantage, friend." He patted Hugh's shoulder. "I think that we should ask if we might see King Malcolm. Even for a brief moment. At least ask permission."

Hugh let the other go across to seek the prince's agreement. He came back nodding. They bowed to the royal back, and took their leave.

Upstairs, the abbot's presence got them past the guards at the doorway and into an anteroom where two physicians and the King's chaplain sat by a fire. They made no difficulties about allowing the Vice-Chancellor into the royal bedchamber, but warned that His Grace was unlikely to recognise them or speak. He was conscious, they said, but only just, barely alive any longer. His heart, they judged, could cease to beat at any time.

Ushered within, they saw the shrunken figure on the great bed, a mere shadow of his former self, and this at the age of only twenty-six. They bowed deeply, but the open eyes did not turn towards them. Moving over to the bed, they each in turn took a frail, limp hand to kiss it, in allegiance. No hint of awareness came into those eyes. The King of Scots was already away in some other land than Scotland.

After a few minutes, sighing, they backed off, the abbot putting up a prayer for the soul of their liege-lord, since his body was evidently past the praying for. Sadly, they left the man whom they both felt should have been up in the Soutra hospital which had been his satisfaction and pride.

The sadness, admittedly, did not long prevail over Hugh's elation at what he had elicited from the prince, even in the unpleasant rain, as they rode back to Melrose. William was not yet king, to be sure, and when he was he might reconsider what he had said — if he remembered it at all. But his attitude did not seem to imply preoccupation with lofty birth and status, so perhaps his support might stand.

Hugh's impulse now was to hurry back up to Arbuthnott, announce his success and claim his bride. But Abbot William advised delay, patience. Olifard might well wish to make his own approach to the crown, doubtful as to Hugh's optimism and claims. And he very likely would wait until it was clear who *wore* the crown. He could well judge that William's word, as only heir-apparent, was insufficient for his requirements. So they might have to wait until Malcolm died — which admittedly could be at any time. Hugh's whole life and future was here involved. It was worth a little patience.

No doubt this was sound advice, but the younger man had his own urgencies. The abbot was not in love, and eager to have that love consummated. Not anxious, as he was, that Margaret should hear of his good news at the earliest, Sir Osbert also, for that matter. His friend said that he could at least help him there. Wandering friars, mendicants, were always calling in at Melrose Abbey, on their travels. He might send a message up to Arbuthnott by one of these, if so Hugh wished. Almost reluctantly that man agreed that this might be best, might serve meantime.

So next day it was back to Aldcambus to await events with what patience Hugh could muster.

In the weeks, many weeks, which followed, he hated to have to admit to himself that he was wishing that King Malcolm would die and the situation could move, he hoped, forward. Assuredly others were hoping the same, for different reasons. Which was a grievous reaction over a monarch who, whatever else, was a good and kindly man.

Hugh's waiting was by no means idle, of course. There was much to see to at Aldcambus, his lairdly duties much neglected, even though Duncan had stood in for him manfully. And it did not fail to cross Hugh's mind that, if all went as he so dearly hoped, Duncan might have to do a deal more standing in hereafter; for clearly if the wedding went ahead he would have to spend much of his time up in the Mearns, learning to be a thane and becoming an Arbuthnott in more than mere name. Duncan might become, in all but title, laird of Aldcambus as well as Redheugh. The said Duncan, as it transpired, was less than enthusiastic about the entire project, whatever extra status it might confer on him. The pity that Hugh could not have found some other woman to marry, nearer home, of less exalted rank, and without all the complications.

The friar who eventually arrived at Aldcambus, in early December, was not, as hoped, come from Arbuthnott with a message from Margaret, but directly from Melrose – this to announce that King Malcolm was indeed dead, having slipped away on the eighth of the month, the fifth day after the Ides of December. Abbot William also sent word that King William had mounted the throne without delay, the first of that name in all Scotland's history. It would be seemly, the abbot suggested, that Hugh should, with him, attend the funeral, in token of their association with the dead monarch over Soutra. This would be held at Dunfermline in four days' time.

Hugh, and Duncan also, had to go, of course.

25

The little town of Dunfermline, on the north side of the narrows of Forth from Queen Margaret's Ferry, seethed with folk. All the great ones of the land appeared to be there, with their bodyguards of retainers, more than Hugh would have expected even for a king's funeral. But it transpired that the new monarch was wasting no time, and was going on from here to the Abbey of Scone for his coronation on the famed Stone of Destiny, there kept. Hence the crowds.

Dunfermline had been Malcolm Canmore's capital and seat where, to his palace, he had brought Margaret Atheling, all but his prisoner, ninety-five years before, and eventually made her his queen. Here their sons were born, three of whom became Kings of Scots in succession, and here all were buried.

Hugh and Duncan found it impossible to obtain overnight accommodation in that crowded town, the palace and the monastic quarters all packed, likewise the hospices and inns. They had to ride back three miles to the firthside burgh of Inverkeithing, in the early dark of the December late afternoon, to find lodgings.

In the morning, they searched for and found Abbot William in his fellow-abbot's quarters at Dunfermline, and thanks to his good offices were able to gain a much more advantageous stance in the abbey than would have been possible otherwise; indeed possibly they would not have gained entry at all, so thronged was it within with the great and the good, with even the clerestory galleries packed. And as they waited for the ceremonial to commence, it was up there, high above the nave, that Hugh saw something which tended to replace due mourning solemnity in his mind. It was to these narrow ledges, on either side of the church, that the women attending had been relegated, from the Countess Ada downwards. And there, a little further back from the chancel, was none other than Margaret Olifard, even at that range her good looks outstanding, for Hugh at least. And as he gazed up, she raised a hand. Sharp- as well as lovely-eyed she must have been to spot him in all that crowd below.

Thereafter it was difficult for one of the late monarch's loyal supporters to pay fullest attention to the proceedings.

Presently, to the solemn chanting of a choir of boys, the Abbot of Dunfermline led in, from the west door, the lords spiritual, practically all of them, the bishops and the mitred abbots, from Bishop Richard of St Andrews, Primate and former royal chaplain, successor to the late Arnold, and Bishop Ingram of Glasgow, the Chancellor, Abbot William, Vice-Chancellor, backed by the other prelates, sufficient rather to crowd the area before the high altar, above the chancel-steps, even before the arrival of the corpse, the new monarch and officers of state. When, heralded by trumpets outside and more singing within, the cortege did enter, even Hugh's preoccupation with the clerestory faded for the moment. For the funeral bier, borne by four heralds, was draped and covered by something unseen in Scotland before, a great yellow banner bearing on it the image of a red and rampant lion. William had not been long in banishing his *bête noir*, the black boar on silver of the Celtic royal house.

Pacing behind the bier and heralds the new monarch himself wore a tabard bearing that same device and emblem. At least he had retained some link with tradition, for although the boar had been the symbol of the High Kings of Alba, the smaller and later Scottish realm of Dalriada, which Kenneth mac Alpin had united with Alba to found Scotland in the ninth century, had had a red lion on gold, but this lion was passant, on its four feet, not rampant, up on its hind legs, tongue out and pawing ferociously as this was. What did this imply, for William's reign? Not a few there, other than Hugh de Swinton, undoubtedly asked themselves that. Had they exchanged a saintly but feeble monarch for a warlike, aggressive one?

The procession of magnates and officers of state behind the King took some time to file up to their reserved places at the front of the nave and up the crowded chancel, and amongst the thanes and justiciars paced Sir Osbert Olifard, walking with his brother and nephew. He would have come south for the coronation, of course, and brought his daughter.

The committal and commemoration service was conducted by the Primate, very movingly, for he had been the late Malcolm's friend as well as chaplain, and owed his preferment to St Andrews to the royal recommendation. The accompanying ceremonial was simple and fairly brief, the Chancellor giving a short oration on the departed's continued support of Holy Church, his concern for his people, especially the poor, the sick and the disabled, as exemplified by his founding of the great Soutra hospital, and his interest in the parish ministry set up by his predecessor and grandsire, David of blessed memory. The glance over at King William may or may not have been a wondering whether his successor would be as spiritually minded. Choir-singing interspersed the prayers and declarations, and then it was time to take the bier to its final resting-place behind the high altar, where opened the crypt for the reception of the royal remains. There was not much room behind there, so that only a few could accompany William to see his dead brother actually interred – his younger brother, David, Earl of Huntingdon, was still a hostage of the Plantagenet in England. How their mother, Adà, skied up there on the clerestory, felt about it all there was no knowing. Singing filled the interval.

Once the King and great ones had formed up and departed, to distinctly more cheerful music, Hugh lost no time, needless to say, in pushing through the crowd and seeking out Margaret. Fortunately the descent by the narrow winding stairway from aloft made her exit delayed, and he was able to meet her as she emerged at the foot, having to restrain himself from throwing his arms around her there in front of all. All that he could do was to grip her arm, and mouth incoherences.

The young woman took charge, for they were blocking the

stair-foot. Taking his hand, she led him towards the great doorway.

"I hoped that you would be here," she said. "I made Father bring me. We go to the coronation at Perth. Or Scone. Do you?"

"Yes. Oh, yes. How good, good it is to see you, my love. It has been so long . . ."

"Yes. Three months . . ."

"You got my message? By the friar. What Prince William said. Now the King. That, that I would make as good a thane as any other?"

"Yes. That was a joy indeed. I was so glad."

"Did your father accept that? Is he now prepared to have me wed you? Is he?" He tugged at her arm.

"He is heartened by it, yes. Relieved, in some measure. But still he wants the new King's own word. Confirmation, he calls it. He must have that, he says. He will be seeking it now, at this coronation."

"He, he was not convinced?" That was tense.

"Almost. But he feels that he has to be assured, himself, Hugh. This means so much to him, you see. To us it is not important. To him . . ." She wagged her head. "You do not fear that William will tell him otherwise? Now that he is King."

"No-o-o. I think not, I *hope* not. He is not greatly concerned with lofty blood and titles. And he thinks highly of my boar-killing. That banner over the dead King – you saw it? He greatly mislikes boars, and has changed the royal banner to a lion, after all the centuries. I hope that we can take this as a good augury. Your boar may be the saving of us! I pray so."

"As do I. But, Hugh . . ." Even amongst all the press of people leaving the abbey, she halted and turned to him. "See you, if he does not, if the King changes his mind, if he does not accept you as heir to the thanedom, then I have decided that *I* can be as decided as my father! That is why I am here today. To tell you that, if all else fails with the King, I will not sit down and accept it. If *you* will, I will

331

leave Arbuthnott. Run off, to wed you secretly! Would you do that, Hugh Swinton?"

Eyes wide, they stared, uncaring of who saw and wondered. "You, *you* would do that, Margaret," he got out. "Defy your father?"

"I would. I have thought long on this. I know that he might then seek royal authority to have the Church annul the marriage. But I think not, for he does love me. And he might destine the thanedom elsewhere. But I would hope, not seek annulment. But – *you*, Hugh? Would you do this? Take such a dire step? Wed me against Father's wishes, secretly? Injure your repute and name, possibly turn the King against you. Give up so much for me! Would you?"

"Lassie, lassie, need you ask that? I would do a deal more – I would give up life itself for you! But you, *you*! Would do it? Make your name, your reputation, of no account! With many. Lose your inheritance. Reject your father. You, you love me enough for that?"

"I do, boar-slayer! But let us hope that it will not be necessary. That King William's red lion is our token, our promise. Hope. For, Hugh, I love my father also. If differently . . ."

Nodding, Hugh realised that they were still standing, a little island amongst all the surging throng, and being eyed most curiously, not least by Duncan a few paces behind, waiting. Taking her arm, Hugh led her on in search of her father and the Abbot William.

Sir Osbert had won lodgings in the palace, so Hugh delivered Margaret there, but could not contact the thane. He and Duncan had a meal in the monastic quarters with their friend, and learned that all were to ride for Perth and Scone in the morning. The new King was in a hurry to be crowned.

They found their way back to Inverkeithing.

From Dunfermline to Perth was some forty miles, quite a long day's riding in winter conditions, especially for elderly clerics and the like, but not, to be sure, for the Swinton brothers. They would have liked to have ridden with Margaret – or at least Hugh would – but based on Inverkeithing as they were, by the time that they got back to Dunfermline the Olifards, and many others, had departed, including the monarch and most of his younger courtiers. At least there was no difficulty in following in their tracks, for the route was preordained, through Fothrif northwards, by Loch Fitty and Kelty to great Loch Leven, then by Kinross through the low hills to Glen Farg and so down into Strathearn. There was a somewhat shorter route, through the Rescobie Hills to Glen Devon and then over the higher hills to Dunning in Strathearn again; but although the winter's snows had not yet begun and closed the passes, that way was contra-indicated at this time of the year, with rivers and streams in spate.

The brothers rode fast, needless to say, and all the way were passing others on the same journey, including the Countess Ada and her ladies. Short of Kinross they caught up with the Abbot William, who was riding in the company of older and less agile clerics. But the young men were not for attaching themselves to such a group of dignitaries, including the Primate and the Chancellor; and although their friend might well have preferred to ride with them, he could hardly leave the others to do so. They pushed on ahead.

They never did catch up with the King's hard-riding party, Brawny Will being that way inclined; but they did come across a group of northern magnates which included Sir Osbert and his daughter, the only woman they had seen thus far forward. Down the narrows of Glen Farg where riders must string out, they seized their chance and, whatever the looks of those they squeezed past, managed to reach Margaret riding behind her father. And the beaming features she turned on Hugh lifted not only his heart but his hopes and spirits. He might be over-optimistic, but he judged that there was something akin to triumph in those lovely eyes.

As he reined in beside her, she it was who spoke first, low-voiced, for Sir Osbert was only a few yards in front. "Good, Hugh – good! He has it, the King's word. You would be accepted. All is well!"

He could scarcely find words to acknowledge that.

"He saw the King last night. Asked him. And was told that he approved of Sir Hugh de Swinton! Oh, Hugh – is it not a joy? We can wed!"

"Thank . . . God!"

Actually Sir Osbert was looking back, in the saddle, and reining up a little. "So you have found us, young man!" he greeted. "And I suspect that Margaret has lost no time in informing you? That His new Grace esteems you worthy. To heir my thanedom in due course. And, I pray, pass it on to a grandson of mine, one day!"

That was an extraordinary statement of intent to be announced, riding down the narrow track of a steep twisting glen, before an unmarried daughter and her would-be spouse, indicative of how much this matter had preyed on the older man's mind.

"I rejoice!" Hugh said, swallowing and glancing sidelong at the presumed mother of his son. "God willing, it shall . . . be so."

Margaret only smiled.

What Duncan thought of it all was questionable – not that that concerned his half-brother.

All rode on, busy with their own thoughts. But every now and again Hugh reached over to press the young woman's arm. Wide Strathearn opened before them.

Across the levels and over Moncreiffe Hill they came to St John's Town of Perth, with the dusk; presumably slower folk would have to put up at Duncrieve, Aberargie or at Ford of Earn. The town was already bustling with activity over the royal arrival, accommodation being sought out and established; for Scone, three miles further, was lacking in such, the abbey comparatively small, however famous, and only its monkish quarters available. The King might lodge there, but most of his court and following must put up in Perth.

In the event, King William elected to remain in the town, no doubt judging its ambience less restrictive and more to his taste than any ecclesiastical premises. Not a few of the nobility had houses in Perth, including the semi-royal Earl of Strathearn, where the King chose to lodge. Hugh, on his previous visit here, had stayed, with Abbot William, at the Cistercian monastery of St James; but ahead of the abbot's party he was uncertain whether there would be room for them there, with all the lofty clerics to house. The Olifards were to lodge, it appeared, in Ruthven House, amongst the great ones, and although Margaret was for Hugh and Duncan seeking quarters there also, they did not want to impose themselves so. It became a matter of seeking accommodation otherwhere – as well that they were amongst the first of so many to arrive.

They found a low-browed inn down at Tayside, amongst fisherfolk and shipmen. There, at least, they did not have to try to keep up with the extravagances of the magnates – for lack of money was always a problem for the brothers. Lairds as they might be, neither Aldcambus nor Redheugh were wealthy properties. They were in fact only large farmers, and Hugh being a knight did not put any silver in his pocket, indeed it frequently caused him problems and embarrassment. It occurred to him now, that one day, part of this thanedom future might result in him having quite considerable wealth at his disposal for a change, the revenues of Arbuthnott. The thought made him feel, somehow, guilty.

In the later evening Hugh, on the excuse that he must find out the order of events hereafter, left Duncan at the inn and made his way up to Ruthven House, near the great St John's Kirk. It was obvious that since not all the important folk would come that night to Perth, including the Countess Ada, the King's mother, the actual coronation ceremony would probably not take place until two days hence, whatever Brawny Will's haste.

Hugh had less difficulty in reaching Margaret than he had feared, for it seemed that she was the only woman amongst all the guests, and had been allotted a small chamber above the servants' wing of the establishment, all the principal rooms being crowded. This was highly convenient for the lovers, for although they could scarcely allow themselves to get involved in any very intimate exchanges, since Sir Osbert might appear at any time to bid his daughter goodnight, they nevertheless

335

did manage to celebrate their splendid news and prospects in fairly suitable fashion, words the least of it.

Next day, awaiting the arrival of the slower travellers, a sort of rehearsal of the coronation proceedings was ordained, at Scone; but Hugh had no especial part to play in the ceremony, so he was able to take Margaret riding in the Carse of Gowrie, new territory for them both, while her father, like the other lords, thanes and justiciars, attended on the monarch. Unfortunately, perhaps, Duncan elected to accompany them; there was no dampening of spirits today, however.

The question now was, when would the wedding be? Admittedly mid-winter was scarcely the choicest time for it, although Hugh would not have objected to that. But not only would Margaret prefer the springtime, but for certain her father would wish to make it a very special occasion, in order to demonstrate, before all the Mearns magnates and barons, who was to be their future thane. Hugh had to concede that this was probably sensible, wise, although wisdom was not what was most on his mind. Early spring, then? But, to be sure, he would necessarily have to come up to Arbuthnott before then to see her and make all necessary arrangements? So they would have opportunity to be alone together, without all this unfortunate concourse of people.

The coronation next day necessarily departed somewhat from the normal, December being scarcely the time for outdoor ceremonial. Usually the crowning itself took place on the top of the Moot Hill adjoining Scone Abbey; indeed it traditionally was quite a vital scene of the proceedings, for the hillock was in theory formed out of earth being brought from all over Scotland, down the centuries, and significantly so. The custom was that here all the lords and landholders came to take the new monarch's hand in their own and, kneeling, swear allegiance, this after having emptied a pocketful of the soil, from their respective properties all over the kingdom, so that their liege-lord could place his royal foot upon it and so seem to receive their homage standing on *their* land, indicative that all the land was the King's to dispose of as he would as superior – thus saving the monarch from having to travel the length and breadth of the realm to obtain the necessary allegiances. But on a cold December day, the actual crowning ceremony was to be done under cover in the abbey itself, and the allegiance-swearing got through in somewhat token style on the Moot Hill thereafter.

So the abbey church was packed for the occasion; and there were no clerestory galleries in this comparatively modest yet famous building. Nevertheless it transpired that Margaret Olifard won a considerably better and more prominent position therein than did Hugh and Duncan, who merely managed to squeeze in at the back amongst the dense crowd; for the King's mother had to be accommodated somewhere suitable, and a place was reserved for her up near the chancel. And with only three ladies with her, and Margaret one of the very few others present, she was included in the Countess Ada's little party, much bettering even her father's situation.

Waiting for the monarch's arrival, Hugh could barely see her, over the heads of the crowd; but at least he and Duncan could see the most significant feature of this great occasion, the fabled Stone of Destiny, placed up there before the high altar, where indeed it was normally kept and where Hugh had seen it on the previous occasion, and not on top of the Moot Hill, as it should have been in kinder weather, for a coronation. The chancel being raised a couple of steps above the rest of the church, it was plainly visible. Still with something like awe, the brothers gazed at this most precious symbol and relic of Scotland's past.

A fanfare of trumpets announced the entry of the principals, led by the High Sennachie and his heralds. First came the Abbot of Scone, with the Primate, Chancellor and Vice-Chancellor; then the great officers of state, the High Steward, the High Constable, the Marischal, the Keeper of the Great Seal and the Hereditary Coroner, or Crowner, the MacDuff Earl of Fife, this last bearing the crown on its cushion, the others carrying the rest of the regalia, the sceptre, the sword of state and the spurs. Then came the monarch, walking alone, resplendent in his lion rampant tabard and cloth-of-gold. He

337

was followed by such of the earls as had dared to attend this ceremony after their so recent risings against the late King. All this to the singing of the abbey choir.

Proceeding up to the chancel, William bowed to his mother before being led to the Stone of Destiny by the Crowner, to stand there, facing the congregation, while the Honours, the crown, sceptre, sword and spurs, were placed upon the altar by their bearers. Then the Abbot of Scone offered up a brief prayer.

This was followed by the High Sennachie making his anything but brief declaration of the rights of this William to sit upon the *Lia Fail*, the Stone of Destiny, for he was William, brother of Malcolm, son of Henry, son of David, son of Malcolm, son of Duncan, son of Crinan and so on, naming all the royal descent not only back to Fergus mac Erc, of the Scots, but to the lengthy and semi-mythical list of High Kings of the Picts of Alba – and all this from memory, without a note or a falter. When at last he had finished, the Earl of Fife, Coroner, seated William on the stone, and led the cheers of the company.

Thereafter the Primate made the oration, went to the altar to bless the phial of holy oil, and then came to anoint the monarch's head with it. The Chancellor brought the crown on its cushion, and the Sennachie called on the Earl of Fife to do his duty.

Hugh was intrigued at this, for the said Earl of Fife had been distinctly unsure of his allegiance during the risings of the other Celtic earls, and at the time of the Somerled-inspired invasion had been reputed to be likely to join the Earl of Mar in a southwards thrust, the same that Hugh had had his hand in seeking to prevent. But these MacDuffs were hereditary Crowners, and this was their duty, even if they were not always dutiful – for it was one of his predecessors who had stabbed to death King MacBeth at Lumphanan, and then crowned Malcolm Canmore instead.

The golden circlet placed on William's anointed head, the other Honours of Scotland were brought from the altar to be presented on bended knee to the monarch by their respective

338

bearers, touched by the royal hand, and then held there, waiting. The Sennachie, turning to the congregation, ordered all to hail their crowned, rightful and lawful liege-lord and sovereign.

"Hail the King!" he cried. "Hail the King!"

Hail they all did, loud and long, on and on, while William, raised by the hand, stood and grinned, the only time Hugh at least had seen him even remotely embarrassed.

Then, to the rhythmic clash of cymbals instead of choristers' singing, the Sennachie, pacing solemnly, led the way out, the King in front now, on the way to the Moot Hill for the allegiance-swearing, or an abbreviated version of it. At least it was not raining.

Up to the top of the mound William climbed, the regalia brought up after him, and there the great ones mounted, to scatter their dribbles of soil, and, with William putting his foot on it, each knelt to take the royal hand between their own two palms and swore the oath of fealty, while the crowd stood around the foot of the hill and watched. Sir Osbert Olifard was one of those selected to climb and kneel, along with his brother, for thanes and justiciars were so honoured, although most of the lords and barons and chiefs advisedly remained below, to await a later and indoors opportunity where shivering was not the order of the day.

This concluded the proceedings and now it was back to Perth. The provost, magistrates and citizens were providing hospitality for all, a banquet for the King and senior magnates, repasts in various houses and hospices for lesser notables in different degrees, and outdoor feasting for the commonality around bonfires in the streets. By choice, Hugh and Duncan joined in one of these last celebrations, near their riverside inn, rather than waiting to be put in their somewhat doubtful places by some upjumped herald. Sir Osbert and his daughter would certainly be at the royal banquet.

Later, much later, but with revelry still prevailing all around, Hugh found his way to Ruthven House, ablaze with lights and all jollity, and managed to see Margaret alone for a space, she, along with the other ladies, having sensibly taken fairly early leave from the banquet, as celebrations there, as elsewhere, grew towards excess. They had a pleasant hour before Sir Osbert appeared, only just sober, and won his agreement that Hugh should come up to Arbuthnott reasonably soon after Yuletide, when weather conditions permitted, to plan their own variety of celebration, their wedding. That had to be all for that night.

In the morning, all took their various roads homewards.

26

How frequently had Hugh de Swinton ridden from Melrose down Tweed the fifteen or so miles to Roxburgh Castle in the company of the Abbot William? He had lost count. But never had he done so in Margaret's and her father's company. And this would be the last time that he did so as Hugh de Swinton, for he was on his way to change his name, this early April day of 1166.

Name-changing was no major affair admittedly, folk of all sorts and ranks frequently doing so, over alterations of occupation or domicile or the inheritance of property and the like; but being a knight complicated the issue. It was a Hugh de Swinton whom King Malcolm had knighted; and to change it to *Sir* Hugh de Arbuthnott required the royal assent. Hence this journey. And since Sir Osbert was Thane of the Mearns and owner of the Arbuthnott barony, he had to subscribe before the monarch, source of all such titles, that this adoption of the name, which on the wedding would become his daughter's, was by his agreement. So the Olifards had to be present at this name-changing process – at least the father did, and Margaret was not going to be left at home over a matter so intimately connected with herself and her loved one. This was why it was into April before travel conditions were suitable for making the long journey. All this had been arranged on the visit by Hugh to Arbuthnott some six weeks earlier, when relevant details had been discussed and decided upon. Father and daughter had ridden to Melrose, where Hugh had met them, and now Abbot William was accompanying them to the King's presence for the necessary royal approval and decree, as witness. All going as was hoped for, the wedding should take place on the last day of this month, which being St Katherine's Day, ought to be propitious, there being a number of places and shrines dedicated to that heroic young martyr in the Mearns, St Kate's Well being situated near Arbuthnott. Abbot William had agreed to travel north in due course to conduct the nuptial ceremony.

They rode by St Boswells, Maxton and Rutherford the fifteen miles, Margaret much interested in all that she saw, this being new territory for her, the abbot expansive on the subject of St Boisel, his first predecessor, who had formed the Columban abbey of Old Melrose in the seventh century, and whose fame and sanctity had brought the youthful and famous St Cuthbert there from his birthplace in Lauderdale, to become prior and then go on to Lindisfarne, from there to convert much of northern England to Christ.

At Roxburgh, as almost usual, they found King William to be out hunting or hawking and, waiting for him, learned that he was now being called William the Lion, after his adoption of that beast for his emblem in place of the boar. Margaret was much taken with this extraordinary and elongated royal castle, with its series of individual towers, and the two great rivers lapping its peninsula at either side, to join at its apex, never having seen the like.

When the King returned, they had a further wait before being admitted to the presence, but when they were, he greeted them well enough, all but hearty, plainly drink-taken for refreshment after the day's sport. He clearly found Margaret interesting, eyeing her assessingly, and making reference to boar-slaying as an aid to romance and female appreciation. Even though Hugh did not greatly favour this sally, it did make the required opening for their mission, the request that His Grace would accede to the transference of knighthood from Hugh de Swinton to Hugh de Arbuthnott, on the declaration here made that Hugh was adopting the latter name, in the presence of His Grace and the Abbot of Melrose as witnesses. To which Sir Osbert added that since Arbuthnott was a barony, of royal granting, the name of it

342

might lawfully be adopted by Sir Hugh, since his daughter and sole heiress was to become his wife.

"Ha! And if I refuse?" the monarch exclaimed, fleeringly. "What then, my friends?"

Uncertain how to take that, the trio forbore to comment. But Abbot William answered for them.

"Knòwing Your Grace's goodwill, and approval of services rendered to the crown, we hope and surmise that approval will not be withheld, Sire, these being your most leal supporters."

"Aye. No doubt. Well, I would be sweir to disappoint this lady! In especial one so ripe for marriage, eh?" That with a hoot – Brawny Will had not altered his behaviour noticeably since ascending the throne. "So, petitions granted. And when will be the day of our boar-slayer's joy? Or night, shall we say, lass?"

Margaret was not the one to be embarrassed by such blatant question. She dipped an incipient curtsy. "On St Katherine's Day, Sire."

"A mercy – and when is that?"

"The last day of this month of April, Sire. You do not know of St Kate?"

"Hech, hcch, there are over-many saints! Though, sakes, never have I met with one! Forby, see you, my royal brother was overlike one for the good of his realm!" Another skirling laugh, and the monarch turned and left them standing.

The four gazed at each other in various degrees of wonderment. Was that it, then? Was that all? What they had come to achieve? Two relevant words, "petitions granted". Just that. All that the Olifards had ridden well over one hundred miles to hear two words spoken, and almost in jest.

Abbot William was probably least surprised. "So, may I congratulate Sir Hugh de Arbuthnott! And, to be sure, his bride-to-be. On the gaining of notable and worthy spouses. And you, my lord Thane, on the winning of your desire, and a fine godson forby! All most excellent. The Mearns, like the Olifards, are fortunate, I think."

Margaret turned and threw herself into Hugh's arms, there

343

in front of not a few of the watching courtiers, even as they bowed, with the King leaving the chamber.

"At last!" she exclaimed. "At last!"

Sir Osbert wagged his head.

"Are you satisfied, my lord?" the abbot asked. "Your requirement gained – and in front of all these witnesses."

"I deem . . . that I . . . must be! But I had hoped for more of it than this."

"Words, maybe! But you have the substance, no?"

They retired. There was still time to get back to Melrose by darkening.

Monastic premises were no place for the sort of celebratory demonstrations of affection and congratulation which the occasion called for, as far as Hugh was concerned, that night; but he did manage a few minutes alone with Margaret, escorting her from the abbot's quarters to a wing of the establishment reserved for visiting females. All had been arranged for the wedding, or as nearly all as was possible at this stage, Abbot William declaring that he would use his Vice-Chancellor's authority to have some ship convey himself, the groom, Duncan and any members of the Swinton family who wished to attend, to Inverbervie, a day or two before the Eve of St Katherine. The church of St Ternan's would provide the setting, so suitably near the spot where that boar had so dramatically brought bride and groom together; and a ceremony thereafter at the castle, before the invited great ones of the Mearns, would formally introduce Sir Hugh de Arbuthnott as royally acknowledged heir to the thanedom.

"So, my love, my dear, my heart's darling, three weeks from now and we will be made one. And I start a new life. I can scarcely believe it truth!" Hugh declared, hugging her, but glancing round almost guiltily, in case any monks were watching. "A new life!"

"Not only for you, sir! Think you it will not be a new life for *me*? Wed to such as you! When, when I might have been married off to some suitable simple, artless and deserving Mearns lordling, without all this ferment and trouble in gaining royal permission! A new life for me, also."

344

"But you *chose* me! Against all the others. It was your choice, as well as you mine."

"Did I choose aright, think you?"

"That I will prove to you, in three weeks' time. If I can live without you until then! And for the rest of our days thereafter."

"I will hold you to that."

"As I will hold you, precious heart, made one with me, for here and hereafter. Praise God!"

She found a little laugh, at that women's wing doorway, where he must leave her. "You believe that God had His hand in this? Or is it just these holy surroundings affecting you! Or that you are now Hugh Arbuthnott?"

"What mean you by that, woman?"

"Just that you have now used our Arbuthnott motto, *Laus Deo* – Praise God! Now it is yours also."

They left it, and each other, at that. But only for a score of days. Then – together for a lifetime.

Postscript

In due course Sir Osbert Olifard went on his crusade to the Holy Land, and Hugh the Fair, as he also became known in the Mearns, did take over as thane thereof, serving as that all the long reigns of William the Lion and his son Alexander the Second. In the fullness of time he was succeeded by his and Margaret's son, Duncan, and then by *his* son, another Hugh, the Blond; in fact thereafter by one of the longest direct lines in our land of ancient families, right down to the present John, sixteenth Viscount of Arbuthnott but thirtieth in descent from Hugh, Lord Lieutenant of the Mearns or Kincardineshire. And, most happily, the other, alternative line, the Swintons of that Ilk, still flourish in the Merse, with General Sir John Swinton, Lord Lieutenant of the Merse, or Berwickshire, at Kimmerghame, with boars rampant still guarding his gates. Blood will out.

Both of these so far distant kinsmen have helped in this attempt to tell this story.